Sword and Silk Books
105 Viewpoint Circle Pell City, AL 35128
Visit our website at SwordandSilkBooks.com

To request permissions contact the publisher at admin@swordandsilkbooks.com.

First Edition: February 2022

Ebook: 978-1-7364300-9-5

For my mother, whose love and stories built a foundation as strong as the Valon Mountains.
And for my husband, whose love and admiration flows as generously as mountain streams toward Lake Clair.

UNRAVEL

AMELIA LOKEN

CHAPTER ONE

Blackwork: a form of embroidery using black thread on white linen
or cotton fabric; iron-based black dye used historically is corrosive
and no known techniques can stop the decay of these threads.

MY THUMBS PRICK WITH TEMPTATION, THE YEARNING TO
thread my magic into the muslin cloth almost irresistible. That cannot
happen.

Not on a burning day.

Clutching my embroidery hoop with sweaty, twisted fingers, I
follow Isabeau and the others in our orderly procession. Sometimes
the magic swells like this, filling me like heavy thunderclouds fast
approaching the Valon Mountains. I must hold it tight, else the magic
will dribble into my embroidery, my clothing, or any other cloth I
brush against.

Voyants are here, close. One glance, and they'll notice the resulting
Otherlight glow. Some voyants aren't as skilled as others, but I'll not
stake my life on such a chance.

We file past the raised stone platform in the middle of the square.
Bundles of kindling lean against firewood lining one whole side of the
knee-high stonework. Enough to make a good-sized bonfire. The stone
pillory stands stark in the center. A pair of stocks usually flank it, but

they've been removed. Today's trial won't end in a pelting of rotten vegetables. Nor with twenty lashings. Not for a trial of the most grievous offense.

Witchcraft.

Fire stops a witch's magic from spreading. Without fire, witchery sweeps from one feeble female to another, like a plague. Or so my uncle says, which is nearly the same as official church doctrine.

But fire doesn't stop witchcraft.

Magic is like breathing, and no one can hold their breath forever.

I've been subtle, figuring out the ebb and flow of my Gift's demands. Making sure I only use my magic when I'm certain no voyant will be around to see my Otherlight aura, or for the two days afterward while I still gleam. Unfortunately, none of us heard about the trial until yesterday, when I was already sloshing full of magic.

We file toward the benches on the south side of the square, already full with the women of St. Clotilde's Abbey. The nornes study every move from the back, three rows of them in charcoal gray. The novices sit before them in unflattering tones of ash, and in front of them sit the postulants in lighter shades of gray wool. The rest of us, their students, wear the pale gray of dawn. We've made no vows to the Seven Sisters of the Pleiades. Not yet. We settle on the front row benches like pigeons along a rooftop. The pillory is only ten paces before us. We have the best view and are on full display ourselves.

The abbey and St. Clotilde's cathedral cast a long morning shadow across half the benches from their perch on the mountain shoulder above us, creating an inviting coolness in the late summer heat. I sit fully under the morning sun's rays. Any Otherlight shine might be less obvious—

A trickle of wayward magic seeps into the cloth. I clench every muscle.

My skin tightens. My embroidery hoop trembles.

I change tactics.

I've a theory I've only begun to test. I've little affinity with wood, or plants, or metal, or stone. Perhaps if my magic isn't flowing directly into thread or cloth, and I'm not purposefully *using* it, any resulting Otherlight will be dim? The magic might soak from the bench into a dozen gray skirts but should still remain faint. My theory has *seemed* to hold up so far.

Fates, so let it be!

I grip the bench, letting magic dribble undirected from my palms, hoping it'll pool on the wooden surface. The tightness loosens. I sigh.

As the rest of the square fills with townsfolk, the abbey Thread-mistress, Sister Egethe, takes her place before us like a field officer surveying infantrymen. We straighten our spines. When she looks down the line, I realize she's already speaking. I focus on her serious expression. She stands to my right, so her words are inaudible. The teachers have been told I can't hear on that side, but they always seem to forget. The left's not much better, but until she moves, I must watch her lips. Something about embroidery and the trial. My hands lift to the silver combs holding tight, dark curls away from my face. A gift from my godmother years ago, they seem expensive but also ordinary. I press them against my scalp; the teeth of the combs bite my skin and her words amplify to an audible murmur.

"... Begin your thread-sketches. Whilst the trial proceeds... stitch the essence... speed, not precision. No colored silks... necessary."

I pull the cloth taut in my embroidery hoop and thread my needle with silk as black as my own hair. Black is good. It's stark, truthful, dyed with oak galls gathered from groves descended from the Valonian Oak. Each of my grandfather's seven thrones are carved from that legendary tree, for none can stand before it and utter lies. With black thread, magic feels more manageable. Less wild.

Sister Egethe's hands move as if offering a blessing. "... Your thread-sketches will be used as references for the tapestry commissioned by the Bishop-Princep."

I tighten my jaw. I've no love for the Bishop-Princep. His Boni-factum Edict issued last year introduced superstition and suspicion throughout Valonia, sweeping through each village, abbey and manor. I keep my expression neutral; catching the eye of Sister Egethe will bring consequences, which might tempt the Fates' notice. Notice brings interest. Interest brings curiosity. And when the Fates become curious, they play with the threads of your life, twitching one here or pulling one there. The resulting upheaval rarely proves beneficial.

So, wrapping my left hand's stiff, twisted fingers around the embroidery hoop, I obediently dip my needle into the cloth. The black silk slips after, again and again, until it outlines the pillory in the middle ground and the three-story guild hall behind it. The building dwarfs a faceless crowd of townsfolk below, indicated with small loose stitches.

The folk grow rowdy until the abbey bells chime Terce hour. The crowd quiets.

My stomach flips. There've been burnings in a few villages since the edict passed, but this is the first in the Clair Valley. The first I must witness.

The Moir Brethren from St. Clotilde lead four manacled women onto the raised pavement. I shudder as the clergymen jostle the women into a line. Stained dresses, once pretty, hang on too-slender bodies. There are books in my grandfather's library with theories that starving a witch takes her power. It's a backward logic that accidentally lands on truth, and those books have migrated from the library to my uncle's chambers. Did he direct his men to only feed these women enough to keep them alive while his magistrates searched for evidence? Someone did. Men seem to find starvation a natural precaution to panicked, desperate magic.

Isabeau elbows me. "Stop staring." She always sits to my left so I can hear her.

Isabeau's seventeen, a year older than I. When we were younger, I pretended she was my sister. She's tall, with hair straight as a mason's plumb line, yet we look more alike than not: brown eyes, freckles, and dark hair. I've trusted her since my first day at the abbey. I'd lined up with the others but missed when a novice gave instructions. Offended at my inattention, the novice grabbed my ear, pulling me toward the door, stating the nornes didn't need a crippled, deaf girl. She tasted

Isabeau's fist before they were both informed that the "crippled, deaf girl" was the princess. Isabeau avoided trouble thereafter... apart from our clandestine puppet shows after lights out and regularly misplacing her embroidery needles. Her current needle darts around the nearly complete central image. My stomach curls at the suggestion of figures tied to the pillory, all nearly engulfed by the stitched outlines of flames.

"He's not passed judgment," I whisper. Though the women will not be found innocent, it seems wrong to illustrate their deaths before it happens. Isabeau returns to her needlework without reply, for the Threadmistress swoops before us.

"A lovely scene, Princess Marguerite." She over-shapes her words as she points to the empty center. "Only the witches left to add."

Solemn drumming saves me from answering. More gray-clad brethren proceed into the town square. Behind the clerics march the Abbot of St. Clotilde and the Lord Mayor of Tillroux. I hunch at the sight of the man marching shoulder-to-shoulder between them.

My uncle Reichard.

Bishop-Princep of Valonia.

He'll preside over the proceedings, magnificent in his black cassock, the Seven Stars of the Pleiades embroidered with diamonds across his chest. He overshadows the two white-clad voyants following at his heels. My uncle brought a dozen of the witch-hunters with him when he returned to Valonia from his duties with the Knights Pleiades. The voyants' faces are scarred from initiation rites they underwent at the end of childhood. Their eyes scan the crowd, searching for telltale gleams of magic. Their hands rest on the pommels of their cold-iron long knives. Everyone knows that when a voyant unsheathes his knife, a witch faces her death.

I curl my twisted left hand further under my embroidery hoop and make myself smaller.

The Bishop-Princep only answers to the Seer of the Stars and the Fates themselves. The only being in Valonia who might check his power is my grandfather, the king, and perhaps my father, the crown prince. My uncle, of course, would never heed a word *I* say. I proceed him in line for the thrones, but I'm too female, too deaf, too maimed, and though he doesn't know it, too magic for his respect.

The drumming stops. The voyants flanking my uncle, not fifteen paces away, turn my way. They squint, focusing their Sight as they scan the crowd. I shiver, willing my body to imitate a well-corked jug.

Isabeau nudges me. "Get back to work. People will notice."

I ply my needle once more, outlining the four figures. Two young, one old and hunch-backed, and the last middle-aged.

The trial starts. The voyants continue looking in my direction, so I keep my head down. I can't hear much at this distance without watching someone's lips, but like Isabeau, I know how this will end. It's better to remember the women's faces before they beg. Before they scream. Before they're consigned to a fiery, "cleansing" death.

The young woman on the far left—her dress has the faintest blue Otherlight sheen—is charged with Skeincraft. The same "crime" I've committed hundreds of times, except my embroidery stitches never kept a child from drowning, and I've never been caught. The next, a rather plain girl, doesn't shine at all. If she ever concocted the love potion she's accused of creating, there's no trace of magic about her now. A subtle, green glow lingers about the third, her wrinkled hands hanging wearily. An Herbwitch—the easiest to find and condemn. If voyants sniff too close, folk merely point them to the nearest healer, then sweep up evidence of their own magic and slip away before the voyants return.

The last, a matronly woman, stands tall and defiant, a golden aura glimmering about the iron shackles binding her hands and feet. The brethren should've used rope to bind a Forgewitch. The woman crosses her large arms with an air of indifference that draws me into the proceedings. When my uncle turns toward me, my eyes follow his mouth and expression.

"… Your children are unnaturally large and strong," I see him say to her. "Nine of them. Half the children of Tillroux fell to the Fates when the red pox came through last winter. Not one of your children died. That seems... peculiar."

The woman doesn't buckle under his stare. "My husband, Stars rest his soul, was a big man, as any blacksmith should be. And I'm not a small woman." Her words are easier to follow, for she speaks boldly. "Fates determined they'd be stout and steady. I've done nothing to alter their destinies, only what a mother should. Fed them, clothed them, gave them work to keep them strong. Can't see how that's defying the Blessed Fates."

My uncle holds up a ribbon with a few dozen iron charms strung upon it. They swing ominously. "My voyants found charms in your shop."

The voyants shift their gaze from the crowd to the woman. I release my breath.

"Those?" She doesn't flinch. "They've hung from the rafters of that smithy since my husband's grandfather's day... hard put to find a smith without such."

"Why is that?" He seems only curious, but it's a trap. *Stop talking.*

"Protects the place from errant sparks. Keeps the smith's eye sharp and his hand quick."

A raised eyebrow. "Don't the Fates have power enough to do that?"

She pinches her mouth shut, finally recognizing the snare, but then lifts her chin. "Fine. Take them all. You won't see my sons using the forge without them." She casts a glare at the townsfolk. "And if you turn my kin out o' Tillroux, you'll have troubled times finding a replacement. See how long you can last without a smith." She says it like a curse and spits to the side as if to seal it.

There's answering movement in the crowd as others spit. Enough to show defiance, but not enough to earn trouble. Through the shifting crowd an Otherlight glow comes pushing to the front, a boy with golden hair clutching a wilted-looking cabbage. He's my age, or a bit older, and wearing an odd assortment of clothing. His wool cloak's too heavy for such a warm day. A sagging tunic, made for a man thrice his girth, is snugged around his waist with doubled-up rope instead of a belt. His leggings are a growth spurt away from being too small, not staying tucked into his worn pair of boots. Strangest of all is his Otherlight gleam, bright as any female magic wielder's and white as lamb's wool.

I've *never* seen a male who used magic. Men can only sniff it out. Women give it form in charms, potions, and embroidery.

The drumming resumes.

Brethren push the women toward the pillory, tying them together, backs to the stone column. Other brethren place the wood and bundles of kindling around their feet. Nausea rises within me. I can't watch. But I must.

"Witchcraft is the most insidious of sins against the Seven Fates." My uncle captures my gaze as he circles the pillory. "Women, formed in the image of the Sisters... imitate the Fates... trying to mold the destinies of others... meddling, mischief, and ultimately to witchcraft... serving Eris, mother of strife and discord. We must purge Tillroux..."

His words fade as he turns away, circling the women. My entire body is taut. Eventually, his voice becomes audible again.

"You, madame, shall have your useless charms." He flings them at the feet of the blacksmith's widow. She shrugs. A brave mistake. He'll seek higher stakes, something to make her flinch. "And each of your children shall be branded. All folk will know what sort of mother they had."

The blacksmith's widow blanches and tightens her jaw. That seems enough, for he moves to the old woman. Her cottage will be burned, her garden plowed under and sown with salt. A waste. Next winter, the townsfolk will rue that they've no herbwoman, no plants to soothe their coughs or bring down their children's fevers.

The girl accused of making a love potion sobs as my uncle steps before her. She begs, perhaps claiming innocence. He steps closer, making the sign of forgiveness.

The girl sags, relieved—but he doesn't release her.

I grip my embroidery tight as he turns to the woman with pale blue Otherlight. "You claim love motivated you to stitch enchantments... your son's clothing... highest, holiest gift the Fates give to womankind... twisted... keep a child under control."

"To keep him safe... prayed as I embroidered them."

"Blasphemy!"

"No—" she protests.

"The *Fates* will keep him safe." He points skyward. "The *Fates* will see to it that he fulfills his destiny, whether that life is long or short. Where is your faith, woman?"

She straightens and glares at him. Bruises mark her face; a nasty burn puckers her neck. The inquisitors haven't been gentle.

"Your Grace never experienced childbirth."

My uncle draws back as if slapped. "Of course not."

"Pain... Hours of it. No escape." The woman juts out her chin. "Your body rips itself open and pushes this child into the world. You stop breathing..." Her face softens. "... placed in your arms. Your child... suckles your breast... such tenderness and fierceness." Her eyes narrow. "You'd do anything, face any foe, to keep that child safe and warm and fed. If it means borrowing a blessing from the Fates and stitching prayers into the very seams of your child's clothing, so be it."

My uncle pounces. "You admit you defied the Fates."

"My husband died before my babe could walk. I did *all* in my power to protect my son."

"Witnesses state the child should have drowned... because his jacket snagged on a tree root, he didn't."

"I thank the Stars every day they kept him safe."

"It wasn't the Stars; it was your *witchcraft*." He plows on. "The Fates allowed the child to stray from your side. The Fates let him slip in the river. They determined the boy should die that day and *you*, woman, snatched him from their loving arms... As Bishop-Princep of the Holy Order, I judge... meddled in the operations of the Pleiades. To appease them, the boy shall die with you in the flames."

"No!" the mother cries.

No. My gut twists.

My needle, tucked in the cloth, pierces the meat of my palm as I clutch my embroidery. I extract it, releasing a breath. Then pause.

Magic fizzes along my fingertips, pricks at my thumbs. My embroidery work gleams with a faint blue light. *Merde!* The ends of the cloth caress the bench. I'm unconsciously pulling magic back from the wood. It soaks the cloth and stitches, ready to be put to use. The Otherlight's still faint, but I dart a glance at the distracted voyants.

My gaze snags on the only person looking my way, the blond fellow who shouldn't be glowing. He stares for a heartbeat, then winks.

Merde!

I jerk my gaze back to the voyants. They're scrambling towards the blacksmith woman. She's freed a hand from the shackles and swings it at the nearest clergyman. She looks like a warrior-saint wielding an odd-shaped flail. She strikes a brother, who falls before her.

"You're no agent of the Fates," she bellows, striding toward my uncle. "You climbed from Eris' bowels."

She's almost to him when the voyants catch her arms. She pulls and bucks, advancing another step, but my uncle meets her with a backhanded swing of his silver judgement scepter. Her cheek splits open, spraying him with blood. His face is freckled with scarlet, but his black cassock absorbs the blood without stain. The voyants force the dazed woman back to the pillory.

My uncle gestures to the brethren below. "Bring in the child."

No. He wouldn't. I flex my twisted fingers. *Yes, he would.*

The blond fellow in the crowd shouts at my uncle. Another takes up the cry on the far side of the square. The townsfolk shift like a windy field of wheat. Someone nearby repeats it, and I hear what they call my uncle.

"Monster!"

I shiver. Blink prickling eyes. They shout what I've whispered in silence for years.

More cries join, like a rising storm. The right spark might turn the crowd into a mob. Purposefully or not, the fellow is sowing chaos, distracting the voyants from looking my way.

A grim-faced brother hoists a boy of about three up to my uncle. The crowd growls and surges forward past our island of still-seated nornes. My uncle gestures a command. Brethren circle the raised platform. A jerk of his hand, and they turn their staves around, sharpened ends pointing toward the townsfolk.

"We are men of the Klothos," my uncle shouts. "We defend the judgments of the Fates. If you feel it's your time to die, then come and meet your destiny!"

The crowd quiets.

"Coward!" The blond fellow stands five paces to my left. He throws his cabbage over the row of staves, hitting my uncle in the shoulder. "Monster!" He bends, then throws a cobblestone. My uncle barely avoids being struck in the head. He orders his voyants into the crowd.

The fellow ducks. Disappears.

Another stone hurtles toward the pillory, missing my uncle by an ell. A cabbage flies from a different corner. Then a beet and a parsnip. Soon, it's raining rocks and vegetables. Girls around me squeal and jostle as the town square heaves in chaos. A norne gestures for us to gather, but I pretend not to see. I dash forward into the melee, unhooping my embroidery and folding it small. I mutter prayers, pouring all my unstoppered power into it. The thrill of the release makes me stumble. Pleasure rushes through my limbs as the cloth glows a clear blue between my fingers, bright enough for any voyant to see.

I crawl forward on hands and knees, wriggling between the armed brethren. Some have Sight. Not enough to become voyants, but enough to detect this bright glow. Scrunching the cloth in my fist, I focus on hiding, being unseen, wishing again that I knew how to trigger the legendary masking effect of embroidery magic. With no teacher, I've only overheard stories and read vague references in history books.

At the edge of the raised stone platform, I kneel and peer about.

My uncle's not in sight. The witches are almost within reach, but a wall of stacked firewood encircles their legs. The child knocks pieces off, trying to get to his mother.

"Go!" she urges him. "Run fast!"

His chubby hands don't pause, unaware of his danger. I reach, clambering onto the platform, and grab the back of his shirt.

His mother struggles. "Get away from him, abbey-rat!"

"I want to help." I thrust my cloth against her bound hands. Her eyes widen, then focus sharply. I hold her gaze, hoping she can sense my honesty. She gives a quick nod.

"His name is Henri." Her fingers tighten; the cloth flares with *her* deep blue Otherlight.

"Henri," I repeat, tying the embroidery around his neck like a kerchief. Henri pushes away. I exchange one last look with his mother as I haul him under my arm and tuck the cloth under his shirt. Henri resists, scrabbling for his mother. I grip him firmly, scooting off the platform. I'm trusting untrained magic to keep him masked. It has no chance of working if he becomes the center of attention. I duck under clergymen's elbows and townsfolk's arms. He's a solid child and not cooperative. I kneel, wrestling him into a more secure position and wishing the ever-bent fingers of my left hand could flex and grip.

"Mama!"

"Hush." I try to think of comforting words, but all are lies. "Hush," I repeat, and press forward. He wiggles desperately. I near the edge of the crowd when Henri arches so violently I nearly drop him.

"I'll take him." The consonants cling together like spring mud. Lowlander accent. The blond fellow, glowing with white Otherlight, is on my left, reaching for Henri.

I clutch the boy closer and hurry away.

Henri halts his crying. He flings himself sideways, just as the Lowlander catches up and plucks him from my arms. It's like being pickpocketed—if the money had a mind of its own and could jump out of one's purse.

The blond fellow dashes away, weaving through the crowd and into a narrow street. I chase after, down another street, joining them in the doorway of a closed shop. The fellow's holding the child as he twists a length of rope in a convoluted mess of loops and knots. It gleams with white Otherlight.

I edge around to his right. I'll not miss a word the trickster says. "What are you doing?"

He cocks an eyebrow. "Trying to save this little *kleuter*."

That's what *I'm* doing, and I'll not trust a Lowlander to do it better. "What's a squelcher like you doing up in Valonia?"

"Long story." He sets Henri on the street and pulls off his cloak. His rope looks like a net woven by a drunk fisherman. He slips two loops over his shoulders. "Hoist him into this."

Eyeing the makeshift harness, I cross my arms. "The voyants will sniff you out. If your magic doesn't tattle, then your accent will. Any Lowlander found in Valonia risks a whipping, and if you're from Brandt, they'll hang you."

He shrugs as if told he'd a bit of mud on his shoes, then lifts Henri. "Let's worry on getting this lad where they won't kill him for a tad of *duw* in his stitchery." He looks me over. "Pot's calling the kettle black—some shine about yourself, yes? And you pretending to be a holy girl in that gray habit."

Never been caught, I want to say. But don't. Boasting only invites the Fates' notice. I can't have them twitching my life threads *now*. If discovered, we might be tied to the pillory with the others. Or my uncle might arrange another—more private—trial.

"Give a hand," he says. "We'll both earn a Fates blessing."

I uncross my arms and, taking Henri, wrestle him into the harness of ropes.

"Horsey!" he says, grabbing at the Lowlander's hair and making him grimace.

I hide a smile as he loosens Henri's grip, then hold out my right palm. "I'll show you the best route to travel." He frowns at my hand. More proof he's not from our mountains.

"It's a map," I explain. "Of Valonia. The fingers and thumb represent the five valleys. Stretching southward, see? This is Lake Clair." I circle the hollow of my palm, then point to the base of my littlest finger. "We're here in Tillroux. Go southeast through the valley. At Ligeron" —I point to the tip of that finger— "cross into Haps-Burdia. That's the quickest way."

He grazes the side of my palm down to my wrist. "What about the northern mountains?"

I pull away, pointing over the rooftops to the blue mountains beyond. "Those have kept us safe from invasion for centuries. Don't try it. And not with a child."

He reaches for my hand and unfurls my fingers, as if unfolding a fine piece of lace. His calloused finger traces a similar path closer to the center of my palm. My pulse jitters. He doesn't seem to notice. "Staying in the foothills 'til here, I could cross the river at Nemeaux."" He taps my wrist.

I shake my head. "The bridge has been gone sixteen years. You'd pay dearly to ferry across to Brandt. No, you'll want to—"

"Continue westward to Hlaandrs." His finger slips back to my palm, then up to my thumb's first knuckle. "River's narrower here, and there's a bridge."

I swallow. Stupid to be all a-flutter because a lad holds my hand. He sees a map, nothing more. It just happens to be my flesh and bone.

"It seems you know your way then." I pull my hand away and focus my attention on little Henri. I settle him more securely in the harness. The blond fellow studies me over his shoulder.

"Does such a brave and helpful maiden have a name?"

"Margo," I lie. "And you?"

He grins. "Tys Owlymirror, greatest acrobat south of the North Sea." He swings his cloak around his and Henri's shoulders so he looks like a hunchbacked, two-headed ogre. I snort at his appearance, and perhaps at his cockiness.

"Bragging earns notice from the Stars, more than magic does," I warn.

"That so? Must tread lightly in your mountains, then." He grabs my hand and looks at it as if reading the map once more. "As should you, Margo. Too much shine. Here..."

He snags one of several odd bracelets tied around his wrists, sliding it over our joined hands and down to my wrist. "It's a charm. To make you less noticeable... to voyants, anyway." It's only a bit of twine that's been knotted in a pretty fashion and tied in a circle, but when I look up, his face is shining brighter than before.

"What about the two of you?"

He flips up the cloak's hood. Henri disappears into shadow and only Tys' face is visible. He hobbles forward like an old man. "I have others." He winks, then totters down the street toward the north gate.

As he disappears around the corner, bells ring out. The big ones from the church at the far end of the square.

I spit to the side like the old grannies do, as if that can hold back misfortune. I can almost feel the weight of the Pleiades' gazes upon me. I don't regret rescuing Henri. I don't regret meeting Tys Owlymirror, but I should've taken more thought. Planned. Like I plan everything.

It all happened so fast. For the first time in a dozen years, I acted without thought. The Fates noticed, I'm sure of it, and they will want their due.

CHAPTER TWO

Running Stitch: a simple needlework stitch consisting
of a line of small, even stitches that run in and out
through the cloth without overlapping

A FOOLISH, WISTFUL PART OF ME WISHES I COULD LEAVE
Tillroux as easily.

I hurry back to the square. There's no smoke. Yet.

I stand on an abandoned wheelbarrow. No flames around the
pillory, either.

The townsfolk still crowd the center, but the brethren have
prodded them into a wider circle with their sharpened staves. None
can reach the pillory now.

My uncle is once more on the stone platform, entreating the
crowd. His voice is nothing in my ears. I'm dozens of ells farther away
than before; his lips are small and impossible to read. He raises a hand
and points northward. Movement ripples through the crowd. Folk spit
or snap their fingers to ward off evil.

"What did he say?" I ask a man to my left.

"Word's come from the northern border. An army, led by the
bloody Duke of Brandt, is gathered along the River Muse."

Fates, no! Every adult remembers where they were sixteen years ago. The Duke, leading the Haps-Burdian army, swept across the Valonian plains, conquering a third of our country in a matter of days —our family, our neighbors, our best farmland stolen from us. We retreated, like an army under siege. The Valon mountains became our fortress wall, the Muse River our unbridged moat. Now Brandt comes again?

My uncle raises his hands higher, turning to collect listeners from all corners of the square. I could ask my neighbor to repeat the Bishop-Princep's words, but water's best from the spring, rather than muddied downhill. Yet I'm probably bright with Otherlight. I hesitate. Thanking the Fates for making me small, I slip through the crowd until I'm wedged between shoulders and bellies, only a sliver of the pillory within view. It's the sliver that has my uncle within it, gesturing passionately.

I press my combs against my scalp, trying to increase the volume of his voice. I catch phrases, bits I try to stitch together coherently. He recites the history of the growth of Haps-Burdia, how the empire gobbled up one kingdom after another, turning them into ducal states. He doesn't mention that some are semi-sovereign, like Brandt, but plays upon our people's patriotism. And fear. He twists them together, warning of worse troubles.

"Our worship... Seven Sisters must be more sincere... our existence relies upon..."

I grasp the narrative thread, but I've heard it enough before. I pull the combs from their places behind my ears, and the world goes quiet as my hair falls forward in a dark curtain. In this small tent of shadows, cradled in my hands, the combs glow with subtle, golden Otherlight.

I'm tempted to retreat to someplace hidden, away from the trouble my uncle brews.

Yet, when I emerge, the trouble will still be there. Isn't it better to know that trouble? To know what our people are facing? What they're tempted with? I can send a messenger pigeon to my grandfather; let him know what his younger son's up to. Not like a tattletale. More like an advisor. A spy. The king's probably up to his eyebrows in war preparations, but... I study the crooked fingers of my left hand curling around the silver combs. The king will *want* to know of my uncle's newest maneuverings. He's very protective of me, our land, our people. I replace the combs behind my ears and lift my face toward my uncle.

"Can you ignore... charms your wife embroiders... children's clothing? Turn a blind eye... herbcraft in the kitchen? Pretend you don't see... neighbor's talismans?"

My uncle paces along the front edge of the raised square, his gaze searching the crowd, reeling in the townsfolk of Tillroux like fish tired of fighting the line.

"... Seems harmless when Brandt's on the far side of the mountain and harvest is good. Yet... Brandt is at our door... the might of the Haps-Burdian empire behind him. If we go to battle... relying only upon our mortal strength... Will the Fates guard us from an early frost, or a long, rotting rain? With the menfolk gone to battle, the responsibility... fall upon the women.... Charms and witchery, but will it save our homes and harvest from the wrath of the Fates?"

It's wrong to take something wholesome, like faith, and twist it. It's wrong to convince our people that their neighbors are enemies as well. Valonians would never allow this if left to their own heart's conscience.

I glance Heavenward. Hasn't he provoked the Fates' notice yet? They could curse him with sudden laryngitis, or a violent urge to evacuate his bowels, anything to silence him and remove him from the town square. My prayer is not answered.

"I tell you all, townsfolk, farmfolk, mountainfolk, and churchfolk: the Fates remember who we choose. Who we rely on... our allegiance, our dedication. We must not waver in our love to the Seven Sisters... the very witchcraft that tempts our sisters, our mothers, our wives, and our daughters..." He turns as his voice rises, pulling the crowd into agreement with him. "... We must do that which is dreadful for that which is best. Let us clearly demonstrate in whom we trust. All hail the Fates!"

It's a rallying call. I hold my breath.

"All hail the Fates," the crowd repeats, the response loud enough to please my uncle.

Merde.

"May the Sisters bless us all. Menfolk sixteen and up, report to your guild masters or valley headmen. Conscription orders will be issued through them." He stalks to the pillory where the bound women struggle. His gaze seems to linger on Henri's mother, on the place where Henri once stood. He holds up his hand to quiet the crowd.

My skin prickles.

"And houndsmen! Report to my office in St. Clotilde's abbey."

Seaux de Merde!

Tys and Henri are in trouble's thornbush; those bloodhounds belong to the office of the Bishop-Princep and have never failed to bring culprits back to face the Fates. Someone should warn Tys. Get him a horse to outrun them.

People start to disperse. Men head toward the guildhall. Is there anyone in this crowd that might be willing to help Tys? Willing to flout the Fates' judgement?

Except this isn't their judgement. It's my uncle's.

He stands near the bound witches, head bent in conversation toward a voyant. The man nods and departs. My uncle lifts the hem of his cassock as if about to leave. Between him and the stairs stands a brother with a torch, still waiting. Almost as an afterthought, my uncle takes the torch and tosses it onto the woodpile surrounding the pillory.

The condemned women scream.

The crowd stills. A tongue of flame licks the wood.

My uncle sweeps his gaze across the people. "Now is the time for all Valonians to prove their faith... the stain of witchcraft be purged...

rise again, stronger... more blessed than ever before. Do you stand with the Seven Sisters, or do you stand with these sin-filled witches?"

Someone will act. Some brave woman or man will stand up to the Bishop-Princep.

The flames lick higher.

The screams turn to screeches. I pull the combs from my hair, covering my ears. Tears blur the flames as I collapse to the cobblestones.

I'm impotent. I have no power. No magic left. The square fills with the scent of charred meat, and charcoal-gray ash settles on clothes, hair, skin. It coats the broken embroidery hoop at my feet, already soaked with the rejected contents of my stomach, turning it black.

AS WE'RE ESCORTED BACK to the abbey like a herd of frightened cattle, I gather my shattered thoughts. There is no *someone* to help Tys. There is only me. No one else knows. I hurry to the dormitories and the room I share with Isabeau.

The door slams behind me. Startled, I turn.

Isabeau leans against the door, the only way to secure it from the inside. She frowns.

"What happened to your regular dress?"

I blink, wrenching my thoughts from Tys to puzzle out her question. "What?"

"The dress you always wear, every day. The one with an ink stain on the sleeve."

I try to remember before the eternity of the past few hours. "A norne told me to change before the trial because of the stain."

"Where's it now? Sent it to the laundry?"

"No." I pull the folded dress from under my pillow. "I had no time."

"Quick! Change dresses." Isabeau's distress is unlike her normal, busy calm.

"Now? Why?"

She steps closer, keeping her hand on the door. Her voice is barely audible in my left ear. "Do you *not* know what you are?"

My cheeks flame. She can't mean what I think she does. Magic has nothing to do with which dress I wear.

"Feel the hem of that dress," she demands.

Impatient with her strangeness, I pull the hem quickly through my fingers. "Ow!" A bead of blood wells up on my fingertip.

"There are more than a dozen of those."

"A dozen of what?"

"Charms."

"In my dress?" I study my roommate. Does she want me to admit my own witchery, or does she already know? If extortion's her game, there's much she can demand for her silence. "For what purpose?"

"To keep your power hidden away. From the voyants. From the Bishop-Princep."

I wait, silent.

"I know why your grandfather sends you to school here, rather than tutor you in Boispierre. You're not the only one who must hide all you are. Not that you're sufficiently cautious; I can feel the hum of your magic from here. You must've been bright as a bonfire this morning. It's a wonder the voyants didn't catch you."

I shiver as my mind grasps the full import.

Isabeau sighs. "Guard the door."

We exchange places. She pulls up a loose floorboard and brings out a little box. It has no Otherlight glow—until she opens it. Golden Otherlight shimmers. There must be more than a hundred charms inside. They're not made of the usual copper coins or old iron nails; slender, silvery wire wraps around itself to make the symbols. I peer closer.

"Are those...?"

Isabeau nods. "All the needles I've 'lost.' When it builds up" — she's careful not to name *it*—"only metal can take it from me."

"You embedded them into my clothing?"

"Your Gift is sometimes obvious."

"I bleed it off all the time," I protest.

She bites her lip, holding back a too-honest answer. "I sewed charms into all your clothes, and a few extra in that one since it's your favorite. It dampens the hum." At my look of confusion, she explains. "You know, that sense that something or someone is *more*."

I nod. I depend on my Sight, which, as a girl, I shouldn't have. Other witches must use vibrations. I lean against the door as Isabeau hides the charms.

All these years, I've shared a room with another witch. I could've gone to her about magic the same way I had when I'd started my menses. She'd have answered my stupid, anxious questions in the same prosaic way she discussed monthly cycles and cramps. It'd have seemed ordinary, nothing to stay awake worrying about. "Stars! Why didn't you tell me before?"

Isabeau takes my place against the door and points at my dress. "Change."

As I wriggle into the other dress, the air snugs close against me. How often have I felt this and never noticed? Only assumed it was the thicker wool cloth? I know Skeincraft, and I'd not recognized this magic.

"Good." Isabeau nods. "Now, *what* are you up to?"

It's tempting, especially since she's been so helpful, but *I* don't even know what I'm up to. I've no plan other than horse, Tys, safety.

"My grandfather called me home."

Isabeau lifts an eyebrow, but doesn't call me a liar.

The only way to keep her safe is ignorance. "Yes. He feels I'll be safer at Boispierre." I gather my cloak and riding boots. As I pass, Isabeau grabs my arm. She waits until I look at her.

"Marguerite, if your grandfather doesn't confirm your story... the abbess won't strip your privileges this time. You'll be tossed in the Closet."

It's not the possibility of long, dark hours and visiting rats that makes my jaw tighten. It's the possibility of discovery by my uncle.

Since his return from service in the Knights Pleiades, he's kept busy climbing his way to the post of Bishop-Princep, and I've kept out of his way. Yet the Fates brought our paths together again today. He's hunting for witches and I'm fool enough to set myself against him. Any mistake, and I could lose my other hand or even my life.

"My grandfather will confirm my story."

Isabeau's eyes search mine. I plead silently. Her grip relaxes. She looks away. "If anyone asks, I'll say you received a message from the king. May the Stars bless you."

I give her a swift hug. "A thousand thanks."

Entering the dormitory corridor, I offer my own prayer for a Fates blessing. As I step into the courtyard, I quickly retreat. A dozen bloodhounds pass, straining on their leashes, their voyant handlers looking eager to let them go.

I mutter an amendment. "At least turn a blind eye to my next bit of folly."

THE PORTER'S out in the road watching the hounds being brought to heel as I ride out the gate. Preoccupied, he waves me on. The guards at the city gate are equally distracted as they wager over how soon the Brandt army will attack. At the first crossroads, I study the ground, trying to discern if Tys Owlymirror continued traveling northwest. A faint sound, like someone in pain, pinches my ears. I turn, trying to determine its source. I press my combs hard against my scalp and hear it once more—the long bay of a hunting hound. The scent's been found.

I hitch my skirts and swing my leg, so I'm astride the saddle like a man. I press my heels until Etoile reaches a mile-eating canter. The northbound road soon buries itself in the wooded foothills of the mountains. On the road ahead, through the woods on either side, there's no sign of Tys or Henri.

Perhaps they took a different route or are so far ahead the hounds will never catch them.

If I turn back now, I can salvage everything.

But I might cross paths with the hounds. If Henri's scent clings to me from when I carried him, they'll chase me down. Meanwhile, I left the abbey without permission. How will my uncle interpret the timing of such behavior? I shiver. Much safer if he learns of my departure *after* I'm safely tucked in Chateau Boispierre with my grandfather guarding me.

Merde. No choice but onward.

I spy the rope strung across the road just before it catches my shoulders.

Snaps my head back. Sweeps me off the saddle.

I land on my back, the hard-packed road driving all breath from me. The Seven Stars of the Pleiades explode behind my eyelids. My mouth opens and shuts uselessly. Pain echoes around my ribs.

I open my eyes, staring into the leafy canopy high above as I struggle to draw breath. A face appears. Its expression changes from smug to concerned as I stare helplessly upward. The face disappears. Still no air. I panic, clawing at my chest. The face reappears, closer.

His lips move. I hear nothing. My combs! They've been knocked free.

I scrabble in the dirt. Twist. My chest aches. My mouth opens—still no air. A silver glint in a wagon rut. I snatch my comb and curl into a ball, which seems to unlock whatever binds me. Cool, glorious air slips into my lungs. I draw breath after breath and finally sit up, tucking the comb behind my left ear. Etoile crops grass a quarter mile down the road.

The perpetrator stands, proud as a rooster, on a lower branch of the oak, Henri peeking over his shoulder.

"Tys Owlymirror!" I croak.

He gives a slight bow. "At your service."

I scowl. "You... you..."

He chuckles. A dimple appears in one cheek. My breath hitches.

His chuckle turns to belly laughs. "Should have seen... Should've seen yourself." He opens and shuts his mouth in imitation. "Looked just like a landed fish."

My scowl deepens. "Are you always such an impertinent ass?"

He grins saucily, arms spread wide. "Behold the King of Impertinence."

"Careful! You'll fall, then I'll have risked my neck for two dead corpses."

"Most corpses are dead, *kleintje*. Not to worry. Perfectly safe up here."

I clamber to my feet and find my other comb along the grassy verge. He's too casual, treating this all as a joke. I jeopardized more than my place at the abbey. I curl my movable fingers into fists as I march toward my mare. I risked my skin for him.

"Have fun larking in the woods," I call over my shoulder.

Several paces down the road, something hits me square in the back.

"Ow!" I turn on my heel and glare. An acorn bounces away into a rut.

"You came to help, yes?" Tys Owlymirror calls.

"I've had second thoughts."

He cocks his head. "You resemble a terrier, you know, with that shrill little bark and—"

"You like dogs? You'll see more soon. Bloodhounds are on your trail." I give a mock curtsey. "So nice to meet you, King of Impertinence. Farewell."

"Wait," he calls. I ignore him for a few paces before I turn. He's pointing upwards. "... Through the trees for half a league so's not to leave a scent trail... slow going... I set a trap. Didn't plan to hurt anyone. Just needed a horse."

Half a league of tree-traversing is impressive, but I frown. "You could've asked."

"Didn't know it was you, riding astride and all."

"You almost beheaded me."

"Sorry. Planned for a man on a horse, not a short girl. No permanent damage, eh?"

I huff. "Was it a fairy or an imp that presided at your birth?"

"Fairy. Doing good deeds, aren't I? Rescuing Henk?"

"Henk?"

Tys points over his shoulder to little Henri.

"You changed his name?"

Tys shrugs. "Got nothing left here, has he? Needs a new life in a new land. Needs a name that sounds like all the rest of the *kleuters*."

"But–"

Tys puts up a hand, cocks his head. My ears can't detect it, but I know what he hears.

"They've found your scent." I whistle for Etoile, mount up and ride to the branch where Tys stands. "Give Henri, *er* Henk, to me. Then you—"

"You're not leaving me behind." Tys scrambles onto Etoile's back, steadying himself with a hand on my shoulder.

"Hey!" I protest.

"Thrutch up." His voice is close as he nudges me forward. "Plenty of room for both of us, seeing you're so small." He squeezes into the saddle behind me.

I don't mind cramped spaces, but I do mind sharing them. Especially with a too handsome boy. His keen eyes and the scent of wildness about him prickle my skin.

"This is *my* horse, and *my*—"

"Bloodhounds. Let's go." He digs his heels into Etoile's ribs. Anger simmers in my still burning chest, but I focus on the mare's gait. Tys snakes a hand around my waist. I smack it. He doesn't change his grip, but I feel him twist in the saddle.

"Roast pheasant in your saddlebags. Good thinking."

"Keep out of my provisions." I make to grab it. "We'll eat later."

The pilfering sneak has the dexterity of a juggler. He pulls off a leg and tosses it into the road.

"What are you doing?"

"For the hounds." Despite the whistling wind, his voice is audible, his lips too close to my left ear. He hands half to me. "Throw a few pieces at each crossroads. Confuse them."

My anger and admiration battle. Finally, I nod. I nudge Etoile faster. Both of Tys' hands grip my waist. I stiffen.

"Must you?"

"What else can I hold on to?" His voice is too innocent. I grind my teeth.

He moves one hand, reaching for the reins. I grip them tighter. *I'll control Etoile, and if I can keep my thoughts from Tys Owlymirror's hands, I'll keep her at a good pace.* I drive my heels into her sides, a bit more roughly than I should. She transitions to a brisk gait, and we wind our way into the North Valon Mountains. I pray we gain a few leagues of road between us and the sharp teeth of my uncle's hounds.

WE MAKE GOOD PROGRESS. A hound scenting quarry will have difficulty catching us. I hope that after Tys and Henk took to the trees, their scent on the ground weakened. Now that it mingles with horse, it should be impossible to detect.

I hope.

Tys says he's heard no baying for a while. I offer silent thanks to the Heavens.

Only five miles later, the Pleiades' favor sours. Etoile's movements change. She could be tiring, though I've alternated gaits to give her rest, but her pace is wrong, with an odd head bob. I pull her to a stop.

"What is it?" Tys asks, rubbing his back as I slither off the saddle.

Feeling as superstitious as a mountain villager, I don't voice my thoughts, as if saying the word *lame* might cause it to happen. Peering at Etoile's legs I see no obvious cuts or wounds, yet the way she holds her left foreleg, as if she wants no pressure on it...

"*Merde.*"

I pick up Etoile's hoof. There it is—a jagged little stone lodged between the tender foot and the hoof wall.

"Hey!"

I look up. Tys sits in the saddle, his impatient expression a familiar one. No one likes being ignored, and no one ignores better than a deaf person who never heard what was said. Exhaustion washes over me. I'm tired of the journey, of being squashed hip to pelvis with the handsomest boy I've ever met, of the treasonous weight of smuggling a Lowlander through our mountains.

"My mare picked up a stone. She might take us as far as Boispierre, but no farther."

"Boispierre," Tys splutters. "Home of Rotten Reichard? *His* hounds are tracking Henk. You know this, right?"

I concentrate on prying the stone from Etoile's hoof. "My grandfather's there. He'll help us."

Without seeing his lips, Tys' answer is submerged into murmured half-silence, but the pitch of his fear carries. I look up and catch the end of his tirade. "… endanger your family, by landing on his doorstep with the houndsmen's prey?" He jerks his thumb to indicate Henk.

"No one of consequence will see us."

"No one…? That castle's filled with Reichard's foul kin."

I straighten and glare. "I beg your pardon!"

"Boispierre's as dangerous as a pit of vipers." He shivers, as if truly scared.

I've not mentioned my family name, and I lied about my first name. He doesn't know I'm a princess, that my uncle is Rotten Reichard, that my grandfather is King Gauthier. Still, his assumption stings. Etoile butts my shoulder, bringing me back to our predicament —the warm tissue inside her hoof.

"Boispierre. I removed the stone, but she can't take us farther."

When I look up, Tys is pointing upwards. "… string a hammock between the trees. Hide here until she recovers." His hands describe ropes in the tree branches.

I rub my temples. I understand waiting out danger, even if I can't imagine waiting in a tree. The sun is only halfway down the western side of the sky. "The hounds will be out hours yet, tracking us. We can't stop now."

Henk wakes, cranky and crying for his mother.

"… Bring all the hounds upon us, with that fine pair of lungs," Tys complains.

He untangles Henk from the sling and sets him in the saddle before him. I lead Etoile, ignoring Henk's howling. When he finally quiets, I turn around. Tys is singing. Each phrase has hand gestures that cover Henk's eyes or pat his cheeks or tugs at his ears. The boy giggles. Tys catches me staring. Even in the green, leafy light, his blush is obvious.

I pretend not to notice. "He'll be hungry soon. There's not much food."

"Between your saddle bags and mine, there'll be no hollow bellies." Tys pulls out a sausage, half a rye loaf, a narrow wedge of cheese, and divides them. I walk beside them as I eat.

"And for dessert…" He holds up two golden pears.

"Where did you find such delicacies?" They certainly don't grow here. The season's too short in the Valon mountains.

"Ligeron, two days ago. Villainously priced." Tys cuts slices with his boot knife and hands one to me. "Smuggled in from Brandt."

The fruit is honey sweet. I hold out my hand for another slice. "It's delicious."

"Because it's from Brandt." He gives it to me and cuts into the second. "Everything from Brandt tastes better. The wine, the cheese, the fruit, the mutton."

The truth is obvious. "You're homesick."

His knife stills. Slowly, he continues slicing. "Perhaps I am."

He admits he's my enemy.

"Why'd you travel to Valonia? Everything from Brandt is outlawed. Even you."

"Fastest way home." His bleak expression adds depth to his words.

"And you're traveling from…?"

He doesn't answer, instead wiping his knife on his leggings, sheathing it, then tossing the cores to the roadside. His lips move as he's half turned, his answer unintelligible. He faces forward, silent. Frustration nips like fleas. I say the words I've never directly told anyone.

"I can't hear. Not much anyway. If you turn, I don't know what you're saying."

His brows lift, then settle in understanding. "Oh." I brace for the inevitable nosy questions, but he surprises me. "I said, soon a bit of Brandt will grow in the Valon Mountains. Can they outlaw that?"

Trees rarely bear fruit in high altitudes, but I just shrug. "You said you traveled from…?"

His saucy grin peeks out. "Persistent girl." He loosens Henk's grip on Etoile's mane as I urge her into a brisk walking pace. "Shipped out of Aemsterhaven."

"I thought you were an acrobat."

"Didn't choose life at sea." Tys plaits Etoile's mane into long, rope-like braids. I watch his lips, not wanting to miss any of his story. "Passage went well enough 'til we reached the far side of the Middle Sea. Knights of the Pleiades pressed us into service."

"Oh, no." The monastic, military arm of the church is known to be tough, the opposite of the pale, land-bound friars. Knights defend coastal cities and merchant vessels in the Middle Sea. On the Fates' behalf, of course. Pirates caught are summarily killed; confiscated plunder enriches the Knights' treasury. My uncle was a very skilled knight.

Tys shrugs. "Fates blew us close to a Knights' galley. Forced a dozen of us to come aboard their ship and work for half-wages. Our captain couldn't say nay."

"That's unfair."

Tys nodded. "Knights will flog a lad if too slow sluicing blood off the deck."

I swallow, trying to imagine such a life. "Was there a lot of blood?"

"Enough. After a year, I feared I'd tempted the Fates too long. Next battle might be my last. So, next harbor… I left."

"They let you?"

"No." His laugh is humorless. "Jumped ship. Almost caught too." He rubs his shoulder. "Gave me a token, so I could remember them."

"How long since you left the sea?"

"Four months."

"That long?"

"I've been *walking*. It's not exactly near, the Middle Sea."

"How far is it?"

"Two hundred leagues." He cocks his head. "More or less."

"Two hundred leagues? How did you survive?"

He gives a quick, forced smile. "Juggled for my supper."

"You really are an acrobat?"

"Never joined a troupe. Struck out on my own." His gaze flicks my way. "I can do all their tricks. Juggling. Tightrope. Legerdemain."

"Will you show me?"

He shrugs. "Perhaps tomorrow."

At the next crossroads, we head down into the foothills. Tys returns Henk to his sling and covers him with his cloak. Villages appear as the sun lowers. We pass laborers heading home from the fields, milk maids carrying full buckets on shoulder yokes, and children with bundles of kindling. The normal activity feels strange.

Tys reports no baying since mid-afternoon. I send thanks Heavenward.

The road dips and curves with the foothills, and as we crest the last, the gray stone walls of Boispierre appear on the opposite side of the valley. The great oaks on the mountain circle its shoulders with a mantle of green. The buildings of the town, constructed around the lower hillside, settle at the castle's feet like small children waiting for a story.

"Boispierre?" Tys says.

"Beautiful, isn't it?" I want to race home to my grandfather's arms. I'll tell him all the terrible things that've happened; his brow will cloud, and he'll start setting it right. He always does.

Tys pulls the cloak closer. "Looks over the Pilgrim Road. Anyone could be watching right now. You want to just march in? Snatch a new horse?"

"It won't be like that." I pull my own hood up. Just in case. "I know a secret way inside. Stay on the Pilgrim Road for now."

The road follows the valley. I keep stealing peeks at the castle, though we don't turn that way. I stay patient until we round the shoulder of mountain that hides Boispierre from sight once more. We're the only ones left on the Pilgrim Road. It's narrower here, more overgrown.

Another stream comes into view, tumbling down the steep mountainside in a series of small waterfalls. I step off the path and wade in. When the water is knee-deep, Etoile stops following. I look behind. Tys sits in the saddle staring after me.

"Come on."

"Get my feet wet?" There's something wary in his too casual expression.

"What's wrong?"

"Nothing."

I huff impatiently.

"By Fate's miracle we escaped the hounds." He leans forward. "Traipsing into the wolf's den is too confident by far. Safety's only a few leagues away." He gestures north. "Henk and I could be in Brandt by sunset."

"You've nothing for the ferryman," I counter. "You need something valuable."

"How valuable? I'll not have you take your grandfather's last coin, nor have you turn thief for me. Henk and I'll take it on foot from here." He turns again to the northern pass, studying it. He's serious.

"My grandfather's not poor. I have a few valuables no one will miss." He starts to protest but I keep going. "Besides, your journey doesn't end at the riverbank. You've no food left for your journey to Aemsterhaven. Let me do this."

Tys turns his full attention on me.

I cross my arms. "I don't want to worry. About Henk."

He smirks. "That'd mean thinking about me."

I roll my eyes, unable to lie.

"Oh, you'll be thinking of me." He swings down from Etoile, taking care to keep Henk steady, and strides through the stream until he's beside me. "Won't be able to resist wondering whatever happened to Tys…" His voice is warm, prompting shivers down my neck and arms. Then he looks over his shoulder; his voice lightens. "… and that little *kleuter*, Henk. Must be growing like a weed, that lad."

I give his arm a shove. "Come on."

We leave Etoile to soak her sore hoof in the stream and climb the waterfalls. We're sopping wet and tired when we reach the high meadow beside the stream. A huge oak spreads its arms wide in the center of the fallow field, and an old charcoal burner's hut leans precariously against the granite outcropping.

"So," says Tys as he massages where the rope harness cuts into his shoulders. "How to get into the castle?"

"The hut."

"The hut what?"

"The hut conceals a hidden passage into the castle."

Tys goes pale. He follows me across the meadow, but slowly. When I reach the hut, he's five ells behind.

"It's a tunnel, not the entrance to Hades."

He comes no closer.

"You don't like dark, tight places?"

He stretches his arms. "Give me wide-open land and all its danger, and I'm a happy fellow." It's not wise to tempt the Fates with such bold talk.

"Fine. This task requires one pair of hands, and I know the castle well." Ignoring the relief on his face, I point to the oak. "Go, make yourself a hammock in that tree."

I leave Tys and Henk, slipping into the dark of the forgotten hut.

CHAPTER THREE

Tyrian Purple: an ancient dark red dye also called
Royal Purple, extracted from predatory sea snails in
the family Muricidae

I USE A TINDERBOX AND CANDLE STASHED UNDER A hearthstone and descend into the passage. Second thoughts assail me. The original purpose of the passage wasn't for entering the castle, but to provide escape. A bolt hole. Only five people know of its existence.

And now Tys.

I shouldn't have told him. I shouldn't have revealed so much. About me. About my defect. What is he thinking right now? What was I thinking?

I halt. One side of the tunnel's partially collapsed. Thick tree roots protrude into the passage around the fallen stones. The opposite wall bulges, making the resulting space narrow and cramped. I exhale. I've acted the fool all day, but this secret is as safe as Valonian silver. With his fear of tight places, Tys will *never* use this passage.

The passage veers upward again. I climb two sets of stairs and face a door. It's heavy and stiff, weighted with centuries of secrets. I hope it doesn't squeak with rust. I push ahead through dusty spider trails, lifting the candle high. The passage, one of six I discovered during my childhood, meanders like a termite's path through the thick walls of the chateau.

I pass the turn that leads to my father's chamber and my uncle's. Since their birth within an hour of each other, they've occupied neighboring rooms. Considering their opposite personalities, it's a wonder my grandfather never separated his twin sons. Perhaps if Reichard avoided reminders he's the second son, he'd not have become bitter and cruel. I've never understood why he adores the Seven Sisters, despite knowing the Fates held him within the womb while my father, Julien, slipped out first. Their wisdom denied Reichard the right to inherit the crown, yet he's never seemed to blame them.

A shift in the dank air. A fresh scent. I pause.

The far-off glow of another candle is faint but intensifies. I blow out mine and retreat behind a bend in the passage. The illumination grows brighter. I retreat again, but the light dims. I dare a peek around the corner just as the light narrows to a rectangular beam, then a sliver. It blinks out. Someone has snuck into Lady Ulrica's chamber.

My neck prickles.

Lady Ulrica fostered here as a child, while the Eastern hordes harassed her parents' kingdom. When it fell under the weight of the onslaught, Ulrica lost home and family in one blow. My grandfather tried to lessen her pain by adopting her into ours. She chose to never marry, becoming chatelaine of Boispierre when my grandmother died. The kitchen, pantry, dining hall, and wine cellar are all ruled by her iron fist. Overseeing matters of the household herself, she rarely lingers in this wing during the day.

None deserve to be surprised in the sanctity of their own chamber. With patient movements, I pull the latch, easing the door open, hoping it's silent. I push back the tapestry that covers the wood paneling, and the hidden door.

Surprisingly, Lady Ulrica *is* in her chamber, pacing, agitatedly speaking to someone. I catch none of it until she stops and says clearly, "His chamber reeks..." She makes a sour face and continues pacing as she listens to the other person. She shakes her head, patting her side under her arm. "... The skin is crusted... succumbing... putrefaction..."

I'm confused, certain I'm misreading her lips. Why is Ulrica nursing castlefolk?

Her brows lower and she stalks closer to the person on the other side of the tapestry who earned her ire. "You don't *want* to know... sweep cobwebs from the kingdom... leaving dung heap duties to me." Her glare's intimidating. I'm not envious of her visitor.

I need to gather saleable items for Tys' ferry ride. I must keep moving. Before I do, Ulrica's bleak expression halts me.

"*You* are not watching him die, Reichard."

Reichard. My uncle. He's here.

My heart thuds against my ribs. When did my uncle leave his houndsmen? Did they give up the chase? Have Brandt soldiers invaded already? Why discuss a wounded man with Ulrica?

She grasps his sleeve, dragging him toward the chamber door on the far side of the room, into my sight. "Let me give him comfort. Water, at least."

No water? He must be a vile criminal in the dungeon.

My uncle resists, turns. "And if he lives? If anyone suspects the truth..."

"He won't live, Reichard."

"Perhaps I should smother him to have done with it."

Ulrica looks shocked. "That's regicide—"

He turns, quick as an adder. Ulrica retreats, apologizing. I stare, breath stuck in my throat, as if I've been knocked off my horse again. *Regicide*. It's no criminal—the dying person is my grandfather, King of Valonia. My thoughts tangle.

Where's my father?

Does he know?

How long has my grandfather suffered?

Is he in the dungeon? Or kept prisoner in his own chamber?

I take three steps down the passageway, then double back to close the door. Reichard cradles a crying Ulrica. His lips move against her ear. Gossip says Ulrica and my uncle were sweethearts when they were young. Then he took vows dedicating himself to the Seven Sisters and to love no mortal woman. They couldn't still be lovers, but it seems they are partners.

I slip the latch into place with trembling fingers and scurry up the last set of narrow stairs that leads to my grandfather's private rooms. Could he be already dead? I need a chance to save him. To say good-bye, at least.

HIS BEDCHAMBER SEEMS EMPTY, the air unnaturally still. Like a tomb.

The bedchamber's huge, befitting a king, and his bed is on the far side. I draw close, peering into the shadows of the curtained bed. I rush forward. He looks like a corpse. Smells like one, too. His shoulder-length white hair is a tangled mess, his silver beard frames cracked lips.

"*Grandpère?*"

A slight rise of his chest, but he doesn't wake. My heart stutters. Fumbling, I pull the coverlet away. His hands, crossed on his chest, are nearly skeletal and so very cold. I rub them. The movement will generate heat. Perhaps even consciousness.

Yet there's dark seepage staining the side of his nightshirt, a crusted mixture of greenish-yellow and rusty red.

"What do I do?" I pray aloud in frustration. The Fates hear me, for I recognize what surrounds my grandfather. Thread. Fibers. Woven into sheets and pillowcases and coverlet.

He's enveloped in cloth, and I *know*.

I've never used my magic for healing but...

Before the Bonifactum Edict, the market fairs sold rolls of bandages that kept a wound clean and prevented sepsis. No one ever *said* they were endowed with Skeincraft, but they glowed with blue-green Otherlight. I thread my needle and wish, not for the first time, that I'd been trained properly. I've always known needle and thread harnessed my magical power, and always known not to speak of it. I'd find excuses to hang around market stalls selling Other-lit embroidered items. I noticed special stitches on clothing, on bedding, on purses of coin. I caught phrases, learning how storytelling and music enhanced Skeincraft because of its connection to the element of air. I gleaned the rest by guesswork and intuition. I'd *never* ask a woman to risk her life to train me.

My needle hovers, uncertain. I'm empty, my power elusive, unwilling to be coaxed out of hiding. Except... Isabeau cloaked that power. I search for a knife, any kind of blade. I find one by the tinder box and rip the stitches from my hem. Tiny silvery charms fall like scattering hail.

My lungs expand. I'm a windmill, sails filled with the autumn breeze and windlass churning. I gather magic from the corners and crevices of my body. The warm, delightful tingle pulses as I push it out through my fingers and into the needle that bobs in and out of the silk coverlet. The thread fastens my magic to the cloth. I push as I pull the needle. Blue as Lake Clair, the power spreads to the sheets and his nightshirt. It cocoons him, offering strength.

I need specific stitches, special knots, but don't have them.

I can only push my magic toward that festering wound and hope.

I steal strength from my own body. Warmth flees. Knees buckle. It doesn't feel good anymore. I shiver, focusing on the wound, speaking to my grandfather. Mooring myself to him with my words. I weave the tale of the witch trial. Tys. Henk. Our flight through the mountains. Otherlight shimmers around my grandfather.

His fingers tremble atop the coverlet for a moment, then reach towards me.

"*Grandpère!*" I set aside my needle; my tears splatter our twined hands.

His eyelids flutter as words creep out of his throat. "Your father... tell him..."

"I don't know where he is." He could be anywhere in Valonia - overseeing tax collecting, or road repairs, or settling judgements.

"With men... along northern border." He gasps for air. "They watch for... Brandt soldiers." I'd forgotten about the war brewing. His fingers tighten slightly. "Anything happens to your father, you are... queen."

The word weighs heavily between us. No one has *ever* said I could rule. By myself.

Because I'm deaf or because I'm a girl, I don't know.

I love Valonia. I know to put duty first, as Grandpère always has, and I've sometimes imagined wearing the crown. I'd be gray-haired with grandchildren of my own. Wise. Experienced. Appropriately deaf. Folk don't seem to mind if old people can't hear. They're patronized, yes, but *young* deaf people are considered incapable.

"You must go." His brow furrows. "Must be kept safe." His fingers twitch and stumble over each other. "Take this ring."

He has two. One's a delicate silver band, worn on his smallest finger. The other, a heavy gold signet, silently announces his identity as King. He plucks at the silver ring, trying to work it over the knuckle.

"Find Tatienne du Rjasthani." He collects his breath. "Wise woman. Of the Mirvray. On Isle Dinant. Tell her I wish to redeem... the promised favor. *Valorificati favoarea.*"

The Fates have found my destiny thread and are playing tug of war between themselves. Stay. Go. Tys. Grandpère. Boispierre. Isle Dinant.

He tremblingly holds out the ring. The island isn't far, sitting in the middle of the river that separates Valonia from Brandt and the Empire. Where the ferry crosses.

I take it, repeating the name, location, and keywords.

I can't leave, though. He needs me. Needs my magic. Long enough to get a physician.

"She's to keep you safe until a truce is declared." His breathing is labored. "Return you to..." He pauses and stares at the chamber door. "Voices. Reichard."

Stars! I must hide.

I stand, focusing on the secret passage... and step on Isabeau's charms. *Merde!* I sweep armfuls under the bed. Find more telltale bits of twisted steel. Push them into shadow.

"*Chérie!*" A hiss of warning.

Too many ells of hardwood floor separate me from the passage. Only my grandfather's shield stands propped in this corner, beckoning me to safety. I toss the last handful of charms out the window and pull the broad, kite-shaped steel away from the wall and wedge my back into the corner. I press my feet against the floorboards. The vibration of my uncle's steps informs me better than my ears can. Steps circle the room. He approaches. I shrink smaller. The metal of the shield presses against my head, causing one comb to bite into my skin.

"Holy Heavens, the stench is terrible."

I nearly jump out of my skin; my uncle's voice is so loud, as if he speaks right into my ear. I hold my breath. The footsteps pace to the window, then back to the bed.

"Not nearly as dead as I'd hoped," my uncle says, too loud for such treasonous words.

"Sorry... to disappoint you." My grandfather's voice is thin but audible, as if I sat beside him. I angle my head up and around to see what's happening on the other side of the shield. I glimpse the curtains around my grandfather's bed and my uncle's broad back as the world quiets. An idea. I turtle my head down and press it once more against the shield.

"... So wretched, Father. You're giving your life for your country." My uncle's voice is as clear as if I'd been born with normal ears. The shield. Somehow, it magnifies the sound collected by my hair combs. The metal perhaps?

"I always hoped to... sacrifice on the... battlefield." Even with the magnification, my grandfather's voice fades.

"A different sort of battlefield. You shall save many Valonian lives."

The quiet grows heavy. I resist the temptation to look again. In the silence, a slight sound. One I can't place. Concern tightens my belly.

"Poison," my grandfather wheezes. That sound—a bottle uncorked. "Not very trusting of the Fates."

"They are always opening and closing doors. If I keep one opportunity propped open or keep another one locked tight, I can't see how that violates divine doctrine. And here you are, mortally wounded, just as Brandt musters an army at our doorstep."

"The *Mors Regiis* pact," my grandfather mutters.

"Yes. It will keep Brandt from invading. Yet, if Brandt assassinates Valonia's newly crowned king on the day of his coronation..." He *tsks*. "Such treachery, it will be only right to bring bloodshed upon them. If we regain all the land that once belonged to Valonia, it only proves the Fates are with us. And with me. All hail the—what is... that?" His voice rises.

Steps.

"A witch's charm?"

Merde. I missed one.

"A pair of twisted needles?" Steps back to the bed. Rustling. "These stitches... Who's been here? Ulrica never... Marguerite's still at St. Clotilde's..."

I tuck my head farther.

"Already left," my grandfather murmurs.

"The long passage?" My uncle's footsteps march across the room towards the secret door. On his way back, he flings open chests and turns over chairs, sounding like the thunder of an approaching storm. I huddle smaller, cradling my left hand. "Who did this?"

"I do not know... A woman."

His voice rises louder than I thought possible. "A *stranger* found the long passage?" His footsteps stop beside the bed. "No, Father." His voice drops in volume. "You've sat too long on the Oak Throne. Lies do not sit comfortably on your tongue."

I'm an animal cowering, my breathing erratic.

"A woman, yes," he murmurs. "Only family knows the passages, and it wasn't Ulrica." A faint noise. "I could have sworn to the Stars that Marguerite was on the front row in Tillroux. I'll send a pigeon to the abbess to check the dormitory. How long has Marguerite been here?"

A *snick*, like a blade through paper.

"How long?"

My grandfather's breath wheezes. Then stops.

I can't resist peeking. My uncle lifts a knife from the mound of blankets that was my grandfather. The blade gleams, no blood upon it. Another wheeze. *He's alive.*

He didn't plunge it into my grandfather's chest, only the coverlet.

"Perhaps the Brandt assassins will stumble upon Marguerite as well."

My heart pounds so hard, I almost ignore a new, faint sound—the baying of hounds.

Tys. Henk.

My uncle strides to the window. "The witch's boy made it this far without being caught? He had help." His steps return to the bed. "None can outwit the Pleiades. Not you. Not Marguerite. Not anyone."

My uncle stalks past my hiding spot and opens the chamber door. He speaks to the King's Guards always posted outside, ready to stop an enemy assassin. "The king is ailing." My uncle sounds heartbroken. "Redouble your prayers." The door shuts.

I wait a moment only, then slip from behind the shield. I scurry to the bed. My grandfather gasps for breath, his arms outstretched. Feathers litter his coverlet; the threads of my spell hang limp and powerless.

"Grandpère." My hands flutter, trying to find a way to repair it, to renew the magic keeping him alive. Tears burn behind my eyes.

"Go." His voice rattles.

I step to the window. I have a clear view of the meadow and that single oak where I told Tys and Henk to take refuge. Hounds circle it. My stomach heaves.

In the bed, my grandfather struggles to push himself upwards. I rush to his side, brushing the matted hair from his face.

"I can't help them." Tears slip down my cheeks. "I can't travel through the long passage in time." I imagine Henk's little body mangled. Tys trying to fight off the dogs but falling under the weight of furry bodies and snapping teeth. I grip the coverlet. "I can still save *you.*"

His gaze fastens on mine. "Go."

"I can't."

He holds up his left hand. "Ring."

I clasp it. "I have it. I'll find Tatienne du Rjasthani."

He squeezes my hand. "Rrrring…" The gold signet on his finger presses against the silver ring on mine. "… Is a key."

"The silver ring?"

He shakes his head.

"The signet?"

He nods.

"Key to what?"

His eyes roll up in his head.

"Grandpère!"

He stares at me once more. Slowly, he angles his chin, looking over his shoulder at the carved headboard behind him. I'm baffled.

"Seventh… passage."

Of course. Everything comes in sevens. Seven Sisters. Seven hours of the day. Seven compass points surrounding true north. Seven castles of Valonia. Why only six secret passages?

"Seventh? Where?"

Again, his eyes roll. This time I understand.

"The wall behind you? The headboard? The signet is a key?"

His eyelids close like a nod.

"I'll get you out of here. Down the passage."

His fingers flutter; his head moves side to side, sawing my heart in half. My chin wobbles. I can ignore his wishes. Save him.

His hands flutter again, pointing downward. "Stable."

I blink. I'd never realized the residence towers were stories above the stables. Although, the Valonian kings in days past did sit uneasily upon their thrones. Another bolt hole, I guess.

"If you're sure."

He squeezes my hand. I squeeze back. The whisper of baying hounds reaches my ears.

"Go."

I pull the ring off his finger. My obedience tastes like betrayal. "I love you."

His gesture is one used to shut up long-winded courtiers. I clamber onto the bed and find an indent carved within the ornate headboard. It matches the ring exactly, down to the gouge cut across one edge. Like a key. I turn it to the left; the headboard clicks apart, opening like a pair of doors into the dark passage. My grandfather shoves at my hip, urging me onward.

I kiss the top of his head before slipping into the tunnel.

⁂

MY BORROWED mount weaves downhill through the trees. The mare I snatched for Tys keeps close behind. Undergrowth and the steep slope slow us as terrible scenes of carnage flash behind my eyes. Blood. Bone. Torn flesh.

"Faster!"

Something hits the back of my neck.

"Margo!"

I halt. There's no one.

"Up here."

I peer into the golden-red leaves. There he is, high in the branches, Henk strapped to his back. Ropes drape across the tree canopy. The Fates made him half-squirrel.

He descends hand by hand. Too slow.

"Hurry!"

"Ever had rope burns?" His face is taut with exhaustion. How far did he travel through the forest by rope? Two hundred ells? More?

The hounds' murmurs fall silent. Tys scrambles.

"Houndsmen arrived. Found nothing in that oak but the cloak I fastened there." He lowers himself onto the mare's back, then claps his heels. I follow close as a shadow, plunging downhill through the undergrowth, dodging trees. The terrain flattens.

Tys swivels his head, shouting something.

I glance back. Nothing. Then the underbrush ripples. Dark shapes surge over the ground.

"We're too slow!"

I glimpse lighter ground up ahead through the trees. The road.

How close are the hounds? I dare not look again. I can't slow for even a heartbeat.

The ground evens out. I lean over my horse's neck, gaining speed. We emerge onto the Pilgrim Road, our mounts stretching their legs in a thundering gallop.

The hounds shoot out of the woods like cannonballs. We swerve. They leap at us. Jaws snapping. One wraps its teeth around the heel of my boot. Loses its grip. Falls to the ground.

Tys cries out.

A hound dangles from his calf. Its teeth clamped around muscle. Tys pummels the dog. It remains firmly attached, swinging as we gallop onward.

Hounds leap around us. They're a large, heavy breed. If they go for the horses, we're doomed. I urge my mare closer to Tys' mount. He struggles to pry the dog's teeth from his calf, not directing the horse. We're nearly neck and neck. Then he's falling behind.

"Tys!"

He rallies his mount; it leaps ahead beside my horse, the hounds at our heels. We race up hills and down as the road descends toward the Muse River. The dogs tire and slow. The only one remaining is clamped onto Tys' calf.

His leggings are dark with blood. The hound's jaws are stubbornly locked. If it hangs much longer, it'll widen the wound. He'll bleed to death. Tys grips his boot knife in one hand, holds the reins in the other. He turns to me, saying something.

"What?"

But he's bending, plunging the knife into the hound's throat. Blood sprays my face. When I look up, Henk's slipping off Tys' back.

"Hold tight!"

Henk screams, panicking.

"Hold on, dearling." I ride close, haul him up by his shirt. His little hands grab around Tys' throat. Tys doesn't straighten. *Stars!*

The hound's body drops onto the road. Tys sits up, shoves the reins between his teeth. His empty, red-stained hands pull Henk over his shoulder and into the saddle in front of him. I release a breath.

We near a sentinel tower. I point. "We should stop. The guards will help. Bind your leg."

Tys shakes his head. "I'm... Brandt!... Arrest me..." We gallop past. He looks over his shoulder. "... Not safe 'til... river..."

We crest the last ridge. The road unspools down to the wide, sparkling blue of the Muse River. In the middle of the river sits Isle Dinant, like a large, mossy turtle shell. On the far side are the gray walls and thatched roofs of Nemeaux. I've never been this close to the city of my birth. It belongs to the Duke of Brandt's spoiled younger son and, if my uncle's report is correct, it's crawling with enemy soldiers.

A blunt-prowed ferry boat leaves the island and rows toward us, its wake a wide V. *Thank the Stars.* The ferryman can take Tys and Henk to Brandt, then return with me to the island. I'll find the Mirvray wise-woman, Tatienne du Rjasthani. Kill two flies with one slap.

My satisfaction slips when I glance at Tys. He's pale, his face tight with pain. One arm is wrapped around Henk, who's flushed and howling. I measure the distance to the edge of Valonia. Still a good mile. *Fates, we need luck!*

The road takes a sharp bend. Tys slips sideways, then straightens, a grim set to his mouth.

Please.

The ferry nears the bank. It'll arrive as we reach the shore.

Two hundred ells to the riverbank. Tys' torn legging flaps around the mess that's his leg.

One hundred fifty ells. He glances backward. Says something. Kicks his mount faster.

One hundred twenty ells. I look over my shoulder and see them. Mounted archers and pikemen, racing over the crest of the hill behind us. Soldiers from Boispierre?

One hundred ells. The ferry halts a few ells from the bank.

Eighty ells. The ferry turns. They'd leave without us?

Seventy ells. We shout. The ferrymen pay us no heed.

Fifty ells. I yell, *"Valorificati favoarea!"*

Twenty ells. We're almost to the bank, but we don't slow. I'm determined to get on that ferry. Or angry enough to sink it. We plunge into the water. The spray makes it difficult to see the ferrymen, but they call out. Words I can't hear.

"Valorificati favoarea." I assume the words are Mirvraan, and they'll understand.

They're still in the shallows, drifting a bit downstream. We urge our sweaty, trembling horses aboard. The weight settles the flat hull against the river gravel. The ferrymen shove with their long oars. The ferry doesn't move. I glance at the pikemen and archers racing down the road towards us and scramble off my horse.

Tys catches my shoulder. "We need to let one horse go."

I slap my mare's rump. She plunges over the side. The boat rocks with her departure. The ferrymen yell in their foreign tongue.

"If we don't move, we're all dead."

I point over their shoulders to the armed men fast approaching. They stare quizzically. One reaches forward and tries to grab my hand. I jerk away. "Row now, or we die!"

They're good at their business, maneuvering the boat. Still, the army has bows, and we'll be within their range soon.

Tys passes a sobbing Henk to me. "Protect him. He's the reason we started this."

We settle in the bow, Henk in my lap. He's shielded from the sight of danger and any possible arrows that might come our way.

"Do you know the story about the *djinn* and the stork?" I ask. His cries don't pause. I start in on the tale. Henk's sobs slow. While I speak, I tear strips from my undershift. Tys clings to the saddle, standing on one leg. I shift Henk so I can reach Tys.

I press against the mangled skin and muscle. I bear down on the story, describing the villain's long, scraggly hair and pockmarked face, and push that energy into the cloth. There's no extra tingle as I tuck loose bits of skin together, wrapping it tight, from ankle to knee. I pray the pressure will stem blood loss and that any magic can protect it from infection.

"Arrows!" Tys warns and pushes us down.

Thock. Thock. Thock.

Thock. Thock.

The vibrations echo through the ferry's frame.

Then, sharper vibrations. Iron-shod hooves stamp against wood. I glance up as the horse rears. I grab Henk, rolling away from those hooves. The ferry bucks. I grab the side of the boat and curl us tight against it. Henk screams. The boat dips violently again. I scream too, as we nearly fall into the river.

Someone snatches the back of my dress. I cling to Henk as the boat jerks upward. We're thrown against the ferry's planks and something softer. The rocking boat settles. The horse plunges through the water, two arrows protruding from its side.

I shift. Tys, the soft thing I'd landed on, releases my clothing. A ferryman crouches beside Tys, loosening his own grip from Tys' sleeve.

"Almost paid your debt to the river god." His voice is gruff, accented. "That'd be the end of that, huh?"

"A thousand thanks," I say as Henk starts bawling again.

"Thank us when we touch land."

"Take us all the way?" Tys asks, teeth clenched. "To Brandt?" He points to the far side of the river.

"Don't you want to stop at Isle Dinant?" The ferryman looks to me as if I'm the one making the decision.

"No," Tys answers, as I ask, "Is there a healer? A good one?"

"Yes." The ferryman nods.

"I must get to Brandt," Tys says.

"You want to go there?" The ferryman points past the eastern tip of the island. On the far bank, their gray and green uniforms blending in with the mossy stones of Nemeaux's docks, are several dozen Brandt soldiers. They hold pikes and halberds as well as longbows. Death awaits on either bank of the Muse River.

I touch Tys' shoulder. "You need a healer." He doesn't meet my gaze. "Please."

He nods.

"The island," I tell the ferryman.

CHAPTER FOUR

Darn: to mend, as torn clothing, with rows of stitches,
sometimes by crossing and interweaving rows to span a gap

THE TWO FERRYMEN HOLD THE BOAT STEADY AS WE clamber ashore. Tys leans heavily on my shoulder. Once on firm land again, I check the Valonian archers. They stand, bows at their sides.

"Why not send another volley?"

The talkative ferryman spits. "Valonia has an agreement with our queen. All on our island are safe. If they send arrows, they risk" —he seeks the right word— "retribution."

He savors the word, making my neck prickle.

I remember that they've not asked for payment. Yet.

We're stranded on an island with nothing of value except my grandfather's rings. Even the horses are gone. When they demand payment, what will I have to give them? I bend over and pretend to retie my bootlaces while stuffing the gold signet down inside. Hopefully, they will be satisfied with the silver ring, once I find Tatienne du Rjasthani.

When I stand again, too many Mirvray folk have appeared on our spur of rock. We are quite outnumbered. Henk grabs my skirts and I hoist him onto my hip. I stand there, as Tys tries, without success, not to lean so heavily on my shoulder and will myself to look calm. They speak with the ferrymen in their language, so I glean only their expressions and gestures. Perhaps they're only here to greet us? A couple brings a litter and convinces Tys to lie upon it. They look like the Mirvray folk that seasonally traverse Valonia, in loose clothing and more jewelry than most folk are wont to wear. Supposedly, many have the Sight, but none are voyant-scarred.

Two women come forward, making eyes at Henk. He buries his face in my shoulder. I wish to hide too. One motions for me to hand Henk over. I shake my head. Henk's my responsibility.

Tys props himself on his elbow. "Hey!" He follows with a string of Haps-tongue. Though he looks ready to faint, he summons an air of authority. The Mirvray nod. Two lift him and start inland. The crowd follows. I can't stand here alone on the riverbank with night drawing near. I hitch Henk a little higher on my hip and follow the Mirvray, praying the Fates will protect me from whatever mischief might lie ahead.

I trail after until I'm caught in the embrace of narrow streets and multi-level homes. Up ahead, the Mirvray greet neighbors leaning out their windows. They don't seem dangerous exactly, more... uninhibited. They call with shouts and gesticulations, too exuberant for a street so Valonian in architecture.

Sixteen years ago, when Nemeaux fell to the Brandt army, Isle Dinant was abandoned. Few were surprised when the Mirvray settled here. They're brave, certainly; they travel the continent making trade at fairs and markets. Few doubted they'd find a way to profit from an abandoned town in the middle of a river. They always wring a profit, folk say, even if they must pick your pocket while promising a bargain.

The crowd of Mirvray don't *seem* like pickpockets. They've not the lean look of kids roaming the markets stealing coin to fill the belly their parents can't feed.

The crowd gathers around a house at the far end of a modest square. Someone knocks. The door is flung open, and a woman stands in the doorway. I gasp. The sun's sinking behind the island, but she glows with a pulsing amber Otherlight that rivals it. It shines from her wild hair, unbraided, uncombed, and curling past her shoulders, to her boots trimmed with little tin bells. The ring in her nose gleams, as do her earrings and multiple necklaces, with more than reflected sunlight. She advances towards the crowd, shifting the weight of the bundle she holds with one arm. The bundle moves. A tiny fist pushes the blanket aside. The woman's blouse is open, most of her right side bare as the baby suckles her breast.

The woman's attention isn't on the baby, but on Tys and the men carrying his litter. She speaks sharply in her native tongue, her free hand gesturing in a choppy motion. The men drop their gaze, shifting guiltily. She speaks again. They straighten and jog off, carrying Tys down a side street and out of view.

"No!" Tucking Henk close, I push through the crowd. "Where are you taking him?" A dozen steps, and I can see Tys' litter. "Stop!"

The Mirvray men ignore me. I hurry after, but one ferryman catches my arm.

"Are they taking him to a healer?" I ask. "I should be going too. Tys is my responsibility."

He pulls my hand in the air and faces the crowd. In his own language, he speaks animatedly while pointing to Grandpère's silver ring. Is he demanding payment? Claiming he was cheated? I can't give it up yet.

I wrench away and tuck my hand around Henk. "I asked for a healer. You said there was one here. Is her name Tatienne du Rjasthani? I need to see her. *Valorificati favoarea.*" My gaze bounces between the ferryman, the crowded square behind him, and the empty street where Tys and his litter have disappeared. "Please."

"Girl!" the woman with the baby calls in my language. The crowd parts for her. She is so *bright* with her Otherglow. "I will take you to Tatienne du Rjasthani. You will tell me what you want with her and we shall discuss the fate of your friend. Yes?"

I nod warily and hitch Henk up on my hip.

"Feroulka." She gestures for a girl about Tys' age to come forward. "Take this little fellow to the children's paddock so we can speak freely."

I pull Henk tight. "Children's paddock?"

The woman motions for folk to disperse and smiles at me. "Protective, eh? Slow to trust? Good. Come, I will show you."

She gestures for me to follow her down the sloping street. I follow, but slowly. Trusting my grandfather's dying words led me here, but what if he was wrong? What if I misheard him?

Feroulka walks beside me. "You look scared out of your wits." Her smirk is patronizing.

I try to smooth the fear out of my expression. "Who is that woman?"

Feroulka looks offended. "She's queen of the western Mirvray."

I don't like her tone. "A queen? She's wearing an apron. And where's her crown?"

She shrugs. "The queen has power enough, crown or not."

Magical power, that's certain, even if it's stored in the jewelry around her neck and pierced through her ears and nose. Still, I hurry my pace until Feroulka and I are walking with the queen. We wind through the streets of Isle Dinant until we come to another, larger square. It's unlike any I've ever seen. Nearly all the paving stones are gone, replaced with grass. It's enclosed with a low fence. A few dozen children chase each other or climb the wooden structures scattered around the little field.

"You pen children like chickens?" I ask.

Feroulka scowls, but the queen answers.

"We are on an island, and the river is swift. Here the children are free to play within safe boundaries."

I'm not fully convinced, but Henk wriggles, eager to get to the ground. He's been confined to harness or horseback most of the day. He wants to play. I lift him down inside the fenced area.

"Ball," he says happily, finding one and holding it up. I nod as he runs off to play.

"He will be fine," the queen says, inviting me to sit. "Now, let us speak together."

I hesitate. "Tys. Where've you taken him?"

"To our healers. He will be fed, as will the child, when he remembers his hunger." She indicates a tray of food placed between her chair and mine. I keep a wary eye as we eat fruit, cheese and foreign-spiced pastries. The queen shifts the baby from her breast to her shoulder. Patting his back, she turns her gaze upon me. "I hope we can speak truth to one another."

I nod. The Common Law of Hospitality respected across the continent binds host and guest to speak truth. If either lies, the oath is broken, and we're both vulnerable to treachery.

"I am called Tanja," she says.

"I'm called Margo." Only Tys called me that, but half-truths are acceptable.

"Your companion was severely injured. We heard baying. May I assume a dog bite?"

"Yes. We were hunted by the Fates' Hounds, the ones belonging to the Bishop-Princep." It feels like I'm shouting for the Stars to meddle with us. I tug at Tys' bracelet around my wrist.

"Was your crime felonious in nature?"

"No. Heretical."

"Ah." Her baby lets out a tiny belch. "You and the young man?"

My cheeks flame. I want this truth clear. "The boy's mother" —I point to Henk— "was burnt for embroidering spells that kept him from drowning." I close my eyes to block the memory of the conflagration, but it's no use. I open them. "The Bishop-Princep thought full justice included the death of her son. Tys and I felt differently."

Her face softens. "So, you were hunted. And nearly caught."

"Yes. I thank you for your hospitality and the swift work of your ferrymen." I tuck a peach into my pocket. "I... we hoped one horse would be sufficient payment. Yet we seem to have lost both."

"We shall recover them." Her eyes gleam with humor. "Our folk are known as vagrants and horse thieves. We cannot let that reputation die before my son becomes king."

I risk a smile at her joke as we're interrupted by a runner. He hands a slip of paper to Tanja, then dashes away. The woman reads the lines and her face grows serious.

"Your friend's wound is bad; the muscle is badly savaged. Also, with bites come infection. It will be difficult to repair the damage, but to amputate successfully will take tremendous energy I am not willing for my healer to waste. Not for a stranger, even if a guest."

With each sentence, it seems the Fates hammer judgement upon Tys.

"Amputate? No. He's an acrobat."

She raises her eyebrows. "Truly?"

"Yes. An amputation will cripple him."

"You would rather he die slowly of gangrene?"

"No. I'd rather you heal him. Mirvray folk have magic." I look around. "This island must be full of herbwitches. Can't they do the work necessary to heal him?"

"For a fellow Mirvray, yes, but I will not ask it of them for a guest."

"Why not? Fortify them with charms. Your Otherlight shines clear. Spare some power for Tys. He risked his life for an innocent child. He ran and climbed and carried him all day. Why withhold your healing?"

The stillness of the square draws my attention from Tanja. All the children, and the adults attending them, stare at me; the air bristles. I slide back from the seat's edge, lowering my gaze.

"I apologize, Your Majesty." The words stumble from my mouth. "I shouldn't have raised my voice."

When I look up again, she smiles. "You have answered the question I would pose. Are you willing to stand as the source for his healing?"

"Me? I tried to heal my grandfather this afternoon." My voice catches. "I... used all I had. I've nothing more."

The queen leans forward, her expression intense. "Are you willing?"

"Yes."

"A second question: who is your grandfather?"

His name sticks in my throat.

"Did he give you that silver ring?"

I straighten. Tanja seems so motherly and harmless. How have I *not* seen her guile and perspicacity? Two young people approach. One takes the tray, and the other takes the baby. When they leave, the queen leans forward, almost conspiratorially, pointing to my finger.

"I wore that ring years ago. As a girl, I gave it to Prince Gauthier. He saved my life, and I owed him a debt."

My grandfather said *wise woman*. I expected a hunch-backed, gray-haired vessel of knowledge, not this vibrant person. "I thought your name was Tanja," I accuse.

"You said you were called Margo. It seems neither of us was fully truthful. Tell me, what favor does King Gauthier require of me?"

I speak low. "If you're Tatienne du Rjasthani, he asks that you keep me safe until a treaty is made and I can return to my father's care."

Tanja nods. "I am, and I pledge to fulfill this favor. It is easily done."

My shoulders relax. "A thousand thanks."

"With that information as to your parentage, I assure you that you have the magical capacity necessary to heal your friend."

"I'm no healer."

"I shall provide the healer. You only must let the healer use your strength and power to facilitate the healing."

"How?" I might bespell bandages or bed linens as I'd done for my grandfather. Tatienne du Rjasthani seems to want something else from me.

"I will show you." She stands. "You had enough to eat?"

"Yes, thank you." I stand and follow. "I've never heard of a witch lending power to another."

"You are not a witch."

I stop in the middle of the street. "What?"

She smiles over her shoulder. "You are a mage."

"Mage?" The word's unfamiliar.

"One capable of both sensing *and* performing magic." She gestures to continue. I follow.

"No. Women perform the magic and men can see it. That's how it works."

She chuckles. "That is what seems to happen when magic is thinned out. Yet, here you are, able to do both."

"How do you know that?"

"You told me yourself. You sensed my aura."

If I wasn't so flustered by this news, I'd kick myself for being a flap-jaw. "This will help Tys?"

"Yes. The infirmary is just ahead." She points to the westernmost tip of the island. An assortment of watermills and other mechanical devices spring from a low-slung building. "And you are certain you have had enough to eat?"

"Yes." I slow, remembering tales of witches eating fat little children. "Why is that important?"

"A starving witch or mage can do little, even with the tools she needs before her." She points to the watermill. "Like a mill with nothing to push it. If I let you assist my healer without feeding you, we would have little success. Come." She opens the door into the building.

I follow her down a hall and into a whitewashed room, well-lit by oil-filled braziers. In the corner, a trickle of water descends from a hole in the ceiling into a basin. Tys lies face down on a draped table in the center of the room. A huge bear of a man stands behind the table arranging pots and bowls, helping a girl my age.

"The healer's no older than I am." No wonder the queen wants me to help her.

"No." Tatienne points to the girl. "Adrenna is assisting our healer, Gaspar."

She then points to the bulky man. He wears his shirtsleeves short, with large brass cuffs around his biceps. He looks nothing like the university-trained physicians in Valonia, but rather like a sun-burnt farmer, ready to wrestle for a prize at the harvest fair.

"He is a true healer," Tanja says. "A mage, like myself. Like you."

He does have a glow about him…

"A *male* healer?"

"One of many mysteries in the world." Her mouth twitches upward, then turns serious. "Gaspar is ready. I shall demonstrate what you are to do." She stands behind him, placing her hands on the arm cuffs. "I am a Charm-mage, so I send my power into the metal that rests against his skin."

It's difficult to see Otherlight in such a bright room. Still, as she closes her eyes, her golden aura flares. The healer pulses a bright green. Then it ebbs, and the queen opens her eyes.

"You, of course, being a Skein-mage, will place your hand upon his back, your power flowing through his shirt."

My breath comes rapidly. So much information about myself, about my power, and now, assisting a strange man perform a miraculous healing? My gaze catches on Tys' face. Pale skin, slack expression; even his curls droop. The life and energy that drew me to this boy and kept me by his side are gone. I miss his smile, the mischievous gleam in his eye. If he can't walk properly, who's to say he'll ever perform again, or that I'll ever see his smile once more.

I step forward. "I'll do whatever's needed."

※

DRAWING magic from my center to my fingertips feels like drawing water from a well. I focus on pulling the magic outward. If I falter, it's like letting go of the windlass, the bucket tumbling down into the well's depths.

Standing behind Gaspar, I can't see what he's doing. His cavernous chest vibrates as he speaks. Sometimes his efforts pull power from the cloth underneath my fingers, and his sentences are brief. I pour extra strength then.

My arms grow tired pressed upon the healer's back. The fingers of my left hand ache from the forced straightness. No obvious scars from the old injury, only loss of dexterity and a tendency to twist. I let them curl naturally into a fist, pressing my knuckles into Gaspar's back. I close my eyes. I puzzle over Tys and his white glow. I ponder Tatienne du Rjasthani's words. If I'm a mage, able to do both sides of magic, is Tys one as well? He can see Otherlight—he told me so—and he must be able to perform some sort of magic, though I've not witnessed any. No magical affinity I know of produces a white glow. Something to do with acrobatics or the tightrope?

The healing drags on. The windlass of my well becomes rusty. My stomach growls. I want the peach in my pocket, but I need both hands on Gaspar's back.

My strength ebbs. Head aches. Muscles cramp. I'm lightheaded. I need more…

Storytelling… that focuses my energy.

"Once there was a dragon…" My words whisper. Thin and wispy, a thread ready to snap. I swallow and speak again, louder. "A terrible dragon…" I close my eyes, feeling past how my words hang in the quiet room, testing if they're strong enough to draw magic from the air. "… who controlled a large valley. All that happened within his domain, he watched with a jealous eye."

I imagine Tys and Henk listening; drawing magic becomes easier. I let the tale meander, getting the feel of its shape, then let the story spin out. It twists and turns; I'm lost in the weave of breath and weft of timbre until my voice tires and words become grit in my throat.

Someone touches my shoulder. I jerk. Open my eyes.

"We are finished." It's difficult to focus on the girl before me. "You may rest."

I WAKE in a small room bathed in the blue light of dawn. My arms ache. My head hurts. My throat's dry as a butcher's smokehouse. Beside my bed, a dark-haired girl scowls at me.

Isabeau? I blink. It's not my roommate. Green eyes instead of brown, earrings dangling on either side of her face. I search for her name. *Feroulka.*

"You used magic until you passed out? How stupid are you?"

Wincing, I sit a little higher in my bed, so Feroulka can't look down her nose at me.

"Head hurt?" she asks.

I nod the tiniest bit.

"No more than you deserve." She hands me a mug. "This should help."

A stalk of mint steeps in dark tea. I sip. It's strong and sweet and nothing like Valonian tea. I like it all the same. I drink half before she takes the mug and pushes a tray toward me.

"Eat, too. Fastest way to get rid of the headache."

Dishes crowd the tray. "It's enough for three people."

"You did the work of three people," Feroulka says. "My uncle's rather impressed."

"Your uncle?"

"Gaspar, the healer."

"How is Tys?"

Feroulka shrugs. "He won't need an amputation."

I frown.

"That normally happens, when a limb looks more like meat than muscle." Her attitude softens. "Because you worked in tandem so long, my uncle was able to repair more than he thought possible. Your acrobat will probably limp, but he'll walk."

Relieved, I sag against my pillow. "Can I see him?"

"He'll sleep the rest of the day. You need rest, too."

Obediently, I eat and sleep. When I wake, the golden afternoon sunlight fills the room. Another tray of food is on the table beside my bed, along with my combs. I replace them and slide my feet out of the bed and cautiously make my way to the window. I'm still weak. I grab a slice of bread and butter from the tray and eat as I stare across the river at the moss-covered stone walls of the city of Nemeaux.

I haven't been this close since the day I was born. The day we fled. The day Nemeaux was captured by Brandt for the Haps-Burdian empire.

"... Ferry brought Valonian soldiers... white flag... Brandt this morning."

Snatches of conversation drift upward from the courtyard, a story below my open window. I look down. Two Mirvraan women are hanging laundry and sharing gossip I'm desperate to hear.

"... waterfront full of soldiers cleared quickly..."

"My man ferried them across... had a document with a lock of white hair embedded in sealing wax..."

No! I press my forehead against the window frame. All the dread and fear I felt in my grandfather's chamber rises to swallow me. I know what news was brought by ferry.

"The king is dead..."

Tears come like rain in a spring storm. I left my grandfather alone and dying in Boispierre. He told me to go, but I could've stayed. I could've pulled him from his bed and brought him down that passage with me. He was skin and bone, light enough to carry. He could be lying in a bed like the one in this room, his ring still on his finger.

He died. Protecting me. Just as he'd always done.

Someone shakes my shoulders. "Margo!"

I peel my hands away, tuck my combs more securely in place. Tatienne du Rjasthani peers at me.

"King Gauthier is dead?"

The queen nods and gathers me to her bosom. I don't know what to do with her arms around me, her necklaces pressed against my cheek. I go limp, breathing in her scent. Herbs and smoky copper.

I finally straighten, wiping my eyes.

"The news came this morning," Tanja confirms. "I'd hoped to tell you myself. My men ferried a party to Brandt. They had a document stating the king is dead and, under ancient treaty laws, Brandt must swear nonaggression for three months. The commanding general at Nemeaux made the oath, promising to deliver the news to the Duke of Brandt."

"Three months," I say. "Firmly into winter. What happens then?"

Tanja raises a brow. "Doubtful they will start a campaign in the middle of Yuletide."

Comforting, yet no one's mentioned my father. "Who signed the document?" I ask.

Tanja answers, "Bishop-Princep Reichard."

"Not Prince Julien?"

"No." She squeezes my shoulder. "I am sure he is safe."

"He was in the mountains with his men, watching the border." I take a steadying breath as I gamble with my trust. "Before I left Boispierre, I watched my uncle poison the king. He said he'd arrange for Brandt assassins to kill my father on his coronation day."

Tanja watches me steadily, as if she believes me.

"And me too."

"We will do all we can to warn your father, my dear." She takes my hand in hers and touches the silver ring. "I have a life debt to repay. Upon my honor, I swear the Mirvray people shall keep you safe."

CHAPTER FIVE

Applique: a sewing technique that involves stitching a
small piece of cloth onto a larger one to make a
pattern or design

WHEN A KING OF VALONIA DIES, THEY SAY THE ENTIRE
kingdom holds its breath. Though the next in line to the throne is
acknowledged as the new ruler, he's not crowned, nor holds administra-
trative rights, until seven weeks of mourning pass. My father doesn't
hold the full weight of the king's power. Not yet.

I write a letter to my father that afternoon, explaining all I
witnessed in my grandfather's chamber, and how I found hospitality
with the Mirvray folk. I take my grandfather's signet ring from its
hiding place in the toe of my boot and press it into the cooling wax. I
worry already. If it falls into my uncle's hands, he'll know I witnessed
his perfidy. He'll know where to find me.

Tanja assures me her courier will never make such a mistake. I
hand Tanja the letter but snatch it right back.

"They're identical, you know," I say. We sit side by side, watching
Henk play with the other children in the paddock as she feeds her
baby.

She smiles. "I know."

"It was easy to mistake them for each other, before my uncle donned the cassock."

"Trust me. I can discern Julien from Reichard de Perdrix. So can my spies and couriers."

Feroulka joins us. "I can't smuggle a letter you're still holding."

"You're the courier?" I ask. Or perhaps spy.

"Why not?"

"My uncle would rather spit on you than let you in Boispierre. He has little tolerance for anyone not born on Valonian soil. Such an obvious Mirvray would be conspicuous."

They exchange a look. Tanja says, "… I rather think that has more to do with Ruxandra than Feroulka herself."

"Ruxandra?" I tuck away my explanations about sentinels and guards. "That was my mother's name."

Tanja nods, shifting her baby to her other breast. "She was my younger cousin. We grew up together. The story of a prince rescuing me from townsfolk—my giving him my oath ring? That was her favorite."

She can't mean…

"The others grew up and grew tired of it. Ruxandra never did. When the lads came around, wanting to pair off, she couldn't see past the dirt under their fingernails. She had loftier dreams. We argued until, finally, she seemed to settle."

Feroulka crosses her arms "She didn't settle."

I glance between them. My exotic mother, brought by the Fates from the Far Lands… was no more than a rebellious Mirvray girl? One who thought she was too good for her own people? Impossible.

"One morning," Tanja says, "I found her gone, along with our grandmother's jewelry."

"No."

"Ancient pieces, the dowry to be divided when we married. She took it all."

I imagine how angry Tanja must have been.

Her hand encloses mine. Tanja tugs me closer on the bench, turns so our eyes stare into each other's. Whatever anger might have been there has burnt out. She speaks carefully, as if wanting no misunderstanding.

"I was not surprised when I found her with King Gauthier and the twin heirs. She wore our jewelry, spinning a sad tale about being a princess from the Far Lands. Kidnapped. Shipwrecked. She was a story weaver *non pareil* and Prince Julien was absolutely smitten." Her smile turns to chagrin. "Prince Reichard less so. He did not believe her tales. Determined to prove her a fraud, he set up elaborate tests to prove her royal blood."

"Sounds like my uncle."

"For the last one, he gathered nearly every mattress in the chateau. Stacked them atop one other; a princess sleeps on the softest bed possible. Your uncle told the King's Council that he had placed a single dried pea underneath the bottommost mattress. When your mother left the chamber the next morning, she complained she had not slept a wink. Reichard did not believe her, but she insisted on a physician's examination. He found tiny bruises all over her back and sides."

"How?"

"Ruxandra poked and pinched herself all night long, to prove she was a princess." Tanja shrugs. "She was *that* determined to wrest her destiny from the Fates."

I stare mutely as my thoughts catch up with her story.

I am Mirvray?

Emotions cascade over thoughts, which tumble over reason.

I am Mirvray.

Tanja takes my left hand. I don't breathe as she traces grooves on my ever-curled palm. "Some say our folk are gifted in knowing what the Fates have in store."

I swallow. She slides her hands away in a strange gesture, as if drawing something invisible out of my hand.

"Yet one's path isn't written here. It is determined *here*." She points to my heart. "And most often can be seen here." Her fingertips graze my forehead, circling around my cheekbones and jaw. "Especially in the eyes."

I blink away tears. Anger, fear, and this *yearning* for family are all tangled up inside.

"You remind me of her," Tanja continues. "Brown eyes, dark hair like all the Rjasthani family. The same way of pinching up her eyebrows when she was angry. That determined set of your chin—just like your mother." She sighs. "The freckles are a nice addition. Your father's side, yes?"

I nod.

"I am sorry you never had the chance to meet her, Marguerite. Your mother was a lively, complicated woman. She loved your father fiercely and looked forward to your birth. She asked me to be your godmother, before... everything happened."

The avalanche of emotion suffocates me as my world turns upside down.

I race from the square.

TYS IS AWAKE, sitting in bed, when I burst into his infirmary room. He yanks bedclothes back over his bare, bandaged legs at the sight of me, but I don't apologize for not knocking. I collapse into the chair beside his bed.

"What's the glare for?" he asks, half laughing.

"I'm not glaring. How are you?"

His skin has lost the chalky, gray pallor of before. "Not terrible. Thanks to you, I hear."

I shrug away his gratitude. "I'm not some angel of healing."

He squints and cocks his head. I don't like being studied. I stand and pace.

"What's wrong, *kleintje*?"

"You know what I just learned? Apparently, I'm part Mirvray."

Tys doesn't seem sufficiently troubled.

"You know what this means? I thought my mother was this beautiful, ethereal, exotic…" I gulp, remembering what my uncle once said. "Maybe she truly was a greedy, conniving, ambitious witch who used her wiles to bed my father."

"*Kleintje!*"

"Why did no one *tell* me? I've lived for *sixteen* years. *Someone* should've said *something* before now. I feel tricked. Duped."

Tys looks confused.

"Everyone says I look like my mother." I sniff. "I never considered that she was a common, lying Mirvraan." The cauldron of hot anger and shame spills into tears.

Tys snatches at my hand as I pass his bed. "Margo!" He looks disappointed. "Didn't know you had a problem with Mirvray folk."

I sit. "I didn't. I don't." I want to explain, but tears clog my throat. Finally, my thoughts and voice clear. "My uncle never liked me. I thought it was because he suspected witchcraft. Or because I can't hear. Maybe it's because of my mother?" I hold up my left hand, wiggling the thumb and forefinger while the others stay uselessly curled. "He did this. Took me to the farrier's anvil, placed my hand upon it, and brought the hammer down." I still have nightmares—the anvil's warmth soaking into my skin, then excruciating pain. "He was so… angry."

"*Kleintje.*" He releases my right hand and tenderly takes my left. "Such cruelty."

We sit in silence for a long while.

"He's one man," Tys finally says. "You're here now. Never have to see him again."

"I do." I groan. "I must go back."

"No, you don't. Fates brought you here. You can stay. You're Mirvray."

My grandfather's signet rubs against my toes. "I'm also *very* Valonian."

He strokes my clenched hand. "So, you eat songbirds roasted in dung by moonlight?"

"What?" I jerk away.

"Does every fellow have the Partridge and Oak tattooed on his back?" His mouth twitches. "Heard every Valonian's born with an extra finger, but you don't have one. So perhaps untrue. Or perhaps you're a freak?"

"Tys Owlymirror! You…"

His mouth opens wide in a laugh. He snaps it shut, trying to look repentant, but laughter bursts out again. A smile tugs my lips upward. Tys leans against the pillows, he's laughing so hard. Finally, he begins to speak, interrupts with a chuckle, then manages a few words. "Apologize… Wanted to make you laugh again…"

I remove my boot and catch the ring. I'll tell him quickly, like a merciful death. "I am the daughter of Prince Julien. King Gauthier is… was my grandfather."

More laughter bubbles out of him. "That's funny, Margo."

"Marguerite." I hold my palm toward him. My grandfather's signet gleams in the late afternoon light.

His amusement slides away. "Marguerite?"

"Marguerite de Perdrix." I swallow against the rough feeling in the back of my throat. "After my father's coronation, I'll be the Crown Princess."

His face settles into serious lines that make him look so much older. "Crown Princess. Should I start saying 'Your Highness?'"

"Of course not," I huff. "You seem to like calling me *kleintje*. I'll accept that in its stead, King of Impertinence." I give a mocking bow. His eyes crinkle.

"So, you outrank Rotten Reichard." The seriousness hasn't melted yet. "Your uncle."

I nod.

"Should've aimed that rock better. World would be better without that monster."

We retreat into silence.

"Men who bully women…" he starts. His face tightens. "Anyone who hurts another... With purpose or cunning. Those deserve the punishment of the Fates."

I recognize the careful way of telling the truth. "Who hurt you?"

He's slow to answer. Perhaps, like me, his accusations remain mostly unspoken. "My father. Never bruised my mother, but as years passed, he stripped her of worth and power and everything she loved." He looks down. "My half-brother drove me to leave home, though. Sly as a fox. Enjoys cruelty. Whips. Knives. Words."

"It takes courage to leave home," I offer.

"Or great pain."

THE NEXT DAY, as I play with Henk in the paddock, Tanja settles in the shade and watches the children. I wait. She catches my eye. Smiles. Waves. She doesn't seem angry that I ran from her yesterday.

She might be hiding her emotions. It's easy, when done often enough.

I wait until her baby sleeps on her shoulder, then approach. I stand out of reach, asking for news from her spies. The conversation is awkward at first, like a dress made to measure for another person, pinching and sagging in all the wrong places. I pull the silver comb from behind my right ear. It never helped much, anyway. I drop it in Tanja's lap.

"I was told these were a gift from my godmother."

My heart trips down the stairs of my ribcage as Tanja smooths her thumb over the etched silver oak leaves along the edge, examining it as if she's never seen it before. She looks up, tears shining in her eyes.

"I wanted to do so much more." She makes an apologetic gesture. "In Valonia, it is rare to have a child born without hearing, but among our families, it is more common." A shrug. "The Fates have decreed it; so instead of letting deafness isolate our children, we all learn to converse with our hands from infancy. It pained me you would struggle, that you would be considered broken. I was tempted to relegate the Fates, to steal you from your family and let you grow up among us, where no barriers would impede your development."

Strange to feel horrified and cherished in the same moment. "Why didn't you?"

"Growing up in Valonia, you were different, but still one of them, able to take the crown if the Fates decide. If I took you away from all that, no matter the advantages, there would be no chance Valonia would ever claim you. I found another way." She fingers the comb. Otherlight gathers tight around it. "This does not give you back your hearing, but I hoped it would help."

"It has." I offer her the other comb, letting the world go silent.

Her fingers coax more shine from the silver, as if she's polishing it, instead of pouring magic into it. Her lips don't move until she's handed them back and they nestle against my skull.

"I cannot change what the Fates have decreed." Her words are crisp, her accent more pronounced. "I can only soften their blows. While you are here, we will teach you again the language of hands." Her hands move in Mirvraan fashion, seeming to add to whatever's spoken.

"Again?"

She sharpens her gaze. "After your mother died, I made sure you had a Mirvray nursemaid. You became quite proficient before she was discovered and... relieved of her position." The delicate phrasing makes me shiver. She places my hands atop hers as she continues, gesturing with her words. "Enchanted combs made it easier for you to assimilate in Valonia." She smiles. "The Fates returned you to us. Perhaps they desire you to become reacquainted with language that does not require hearing."

⚜

I TELL Tys about this secret, second language. He's intrigued, and we practice hand words throughout his recuperation.

"*Kleintje*, know this one?" he says each time I visit, making graceful gestures.

It's a game. A competition. I drink in the language. I pester the island folk, asking the meaning of this gesture, or that sign. Language tutors are everywhere, from the young man baking the morning bread, to children playing in the paddock, to old folk gossiping in the afternoon sun. I watch and I listen. The language I'd not recognized before now flows around me like water, and I snatch meaning from bent fingers and twitched eyebrows.

A few days later, Tys takes his first halting steps, holding to railings.

He's weak, and in ill temper afterward. He ties knot after knot in a bit of rope then throws it across the room. When I offer encouragement, he's surly.

I look him in the eye, signing, "You're a complete ass."

"Better than a…" He signs something I don't know, but roughly translates to sickly sweet dwarf. I should be offended, but I can't hold back my laughter. A moment later, he laughs too.

Each morning and afternoon, when Gaspar's sons take Tys outside to exercise, I come along. He sweats and trembles, but I distract him with elaborate insults. It doesn't matter if it's Langue-Valon or hand language, he volleys them right back.

When his nostrils flare and he doesn't respond quickly, I insult him again.

"Extra point for me!" I crow, even as my heart twists.

"Not so fast." He blinks back tears, taking two more steps. "You pale-bellied, moldy-haired giglet. Daughter of a cross-eyed farrier who couldn't shoe a horse if it were three-days dead and an onion-eyed alewife who brews pigweed and thistles."

Gaspar's sons declare him finished for the morning and he crumples onto a bench.

"Three points for you, then." I shrug. "Cheater."

A sideways glance and the ghost of a smile twists my heart in an entirely different way.

Tys' leg improves steadily. Soon, he's walking farther and farther around the courtyard. The limp's pronounced, but Gaspar says that with proper work, he'll heal.

"He must walk. He must climb. In time, he must run. The only way the muscle will heal is to be used." Gaspar studies his movement and gait. "He should practice magic as well. There are too few of us men who have the Gift—who can keep the Gift. Shame if he lost it."

This is new information. "It's possible to lose your magic?"

Gaspar nods. "Do you not notice his missing glow?"

Tys collapses on a shaded bench. I squint but can't discern any Otherlight. I can't remember when I'd last noticed it.

"How'd he lose it? Is it gone forever?"

"Any magic wielder who willingly takes life loses his magic for a time. Any spell done recently loses power, and there will be days, months, or longer when they cannot perform."

"Tys didn't kill anyone."

Gaspar raises his eyebrows.

"He killed the hound that wounded him," I admit.

"That is enough."

"The dog was biting through his *leg*. Plenty of witches kill mice or wring chicken necks."

"The purpose of killing has some... correlation. Also, the beast's intelligence."

I ponder that. "So, murder, or warfare even..."

"Can hamper your magic for years. Perhaps the rest of your life."

"Preventing the dark magic told about in the old tales."

"Yes." He scratches his thick, black beard. "I believe that is why you do not see as many male mages. The responsibility of hunting, defending, waging war often falls to our shoulders."

My thoughts pick through the tangled skein of his words.

"Stop staring at that boy." Feroulka swats my shoulder. "You're embarrassing."

I startle, looking around. Gaspar's gone. Only Feroulka pays me attention, a wide, knowing grin splitting her face. My cheeks burn.

"Come, the queen wishes your presence."

I obey. Tanja sits in a shaded courtyard, sorting through a box of earrings. The contents and her fingers glow amber. She gestures for me to sit beside her. "Your letter was delivered."

I'm relieved but notice her determined expression.

"These next few weeks, you must practice your Skeincraft—unfettered and unrestrained—so you can access it, and repress it when necessary, instinctually."

"How will I do that?"

"We shall create a wardrobe for you. We have weavers who imbue cloth with magic. You, Feroulka and the others with Skeincraft will make the garments and embroider power into the clothing. I will be sure you have jewelry appropriate to your station, for an extra source of strength." She holds up a pearl earring. The gold filigree shimmers with power, and she nods.

I calculate the cost in my head. Surely, this goes beyond the bounds of hospitality? Even if she's my godmother. "You'll be repaid, I promise."

"This will be a gift." Her eyes seem to see beyond me, or even the courtyard. "A gift that will bless both giver and receiver. When you develop the skills necessary, you shall make a gift for your father. It will be like chain mail but made of linen and worn against the skin. It will protect him from blade or bow."

"I could make such a thing?"

Instead of answering, she takes my left hand and studies my palm. "Do you use this hand when you embroider?"

"No. It was broken."

"Yes, but you have movement enough in these fingers." She moves my thumb and forefinger.

"No." I snatch my hand away. "I never use it."

⁂

OVER THE NEXT WEEKS, I spend much of my time with Tanja and Feroulka, sewing and embroidering. They teach me basic stitches I already learned in the abbey. Sometimes, when Tanja's baby's napping, we take cloth, needles, hoops and thread to the top of an old watchtower and work there. We start *yet another* satin stitch.

"Can we move on to something else?"

Tanja takes my embroidery and traces the threads. "You know the stitches, how they look, their texture and density. Now, *feel* how the stitch is made. When you know how the stitches *feel*, then you can find spells that best complement them."

"I don't understand."

"You have power, child, but you will wear yourself out if you continue to pour magic into every stitch. Let the cloth, the thread and the stitches complement the purposes of your magic. Then let your needle snatch tiny bits of your magic to tack it into place."

"But magic takes concentration. It's work."

"Breathing is work," Feroulka says, "but you don't think so hard about that."

Tanja points to the catapult sharing the top of the tower. "That device can throw an object more than two hundred ells. The arm moves in an arc of less than ten ells. But the lever that releases all that energy, it moves the length of your thumb. *Feel* the magic within your stitches. More focus. Less effort."

※

IT'S difficult to *feel* the stitches, but I sew most daylight hours, constructing my new wardrobe. The gowns take shape. Rich teal and carmine curve and flare around me. The magic woven through them will protect me from whatever the Fates have in store.

Mornings, we settle in the arcaded courtyard where the Mirvray practice acrobatics and swordplay. Tys' leg is now strong enough for such vigor without me goading him with name-calling and insults. He joins those readying for swordplay as they stretch, squat and lunge. He mimics their movements, but Gaspar's sons urge him to do more.

"Lower," they shout. "Kick out farther."

As the morning wears on, my gaze lifts from my embroidery, wandering the courtyard. Swordplay becomes counterpoint to the steady pace of my stitching. As the men and women shift in brisk, fluid motions, my gaze lingers on the athletic pull of muscle. I appreciate the height of a leap, the power of a sword thrust, their abandonment of fear and surrender to the moment's demands.

Feroulka tilts my embroidery towards her and nods. "There. That's what happens when you *feel*."

The stitches aren't that different. A little tighter, smoother, but the Otherlight glow is significantly brighter. Is it because I've relaxed into this new life that demands so much, yet feels so right? Or was it because I was thinking about Tys?

THE DAYS PASS QUICKLY.

A week before the coronation, I take a break from stitching the linen armor I'm preparing for my father. It's long after morning practice, so I cut through the arcaded gallery. A figure lies stretched on a bench, his bare back soaking up late September sunshine. Blond curls and pale skin. Tys.

I'll not disturb him. He worked hard this morning, trying to match the able-bodied men.

As I pass, though, my gaze catches on where he's rolled up his leggings. A purple, jagged scar stretches across his calf. It's the first I've seen the wound since he was bitten. I step closer. The purple tissue is warped and wrinkled. Yet there's no redness. No pus or infection. It's ugly, but it's whole. No severed limb. No amputation.

A complete, healed leg.

I run my finger lightly over the scar. My power, harnessed with a healer, did that. I trace the path where those teeth tore...

He twitches.

I jump back. Heat floods my cheeks. I tuck my fingers out of sight and hurry toward the nearest exit. I'm almost there when what feels like a pebble hits my shoulder. I pause and turn, trying to look innocent. Casual. But my gaze sticks on Tys' bare chest and the knotted necklace that drapes over his collarbones like a twine cobweb. Dangling from its center, resting against his sternum, is a small golden ring. I rally my thoughts once more.

"Oh, Tys. Hello. I didn't see you there."

His gaze sharpens, but instead of calling me a liar, he sits up on the bench. "Practice was brutal. Only meant for a quick rest." He stretches. Pulls his shirt back on. My arms unfold. My fingers fidget with a seam in my dress. I cross my arms again.

"Gaspar's sons seem to know their trade," I offer.

He gives a bitter laugh. "Reichard could hire them as torturers, they're that good."

I wince. "Tys."

"Sorry." He pats the right side of the bench. An invitation. My insides somersault as I sit. He says, "You're leaving soon."

I nod. Silence stretches.

Tys raises his eyebrows.

I look away. I don't want him to see my yearnings.

His fingers tilt my chin until I look up. "Must you return?"

"I should be there for my father's coronation. My absence will be misconstrued. My uncle could turn it to his advantage."

"You're a brave girl, *kleintje*." His thumb strokes my jaw. I watch his lips but can barely focus on the words they form.

"I'm not brave. I'm doing what must be done."

"Can you return to Isle Dinant soon? Or come to Brandt?"

I snap the thread of my gaze that's anchored to his lips. "Set foot on enemy territory? I can't betray my people that way." I twine my fingers in my lap, willing my tongue to imitate their stillness.

His hand moves into my vision, reaching for mine. He hesitates, then his fingers form words. "I can visit you."

"Tys, no." Cold washes down my spine. "You're from Brandt... They'll hang you."

He smirks. "Not caught last time."

I point to his leg. "You nearly were."

He opens his mouth to argue. I press my hand against it. The right word, and my feelings will tumble out. "Please, don't come."

We sit, staring at each other, the air heavy with everything unsaid. Tys moves my fingers from his lips, interlacing them with his, and rests them between us on the bench. His face settles into a series of serious lines. I search for something, anything, to give a thread of hope. Of connection.

"Perhaps... we can exchange pigeons. Send messages to one another?"

His eyes spark. "Secret messages with the princess of Valonia? Right under Rotten Reichard's nose?" He grins. "The fellows and I will arrange that."

I imagine a crew of Mirvraans sneaking into the pigeon lofts at Boispierre, smuggling out baskets of birds. "Be careful."

He starts to rise. "When have I ever not been—"

I tighten my grip, pulling him back. Closer.

"Tys?"

He places his other hand over mine. His breath comes faster. "Marguerite?"

I have no words. There's nothing I can promise. The Fates play tricks with promises. I stare into his eyes, hoping he understands. "I *wish* our paths continued together."

His gaze drifts down to my lips. I hold my breath, anticipating. Then he pulls his hands from mine and looks away. Disappointment snags in my chest.

Tys gives my twine bracelet a little tug. "First knot any sailor or seaman learns is a reef knot. For bundling sails in bad weather."

I raise my eyebrows in question.

Tys turns it so the decorative knots are hidden, and the simple knot that fastens it faces up. He unties it.

"Sometimes called the square knot." He holds both ends. "See, we have two ropes coming from opposite directions. This one crosses over and tucks under. Then turns around to go back home, but before it does, it crosses and tucks once more."

He pulls the twine until it makes a sturdy, compact knot. A bracelet once more.

"You and I come from opposite places. The Fates" —he glances skyward— "allowed the threads of our lives to twist together. Once. Twice. Return home, *kleintje*, but don't think you've seen the last of me."

Tys stands and with a brief touch to my cheek, he leaves.

CHAPTER SIX

Featherstitch: an open or looped stitch, in which the
thread is caught by the next upstitch and curved away
from its natural path

A FEW DAYS LATER, IN THE COLDEST HOURS OF THE NIGHT,
Feroulka rouses me from sleep. She holds out my combs and waits for
me to tuck them in place.

"The queen calls for your presence. Dressed in your finery."

"Now?" I'm still sweeping cobwebs of sleep from my mind.
"Why?"

"She called her council and asked for you specifically."

"In the middle of the night?" But I tumble from bed. Feroulka
helps me pull on the carmine red gown with gold oak leaves embroidered around the hem and the wide square neckline. I'll wear it when
I return to Valonian soil next week. Its power shivers through me as
the fine wool rests against my linen underdress.

There's no throne room or council room on Isle Dinant. Instead,
the Mirvraan council meets in the weaver's lodge. Two men guard the
door. I prickle at the heightened security even as they wave me within.
I've never been inside, but it was obviously a warehouse once. It's
large enough that all the island folk could eat a communal meal here

together. The ceilings are high; the half-dozen braziers at the far end of the room barely illuminate the rafters.

Two people stand between me and the light. One turns and steps forward. I freeze like a startled rabbit. My uncle. Here, on Isle Dinant.

He stalks toward me.

"No." I tuck my fingers under my arms.

The torchlight from the doorway illuminates a concerned expression. My father. In a long cloak, not a clergyman's cassock.

"*Mignon!*"

"Papa?"

He claps his hands and holds them out to me as if I'm still four years old. I don't run to him, but when we embrace, I inhale his scent of cedar and oranges. His chest rumbles with words I don't understand. I look up. He kisses my forehead.

"I thought it safer to come to you, rather than you coming to the coronation."

My heart stumbles. No. In the wavering torchlight, I must've misunderstood the words his lips formed. "I'm coming to your coronation."

"Reichard, he..." My father resumes his blank expression of the last decade. "My observations and your letter make it clear. You mustn't return to Valonia until Reichard is... no longer a threat."

His words squeeze my chest.

"My council is assembled," Tanja interjects. "We all would like to hear your news."

It seems to be decided. All that's left for me to do is concede or rebel. I twist my grandfather's signet around my finger. *Valonia. Home.*

My father turns to follow Tanja.

I catch his sleeve and remove the ring. "This belongs to you."

He studies my face before kissing my forehead. "I'm glad he had company, *mignon*, before he joined the Stars."

The tightness in my chest loosens a bit.

At the illuminated end of the warehouse, a circle of mismatched chairs intersperses with the braziers. As we reach the circle, men and women emerge from the shadows and claim their seats. Tanja indicates the two remaining. We sit, and I press my combs tight against my skull. Deciphering this discussion might be difficult.

"May I introduce the Council of the Ten Families?" Tanja names each man or woman, finishing with herself as she sits. "And I am Tatienne of the family Rjasthani, elected queen of the western Mirvray... offer welcome to you, Julien of the family Perdrix, soon to be king of the Valonian people, chosen husband of our own Ruxandra du Rjasthani, and father of our own Marguerite de Perdrix et Rjasthani... gather to hear your petition."

My father kneels. He's never knelt before, except in ritual fealty to my grandfather. When he lifts his head, tracks of tears gleam on his cheeks.

"First, to the Council of the Ten Families I offer a thousand thanks... hospitality and sanctuary... my daughter. There are no words, no reward, that can recompense for this kindness. Now, or in the future, name a boon... I swear... give it freely."

I stare. My father hasn't shown such emotion since I was small. I thought his love had dried up years ago because of something I'd done, or because I was broken.

"Secondly... petition the Council... protective escort for my daughter to some place... out of reach of my brother, Reichard de Perdrix, Bishop-Princep of Valonia. His power is too great... bring our small evidences against him, but... certain he killed the king of Valonia and that he has designs on my life and that of my daughter, Marguerite."

He doesn't glance my way, but his face betrays fear and love and desperation. How had he kept this hidden so long, dammed up like a mountain spring? How had I not known?

"If we can halt him now..." he continues. "... Save many lives... future warfare ... Valonian, Brandtian, and Mirvaan." He lists several places where I could safely stay, some as far as the Middle Sea coast.

This new feeling, being cherished, leaves me breathless. Yet I've no voice. No choice. If I'm sent to the far side of the continent, will I ever see Tys again? When will I return home? Still, I dare not interrupt, for despite the mismatched chairs and the cracked plaster walls, this meeting demands the same decorum required before the Oak Throne of Valonia.

My father sits again, and various council members offer ideas: a stronghold in Brescony, a caravan traveling to the North Sea, or the West Sea, or the Grenwald forest, or the Halpen mountains, or several other places I've never heard of.

I don't want to be banished to any of them. I want...

I tilt my head back, trying to blink back tears and see Tys' telltale white Otherlight up in the rafters. I stare at the oblong glow stretched out along a beam, eavesdropping, then duck my head as if I never saw a thing.

Tanja claps her hands. "It is decided. We will offer your daughter protection and escort to a new sanctuary. Perhaps the final decision regarding the location can be decided by a smaller circle." Her gaze drifts upward, just slightly. Perhaps she spied Tys as well. "As to your first offer, I wish to lay claim upon the boon you offered."

The already quiet room stills as she approaches my father across the circle. She's dressed in a pale gown cut in simple lines, her most elaborate adornments, the jewelry clasping her throat and wrists, piercing her ears and nose. Yet authority encircles her as surely as if she wore a jewel-heavy crown and an ermine mantle.

"I ask this of you, Julien de Perdrix... Remember us." The room suddenly feels heavy, as if the Stars themselves take notice. "Remember that the Fates delight in reversing fortunes. If you ever find one of my people, any of your daughter's people, desperate and in need of sanctuary as she once was, then remember the hospitality given to your child and give equal hospitality in return."

My father returns to his knees; he stretches out his hands in the gesture of acceptance all petitioners make to the king when judgement is given.

"I swear on behalf of myself, and my daughter, under the gaze of the Fates, it will be so. May I ever be found a friend of the Mirvray in their hour of need."

"So let it be." Tanja raises him to his feet. "Now, come." Her glance includes me in the command. "We will decide the safest place for Marguerite."

We follow her through a doorway into a small room. My arms immediately prickle. Moonlight from the window illuminates rows of shelves, laden with glowing bolts of cloth. The scent of cedar and herbs, to deter creatures from nibbling the textiles, fills the air.

"There's magic here," my father says, fingering a bolt of thick velvet. "I can feel it."

My jaw unhinges. "You...?"

My father's bemused smile takes in the shelves of cloth. "There was a time, *mignon*, when I saw all the colors of magic. Now, I only get a frisson here or there, but this room..." He rubs his forearms, as if goosebumps sprouted under the sleeves of his doublet. "Full of power."

"You never said anything."

His gaze flickers to me, then away as he touches several bolts. "Reichard."

I trail after until we reach Tanja, seated on a bale of wool before the dark window. We follow suit, sitting knee to knee in a small pool of moonlight. She resumes the evening's business.

"You want your daughter safe, Your Highness, but you want her to return home something more than just a frightened, obedient girl, do you not?"

He studies me in the moonlight. "Of course."

"There is a place. An abbey."

"Like St. Clotilde's?" I ask.

"No. St. Clotilde's brethren use their Sight to guard against witch-craft among the fold. The possibility of discovery makes for a frigid and restrained environment." She lowers her voice. "St. Beatricia's abbey is all women; one of several in that city. Each has its specialty: musical instruments, medicines, glassmaking. St. Beatricia's specialty is embroidery, tapestries and lacemaking. We sell some of our best cloth to them. We can take Marguerite next week when we bring our shipment."

"Where is this abbey?" my father asks.

Tanja sits straighter, pulling back from our little circle. "Godesbrouk, in Hlaanders."

"Hlaandrs?" The word bursts from my father's lips. He lowers his voice. "Are you not aware of this region's politics? Its history? I can't send Marguerite to live within the Haps-Burdian empire. If her identity is discovered..." He turns his head. "... pawn... continental dominance."

Tanja makes conciliatory gestures. "She will be incognito, of course. There is danger, but is it greater than what she faces within your own borders?"

My father doesn't answer, but he doesn't look pleased.

"The needlework scholarship at St. Beatricia's is unsurpassed on the continent."

I lean forward.

"If you stay until you are a woman grown," she says, "you shall gain an arsenal of skills. Magic you could never learn within the mountains of Valonia, not with its current laws."

It sounds enticing. "I can't learn such skills here, from Feroulka?"

Tanja glances at my father. "You are too easily at hand if anyone comes searching."

My father inclines his head towards her and sighs. "I submit to your recommendation."

Tanja looks to me.

"Yes." It's everything I wished for these many years. "I'll go to St. Beatricia's."

Her body eases into gentler lines. "I shall make the arrangements."

With that, she leaves, and I'm alone with my father for the first time in more than a decade. I study him in the moonlight from the window.

"You never spoke of magic before," I say.

"I dared not confirm what Reichard sometimes suspected."

"Doesn't he have the Sight? He's always *watching* me, despite relying on voyants."

His face pinches before he answers. "He lost it years ago, before any hint of your magic."

"How?"

"I never knew the specific circumstances."

"And yours?"

He points out the window. "Once a great bridge spanned the Muse River here. It connected Nemeaux to this island and to our mountains."

"It was destroyed," I say. "With black powder. To keep Brandt's army from following into the heart of Valonia."

"Yes, black powder." He flicks a glance at me. "It was my responsibility to clear the bridge before it was destroyed." He frowns at the wavy glass, as if he can still see the bridge spanning the water. "People died. Desperate people. Trying to get ahead of the army. When the dust settled, I couldn't... see magic anymore." He's quiet for several heartbeats. "Even without the Sight, *mignon*, never underestimate my brother. When you return, no matter how strong you are, hide your magic until you're ready to deal the final blow."

The truth I should've seen years ago is etched on his face. "You're frightened of him."

"And you're not."

Anger and frustration bubble. "Too long I've been frightened of him, and you've never done anything to protect me. You left that for my grandfather."

He jerks back as if I'd slapped him. Still, he doesn't defend himself. Doesn't explain why he retreated all those years ago, hid his affection, became a stranger.

"Why did you leave me?"

He stands and points out the window, not to where the bridge once stood, but to an empty corner of sky—the location of the Pleiades constellation, if we could see it through the glass.

"I've learned that when I reach beyond the bounds the Fates have set, trouble follows." He stares into the darkness. "Being Reichard's elder brother has always been... difficult. He was always striving to prove he was better. Swordplay. Strategy. Scholarship. He always won. He savored the victory. Archery, however, was my strength. His arrows never beat mine until we were twelve years old. There was a tournament. He cheated."

"How?"

"Does it matter? No one caught him. He was never punished. I knew he'd done it, though, and I seethed. He took the one thing that was *mine*. I confronted him. He just lied. So, I went to the kennel and collected a handful of... er, filth, and I smeared it inside his bed."

I'm delightfully shocked. "You put..."

He nods.

"In his...?"

He doesn't share my glee. "The next morning, my favorite hound was found dead."

"No."

"Poisoned. I learned *others* might pay the price for my petty revenge." He gathers my hands in his. "When your mother came into my life, I forgot all that. Reichard counseled me against marrying her. I responded with careless words. Each time I had to choose between my wife or my brother, I chose Ruxandra."

He falls silent, studying the stars.

"I sowed a bitter harvest. From your birth, Reichard chose you as the scapegoat for all our trouble. I fought him with words or fists, whichever was necessary, for my darling girl."

I have faint memories of riding on his shoulders, laughing beside him as we ate supper, reading together. I sometimes wondered if I'd imagined them, for he never acknowledged there'd been any change.

He lifts my left hand. Kisses it. "I never thought he'd hurt you. I'm sorry."

The anvil. The hammer. My uncle's expression. Mostly, I remember the pain. I screamed, cried for my father. He never came. My grandfather became my champion.

I flex the fingers that can move. "Why didn't you come?"

"Reichard and I argued the night before." He runs a hand through his hair. "Over you, the way you favored your left hand. How you used your hands to speak. He said it was a sign of deviltry. I laughed in his face. He insisted your nursemaid was teaching you magic. I didn't care. He became furious, spoke of Ruxandra and how she'd been a witch, too. That she'd ensorcelled me with magic." He steps away, into the aisle between the shelves of cloth, as if ready to pace. I catch his sleeve.

"I can't hear you if you turn away." And I desperately want to hear this.

He smiles apologetically and we sit again on the wool bales "He... said worse things. We fought. I left him bleeding in the middle of the Great Hall. The next day, while I was searching for a dozen horses that had been 'stolen,' he crushed your hand."

I lean against the window, fitting his story with my terrible memories.

"The satisfaction on his face when he assured me you'd never use that hand to speak or make mischief again... I almost murdered him." He covers his eyes. "Father caught me before I could. He convinced Reichard to join the clergy, become a Knight of the Pleaides. He left for a few years. I knew then that I could never show the depth of my affection; he'd use it as a weapon."

He pulls his hand down his face and stares at me.

"I thought I was being wise, but here I am pushing you away again." He leans closer, fingertips grazing my cheek. "What a price to keep you safe. I wish I *had* killed him." The simmering, lingering anger lifts the hairs on the back of my neck.

"Will you kill him now?"

He looks away, focusing on the stars once more. "I don't know."

I shiver, which seems to bring him back to the room.

"I'm making the first move this time. At the coronation. I'm bestowing the fortress of Roc Ursgueule upon the Bishop-Princep."

I've visited the tumble-down fortress in the southern Valon mountains. It has a menacing, suffocating presence, probably because of its bloody history. Our ancestor, seven generations ago, killed the previous king under the boughs of the Valonian Oak in its center. Though the oak was the legendary source of our kingdom's power, that ancestor cut it down, divided the massive trunk into seven pieces, carved them into thrones, and distributed them among the seven castles of Valonia.

"How will a ruined castle stop him?"

"I'll lay the responsibility of restoration upon Reichard's shoulders under the gaze of the entire kingdom, with the requirement that he must attend to the repairs *personally*."

"The first snows will come soon. How can he, or anyone, stay the winter?" The central keep has no roof.

My father bares his teeth in a semblance of a smile. "He must work fast. And of course, once he's snowed in, we won't hear from him until the spring thaw."

⚜

WHEN MY FATHER leaves Isle Dinant, I give him the linen armor I prepared. It comforts me he'll have some protection in case my uncle doesn't come to heel as easily as my father plans. I wish for another day of embroidery to set the charms more firmly, but he must return to Boispierre before he is missed.

Three days after my father's visit, I also leave Isle Dinant. Feroulka comes as my escort. The ferry's loaded heavily with bolts of cloth bound for St. Beatricia's. Feroulka and I squeeze into the remaining space beside Tys and Henk. I'm relieved they'll be traveling with us. Yet, when we reach the docks of the Nemeaux waterfront and load the cargo onto several mules, there are only two awaiting horses.

"Who's riding longshanks?" I ask, using the Mirvray term for walking.

Tys, fastening Henk onto his back, much like he had all those weeks ago, jerks his chin up. "That's me. Got some family in Nemeaux. Ones worth visiting. Thought to darken their doorstep. Let them know I'm alive."

"Tys Owlymirror!" I plant my hands on my hips, trying to ignore the pit yawning in my belly. "You've family a stone's throw from Isle Dinant, and you said nothing?"

He shrugs. "Won't be going with you to... where was it again?"

Feroulka flicks his ear. "A secret. Remember? Queen's orders."

Tys shrugs again. "Can't blame me for trying."

Feroulka busies herself with girth straps, and Tys gives an elaborate, courtly bow, then claims my fingers for a soft kiss. Henk grabs his hair like reins, making Tys jerk and grimace. Loosening Henk's grip, he smiles again.

"Good fortune on your journey, Crown Princess. May the Fates allow our paths to cross once more." It's a ridiculously formal farewell. Laughter bubbles up, even as my eyes prick. I've nothing witty to say in return, so I blink back emotions and give a deep curtsy, matching his formality.

"So may it be."

I kiss Henk's cheek, then Feroulka and I mount. Tys walks beside us, making jokes. Feroulka joins in, teasing him easily. They speak and sign, but I lose the thread as I glance between them. When I turn to Tys again, he's gone.

He's slipped away with Henk to rejoin his old life.

I twist the knotted bracelet around my wrist until the tangled feeling behind my ribs loosens a bit, whispering prayers that someday I'll see the light of mischief in Tys Owlymirror's eyes once again.

WE RIDE ALL THAT DAY. The flat farmland reminds me of a blanket smoothed over an empty bed. We don't buy our noon meal or supper, relying on the contents of our saddlebags and waterskins. Feroulka says it's best to slip across the land without notice.

"You've been protected by your royal blood in Valonia," she said, "but out in the world, all anyone sees is a pretty girl ripe for plucking." She points out the rows of decorative stitches along the sleeves, hems and necklines of our loose dresses. "These keep us inconspicuous." She describes each stitch and its purpose as we ride. "I'm prepared for all else the Fates may throw in our path." She flips up the hem of her skirt, displaying a sheath strapped around each calf with a knife and a small, corked vial apiece.

Feroulka seems fearless. Could I ever be so confident?

Before the sun sets, she has me practice protective Skeincharms. I'm nowhere near mastering them when I smooth out my bedroll and find a tangled bit of twine. I almost toss it in a nearby thicket, but it's too heavy. Holding it to the firelight, I see it's a network of thin cord making a necklace, the one I saw around Tys' throat. Dangling from the center is a small ring with tiny golden pears all around the circumference. If Feroulka sees this, she'll tease me for the rest of the journey. Removing my shoe and stocking, I shove the ring on my toe and tie the knotted necklace around my ankle. I replace my footwear, burying the evidence of Tys' affection.

We cross into Hlaanders with little ado. After three days heading west and north, we arrive in a broad valley, a river curving toward the North Sea. The city of Godesbrouk straddles the river, surrounded by a star-shaped wall of earth and stone. Feroulka says the river flows through canals that separate the city into seven sections like an orange.

We cross a causeway and three bridges before we reach the abbey. As we enter the dark archway and emerge into an arcade surrounding a broad, rectangular courtyard, I *feel* magic. There's no Otherlight, though. I place my palm against the stone pillar of the arcade. The stone hums, as if thousands of bees make honey within its walls. It's the same reverberating thrill that courses through me when I unleash my Gift—yet magnified.

A norne approaches. We dismount. Feroulka and I curtsy, but the woman scolds us in Haps-tongue. Feroulka answers placatingly and points to me. The norne looks me over, sighs, then shoos us out the front gate, pointing down the road.

Mounting up again, I whisper, "Did we go to the wrong abbey?"

"No." Her mouth twists as her hands move. "The wrong entrance. We're tradesmen as well as Mirvray, so our very presence sullies the front gate. We must use the back way."

"You said all students enter through that gate."

"Or through the orphan door." She nods to a small door in the otherwise smooth wall that runs the length of the abbey. It's a sign and term I don't know. Feroulka smiles pityingly. "Orphan door, where shame-babies are left."

"What?"

"If a woman's burdened with an... unexpected baby, she can bring it there."

I blush. I know babies can come before a wedding, but in Valonia, there's *always* a wedding. And to label a baby as shameful... I shake my head and watch Feroulka's hands again.

"... Has two doors, one inside and one on the outside of the thick wall. It's the size of a cupboard. She leaves the babe in the space and raps on the inner door. Nornes wait a few moments so the mother can slip away, then open the inner door and retrieve the child." She makes a sad face. "And the 'Un-Fated' are left there too."

"The what?"

"If a family has a child that's deaf or blind or lame, some think the Fates cursed them. They bring deaf girls to St. Beatricia's. Each church house in Godesbrouk has their specialty."

Tanja only mentioned St. Beatricia's needle scholarship, not anything about other students being deaf. Or abandoned. I feel tricked, then guilty for feeling tricked. I lose the thread of conversation until we turn the corner and find ourselves facing double doors wide enough for a wagon to enter. Feroulka shrills a whistle, and a norne with rolled sleeves appears, followed by a littler terrier. It's small, but I still flinch as the dog plants himself between us and the norne, proclaiming the abbey his fiefdom with his yapping bark. I can't help but think of the much larger hounds that chased Tys and me from Chateau Boispierre to the Muse River. The norne produces a slender stick from the folds of her habit and swishes it through the air, hushing the dog. Her face neutral, she greets us in Haps-tongue without hand language. Feroulka responds in Langue-Valon, signing simultaneously.

"I've brought my cousin this time. She's a worthy candidate for St. Beatricia's."

The norne looks me over like I'm a sheep for sale, and not one she's eager to buy. She switches to Langue-Valon. "At such an age, she must be well-versed in needlework."

"She is." Feroulka produces a handkerchief I embroidered last week.

It's fine work, but the norne shakes her head, tapping the switch against her skirts. "We're full, I'm afraid. No more beds available."

Feroulka produces a small leather sack swollen with coins. "Perhaps this might pay for another bed?"

The switch stills. The norne's eyes spark with interest before she smothers it. "Perhaps."

"We're willing to reduce the price of these fine goods." Feroulka pats a bolt of cloth.

"How much?"

"That depends."

The haggling begins. It's nearing Vespers bell and enticing cooking scents waft through the wide doors as they finish bargaining. The norne doesn't offer a handshake, just a nod. We shift goods from our mules to the storerooms and they exchange money.

Feroulka murmurs a blessing echoed with her fingers and a final touch to my forehead. Then she's gone. I breathe through the farewell-ache as the norne shuts the doors.

"I'm Sister Treuda, the Almoner of St. Beatricia." The poor who knock at St. Beatricia's door begging for alms must be desperate; the almoner doesn't seem the generous sort. "This is Jacco." I extend my fingers toward Jacco. He snaps at them, and I jump back.

"I'm *uh*... Greta."

She motions with the switch for me to follow. I wait until Jacco follows Sister Treuda before hefting my small trunk. I trail after them between towers of stacked grain and sacks of beans. We arrive in a room full of clothing and supplies. I set down my trunk.

"Key," Sister Treuda barks.

I pull it from my pocket and bend to unlock it, but she thrusts her hand before my nose.

"*I* will open it. Some things aren't allowed..." She turns away as she continues speaking.

"What? I don't understand if you turn away."

Her mouth pinches as she faces me. "Mirvraan *and* deaf? Lucky child." She still doesn't use any hand language. Did I misunderstand there were deaf students here? "I said, I'll make certain you hide nothing."

I cross my arms. So far, neither Sister Treuda nor Jacco are very welcoming.

Sister Treuda shrugs. "You don't like my rules, you're free to leave. Go, run after your cousin. Stitch third-rate charms in a poorly lit road-side camp for coppers a piece. Won't hurt my feelings."

I don't like Sister Treuda, or the way she looks down her nose. I'm certainly wary of her dog. I *should* go. Tanja's council discussed a dozen places I can hide. Yet, Tanja said this was where I can truly learn Skeincraft. I *need* those skills if I ever face my uncle again.

I offer the key to Sister Treuda.

She doesn't take it. "You've not given me any reason to like you." She steps close enough that I smell her yeasty breath. "You *want* me to like you. I decide what food you eat, what bed you sleep in, how thick a blanket you receive, and what chores must be done. You understand?"

She wants to be rid of me, it seems, but I'm not easily scared away. Not if this is the best place to learn needlework. I nod.

She takes the key, unlocks the chest and pulls out my things. She comments on everything. I have too many dresses. My linen shifts are too prettily embroidered. My stockings, shoes and mittens are too fine.

"Putting on airs? Or were they stolen from better folk?"

I grit my teeth.

When she finds my good winter cloak, she shakes her head. "Waste… could make two cloaks out of all this." She's obviously not lived through a Valonian winter, so I hold my tongue.

She lifts my last linen shift; two necklaces fall from its folds. Glowing with the bright, amber glow of Tanja's jewelry, they're long enough to tuck under the neckline of an abbey dress and never be seen. Each has a medallion. One's the Mirvray symbol, a stylized wagon wheel. The other is the Valonian Oak, shaped to resemble the protective Hand of Fortune. These must be Tanja's parting gifts. I reach for them.

"No jewelry." Sister Treuda's ink-stained fingers curl around the gold like a hawk snatching fish from the lake.

"I won't wear them, I promise."

"None at all." She points toward my head. "Including those fine, silver combs."

I clutch them protectively. "They're a gift from my godmother."

She frowns. "Why'd you bring them? To brag… rich godmother… make the other girls feel less than? I won't have it."

"I wouldn't."

Jacco growls and steps nearer as Sister Treuda turns away.

I want to protest, to explain that without the combs my world is silent. But that won't impress her if several inhabitants of St. Beatricia's are deaf. My combs might become a valued commodity. I might never see them again. I pinch my lips shut and turn my back on Jacco.

Sister Treuda sets a small chest carved with bluebells on the table and produces a ring of keys. The smallest one unlocks the chest. It is nearly full of jewelry, likely from other hapless girls who didn't know the rules. Sister Treuda places both necklaces and my combs within, then snaps it shut.

"You may have… when you leave."

"How will you know which pieces are mine?"

She taps her forehead. "Sharp memory."

I open my mouth to protest, but Sister Treuda slaps the switch on the table threateningly. "We live…" She turns away, making a half-formed gesture that might mean *equally*.

I nod, but I think of that tiny key. One rainy afternoon on Isle Dinant, Feroulka produced a handful of slim tools and taught me to pick locks. It didn't come as naturally as Skeincraft, especially with my weak left fingers, but I succeeded on a few.

Tonight, I'll take a midnight stroll. Retrieve what's mine.

I just hope Jacco isn't prowling about.

SISTER TREUDA ESCORTS me into the abbey proper. She points to various rooms. Without my combs, her voice is a whisper when she stands to my left and otherwise inaudible. I should be scared, but my chest burns with anger.

I mentally map each corridor. The architecture is regimented. Each building is squared off, every wall filled with dozens of windows equally distant from each other. Impossible for a single hidden passage in this place. I frown.

Tall windows fill the rooms we pass with plenty of light. Women bend over fabric-draped embroidery stands. Girls practice with small hoops in their hands. Wrinkled nornes supervise stitching of a wall-sized tapestry. Some rooms are full of women making lace, others with looms; the steady clacking vibrates the floorboards like a heartbeat. I brush at my arms to stop them from prickling. Though I can't see individual auras, I can't deny the power here.

We pause in a room where I spy a jar full of crochet hooks, some slender enough for fine twine. They're similar enough to Feroulka's lock-picking tools. I swipe two.

Sister Treuda ends the tour on the ground floor, still moving her mouth. She opens the door to the dining hall. The scent of meat and vegetables prompts a murmuring complaint from my stomach. A dozen girls at the far end of the hall set out pots, spoons and dishes. Two scramble to open the kitchen doors. A girl, no taller than me, strides from the kitchen carrying a board of chopped greens. She scrapes them into the large pot of soup that sits in the center of the long table. As she stirs the soup with a ladle, the flare of green Otherlight is unmistakable. A kitchenwitch.

Sister Treuda advances upon her. The kitchenwitch looks up as we march across the dining hall. The norne points to me and continues speaking.

The kitchenwitch betrays a flash of anger before covering it with a neutral expression. "As you say." She uses hand language simultaneously, but doesn't speak much after, only saying, "*Ja*" and nodding to everything the norne tells her. Still, her marmalade-colored hair bristles, and her chin juts.

Sister Treuda jostles my shoulder. I frown up at her, and catch the word "… Introduce…"

"Hello, my name is Greta," I say, forming the words with my fingers as well.

The kitchenwitch points to herself and says a name, the shape unfamiliar. I frown, and she finger-spells, "Renata."

I repeat the name. She nods, but still doesn't smile. When Sister Treuda continues speaking, Renata's hands move. It takes a moment before I understand. She's repeating the norne's words in hand language, becoming a bridge between Sister Treuda and myself.

"Renata's the only girl here who speaks Langue-Valon," the kitchenwitch signs. "So she'll tutor you in Haps-tongue, and hand language if you like." Sister Treuda shakes her finger at me. "Obviously, she has other duties, so you'll learn quickly, won't you?"

As if learning a new language is as easy as baking bread, and only lazy folk learn slowly.

RENATA SEEMS to take pity on me. She directs me to stand behind the serving table with her as nornes, novices, postulates, and girls file into the dining room. She keeps a running commentary in hand language and Langue-Valon as she ladles up soup, providing all their names. I immediately forget them, for as she ladles soup and gives out slices of bread, Otherlight flashes and gleams. She doesn't add magic to everyone's food, and I can't discern a pattern. But I do see everyone's smiles as they receive food from her hands. Is it because of magic, her friendliness, or good food?

We finally sit down. She eats voraciously, hands moving constantly. I guess most of St. Beatricia's inhabitants *must* have hearing loss. *Everyone* is using hand language, even Sister Treuda. Yet, they sign in a rapid cadence, faster than the Mirvray. When the girls sign to me, they have to repeat themselves. I rarely understand the first time. Watching lips proves unhelpful, for they speak Haps-tongue, if they speak at all.

I ask Renata if she can hear; her response is indignant. "Of course."

After supper, cleaning the kitchen, and evening prayers, it's finally time to go to bed. I lift my trunk with aching arms, following Renata across the wide courtyard to the dormitory wing. She opens a door, and I step inside a small, plain room. I set down my trunk. Two beds, with barely an ell between them, stand underneath a window. A shelf sits above each bed. One's full of gray wool and white linen, the other is empty. That's my side, then.

Renata sets the candle in the windowsill and signs. "Valonia or Pranzia?"

"Pranzian," I lie.

"That explains your accent."

Heat rises through my neck and cheeks.

"Never mind. I truly don't care." She crosses her arms. "I'll teach you the basics, but I'm not your bosom friend, understand?"

I nod, but the shift from friendly to brusque leaves me wary.

"How old are you?" she asks. "Eleven? Twelve?"

I clench my teeth. "Sixteen."

"Truly? You're short." She eyes my chest. "And with little where it counts."

I cross my own arms. "How old are you?"

"Almost fourteen."

I turn my back and prepare for bed. The irony of the Fates: leagues from home, and the *one* Valonian here, my roommate, the friendliest girl in the abbey, is hospitable as a hedgehog.

HOURS LATER, I creep out of bed and wander in the darkness to the provision room door. It takes time to manipulate the crochet hooks. I half wish for Tanja's Gift. Iron locks would be easy to manipulate. The door finally opens.

I whisk inside and wrestle the bluebell chest's lock. Time slows. My fingers ache. When the mechanism releases, my necklace with the wagon wheel medallion is on top. The combs, however, are gone and my other necklace is missing.

"*Merde.*"

I sift through the contents. Rings and tangled necklaces fill the chest, a snarled magpie nest. A few are tarnished silver, but most are copper, tin and brass. Keepsakes rather than valuables, from loving parents perhaps. Are these the dregs, the worthless leftovers after she's taken other, more valuable items and sold them? Kept them?

Anger simmers, mixing with panic. Those combs keep me equal with hearing folk. Or closer to equal. I'm in an abbey full of other deaf females, but I'm *not* ready to live without sound. I want them back, no matter the cost if I'm discovered.

My neck prickles. I turn. Candlelight reflects on a pair of eyes low to the ground. Jacco emerges from the shadows, obviously barking. I hear only a distant, grating murmur.

I scoop up the chest and run towards the door. He leaps at me. Nipping. My skirts tangle around my legs. I reach the door. He jumps, trying to bite my hand. I flinch. Fumble the chest. Fling it towards him. It crashes to the floor, scattering necklaces and rings. He dodges, scampering around the mess and back toward me. I wrench the door open, slip out, and close it quick. The door vibrates as he throws himself against it. He's probably making enough noise to wake the entire abbey.

Merde. I still have Tanja's necklace in my fist, but I left wreckage in Sister Treuda's office with all evidence pointing toward me. *Seux de merde*.

I hurry away, back towards the dormitory. I slip into a dark alcove and pull up my skirts. I wrap my remaining necklace once, twice, three times around my knee, just above the bulge of my calf, and fasten it. The magic against my skin comforts but still my pride itches. In a place of sanctuary, I must hide both Tys' ring under my stockings and Tanja's necklace under my skirts.

WITHOUT MY COMBS, I can't hear the bells chime. Renata shakes me awake for midnight prayers. I already resent her. Resent depending on her.

I follow the others through the dormitory hallway. We march across the starlit courtyard toward the chapel. When we enter its candle-warmed glow, Sister Treuda and others wait in the vestibule.

"Surprise inspection," they sign. With sleep-mussed hair and pillow creased faces, the girls acquiesce easily. When it's my turn, Sister Treuda examines my hands and wrists, ignoring Tys' knotted bracelet as she pushes my sleeves back. She runs her finger around the neckline of my gown, but she finds no chain. I try to keep my expression devoid of anything except exhaustion until we're past and Renata pinches me.

I glare, then follow movements down in the folds of her skirt as she signs surreptitiously, "You left earlier tonight. Why?"

I answer likewise. "Looking for the garderobe." No matter the country or language, folk understand midnight urges to relieve their bladder.

She raises eyebrows as we file between benches. "There's a chamber pot."

"I didn't know." I shrug and kneel.

Renata follows, studying me a moment before folding her hands in prayer.

In the front of the chapel sits a bent old woman in a pure black cape, the Mother Abbess. Piously, Sister Treuda sits down beside her. My eyes burn, imagining Tanja's necklace hidden under the almoner's collar, or my combs tucked beneath her wimple. I won't cry. Sister Treuda's sins can't crack me open.

CHAPTER SEVEN

Cutwork: open embroidery in which the ground fabric
is cut out around the pattern. Often, ornamental
needlework is added to the open area as embellishment

AFTER BREAKFAST, SISTER TREUDA LEADS ME TO THE UPPER
floors of the abbey and presents me to a tall, willowy norne. The
room, busy with movement and fluttering hands, falls still.

"This is Sister Famke, our Threadmistress." Sister Treuda's hand
movements are abrupt and half-formed, as if she can't be bothered to
sign more clearly.

I curtsy. The Threadmistress nods gravely.

Sister Treuda doesn't finish the introduction but continues. "You'll
spend your day with her. Show her the extent of your needle skills. A
sampler first, with any embellishments and specialty stitches you
know. Florals, ribbon work, beadwork, stumpwork, cutwork…" She
lists several other kinds of needlecraft I've never heard of.

I suck in a breath to calm the flutter growing in my stomach. I've
gambled for this, but perhaps it *is* beyond me.

Mercifully, the Threadmistress silences the Almoner with a hand
on her shoulder, then turns her to face the door. Sister Treuda gives a

brief, false smile and leaves. She might be Almoner, but nobody trumps Threadmistress in such a place, except the Mother Abbess.

The Threadmistress points to two chairs by the windows. One has a cushion. Knowing my place, I take the one without. Sister Famke sits, handing me an embroidery hoop, a length of creamy linen already in place. Long basting stitches sketch out five parallel lines. A sampler.

The Threadmistress extends her arm toward me, a dozen different needles tucked in the cuff of her sleeve. I glance at her face. She nods towards the cuff. I study the cloth in the hoop. I judge the weave, the size of the stitches I'll use, and choose a needle.

She places a tray of colored threads on her lap. She fans her fingers toward the slender skeins, offering me my choice of them. St. Clotilde's strictly rationed colored thread. Dye is expensive. There are nearly sixty skeins before me. Yet, my hand goes unerringly towards a bundle of black silk. As my fingers touch it, I pause.

She's offering me, an unknown girl, free choice from costly embroidery silks. Why? I fold my hands in my lap. The Threadmistress raises an eyebrow but says nothing. I glance at the other occupants in the room. The women and girls stare back, unabashedly curious.

Clearly, this is a test.

I place the black thread in my left hand. Oak-dyed. Vibrations stir the sole of my slipper, like a bee's hum from the abbey's foundations. It resonates within my core, stirring me. Soothing me. I *know* threads and cloth. My emotions might be a tangle, but this is my strength.

My right hand moves toward a skein the shade of robin's egg blue. I roll the free end through my fingers, testing its texture. I sniff it and catch a whiff of quality color fixative. It's a lingering stink but guarantees the dye won't run the first time the cloth is washed. Or the twentieth.

I catch a brief smile from Sister Famke, but don't react. I pick out superior skeins in golden brown, sunset orange, greens the color of moss and leaves, scarlet—warm hues that complement the linen— several of which, under closer inspection, gleam with Otherlight. I pick three more skeins of blue, darker versions of the first. One reminds me of Tys' eyes.

I have a dozen skeins of embroidery silk on my lap. I look to the Threadmistress and nod my head decisively. I have what I want. She nods in return, hands me a small pair of scissors, and puts the tray away. I thread my needle with blue silk and slide it into the cloth near the first basting stitch.

This is a test, perhaps my only chance. I'll prove my mastery of basic skills as well as more elaborate stitches. Movements tease the corners of my vision as the others resume conversations, but I keep my focus on outlining the letter 'A' straight and true. Breathing in a long, steady rhythm, I remember Tanja and Feroulka's lessons as I fill in the outline with a satin stitch smooth as a baby's cheek.

I'm stitching 'C' with the golden-orange silk when everyone stands to leave. Mid-day prayers. I stretch and follow to the chapel, planning all the while. I eat lunch without noticing the soup's flavor.

Once more in the embroidery room, each stitch seems to bind a part of me to the cloth and to the stones beneath my feet. I'm knotting the letter 'F' when someone taps my shoulder. I gasp, as if coming up for air. Blink. Fading golden rays filter through the windows.

"Vesper bells," the girl signs. I put away my embroidery and follow her.

Before worship, Sister Treuda gives a brief but passionate speech about the evils of thievery while a novice interprets it into hand language. Everyone nods until she announces she'll search dormitories as well as workrooms, classrooms, dining hall and kitchens. I flex my leg, feeling the reassuring weight of Tanja's necklace. It seems the best hiding place for now.

I finish eight letters the next day, each more impressive than the last. My fingertips tingle as I work. At the week's end, I tuck my needle into my sleeve. I stretch like a languid cat, replete with magic. My finished sampler rivals everything I've ever embroidered.

Shortly after, I'm escorted to the Threadmistress' office.

Sister Famke stands when I enter, stretching forth her hand for my embroidery. I offer it and wait. She studies it in the sunlight, her long fingers tracing my needlework, front and back. She makes no comment, but her eyes smile. She sets it down and faces me. Using graceful hand language, she says, "Thank you for sharing your best work."

I realize that in all our time together, she's never mouthed anything.

"Are... are you deaf?" My hands form the question.

The Threadmistress nods, signing, "Yes, I'm deaf. Are you?"

I'm not *that* deaf. Yet I remember Renata's answer, her pride in her hearing ability. How she and Sister Treuda have an air of being better than other abbey folk.

"I could hear some things... before," I sign. "Now, I hear nothing."

"Several here experienced such hearing loss." Her expression is sympathetic. "We don't have many newcomers as old as you. Our way is unique. Deaf and hearing, working together." She touches my embroidery and turns serious. "You have..." She makes a sign I don't know. She rephrases, then rephrases again and I understand. "... potential."

The Threadmistress hands back the best embroidery work I've ever done. *Potential?* I stare at my lap, my jaw set against tears and the simmering indignation in my gut. When I look up, my planned response dissolves.

Otherlight shines from the length of silk she unrolls. The embroidery is exquisite—a fairy-tale scene with a huge dragon that ripples as if it breathes. When I tear my gaze from the cloth, I find the Threadmistress watching me with a pleased expression. She points to the embroidery.

"To create such a masterpiece, you must be diligent, learning even more skills."

I nod, my fiery emotions turning to eager curiosity.

"I'll tutor you twice a week for the next month. If you make progress, I'll consider taking you on as my student." From her expression, the way she phrases it, I understand this is a rare opportunity. *This* is the reason I left Isle Dinant, the promise of learning *such* skills.

I curtsy low, signing my deepest gratitude.

OVER THE NEXT MONTH, I grow callouses on my fingertips. Every night I soften my hands with a lanolin-soaked piece of sheepskin, so I won't snag the embroidery silks. The lessons with Sister Famke are revelatory as she shows me new techniques. Certain stitches take on Otherlight easily. Some make colors more vibrant, others enhance the hand of the fabric.

I learn from the other girls too. Some embroidered since they could walk. I observe how they hold their needles, how they keep the backside of their needlework almost as faultless as the front, how they combine ordinary stitches to make patterns I've never seen before. I combine these with the Skeincraft skills Tanja and Feroulka taught me.

Despite this, I'm lonely. I miss Tys and Henk and the Mirvray. Though the Threadmistress signs slowly during our lessons, no one else in the abbey takes my basic language skill into consideration as they converse. I catch only half of dining hall conversations in hand-language, and very little in Haps-tongue.

Renata spoke true. She's not my friend; she barely fulfills her responsibility to teach me vocabulary. I know the basics: bed, clothes, eat, drink, soup, bread, chamber pot. She teaches me the necessary words for work: needle, thread, bobbin, silk, cotton, linen, wool, scissors, fine, thick, weave, warp, weft, knot, stitch. After that, she's done.

It's not that she can't be friendly. She knows everyone in the abbey and speaks to each person as they go through the line for meals. Sometimes her green Otherlight flashes as she hands bread to a girl or ladles soup for a norne. I wonder what she adds. Flavor, comfort, medicine, nourishment? I don't know, only that she never adds anything to mine. I ask Renata about her days in the kitchen, hoping a bit of honey will extract kindness. She gives brief answers, then ignores me. I notice the kitchen work turns her hands rough, so one night I leave my bit of sheepskin on her pillow.

"What's this?" she asks when she comes in.

"I noticed you don't have one. There's enough wool grease for the both of us."

"Don't need your pity." She tosses it on my lap.

"It's not pity."

"Just because I don't laze about embroidering silk, doesn't mean my work is worth less." She always speaks as she signs, and her irritation is clear in her exaggerated motions.

"Your Gift is equally important, perhaps more so."

She goes still. "Gift?"

Careless. A month out of Valonia and I flap-jaw about magic. "You're a marvel in the kitchen." I flounder, trying to untangle my mistake. "Last week when you were ill and didn't cook, the porridge was lumpy and had too much salt. The parsnips in the soup were hard, and every bread loaf was scorched. I doubt you're given enough praise for all you do."

Renata steps across the room, intimidatingly close. "I don't want praise."

"Fine." I push back, just a little, to get what I want. "Perhaps you can teach me more Haps-tongue or hand language?"

"Perhaps." She snatches the sheepskin out of my hands. Her fingers catch on the cord Tys tied like a bracelet and it snaps. She glances at the broken string, shrugs and retreats to her bed. I stare at the broken twine, not daring to retrieve it and reveal its importance. I force my eyes upward.

"… some of the girls call you behind your back…" She signs a few things as she speaks Haps-tongue. Then a sign I recognize.

"Turtle?"

"You're quite slow. In stitching, in signing, in understanding signs. Perhaps if you used *all* your fingers, you might gain a little speed and grace." She says it carelessly.

I have no response. A hollow place yawns open inside of me. I can't breathe.

"And if you want to threaten me," she continues, "talking about Gifts and such, here's another word for you. *Opsluiten.*"

I gulp a breath. "What does *opsluiten* mean?"

Renata pulls the covers up to her ears and turns her back to me. She thrusts one hand out of her cocoon, making a very rude sign that, essentially, means shut up.

THAT CONVERSATION CHANGES my perception of the abbey. While eating breakfast, scratching my naked wrist, I catch the sign for turtle and the way others claw their left hands soon afterward as their eyes dart toward me. It's done mostly by girls sitting at Renata's table. She doesn't look at me, and she never signs it, but she does nothing to stop it either. Each gesture pricks like a needle. As I do my work, I make plans.

At supper, I bolt my food and leave the dining hall. It doesn't take long to prepare for Renata. Only a few dozen stitches are needed in her blankets. I breathe in the magic that sits heavy in St. Beatricia's. I pull it carefully through my anger and send it down into my fingertips. Otherlight gathers at each corner as I stitch. It's not much, but it'll have teeth behind its intention. I tuck the needle into my cuff, undress, and slide into bed with a smile.

I watch the window-shaped moonlight shift across the floor as my fingers twist Tys' twine underneath my pillow. Finally, Renata comes in. I keep my breath deep and even as if I'm sleeping, but don't *quite* shut my eyes. She pulls her day dress off and hangs it on her peg. Wearing just her linen shift, she slips off her shoes, but she doesn't get into her bed. She steps toward mine.

My heart races. I steady my breath. Will she attempt some mischief while I 'sleep?' I've heard of girls tying knots in others' hair or placing a hand in a cup of water to make them wet the bed. *Just try it. I'll pay you back in kind.*

My bed shifts as she sits beside me and shoves at my shoulder.

I scrunch my face and pull my blanket tight around me. "Go away!"

She shakes my shoulder again.

I pull the blanket away and glare at her. "What? Is it midnight prayers already?"

"No." Her face is close; the moonlight illuminates her pointed chin and mass of freckles. She looms over me. I sit up, trying to put us on equal ground.

"What did you do to make Sister Treuda not like you?" she signs.

A chill shivers through me. "Nothing." I make a confused face, though my thoughts race. "She doesn't seem to like Mirvraans."

Renata stares appraisingly. Not signing.

"Why? What has she said?"

She still doesn't answer.

I throw my hands up. "What is it? Why did you wake me in the middle of the night?"

"Sister Treuda put something in your soup tonight."

"What?"

"You didn't even notice. I switched bowls with you."

"You ate it?"

"I made an excuse and returned to the kitchen. I dumped it into a… special bowl." I wonder what kind of special bowls, pots, and tools she might have. "It wasn't poison or anything straightforward like that."

I sit up straighter. "Why would she want to poison me?"

"That's why I'm asking."

I can only shrug. My bewilderment seems to satisfy her.

"It was a compound, ingredients I'd never think to put together. Not sure what she intended. But it wasn't poison."

I sag against the wall. "What should I do?"

"I'm the only witness. We can't do anything." She holds up a hand to stop me from speaking over her signing. "But we will both watch for her. You'll only take food from my hands, and don't let anyone touch it until the bowl's empty, yes?"

I nod.

She stands and climbs into her own bed. "Lessons start tomorrow. *Goede nacht.*"

It's *not* an apology. But maybe a truce? I glance at her blanket.

I rub my naked wrist and keep silent, burrowing under my warm covers.

Renata shifts. Stills. Shifts again. Movement, hands scratching at skin. More shifting. More scratching. She sits up and stares at me. I breathe slowly as I peek through my eyelashes. The prick of rough threads might feel like fleabites, but they aren't real, and the rash won't last longer than a day or two. It won't really hurt. No more than words in another language or a broken piece of string can hurt a person.

My breath hitches. I'll take out the stitches.

Tomorrow.

Or perhaps the day after.

RENATA'S RASH lasts only three days. She confides that Sister Treuda *must* have put something in my food that caused a rash when she touched it. We both keep an eye out for any mischief from the Almoner.

Nobody else gets a rash.

I suffer through lessons with Renata, knowing they're necessary, but they're awkward. I learn more insults and epithets than I'll ever need. As Yuletide draws near, lessons grow shorter and fewer. Renata spends long days in the kitchen, preparing boiled puddings and whatever else is customary in Hlaandrs. I sometimes use my long evenings alone to explore the abbey, but mostly I invest time in my Skeincraft.

The day before Yule, I leave Sister Famke's office with my thoughts spinning together the new principles she taught me regarding movement and illusion. I'm eager to apply them to my new project, so I don't notice anyone unusual until he careens into my legs. I look down at his blond head, but he barely looks up as he dashes off again and ducks behind a large pillar.

"Henk?"

I find him in an alcove, his chest, chubby hands, and face pressed against the honey-colored stone. His smile is rapturous, his eyes tightly closed. I put my hand against the stone and the vibrations send a warm thrill through me. Henk must have some sort of Gift passed on from his mother that makes him sensitive to magic.

"Henk?" I say again.

His eyes pop open, and he looks prepared to run, but he stops. "Margo?" His lips form my old false name.

I put a finger to my lips. "Call me Greta now." I look past the pillars into the arcade, but no one else is there. "How did you get here?"

His lips move, but I can't decipher his words.

I use hand language. "What?"

He grins as he signs. "I hiding."

Despite his smile, chill prickles my skin. "Hiding from whom?" I sign.

"Aunty."

"Who?"

Several nornes rush past us, then a woman in a pale blue gown. She returns a moment later, striding toward us. I hear a whisper of Henk's high-pitched squeal before he dashes away.

"Why are you chasing him?" I demand of the woman. She's beautiful, though her elaborately styled golden hair has streaks of silver. She says something as she hurries past, chasing Henk.

I grab her wrist.

She stops. Turns. Her expression is startled. I keep my heart firm. Determined.

"Why are you chasing my Henk?"

Her eyes widen. "Your Henk?" Her cheeks flush. "I think you're mistaken." She answers me in Langue-Valon. I can read her lips. I hadn't even realized I'd asked in my language.

Sister Treuda's switch smacks my hand. I jerk back with a yelp. I clutch at my hand, my good hand, trying to massage the pain away while her scowl says more than her stream of unheard words. Two other nornes arrive, fussing over the woman in blue.

I glance around the courtyard but see no sign of Henk. At least he escaped.

Sister Treuda grabs my chin and jerks my face towards hers. She points at me, then at the dormitory wing. No need to read her lips. I try to look chastened and nod.

Before I can leave, the blond woman and the nornes turn as one. I turn too. On the far side of the courtyard is Henk, sitting on the shoulders of…

"Tys." I breathe his name, but it can't be him. He's dressed in fine, bottle-green velvet. His shirt collar and cuffs trail lace. Henk is dressed finely too, though I was too busy to notice before. I don't understand.

Tys tickles Henk as he says something. They're both grinning as Tys strides across the courtyard. The nornes and the woman smile in return. *What are they doing in my abbey?*

Henk points towards me, and his lips form "Margo." Tys' gaze searches. Finds me.

"G-R-E-T-A." I spell with my fingers, yet all the nornes stare at me, and they can read fingerspelling as well as Tys. "Henk's nickname for me," I say, hoping to salvage something of this Fates-crossed situation.

The blonde woman meets Tys and puts a possessive hand upon Henk. A norne interprets her words into hand language. "You knew my nephew before he came into my care?"

Thoughts tumbling, I bite my lip.

Tys' hand moves up to his chin, too casually. He seems to itch it with his thumb, but I recognize the covert sign for 'mother.'

"I… er, knew Henk's mother. I helped care for him briefly, after her death."

Sister Treuda's narrow gaze presses upon me, but the woman's face softens. She glances at Tys and Henk, then steps forward. "Then I am grateful to make your acquaintance... Greta."

I should nod or curtsey or something, but I still have no idea who this woman is.

Sister Treuda's jerky hand language resolves that issue. "Should you not give reverence to the Duchess of Brandt?" she signs.

Brandt...? My mouth falls open. Hate. Fear. Confusion. All swirl within me as I stare at the woman who married the Bloody Duke of Brandt. Sister Treuda advances, her switch tapping her skirt threateningly. I make a deep curtsey as my action weighs like bricks upon my shoulders.

"Y-Your Grace," I mutter toward the pavement. "I apologize for my... impertinence."

I stay lowered until the switch nudges me to rise.

The norne who interpreted before continues signing the Duchess's words. "Apology accepted. It seems you were trying to protect *my* nephew, and I cannot fault you for that. *However*, you can rest at ease that he is now *well protected* by the House of *Brandt*." The norne emphasizes certain words, and I'm not sure if that's because the Duchess herself emphasized them. I wish I had my combs. I wish I could hear for *myself*.

I give a meek nod, and that seems to satisfy everyone. All the women turn toward each other and start speaking.

I am excluded. No longer part of the discussion.

Tys and Henk watch me, though. Tys, one hand on Henk, signs, "Meet you later—"

I hold up a hand to interrupt. "Everyone here signs." I indicate eyes watching from all the surrounding windows. We can't communicate, secretly or otherwise.

"I meant," he signs exaggeratedly, "if you'd like to see Henk again?" I see the double meaning in his expression. *If I'd like to see Tys again...*

Longing suffocates me. "I wish I could." I shake my head and blow a kiss to Henk, then turn and walk away. I only make it five steps before I look over my shoulder. Henk stretches toward me, his mouth open in a howl. Tys barely keeps him from falling off his shoulders.

My steps slow. It's as if a thread stretches between me and them, the way we watch each other. I'm at the door far too soon. I duck inside and hurry upstairs as hot tears scald my cheeks.

ALL AFTERNOON AND EVENING, thoughts of Tys and Henk are an itch I cannot scratch into submission. No matter how many prayers I say on their behalf, or how I wrestle with thoughts of how Tys got mixed up with the House of Brandt, or why the duchess thinks a low-born Valonian child is her nephew.

I wish, how I wish, I had the courage and skills to sneak out of the abbey and find them. But I haven't the language, I don't know the city, and it's likely that if I found them, they'd be surrounded by Brandt-liveried servants or warriors. It's a fool's errand, and I hate that I'm not fool enough to try.

Long after Renata falls asleep, I'm at our window, staring up at the stars. The constellation of the Pleiades glides up over the abbey rooftop, and I pray again. If I could just have another chance to see Tys, to converse with him. I find myself bargaining, promising stricter obedience and stronger faith, if only...

I let out a long, slow breath that fogs the window. Bargaining with the Fates is risky at any time of year, but tomorrow, Yule begins. The veil between the heavenly and earthly realms will be thin for the next twelve days. The Seven Sisters might amuse themselves by meddling in my affairs; there are plenty of ways for them to make my life uncomfortable.

As the fog on the window shrinks, a shadow runs across the abbey roof, across the courtyard. I blink. I rub my sleeve across the glass. I'm tired. I imagined seeing some...

Merde.

The moonlight shines on the shadow's blond hair.

I have never had a prayer answered like this.

It doesn't matter. I wave my arms, hoping he'll see me through the glass. The windows in the abbey don't open, so I can't call out to him. Fumbling, I find the tinderbox and light our candle. I set it on the windowsill, but now, my eyes can't see anything past the glass.

I grab my discarded day gown and wrestle it over my linen shift. I pull on shoes and reach for my cloak when a shift in the light and shadows makes me turn. The candlelight illuminates a figure standing in mid-air outside my window, like a ghost or a fairy-lord.

Or my favorite acrobat, dangling from the roof on a rope.

"Tys! What are you doing?" I sign.

"Searching for you." He grins, pointing to the candle. "Thanks for the help."

"Wait there, I'll come out to meet you."

"No. A dog's down there. Knows I'm here but can't figure out where."

"That's Jacco."

He looks over his shoulder. "Barking again. Blow out the candle."

I do. It takes time for my eyes to adjust. When I can make out his face once more, I sign, "I missed you."

His smile is soft. "I missed you, too." My pulse flutters. I want to reach past the glass. To touch his face. To have him touch me.

I gather my thoughts. It takes effort.

"How did you convince the Duchess of Brandt that Henk is her nephew?"

He ducks his head, perhaps checking his rope. "I... told her the truth."

My gut tightens. "How much truth?"

Tys looks up, holds my gaze. "Everything."

I have no breath. "The Bloody Duke's wife knows who I am and that I'm here?" I rap my knuckles against the glass. I'd rather hit his flesh. Preferably somewhere soft and sensitive. Somewhere that will make him howl with hurt.

Renata rolls over in bed. The Fates are twitching my life threads, I can feel it.

"Do you want me dead? Or taken as hostage? Or worse?"

"No. No, no, no, no, no. Listen. The Duke knows nothing." He presses his palms against his eyes before continuing to sign. "I wanted to tell you before. Wish I could tell you an easier way. Wish—" He stretches his palm against the glass.

"*What* do you wish?" I sign big, so he can see all my anxiety and exasperation.

"The Duchess of Brandt is my mother. We didn't tell my father anything. My mother happily lies about Henk being her nephew."

I stare.

This is a dream. A nightmare. It's nearly Yule; perhaps the Fates are playing with my mind. Having a little jest on my behalf. But Tys continues signing.

"My full name is Mattias VandeBrandt."

"This is no lie?" My hands tremble. "No trick?"

"I'd never lie about—" He twists around and looks down. "Dog got out. It's raising a hell of a ruckus down there." He turns a hopeful face toward me. "Meet me. Tomorrow night. In the bell tower. Moonrise."

"No!" I sign.

He's already climbing his rope. "Tower. Moonrise."

And he's gone.

The Stars have trussed me like a Yule pig ready for roasting. Damned if I do.

Damned curious if I don't.

CHAPTER EIGHT

Shuttle Lace: a delicate, handmade lace formed by
looping and knotting with a single cotton or linen
thread and a small shuttle; also called tatting

ON THE FIRST DAY OF YULE, BEFORE NIGHT FALLS, ST.
Beatricia's gates are locked tight. The outward facing windows are
shuttered. Whatever revelry the townsfolk might do to celebrate, the
abbey inhabitants turn a blind eye, observing the holiday in a more
subdued manner.

I sing and circle the bonfire in the abbey courtyard with the rest
of the girls, my thoughts drifting unrepentantly elsewhere. I'd
assumed Tys didn't want to talk about his home and family on Isle
Dinant because our stations were so vastly different, not because our
families were mortal enemies. Conflicting thoughts battle for
supremacy until Compline bells chime. We pray to the Seven Sisters,
their starry gleam just rising above the abbey wall, and I decide.
When the vigils start, I let myself be picked for the least desirable
middle hours.

Instead of going to bed, I creep through the dark corridors and up
the tall tower's many stairs. I'm nervous. I pray no one has a sudden
urge to visit the belfry in the middle of the night. The starlit sky

stretches above my cloudy breath, inspiring a restlessness I can't fight. Down in the streets, bonfires light the squares like larger, closer stars.

Something startles a covey of pigeons from the rafters above. I duck as they buffet past. I probably disturbed them, making noises I can't hear. With constant watch over the bonfire, and no secret passages to duck into, it's inevitable I'll be caught. I pace the tower. If I have one conversation with Tys, it'll be worth the punishment.

An object the size of my hand sails through the casement opening, hits the floor, then slithers back toward the casement. A small anchor with four curved prongs. Attached to its end is a rope thick as my thumb.

"He wouldn't…"

The anchor lodges in the corner of the stone casement. I sidle closer and peer down into the darkness. A figure stands on the ridge of the abbey roof, two stories below. The rope tautens. The figure ascends, hand over hand. I draw back to the far side of the tower.

A pale hand appears, grips the edge. Another hand. An elbow. Then a face.

"Tys!" Warmth and chills skitter through me.

He vaults over the bell tower railing.

His lips move. *"Kleintje!"*

I want to run forward. To strike him is my first instinct, to embrace him is a close second. I do neither and stand my ground, ten steps away.

"Didn't know how to tell you," he signs. "Not without tangling everything. I'm sorry."

I tighten my arms across my chest, against the cold and the war within.

He takes a deep breath and takes a step forward. Something in my face makes him retreat. "Didn't know how to announce my identity on Isle Dinant after learning yours." He gives a mocking bow as he signs. "Pleased to meet you, Princess. I'm Mattias VandeBrandt. My sire, unfortunately, is the fen-sucked braggart who keeps invading your kingdom."

"Ha, ha." I keep my face expressionless. "And what were *you* doing in Valonia?"

"Trying to get home–"

"You were that desperate for a shortcut of what? Three days? You could've been killed just for stepping foot on Valonian soil."

"Yes. I was desperate." His eyes are wide, guileless. I hate how I believe him. "Told you the truth. I jumped ship. Left the Knights of the Pleiades with my brother's crossbow bolt buried in my shoulder. Was making my long way home. I *had* to tell my mother I was alive." His throat bobs. "She couldn't take losing another child."

"You stayed on Isle Dinant for seven weeks!"

"No. I slipped across with Razvan one night once I could walk."

"Then you *returned* to Isle Dinant?" I pace to the trapdoor, ready to escape down the stairs. "You're a fool."

"Yes, I am." He steps closer. "A fool for falling for you—" He holds up a hand so I won't interrupt. "You're beautiful, of course, but you have spark and flame inside of you. You fight for yourself. You fought for Henk. You... you fought for *me*."

He retreats. Swipes at his face. When he turns back, the moonlight reflects too brightly off his cheeks, though his face is composed.

"Our families have broken people. Twisted by misplaced zeal. Taking out their resentment on the innocent." He points to us both. My heart softens. I want to believe him, to grasp any thread to bind us together, but there's so much that's been false between us.

"I should go to bed."

"Please... I wanted..." He pulls a bundle free that's been strapped to his back and holds it out.

"What is it?"

"Thought we could go out into the city," he signs. "Explore a bit. First night of Yule."

A hundred reasons why I *shouldn't* rush through my mind.

"Haven't you yearned for another adventure these past months?" he asks.

"With a lot less blood and danger, though."

"Come on." He tosses the bundle to me. It's a pair of woolen trousers, a thick knitted sweater, and a cap like his. "Can't climb down a rope in a dress, right?" Tys cocks his head.

So sure of himself. I push down the yearning simmer inside and shake my head.

He turns away, his lips forming words I can't decipher.

"What?"

He doesn't face me. I pull at his shoulder, but his expression isn't angry.

"What?"

He puts a finger to his lips, then signs, "That thrice-damned dog."

"Where?" I look over the edge, but Tys pulls me back.

"Coming up the stairs."

I hurry to the trapdoor. Peer down. There are no torches in the stairwell. Do I trust Tys? Mattias? I put a hand on the trapdoor, ready to lower it, but I hesitate.

Then, in the darkness, I catch a brief glimpse—a pair of glittering eyes racing towards me up the stairs. I yelp and push the trapdoor closed. Tys covers his ears and winces.

"Between the dog's barking and your slamming, half the abbey will be up here in a trice. You want to wait here?" He crouches. "Or come with me?" Tys jerks his chin toward his anchor and rope.

"First night of Yule," I mutter. "The Fates are already pulling their strings."

"The Fates brought us together again. They'll keep us safe." His hand moves to my chin, and I meet his gaze. "And even if they won't, I will."

Stars! Mattias VandeBrandt is a handsome fellow. And too full of charm.

The trapdoor shudders under my hand. Jacco must be throwing himself at it.

"The belfry is seven stories. I should trust a skinny hemp rope in a December wind?"

"You understand thread." Tys shrugs. "Rope's just longer and thicker."

I stare, letting him feel the weight of my choice. "Tie those ropes securely."

Tys grins and gives a salute. I stand on the trapdoor as I pull on the trousers, tuck up my skirts, and slip on the orange sweater. Jacco continues to slam into the trapdoor. The little beast is incorrigible. I don't think he's strong enough to lift it, but I push a heavy box from the corner on top.

"Now, to put you in a harness…" Tys eyes my hips as he twists and loops the rope in a similar fashion as he had for Henk all those months ago. He kneels, holding it before me. Heat flushes my cheeks. I step into the rope harness. I'm acutely aware of the Tys' hands as he moves it up my legs and hips, especially when he pulls and it tightens.

He looks around and signs, "Voices. Coming up the stairs."

Quickly, he fastens my new harness to the rope dangling from the belfry rafters, over the balustrade and down the side of the tower. They glow with unmistakable power. "You ready?"

Ropes are like thread, just longer and thicker. I nod.

Tys squeezes my hand. "I won't let you fall."

"I know." I grasp the railing and swing my legs over.

He snugs up close and signs with his arms around me. "Not until you learn how to fly yourself."

I won't fly alone any time soon. The rope bites into my palms as I lower myself over the side of the abbey. Tys keeps looking upwards, keeping a swift pace. My arms tremble with strain as I pass the fourth story windows, and the third and the second. By the time my feet touch cobblestone, I know we'd best find another way inside when our adventure finishes. I tug my skirts from the pants' waistband and smooth the wrinkles.

Tys pulls me around a corner that has a wide overhang. He winds up his rope and signs, "Not bad for a greenhorn."

I roll my eyes.

He laughs. "Wasn't any better when I forayed into the ratlines of my first ship. Graceful as a bit of dunnage, even with my Gift." He looks upwards once more and urges me onward. After two more corners, he ducks behind a wheelbarrow and emerges with something dangling from each fist. They sparkle in the moonlight, and not from Otherlight.

"Skates?" The abbey girls said they're popular here, where plentiful canals become frozen, icy streets every winter.

"Might be a fun way to see the city."

"I've not skated since I was little."

Tys hands a pair to me. "Like riding a horse, you never forget how."

"And when I fall flat on my *derrière*?"

"I won't laugh."

I raise my eyebrows.

"Won't laugh loudly."

We walk towards the mooring posts along the canal's edge. The frozen water's empty of boats, of course. I sit on the stairs descending to the ice and tie on my skates.

"If I fall and you laugh, I get a point. If I fall and you don't laugh, you get a point."

"What if *I* fall?" he asks.

"I'll laugh and not lose any points."

He sits beside me, his expression thoughtful. "Well-crafted diplomacy I expected, but if it's war you want, I'll oblige you." He waggles his second skate under my nose. "And the prize?"

"Winner's choice." Perhaps a well-thrown snowball right between the eyes.

Tys nods with matching gravity. "As you say." He offers his hand. We shake to make it official. I ignore the flutter in my stomach and step out onto the ice.

"Hurry up, slowpoke," I sign, and promptly fall.

Tys' mouth opens wide in a laugh I wish I could hear.

I grin from where I sprawl. "One point for me."

He slaps his hand over his mouth.

"Too late." I beckon for him to come help.

He ties his last knot and glides out. He pulls me to my feet, keeping hold of my hand as we skate. I breathe icy air, my mouth stretched in a smile. Skating into a larger canal, we find more people. I wobble as they pass too close. Tys pulls me closer, tucking my hand into the crook of his elbow.

"You don't have to," I say. He shouldn't, really. He's a VandeBrandt.

He glances down, then back up. "I do, though." His expression is serious. "Doubt I'll resist laughing when you fall. Only way to guarantee my victory is to keep you on your feet as long as possible." He winks.

"You're terrible." I punch his arm. It's very firm.

"Hey!" Tys flinches, as if it really hurt. "No assistance wanted? Very well." He slips my hand from his arm to his fingertips. He pushes off and lets go.

Gliding away from me.

"Wait." I dig my skates into the ice and launch after him. He looks over his shoulder. Eyebrows raise. Then he dashes away on his skates.

"You'll not be quit of me so easily," I shout.

He grins.

I skate around two middle-aged women and gain a few feet. Up ahead, half a dozen children hold hands in a long line. Tys slows as they swerve in front of him. It gives me the extra moment I need. I grasp the back of his jacket.

"Caught you!"

I have too much momentum. We careen toward the children. I skate farther to the left. Tys overbalances. His hand extends. Catches me under the elbow as my skate hits a rough patch. The next moment, Tys and I are a tangle of skates and limbs, sprawled on the ice.

"You hurt?"

"Only bruised."

"Nothing broken?"

We sign at each other as we right ourselves and move out of the way of the other skaters. In the glow of a brazier on the edge of the canal, we look over our injuries. Tys' thick leggings have a tear. I reach for my needle and thread, but he turns away. I follow his gaze. Up on the bank of the canal, several fellows gathered around another brazier gesture at us.

"You know them?" I whisper.

Tys raises a hand in acknowledgement, his cheeks flushing, then signs. "Met two of them a while ago, before I went sailing."

The fellows call enthusiastically, urging him to come up from the canal. Their clothing marks them as journeymen—a carpenter, a silversmith, two blacksmiths and a pair of stonemasons, judging by the emblems on their sleeves.

"They know you as the acrobat, not the aristocrat?" I ask.

He nods.

"Seems they want you to join them."

"Hey, you scum!" He shouts and signs for my benefit. "Can't you see I'm out with my girl? Shove off." My cheeks burn with the possessive term. The fellows laugh and shout back. One, however, addresses me.

After a moment, Tys' hands move, conveying his words. "Come, girl, don't disappoint us. It's First Night. He'll have a better crowd than market day. You can make him take you out to a fine supper afterward on the coin he'll earn."

I glance at Tys. He stands too casually, too still. I haven't noticed any lingering limp, but perhaps he no longer has the necessary skills.

"I'm curious about this act of yours, Tys, if your leg permits."

He stares at me for a moment. "Forever I'm indebted to you for that healing, *kleintje*." He throws his arms outward and faces the crowd. "Very well." He skates in a small circle, catching the attention of those on the ice and others up on the pavement who haven't yet noticed him. He signs in large movements as he announces, "The Fates heard your yearnings and I'm brought to you by their mysterious ways."

He points a little eastward. "Tys the Rope Juggler shall perform in Chandler's Square. Hurry, to get the best spot."

Finishing his announcement, Tys grasps my hand and skates toward the nearest steps. We remove our skates and hurry upward toward the square. The doors of the nearby tavern are open, and plenty of folk stand around braziers, cups in hand. Garlands and streamer flags stretch overhead across the open space. Several flutter to the pavement as two men clear a space for the long rope they're securing between opposite third-story windows.

As we draw closer, Tys transitions into the performer before my eyes. No duke's son here. As the fellows tease and throw fake punches, Tys jokes and punches back. Torchlight illuminates blond stubble along his jaw. His eyes have a roguish light; his mouth is wide and smiling. Attraction tugs at me. The Fates brought Tys into my orbit, and I desperately want him to stay near.

Which is ridiculous.

We reach the empty area of the square, almost underneath the rope. A fellow leaps onto an overturned box and holds his arms wide, calling the crowd nearer, then gestures towards Tys. His face is animated, teasing, whetting the audience's appetite. He lifts his hands to the Heavens.

"Hail the Fates!"

"Hail the Fates!" the crowd echoes.

Tys stands there a heartbeat too long, as if regretting his decision. I squeeze his hand.

"Set your magic loose."

He inhales deeply, his chest expanding. Tys steps into the empty corner of the square and faces the crowd. He calls for rope.

Someone in the crowd tosses a length to him. Tys catches it, ties it into a loop, then flings it high. He snatches another out of the air, ties it faster than eye can follow, and launches it upward. A third rope smacks his chest. He catches it before it touches the ground and throws it without knotting. Catches the other two and sends them into the air once more. Snatches the third, ties it and juggles in earnest.

The crowd cheers. Has no one noticed the loops glow? Two more rope lengths fly towards him. Tys hurls the three loops higher yet, then uses those heartbeats to tie the others. He juggles five rope loops.

Applause echoes around the square. Tys grins.

He banters with the crowd, juggling the loops in an arch, then in a figure eight. He sends them behind his back and under his legs. Then, two loops join. I blink. Another pair. Then a trio. I squint. All five are linked in a chain. It writhes like a snake overhead.

The crowd's roar of approval is a murmur in my ears.

Tys moves directly under the tightrope. He throws the chain higher, arcing it over the tightrope. Circling the tightrope again and again, it grows longer. Not five conjoined loops, but seven. Then nine. Then a dozen.

Impossible.

I count fourteen when the last loop catches on the tightrope. The people groan as the chain snarls into a knot. Tys shouts to the fellows in the upper windows.

The men shake the tightrope. The loops stay tangled.

The crowd joins in, shouting encouragement and mockery. The men shake the rope until it undulates and jitters. Tys nods. He claps out a well-known work song. The crowd sings along. The rope shakes in rhythm and the loops untangle. Only one remains attached to the tightrope; the fourteen loops dangle three stories to just within Tys' grasp. He gives an experimental tug.

I'd not trust it, except it shimmers with Tys' Otherlight. Tys toes off his thick-soled shoes and climbs the loops like a ladder. The crowd murmurs. Before stepping up onto the tightrope, Tys looks over the crowd and says something. He takes his hands from the rope-ladder, gesturing to the fellows in the windows.

I gasp. The crowd shifts.

Tys apologizes with words and sign. He peers down, shaking his head as if imagining the mess he'd make on the cobblestones.

He throws his arms wide and this time, he does fall.

My heart stops.

Tys arches backward as he falls. At the last moment, his feet catch in the loop he stood on. He swings down and out over our heads.

"Halloooo!" he calls from his upside-down, pendular swing. Once, twice, three times. A twisting flip. He lands on the tightrope, glowing bright white, as if he meant to do that all along.

My heart thunders back to life.

Tys runs along the tightrope to one window, tugs at the knot securing the tightrope to the ironwork underneath. It flares with Otherlight. He runs to the other. That knot flares, too.

The crowd shifts. Pushes against me, then pulls away. I turn. Folk are looking at the ground, parting, like someone is crawling through the crowd. Who's distracting from Tys' show?

"Jacco?" *That demon dog!* He's almost reached me.

Damn the Fates!

I push my way to the empty area under the tightrope. "Tys!"

Jacco dashes out of the crowd and straight at me. I run. He jumps, snaps at my skirts and closes his jaws. I scream. My calf burns. I reach for the rope rings. Grab. Pull. Lift myself.

Jacco jumps again. "Get off!" I kick. Scramble to get higher.

Several fellows break from the crowd and try to grab the dog. I climb higher. Both my ankle and calf now throb, but I climb. One more. And another. I recognize a white wimple and charcoal habit weaving through the crowd.

Merde!

I climb until I'm clinging to the top. Tys pulls me up into his arms. I want his safety, but now I'm ells above the ground with only a rope and Tys' magic to keep me from breaking my neck. The thought makes me dizzy. The horizon tilts. I teeter. Cling to him. Bury my wet cheeks against his shirt. His arms tighten. His feet shift, bracing mine.

"Sister Treuda," I whisper. "She can't find me out here. She can't."

Tys strokes my cheeks, wiping them dry, then snugs the cap a little lower on my head. His chest vibrates with sound. He's shouting. I peek and see the crowd staring up at me, at Tys, who's glaring and shouting down at someone. I dare peek a little farther. Sister Trueda. I'd recognize that scowl and that switch anywhere. She's not scowling up at me, but at the fellows shoving a covered basket into her arms. The top's been tied shut. She takes it and leaves. The crowd parts for her, then turns their backs. She disappears into the dark of the night.

I shudder. *Fates, I hate that dog. I hate that woman.*

Tys' arms tighten around me. I feel his breath against my ear but have no idea what he's saying. I look up. He points his chin behind me and mouths the word 'window.' I nod.

"Turn."

I shake my head. *I can't.* I can barely feel the rope under the soles of my shoes.

His lips form the words "You can."

"How?"

"Trust me. Trust my magic."

I let my gaze leave his face and gasp. He's glowing bright as a white bonfire. I swallow. Then nod. He nods in return.

"Lift your arms," he mouths. I do. "Above your head." I lift them higher. His hands shift from my back to my sides… to my hips. Slowly, gingerly, he turns me around. Somehow, my feet stay steady upon the tightrope. I'm facing the window, but I can't take a step.

Tys snugs one hand tight around my waist, then touches each shoulder with the other, guiding my arms lower until they are extended. I'm balancing. Feeling steady. Almost.

His foot nudges under my right foot. I move. Step forward, my foot on top of his, on top of the tightrope. He nudges the left. I follow his lead, stepping where he guides me. His chest breathing in and out against my back. I'm reminded of being in the saddle with him months ago. Why did I think that so uncomfortable before? Another step. And another.

We reach the window. He lowers me until I'm sitting on the ledge.

A woman is there with a bowl of soapy water and bandages. I turn back toward Tys. He bows and blows me a kiss, then he's somersaulting away, down the length of the tightrope.

The loss of his closeness is like hunger.

But the woman pulls my leg onto the sill. She flips up my skirt and cuts up the side of the trousers. She says nothing as she cleans the cuts and puncture wounds left by Jacco.

I hope the Fates have a proper punishment in store for that dog.

The woman wraps my leg in a bandage. She puts my shoe back on, then retreats from the window and out the room. And I—I'm stuck on the outside of the windowsill. Should I follow her inside? I look to Tys, who has removed the rope links that were my ladder up to him; he juggles them overhead. He's laughing with the crowd as he flings one, then another of the rings out to them. The crowd seems to find this entertaining, jumping and cheering him on.

Soon, all the rings are gone, and his attention returns to me. The eager light of performance in his eyes softens to concern. He turns to the audience and raises his arm in a commanding manner. They still, as if he's thrown a spell over them. A person moves toward the front. Carrying something. Carrying... a bolt of cloth.

I frown at Tys. What in the Fates' names is he up to now?

The fellow with the bolt hands the free end of the cloth to another, then starts unwinding it. Common, dun-colored wool from the looks of it. At a signal from Tys, the bolt is tossed in the air. As it soars upward, it leaves a long tail of pale brown, like a grubby rainbow. Tys catches the bolt, and the crowd cheers. This is the strangest show any of them must have ever seen. Either that, or Hlaandr folk have odd tastes in entertainment. Tys takes the bolt and passes it once around the tightrope, so it's looped around, then walks toward me, carrying the cloth.

"Come," he signs. "We'll get you down, without more damage to that leg of yours."

"How do you plan to do that?" I ask.

"Just like lowering a bit of dunnage onto the deck of a ship." He indicates the cloth. "This should be more comfortable than a mass of ropes tying you up."

He passes the cloth around me once. Twists it. Reverses. Wraps it around twice.

"We're going to trust your weight and mine to this wool. Is it strong enough?"

I smile. "Of course." So many fibers twisted, woven together. The weft and weave of it would be stronger than many of those ropes he likes to use. "As long as you don't have a pair of sharp shears, this cloth will hold." Still, I run my palm against it, adding strength, flexibility. It flares blue.

Tys' eyes sharpen. He moistens his lips. "You glow like a saint's candle is lit inside you. Every time…" A call from the crowd pulls his attention away, and he raises his hands, smiling. He catches my gaze again. "Trust me," he signs before scooping me into his arms, wool and all.

A little protest escapes me, but I don't struggle. I'm wrapped in cloth, held in his arms, three stories above ground, as he walks a tightrope. I don't want to disturb his concentration. He talks the entire time, some sort of patter for the crowd. I watch his lips but get distracted from the message as I focus on their movement as he speaks, as he smiles.

Tys has a dozen different smiles. He's giving the bright, inviting one to the crowd. But he has others, smiles that seem mine alone: hopeful ones, self-conscious twists of his lips, mischievous grins that make my blood rush, and smiles that don't touch his lips, only crinkle his eyes. I want one of those tonight, if we can just leave this tightrope and this crowd. Find a little privacy.

He shifts me in his arms. Lowers me.

"Trust… me," he mouths.

And I fall.

Briefly.

The cloth tightens, and I jerk to a stop. I'm dangling in a cloth hammock only a half dozen feet under the tightrope. I peer down at the crowd that peers up at me. Tys lowers himself, hand over hand, to my side. His rolled sleeves reveal fascinating muscles that shift and flex.

It's mid-winter and he should be freezing.

Though I'm not cold. I'm very, very warm.

Tys twists the loose end of the cloth between his ankles, then reaches upward. I slip downward. I gasp. Tys is beside me in an instant.

"Slower," he signs, reassuring me.

It's tantalizingly slow as he rearranges himself in the air around me, seeming to defy gravity. As he lowers my bundled form, each twist and movement shows off his strength. He keeps it entertaining for the crowd, performing the slowest of cartwheels and flips all around me in midair. Such strength. I want to reach out, to pull him closer. The thought dries my mouth. I wet my lips. Tys' gaze that had been flicking between the crowd, the cloth, and me, focuses on my face, even as his body slowly cavorts in the air around me. I don't have a name for what's happening between us, but it feels dangerous... and as necessary as my next breath.

Tys pulls away, breaking our eye-contact, and wraps the dangling end of the cloth around his arms, chest and thigh. It looks like a complicated knot wrapped around his body, but then he releases something and his body twists. Somersaulting. Soaring. Upward.

As I descend.

A crowd of fellows surrounds me before I hit the ground, lifting me out of the swaths of cloth. My feet never touch the ground. Then Tys is there beside me, scooping me into his arms. The fellows fall back, and the crowd is cheering, loud enough to be audible even to me. Their arms wave victoriously. Their faces are bright, their smiles exultant, as if they themselves had rescued me from the danger of the tightrope's height.

Perhaps that's the magic of a good performer, to make their audience feel as if they too have risked something and have come through on the other side triumphant.

Tys acknowledges their applause, then gestures towards the fellows who helped with Jacco and catching me. The audience is happy to include them in their praise. Tys lifts me higher in his arms and twirls about. He says something I almost don't catch the shape of.

"... the prettiest girl south of the North Sea."

The crowd roars its approval and surges forward. Backslaps. Gripped hands. So many faces. A wheelbarrow is provided for me, padded with a couple of cloaks. I nestle in, and nod to all the folk while Tys pulls on his shirt and jacket. His cap is in my hands and coins are thrust into it. It grows heavy with their abundant goodwill. If Tys was truly an itinerant performer, the money gathered could feed and shelter him for a month.

Finally, the crowd dwindles to the half dozen journeymen who'd persuaded Tys to perform. They escort us out of the square and up a twisting road. Someone deposits our skates into my lap. My ankle's too sore to venture back out on the ice, but I clutch them close, wishing Tys and I were alone once again.

Our little brigade stops outside a tavern, its windows glowing invitingly. Tys gives a generous handful of the coins to the group with a dismissive gesture. He softens it with a sidelong look at me. The fellows understand; they laugh and jostle him, then migrate into the tavern. Tys doesn't quite meet my eye before he takes the handles of the wheelbarrow and continues along the street. He takes a meandering route. I've lost my sense of direction by the time he pauses to roll his shoulders and shake out his arms.

"Where are we?" I ask.

"You can see the abbey bell tower over there." He points over the rooftops on the far side of the street. We're close.

Merde. Despite the pain in my leg, I don't want to go back. Not yet.

"Help me out."

When I'm standing on the cobblestones, I test my weight. I can stand. I can even walk, though it's painful.

"Let me help..." Tys wraps an arm around my waist. I put my own arm around his shoulders. They're muscular and firm, and a little thrill goes through my belly. I take a few experimental steps with his support until he stops and faces me.

"I am sorry." His expression is shadowed by the night, but his Otherlight gives him a luminescence that draws me in like a moth to a flame. "This is all my foolish fault. You're injured, and that norne knows it. I should've let you be. I should've seen the signs of the Fates meddling with us. Crossing our lives. Tangling us together. I wish…"

I place a finger upon his lips. "Hush. Do not wish that."

His lips kiss my fingertip before he murmurs, "You do not know what I was going to wish." His warm hand curls around mine and he kisses my palm. I forget how to breathe. I forget words. I can't find the right ones in Langue-Valon or Haps-tongue or hand language. Are there any such words for this feeling? Any in all the world?

I press my other hand against his chest. Layers of wool and linen lie between his heartbeat and my palm, yet I'm certain I can feel it.

"Marguerite." His face holds longing and hope.

"Tys." This corner of Godesbrouke is dark, without activity or torchlight. It gives me courage. "I missed you."

"Stars, I missed you, too." He pauses his signing, curving his hand around my jaw before he continues. "Twice tonight, when you were in danger, you turned to me. In the tower and on the tightrope. You trusted me. That means the world, *kleintje*."

The tightness around my chest loosens. New words bubble up inside me; truth too buoyant to swallow. But I can't say that. Not yet. Not when he is more than Tys, and I'm more than an abbey girl.

I find different words. "Then I claim my prize for winning our little game."

Tys blinks.

I try to smirk. "I'm still ahead by one point."

His smile returns. "Ah. What prize will you be claiming, fair victor?"

Be bold. "I claim a kiss from the famous rope juggler, known throughout the land as Tys Owlymirror. Can you arrange that?"

His smile widens. "I can."

I cock my head. "You'll need to bend down a little."

"You need to grow a bit, *kleintje*." He bends down anyway. I lift my chin, meeting him halfway. His lips are soft at first, a sweet, gentle kiss. I close my eyes and lean into him. Tys answers with his own insistence. Whispering, without sound, of yearning and hope.

When finally we part, I can't help smiling.

"*Goed?*" Tys leans his forehead against mine.

"*Erg Goed,*" I answer.

In an abbey full of girls, talk of kisses is reserved until after lights out when, hushed and giggling, someone shares what an older sister has told them. The fantasies that built up in my imagination were as firm as milkweed fluff. Our kiss is different from what I expected. It's only two pairs of lips, after all. It doesn't magically transport me. Yet, as I breathe in the cold night air that smells of Tys and danger, I want more.

I lift myself on my tiptoes and kiss him again.

CHAPTER NINE

Couching: a method of embroidering in which a thread, often heavy,
laid upon the surface of the material, is caught down at intervals by
stitches taken with another thread through the material

TYS SAYS THE WHEELBARROW IS TOO LOUD ON THE
cobblestones, so he carries me the rest of the way to the abbey. As we
draw nearer, his pace slows.

"Shall I tempt the Fates and visit you a third night?" he asks. "Perhaps somewhere warmer than the belfry."

I'm tempted, but… "Better not."

Tys steals another kiss. "Imagine the mischief we could get up to,
though."

I pull away, placing a finger over his lips. "No. If Sister Treuda…"

He kisses my fingertip, then moves down to my wrist. My left
wrist. He doesn't seem to notice the way my fingers curl against his
cheek. My heartbeat stutters.

"Tys." I place both palms against his jaw, capturing his gaze and
keeping my wrists away from his lips for a moment. He puts me
down, encircles my waist and tugs me close. We kiss again. The
longest yet. I close my eyes, enjoying the intoxication. But I need to

return, and not dressed like this. I pull off the cap and the sweater and wriggle out of the trousers.

"Sorry, but they'll need mending."

He stares at them. "I could... disguise myself as a norne. No one would ever suspect."

I giggle at such an incongruous image. Giggles bubble into full-throated laughter. Tys stares down at me.

"What?" I manage.

He brushes a curl from my forehead. "You're a serious girl, *kleintje*, but I could get used to your laughter."

Self-consciousness heats my cheeks. "I should get inside."

"I'll be here." He grasps my left hand once more and kisses my fingertips as I slide away down the alley.

It's a snug fit through the orphan door. I have to be careful with my ankle as I nudge the inner door open. I peek into the weighing room. Dark. Cautiously, I proceed. I hobble down one hallway after another, wending my way to the dormitory on the opposite side of the abbey. Through the passing windows, glimpses of the Yule fire shimmer.

I slip into the dormitory and am almost to my own door when I stop.

Yule fire.

I have the middle shift. Groaning, I lean against the doorjamb, picturing my bed on the other side. I retrace my steps down the hall. The floor vibrates as someone runs down the hallway behind me. I turn. Renata. I push open the door, letting in frigid air.

"I'll be late. My shift at the bonfire."

"Where've you been all night?" Renata doesn't stop signing long enough for me to answer. "Don't lie about being asleep, because you've not been there since I finished my shift." Renata folds her arms and waits.

"I don't want my troubles to rub off on you." I push the door wider, certain she'll back down now. Renata grabs the handle and pulls the door shut. She holds it closed, her expression pugnacious as she signs one-handed.

"Are you stupid? Roommates always share the blame, but since it's you..." Her fingers are almost in my face. "Sister Treuda will get rid of you one way or another." She pinches her face like the Almoner. "'St. Beatricia's no place for a crippled Mirvraan bastard.'"

"What?"

"Her words, not mine." Renata doesn't seem apologetic. She sighs, the attitude slipping. "I'm a cast-off Valonian. I work in the kitchens. I'm no one special here. If I don't report your wandering and they discover the truth, it'll go bad for me."

The vulnerability in Renata's expression surprises me. Quickly, she scowls, daring me to acknowledge her weakness. I understand, feeling powerless, scrambling for the slightest advantage. But I must protect myself too.

"I was spying on Sister Treuda, if you want to know the truth."

"Truly?"

I twitch my skirt. "Jacco bit me. Twice." Embroider a lie with truth.

"Have you cleaned it yet?" Renata becomes a fussing housewife, urging me back to our room. I sit and pull up my skirts, remembering too late Tanja's necklace fastened just below my knee, dangling within view. I push my skirts back down.

Renata signs, "Too late. Already seen it."

I hold my breath as she turns and pulls a box from under her bed. It wasn't there during Sister Trueda's surprise inspection. She opens the lid, pulling out a roll of bandages, two small glass bottles and a little jar. All of it glows with shades of green Otherlight. She dribbles liquid onto some wadding and looks up, catching me staring.

"What? You thought I was just a kitchenwitch?"

My mouth falls open. She just called *herself* a— "You... why are you helping me?"

"You obviously need someone's help. And I know you won't blather about me."

I frown. "Because..."

"Secret for a secret. Yours isn't a Pranzian accent. It's Valonian. Not mountainfolk, but valley-born and rather posh."

I say nothing. I dare not.

She rolls her eyes. "I've not spilled the spice on you yet, so stop worrying. But" —she prods the deeper bite wound on my calf— "that'll need a few stitches, and I don't fancy myself a seamstress. Can you do it yourself?"

The angle would be difficult. And I've never stitched flesh. I shiver as I say so.

"And it'll hurt like Stars falling." Renata nods. "But better than it getting bad and needing to chop it."

It's a nasty business, even with her numbing ointment. I'll smell of cloves for days, but better than the stink of gangrene. As I knot the last stitch, Renata turns her head.

"That's the bell. Time for your shift."

Panic flutters in my chest. "I still must mend the tear in my skirt. Sister Treuda will know it was me if she sees it."

Renata smears salve on my wounds. "Make it quick. You've got as long as it takes me to bandage you up. Much later, and they won't believe you overslept, and that I had to wake you."

The black thread will stand out on the gray skirt. It can only be temporary, for I need gray thread and more time to make the stitches blend in with the weave of the cloth. *Hide.* I plunge my needle in. *Conceal.* And out. *Mend.* Slip under and up. *Blend.* Two more stitches. *Obscure.* And the last one. *Please, please be invisible.*

I snip the needle and thread free.

"That's done." Renata looks up from my bandaged foot. "And..." Her fingers explore the area I just stitched. "Can't see any sign of it, but I can feel it... tingling." She eyes me as if reassessing. Then she gets to her feet. "Best leave, else you'll be late."

I do, wondering if I've mended the breach between Renata and me. Or perhaps tangled myself in a snare.

ALL THE NEXT DAY, I worry over meeting Tys again. If I do, I must be *sure* Renata's truly asleep before I leave. Too many nights out of bed and she'll follow me. To be certain that's *not* tonight, I add a few stitches to her blanket. These are unlike last month's. They're subtle charms embroidered on the blanket's underside, ensuring long and restful sleep.

However, Renata doesn't return at her normal time. The moon rises. I fidget. I pace. Finally, I bundle myself into my day gown and cloak and leave our room. I reach the dormitory door as Renata, breathless, dashes inside.

Finger to her lips, she signs for me to come with her. *Stars, is this the snare snapping shut?* Yet there's an openness in her expression that I think I can trust. I follow her outside, through the shadowed arcades, and into the kitchen. Once huddled beside the fireplace, she explains.

"I thought about what you said last night, about Sister Treuda. I've noticed a few things too, the way Sister Treuda supplies the kitchens. She's quick to get the best bargain, and she hoards the abbey's supplies, yet there always seems to be a shortage. Today, when the other girls chopped vegetables, I snuck into the provision rooms."

"What were you—?"

"Looking through her tally book, I found nothing amiss. But when I searched further back in her desk," she signs, "I found a second tally book."

"Different numbers?"

Renata nods, her eyes gleaming in the light of the dampened fire.

"We'll tell the Threadmistress, or the Mother Abbess," I say.

Renata grabs my sleeve. "Also written in the tally book are appointments with different merchants. One's happening tonight." She points to the provision room door. "We need two witnesses to be believed. You want to be rid of Sister Treuda?"

Triumph and dread swoop through my stomach. "Yes?"

She swats my arm. "Lead on."

"But, Jacco—"

"I took care of Jacco."

I'm unconvinced.

Renata huffs. "Sometimes Jacco comes into the kitchens, and sometimes we give him a bit of sausage." She points to a string of sausages draped along the rafters amidst bundles of dried herbs. "It keeps him friendly with us, you know. Then, sometimes, if we need him out of the way, we take a bit of qualmroot" —she points to the far corner of the rafters where several bunches of turnip-like vegetables hang— "and tuck it in his sausage."

"You are devious!" I whisper, glad that Renata isn't my enemy. *Hoping* Renata isn't my enemy. Still, I follow her into the storerooms. We wander the maze of foodstuffs, cloth, clothing and tools. I press my palms against my skirts and will the cloth to be silent. I do the same for Renata. But the scent of cloves lingers about me, and we're visible to anyone with a lamp.

In the last room, sacks of grain are stacked into towers, snugged cheek-to-jowl. The room resembles back alleys with only a narrow, mazelike path through them. Candle-glow emanates from the far side of several towers. We find a pile to climb on, then climb a higher one. We elbow our way to the edge.

Sister Treuda stands near the double doors. One's open, and beyond stands a wagon. A man, face hidden by his hood, hefts a sack from the wagon and deposits it on a short stack of grain. He returns to his wagon and shoulders one more, setting it atop the others.

Renata listens and signs their conversation. "Two dozen, as agreed."

Sister Treuda pulls a bundle from her robes and unrolls a square of creamy lace the length of her forearm. It's beautiful, and undoubtedly expensive. "As agreed."

He inspects the knots and picots, like a connoisseur. They haggle over how many bags of wheat it's worth. Finally, they settle on the price. The man accepts the rolls of lace and tucks them under his cloak. Then touches behind his ear. I look to Renata.

She signs, "Those combs you sold me two months ago, have anything else like them?"

My combs? I inch closer.

"I've a dozen more bags of grain, if you do."

Sister Treuda is silent. I flex my leg for the reassuring weight of my necklace.

"A couple sides of beef, instead?" he says.

"No. I had another necklace, but it's gone. Seems we have a thief in the abbey."

My anger simmers. *More than one.*

"And the other item...?"

Sister Treuda crosses her arms.

He crosses his arms to match. "I thought we had a deal last month, then nothing."

"The girl became the Threadmistress's pet. Can't confirm she's who you're looking for."

"Dark hair and eyes. Deaf. Crippled hand. How many girls you know like that?"

My blood turns to ice, and I miss some of what Renata signs. I refocus.

"Yet you sent a messenger last night. If I'm to be pulled from my Yule revels, I expect something more than lace." His face turns ugly, dangerous.

"I thought she'd snuck out of the abbey last night. *That* is grounds for expulsion."

"So make it look like she ran away tonight. I don't see the problem."

Renata and I exchange panicked looks.

"I can't have you bring her back if she's the wrong one. I won't jeopardize my position."

The man makes a dismissive gesture. "I know how you covet the title of Mother Abbess. The tincture I gave you is working, yes?"

Renata's eyes go wide. Her hands stop. I motion for her to keep going.

"Just give the girl to me. If she's not the right one, I'll keep her. Or sell her to another."

Renata's hands pause again. I push aside my panic and urge her to continue. She shakes her head, signing that no one's speaking. Down below, Sister Treuda paces. The moment stretches long and terrible.

"Tomorrow," Renata signs for the norne. "I must set the ground-work so it's believable."

The man teases her about her hesitancy, but finally climbs on his wagon and leaves. Sister Treuda bars the doors, gives her newly acquired grain a satisfied pat and retreats with her oil lamp. Once it's fully dark, Renata and I descend the tower of grain sacks as quickly as we dare. When we reach the floor, I hurry to the big doors and unbar them. Renata grabs my arm.

"Someone's looking for you?" She adds the sign for steal, which also means kidnap.

"I think so. I must follow that man."

"So he can catch you?"

I pull away. "Go directly to the Threadmistress. Tell her what we heard, and that I'll be back to be the second witness."

⁊

THE STREETS of Godesbrouk are dark as clouds fitfully cover the moon. I follow the wagon wheel tracks to the nearest square. There, the new tracks tangle with the old. I squint at the snow, trying to deci-pher which is which, when movement across the cobblestones catches my eye.

I turn. A shadow emerges from the depths of the abbey road. He waves.

"*Kleintje!*"

"Tys?" Relief washes over me as I make my way across the square.

"Saw you from the tower. Was hoping you'd come again. What happened?" He flings his arms around me in a fierce embrace before I can answer. I pull away enough to tell him what Renata and I discussed, then witnessed in Sister Treuda's storage room.

"My uncle's stuck in Roc Ursgueule. *No one* should be looking for me, yet…"

"Yet…" He nods. "That feeling in your gut keeps you safe. Come, I have an idea." He pulls me eastward.

"I'm sure the wagon went the other way."

"Good thing we're not chasing it."

"No," I said. "I must find that man. Figure out who's asking about me—"

"Don't hand yourself over like a chicken ready for the pot."

"I'm not, it's just… I need to know how much danger I'm in."

"And I need to keep you safe."

A bitter laugh bursts out of me. "I've *never* been safe! Not with my uncle always lurking in the shadows, watching me."

He pulls me close with one arm and signs with the other. "I know someone who can keep you safe. I'm sure she's nearly as vested as you are in keeping Rotten Reichard from the Valonian throne, but it'll take trust."

"Who?"

"The Governor." He waits, as if ready for the Fates to strike him down.

I step away. "The Governor? The emperor's older sister?"

He shrugs.

"That's like handing me over to your father! She represents the empire. She's my enemy as much as my uncle."

"The enemy of my enemy is my friend."

"No. There's no way. I can't. I won't."

"*Kleintje,* you're incognito in a foreign land, five days' travel from home. Within your sanctuary, someone's arranging your kidnapping, most likely so your evil uncle can kill you. Could the Governor possibly be worse?"

IN THE COLDEST hours of the night, Tys and I stand in a receiving room of a fine house in the central city. A huge but impeccably dressed manservant lights the lamps before he leaves to rouse his mistress. The furnishings are plush, the tapestries exquisite. The room has a lingering scent of rose petals and sugared almonds.

"It's far too late to be calling," I sign close to my side, as the abbey girls do to keep others from eavesdropping on their signed conversations. "What will she think?"

"That something important happened."

"Exactly, but it's not vital to *her*. She'll think I'm making roast beef from mince."

We argue silently until Tys glares, speaking simultaneously as he signs. "What do you suggest, then? Go back to the abbey? Rent a room at an inn indefinitely? Perhaps you'd like to be my houseguest in Nemeaux? I'll introduce you to my father."

He jerks guiltily toward the doorway where a large woman stands with an air of authority. As her lips move, Tys cheeks flame pink, but he jerkily interprets her words.

"Don't introduce the girl to your father. Bram VandeBrandt is strong as vinegar and twice as sour. You'll lose the girl before you earn your first kiss."

Heat burns my neck as I'm introduced to her Excellency, Ilsa Bernadine, Governor-General of the Haps-Burdian Lowlands, and the emperor's older sister. I imagined such a position of power would make her mannish, but she's the picture of femininity. Her plump, pink cheeks might give her a jolly look if her lips weren't set in a firm line.

Though Tys greets the Governor formally, she treats him like a headstrong pup returned home after running away.

"What brings you to my door at this hour with a visitor in tow?" She speaks in Langue-Valon, in deference to me, I imagine, and keeps her sentences brief, perhaps in deference to Tys' untried skill of interpreting. Whatever the reason, I'm appreciative. It's important to know what the enemy of my enemy says. Specifically.

"I'm begging your hospitality for my friend," Tys voices and signs.

She studies the two of us. "Immediate danger?"

"Possibly," Tys answers. "Definitely in the long term, with possibility of death."

She's not impressed. "Will this danger pass in nine months?"

Tys is oblivious to the significance of her words. Ignoring my scorching embarrassment, I speak up. "No, Your Excellency. No possibility of that."

"May I have a little more information? Name? General nature of this problem?"

"Pledge of hospitality first." Tys is stubborn, but adds, "If it pleases Your Excellency."

His answer seems to amuse her. "*Ja, ja.* Hospitality is yours." She gestures, and the servant from before appears with warm drinks. When he leaves, she indicates the well-upholstered seats. "Now, if I may rest my bones and have my curiosity satisfied, then I'll be much less disgruntled about being woken before Prime."

We sit. I'm wary of the power imbalance. I take control of the conversation.

"I'm Marguerite de Perdrix of Valonia. I've been sheltered at St. Beatricia's Abbey for some months now, but I fear some within her walls could do me mischief if I remain."

The Governor-General leans forward, her eyes sharp with interest. "Do explain."

Without admitting that I was wandering when and where I shouldn't, I tell of Sister Treuda's misappropriation of personal items and my repatriation of one of them.

"The norne is a thief," she summarizes. "That doesn't put your life in danger, surely?"

I explain the necessary bits of what I've seen and heard tonight.

"The Sister Almoner's behavior should be looked into," the Governor muses, "though without corroboration or proof, the church court's punishment will likely not be more than a slap on the wrist. Now, if the woman could be caught outside the walls of the abbey breaking the law…" Her gaze slides back to me. "This man didn't actually say he would kill you, did he?"

"No, but he's certainly eager to get his hands on a dark-haired deaf girl with a crippled hand. It's too specific. I am in danger."

She studies me. "Your first inclination wasn't to run home. Nor was it to come here. What did you intend?"

I'll lose her good opinion, but I give the truth. "I wished to find the man. Observe him. Discover who he, in turn, contacts."

She smiles.

"I know it sounds stupid," I say.

"Foolhardy," she agrees, "but not entirely stupid."

Tys' expression reveals nothing as he interprets. I've never seen him so circumspect.

"It shows you have an inquisitive mind," the Governor continues, "and a desire to solve your own problems. That's all to the good." She takes a sip. "Would you care to come as my guest to Winter Court? All the landowners and lawmakers of the Lowlands gather in my palace twice a year. They swear fealty to my brother. We settle disputes. All in the midst of parties, dancing, and sumptuous food. It would be quite the political education for you, Your Highness."

"Your guest?" I repeat.

"Winter Court?" Tys asks. "She'd be a chicken in a den of foxes."

"It resolves things nicely, don't you think?" She snaps her fingers. Her servant appears, and she murmurs something, sending him away again before continuing. "You'll remove yourself from the reach of your uncle, or the Sister Almoner, at least. You'll have the opportunity to see other ways of conducting government, and an insider's view of imperial politics. Quite beneficial for your future life."

Good arguments, but I'm not quite convinced.

"You'll have more time with young Mattias, whom you seem to favor. Did you know he'll be there too? Representing the House of Brandt."

Tys' cheeks flush. "Neither my father nor brother can be there."

She nods. "I look forward to seeing young Mattias make his foray into court maneuverings. Still not convinced? I must sweeten the pot. I'll have you tutored in Broid Cypher" —Tys spells out the term, for neither of us have heard of it— "if you're not tired of plying your needle."

"Broid Cypher, Your Excellency?"

"Look on the table." She indicates a square of lace-edged muslin placed under the lamp. It's lightly embroidered around its perimeter. The pattern alternates in a way that'd make Sister Famke frown.

"It's lovely."

The Governor laughs. "Diplomatic answer, for an abbey-trained girl. The one who stitched that hadn't the advantage of abbey tutoring, but she communicated what was most important."

I wait for further explanation.

"It's a code, you see," she continues. "Each stitch means something different; nobility ranks, amounts of money, various goods, names of countries. There's also a syllabary."

I examine the cloth, hungry to decipher its meaning. "There are quite a few butterflies stitched among the vines. Do they mean something?"

She smiles. "Yes. Those particular ones mean love."

I frown.

"I embroidered that handkerchief for the king of Mgyrok when we were betrothed. It's a love letter none of his advisors could read."

I know the story of the love match between Imperial Princess Ilsa and King Domotor a generation ago. Ten years after they wed, he was killed in a battle. That was when her brother placed her as Governor-General of the Lowlands. She knew royal life, with courtiers, sycophants, and all colors of political ambitions. I'd be foolish *not* to accept her offer.

"If you want a more martial example, the sachet in that corner should suffice."

I examine it. A pattern of strawberries with runners twines around the bag.

"The berries represent battalions and regiments," she says. "Indicated by the number of seeds. The runners show the planned movement of the army."

"It's a map? Made by a spy?"

She nods. "A laundress. I won't tell you when, or where, or which army, for that would give you an unfair advantage."

I like the challenge sparking in her eyes. The opportunity offered. There's one problem. "If I go to Winter Court, my identity will soon be obvious."

"True. Perhaps, in the future, you may visit my court with all the glory of your true self, but for this session, may I suggest" —her servant steps into the room, and offers me a cherrywood box— "a disguise. Open it."

I try. The lid doesn't move. "Is it locked?"

"No." Her mouth tilts. "You'll find, dealing with courtiers, that the straightforward path to your goal is often blocked. Try taking a sideways approach."

I frown, sifting through her words. Like the Threadmistress, the Governor is testing me. Perhaps I need a set of lockpicks. Or perhaps... I remember the secret doors and hidden passages in Chateau Boispierre. Turning the box, I press and manipulate solid-seeming wood. I'm probably making a fool of myself.

The back slides open.

"*Brava!*" The Governor applauds. "You solved the puzzle box rather quickly."

Tys leans closer. "How'd you do that?"

I stare at the contents. Within the velvet lined drawer sits a necklace of silver that looks more like a spider web than a chain. Where each strand crosses, a small gem sparkles. All glows with bright golden Otherlight.

"That's..." I stop before saying *powerful*. "Beautiful."

"It is, and it carries a strong charm that will obscure your features."

I frown. "It'll blur my face?"

"Rather, it will blur others' perception and memory of your face."

The necklace glitters innocently. "They will remember you are pretty, or that you were witty, or that you had a green dress, but details will melt away. In my experience wearing it, I found that even the details of our conversation quickly fade. Others remember what they felt and the general substance of the conversation, but little else. Now try it on. Mattias, do up the clasp, will you?"

I gingerly hand it to him, then lift my hair from my neck. His fingers brush my skin, and I shiver. The Governor gives no indication she noticed, only nods as Tys steps away.

"Yes, I think that will do nicely. What do you think, young man?"

He swallows, then forces a smile. "It works. Don't look like yourself anymore."

The Governor sits back in her chair. "What's your decision, Your Highness? Will you accept my invitation?"

Hope and desire somersault in my chest. *Yes!* I want to shout my acceptance. I pull in a breath to answer, but a thousand thoughts jostle the delirious emotion. The suspicious ones are loudest.

It's dangerous.

It might be a trap.

It must be a trap. Even if kindly meant.

The Governor and Tys. A bright, intelligent mentor with decades of experience in statecraft and a handsome boy with magic that calls to my own. How much I want this. How easy to bend my will.

Tys meets my gaze, searching my face.

Heavens, I *kissed* him last night.

What would come next? A broken heart, if I walk away. A broken kingdom, if I give myself wholly to him. If I marry…

Suddenly I can't breathe. What I want and what I can never have is offered freely, yet twisted tight as a new skein of thread. Brandt and Haps-Burdia want Valonia under their rule, and my dowry lands might only be the beginning. I trust Tys, but…

If I love my kingdom as much as my father does and grandfather did, if I am worthy to one day become queen, shouldn't Valonia come first? Before anything or anyone else?

And if my uncle isn't as securely isolated as he should be, shouldn't I warn my father? Protect him as I couldn't protect my grandfather?

The air is heavy and thick. The Fates are close, still trying to tangle my life threads with Mattias VandeBrandt. What seems so easy now will snag my true desires out of my grasp. I must solve my problems another way.

Shoulders stiff with new responsibility, I stand and offer a deep, respectful curtsy.

"I am sorry, but I must decline the invitation, Your Excellency. It's best if I do not attend your Winter Court."

CHAPTER TEN

Backstitch: a simple needlework stitch in which every
other stitch is doubled back so as to present a smooth,
continuous line

TYS INSISTS HE ESCORT ME BACK TO THE ABBEY. I INSIST
he not.

"That Sister Treuda plans mischief. You're not safe."

"I told you." I hand back the Governor's necklace. "I've never been
safe."

"But, *kleintje*…"

I put my hand up to his lips, hushing him as I did on the island. "I
wish our paths continued together." I wrestle the rest of my words
into submission and throw them between us like a gauntlet. "You
know what happens if I don't turn away now. I lose everything."

He flinches. "Everything? You mean Valonia? What has that land
ever given you? A broken hand and a death sentence."

"It's my home. My people."

"You were sent away." *Stars, he knows how to wound.*

"For safety." I blink back hot tears. "If we were ever to… to
become…" I can't say *married.* It feels too far away. "No matter where I

live, I'll always be princess of Valonia, and your father will demand land as my dowry, and he'll have the foothold he always wanted."

"He may get it, anyway."

I blink. "What do you mean?"

His scowl melts. His face pales. But his lips pinch tighter than Sister Treuda's purse.

The Governor clears her throat. I forgot she was there. "If you wish to return to the abbey, I'll send you with an escort."

I TRUDGE through the snowy streets of Godesbrouk, the Governor's large, intimidating servant following me like a shadow. I arrive at St. Beatricia's just as Matins bells ring out. The morning's still dark, but the eastern sky will lighten too soon.

I send the Governor's servant away, then walk past the iron gate and around the corner to the orphan door. Memories of Tys' smile, his kisses, surround me. I brush them away as I tuck myself into the confines of the orphan door.

I slip into the dark receiving room and creep across the floor. I hesitate at the door to the courtyard, then emerge into the shadows. I follow the bobbing candles held by girls and nornes into the chapel. I slip into the pew beside Renata. A hand grips my shoulder from behind. I look up. It's one of the lacemaking nornes. She pins me with narrowed eyes and makes no attempt to keep her signs private.

"When prayers finish and the others leave the chapel, please stay."

My mouth goes dry. *I've been seen.* The consequences might keep me from being a valid second witness against Sister Treuda. Everything is in jeopardy.

I pray fervently as I kneel. I need inspiration, wisdom to find a way out of this coil. The last amens are finally gestured, and the room empties. I stand at the back of the chapel until there's only the Mother Abbess, the lacemaking norne, and myself.

The norne approaches Mother Abbess' seat at the front of the chapel. I follow.

She signs rapidly, but I understand enough. The norne witnessed me leaving the receiving room. She suspects I left the abbey and returned furtively. She can't formally accuse me, being the only witness, but she believes Mother Abbess should be aware.

The head norne nods and thanks her in hand language.

The lacemaker turns and leaves.

Mother Abbess looks ill in the candlelight. The hollows under her cheekbones seem darker, the wrinkles etched deeper. Too much like my grandfather's. I remember Sister Treuda and her visitor discussing a tincture.

Mother Abbess motions me forward and I obey, kneeling.

"I received a report from Renata a few hours ago about suspicious behavior. Will you be the second witness?"

My shoulders ease. I tell her what I saw, how I followed the man with the wagon and lost his tracks in the square. I falter for a moment, not sure how to explain Tys and the Governor. "I didn't return immediately to the abbey, but instead sought advice from someone who could provide help, or at least insight."

Mother Abbess cocks her head. "And did they?"

"Not in any straightforward way, though..." I remember what the Governor said about crime and the church. "Perhaps they did."

We speak a little longer; I explain what the Governor said and sketch out a plan. Mother Abbess eventually nods and reaches for her prayer beads. Some are wood, some are glass, but a few are intricately knotted silk. She pinches one, and it flashes with dark blue Otherlight.

I gasp. Mother Abbess is a Skeinwitch.

The chapel door opens, and Sister Famke enters, holding her prayer beads up with a questioning look. I catch a glimpse of Otherlight before they disappear into the folds of her robes. In a quick series of signed communications, Mother Abbess explains what I just shared. My gaze darts between them. Finally, they nod and look at me.

Sister Famke signs, "You're willing to risk yourself for this task?"

I nod.

"Then we must hurry."

I agree.

The Threadmistress and I retreat to the back of the chapel. Sister Famke looks over her shoulder at Mother Abbess sitting hunched in her chair.

"Dawn comes soon," she signs, "but also Death. Mother Abbess is dying. You *must* succeed."

I nod again. Sister Famke wraps her fingers tightly around my upper arm and yanks me toward her as she barrels out of the chapel.

"Wait! Stop!" I sign. "That hurts!"

Sister Famke doesn't even look at me. I scurry, trying to gain ground so I can get in front of her, so she can see my hands.

"Stop! I didn't say I want to leave!"

Her expression is stony. With her free hand she signs, "You decided to leave when you snuck out. No matter the reason, that's grounds for expulsion."

"I saw a man taking things from the abbey. He had a wagon. Sacks of grain."

"You're making that up." She continues marching forward.

"No!" I look around the courtyard. A few nornes linger near the bath house and three girls stand in the dormitory doorway. "Please, it's true! I saw a man stealing grain from the abbey. You must believe me!"

Sister Famke hauls me toward the abbey gate as I continue begging, trying to explain. The porter appears and unlocks the gate for us, holding it open. I wrench myself from Sister Famke's grip and sign to the onlookers, who've multiplied.

"Please, can any be my second witness? Did anyone notice things missing from the storeroom? Perhaps Sister Treuda herself gave the grain to him. Sold or traded it."

Sister Famke's hand cracks across my cheek. I stumble sideways, sprawling in the snow. She stands over me. "Now you've gone too far."

The porter, a broad-shouldered norne, hauls me outside the gate. It swings shut before I regain my footing. I cling to the cold, twisted iron and let tears slip down my cheeks until all the onlookers depart. Then I turn and plod down the dark street. I scoop a handful of snow and rub it against my cheek. Becoming bait has few advantages.

⁂

I TRUDGE through the streets of Godesbrouk, my mind racing.

Mother Abbess isn't long for this world. I don't know if it's poison, or a slow-moving illness that's been helped along, but she'll be gone in a few months at most. Is that why Sister Treuda collects extra money and provisions? Is it exchanged for favors? Bribes? To position herself to take over the abbey?

When the Bishop-Princep over a region chooses a new abbess, for continuity's sake, it's usually one of the two lead women in the abbey. Either the norne who leads the abbey specialty craft, like the Thread-mistress, or the Almoner. The right hand or the left.

The wind whips the snow in the street before me, and I hurry.

I must return to the Governor's house.

It's not as easy as I thought. The moon is fitful, hiding its slender length behind clouds. The streets, laid precisely in geometric sections, look too much alike. I backtrack several times. The houses finally become more prosperous, generous in height and breadth. I'm near. A left at that fountain, then a right.

My neck prickles. The urge to look over my shoulder is like hunger on a fasting day. I resist until just before I round the corner, but when I peek, there's nothing but snow and house-shaped shadows.

I trek through the dark streets. I reach a broad gate similar to the abbey's. It keeps the rabble from the front door of the Governor's residence. I pull the bell. In the silence, I must have faith that the jangling rouses someone from bed. I blow on my fingers and stomp my feet. Turn and look around the dim street. I blow on my fingers again. Ring the bell once more.

I'd rather not face the Governor, not after turning her down. She offered that advice about Sister Treuda, though. She has the power to lock the woman up.

The Governor's porter must sleep deeply. I ring the bell a third time.

A glow of candle flame appears behind an upper-story window. Someone's coming. I wave a hand in case they're looking. I survey the street once more and nearly scream.

Jacco races around the corner, dashing straight toward me.

I scrabble for the bell pull and yank. Once. Twice. Thrice.

That demon dog will haunt me 'til I die! So much for Renata's qualmroot and sausage.

Jacco's halfway across the square when a cloaked figure hobbles around the corner. It pulls back its hood. Sister Treuda, gesturing for me to stop. I'm more worried about her dog quickly gaining ground. I hoist myself up the gate, climbing with hands and numb toes.

"Get away."

"No, you don't understand," Sister Treuda signs in her rusty way. "I've come to help."

"Then call off your dog." I scrabble higher.

Jacco's beneath me, leaping, teeth snapping.

"I heard you were thrown out. I can give you a place to stay. Warm bed. Warm food." She could be convincing if I didn't know her plans and if Jacco wasn't trying to sink his teeth into my ankles with such enthusiasm.

"At the abbey?" I ask. *Where's that porter? I'll even take the Governor herself.*

"Nearby. I'll talk to the Mother Abbess, and she'll let you come back. Tomorrow, the next day at the latest."

"I don't know," I lie.

My foot slips. I try to get better purchase, but the norne grabs my ankle. She yanks hard with surprising strength. I kick out, clinging to the ironwork gate with numb fingers.

"Help!" I scream, trying to remember the equivalent word in Haps-tongue. "Help me!"

Sister Treuda pulls on my cloak. The ties cut against my throat, silencing me. I reach for the bell pull; I tug at it, even as she wrenches me down to the ground. I bat her away, scuttling over the snow-slicked cobblestones. Jacco's teeth sink into my arm. *Damn him!*

I shake him off. Stand. Run blindly. Straight into someone's arms.

He smells of milled flour and cheap liquor.

I yell again, clumsily using tricks Feroulka taught me. Stomp foot. Elbow stomach. Slip through arms. Headbutt. Groin.

We both tumble. I kick free. When I look back, my captor is pinned to the ground by a large man, the servant who escorted me earlier. Two other men hold Sister Treuda, endeavoring to bring her within the Governor's gates.

Jacco dashes forward between everyone's legs, not towards me, but returning to Sister Treuda's side. The big servant reaches out and picks him up by the scruff of his neck.

"Demon dog," I mutter and sign.

"No," the servant signs one-handed. "He's a good dog. Can't help being small. Makes up for it by being fierce and stubbornly loyal."

I shake my head and examine my bleeding arm. "Agree to disagree."

※

I SIT across from the Governor once more, pressing the embroidered love letter handkerchief against my arm. I protested using it, but she insisted handkerchiefs are for mopping blood, tears and snot, and the piece had sat idle long enough. The hulking servant who defended Jacco sits beside her, interpreting more smoothly than Tys had earlier.

"How do you know hand language?" I ask him.

"He has a sister in St. Beatricia's," the Governor answers. The stream of servants slows, cupfuls of tea warm my insides, and the bloody gash is staunched and cleaned. The Governor settles by the window at a table with a delicate chess set and gestures for me to join her. The first move is mine. I look up to find the Governor's dark eyes studying me. The sharp light of sunrise reveals fine lines around them and her mouth, making her seem much more canny.

Her first sally is innocent enough. "So, you will return to St. Beatricia's?"

I shake my head. "Not safe. I must go home."

"Return to Valonia? There are far better places to hide."

"Where I can use hand language? There are few of those." Using my twisted left-hand fingers, I move another pawn. "I'm distinctive enough. My uncle will find me again, despite his isolation. I may not have warning next time." We move a few more pawns before she brings out her bishop.

"You'd rather face him on your own ground, Princess?"

I move my knight. "It's my ground. And my father is king."

"Kings are often vulnerable." She moves her king one square. "Their hands are tied by politics and other duties."

"My father will protect me, and I'll watch his back." I'm not sure if the game is meant to emphasize the conversation, or the conversation is to distract from the game.

"I'm certain he will. But from what I know of Reichard de Perdrix, he doesn't play fair."

"I hope you don't infer I should lower myself to his level."

"Merely advice to be on your guard." Her rook advances. "Now, how did you lure that norne out of the abbey?"

The topic change makes me pause. "I named her as possible second witness."

"And lured her out of safety to pursue you." The Governor smiles. "The Queen's Snare. Very nice."

I frown. "That's the name of a stitch. A rather complicated one with three needles."

"Named after a chess move that is not quite as complicated." She nods toward the board, where I thought I'd cornered her queen. "However, the idea of putting yourself or a valuable piece at risk to gain an even greater advantage is one known to chess players and rulers as well." She brings forward her knight. "Check."

I look for an opening for my king to escape. There? No. Or there? No, but possibly...

I move the piece and find her watching me.

"It's a pity our acquaintance will be cut short." She quiets my protest with a gesture. "Relax, I won't tempt you again. Your answer was clear enough the first time." She lifts her hands and signs slowly but clearly. "However, you are a clever girl, and I don't like to see a girl's intelligence wasted."

I smile a little.

"So," she continues speaking, her servant interpreting, "I have a gift for you." She produces a slender book. Each page has at least one small bit of embroidery, like sampler stitches. I handle it reverently.

The Governor answers my questioning look with a smile. "A syllabary for Broid Cypher, within a book of political instruction. How to get power and keep power."

Like honey on a trap. I try to hand it back. She refuses.

"Take it. Read it or not. I promise, your uncle has his own satchel of tricks. But this was written by a woman, advising her daughter how not to be powerless in a world governed by men. I thought you could use it to survive, if nothing else."

I flex my twisted left hand and nod. "Thank you."

"Perhaps we could correspond."

"Correspond?"

"Letters via pigeons, embroidered on strips of cloth."

It's dangerous. She's a known enemy. But she's old enough to be my grandmother.

"What kind of correspondence?"

"Nothing traitorous, dearheart. The weather, what you ate for dinner, the latest gossip. I'll send six pigeons with you. The message can't be more than a few lines. So, a dozen sentences about weather and gossip—what could I glean? Precious little."

Before I can ask my next question, a servant escorts Renata into the room. She gives me a quick smile, then curtsies to the Governor and reports like a lieutenant to a general. She and Sister Famke waited until Sister Treuda left the abbey, then went into the provision rooms and gathered evidence. Renata has both tally books, a satchel of fine needlework pieces found under the norne's bed worth hundreds of gold coins, and a letter from Sister Famke. The Threadmistress wrote on behalf of Mother Abbess, asking that the Governor prosecute Sister Treuda for theft, embezzlement, assault, and a host of other crimes. Since her crimes extended outside the abbey, the church will relinquish its right to an ecclesiastical tribunal.

The Governor looks approvingly at her huge servant interpreting. "Your sister will make a good Abbess." She turns her attention back to me and says, "If you wish to change your mind regarding the abbey, Sister Famke assures no punishment. Indeed, she offers protection."

I shake my head. "I'm not going back to the abbey."

Renata looks disappointed, but the Governor stands, clapping her hands together.

"I'll provide food, a horse, and a bit of coin so you can overnight at inns." A sideways glance. "A basket of birds strapped to your saddlebags supports the story that you're exchanging pigeons between two abbeys."

She and her servant leave before I can answer.

"So, you're leaving?" Renata asks.

I nod.

She stands awkwardly. "Remember your slow turtle signing?"

I stiffen. Nod again.

"No one said that before I started it. I gave you that name sign." Her left hand mimics my fingers' curl, then becomes the sign for turtle. "It was... wrong and hurtful, and I'm sorry."

"Why did you?"

She frowns. "When you get back home, perhaps you'll go up the Fontaine valley," she signs. "Perhaps as high as the village Ariengy. Perhaps you'll meet a carpenter and his wife. He'll have red hair. She'll be blonde. They'll have two boys nearly grown, and another about so high." She places her hand at her nose. "Could you tell them that Helene is doing well? That she... I cook every day. Thick soup and good brown bread." Her lips pinch together. "Tell them that Lilou was happy. Here, it didn't matter she was deaf. She chatted and sang and learned. She stitched beautiful flowers, like the ones in our meadow. Tell them I kept my promise. I cared for her. Kept her safe. We shared a room until two winters ago when... I couldn't protect her from pneumonia." She squeezes her eyes shut.

I try to imagine what it would be like to have a little sister, to lose her, and how I would feel towards the next person to sleep in her bed. Months of hurt are easier to nurse than new sympathy, but I stand and wrap my arms around her. "I'll find them."

IT DOESN'T TAKE LONG to prepare for my journey. The huge servant takes me aside in the courtyard and draws a map using a bit of charcoal on the cobblestones. I recognize the route I took with Feroulka coming to Godesbrouk. I'll trace that route in reverse. I nod. He takes four small stones and places them along the road he's drawn. He scratches the name of each town the stone represents, then draws a picture of each inn's sign. A pair of hissing geese, a crowned swan, a girl carrying two buckets on her yoked shoulders, and a flute and drum. I nod once more.

"If you have any problems with the innkeepers," he signs, "show them this." He holds out a ring. Stamped into its center oval is the Governor's crest: the Haps-Burdian falcon.

I stare at the symbol of my kingdom's enemy for too long, not taking it. The servant waits, not making the choice for me. *Can I align myself with the Governor, even briefly? How much allegiance can I offer? How much help should I accept?*

I pluck the ring from his fingers and offer my thanks.

I turn. There, between me and the saddled horse, stands Tys. He holds the basket of pigeons. His gaze travels between my face and the ring pinched between my fingers. He raises an eyebrow questioningly. With such an expression, he doesn't need hands or voice.

When I refused to go to Winter Court, I rejected him. I professed loyalty to Valonia as my reason. This ring tarnishes that loyalty. Shame heats my skin.

"It's only for safe passage," I mutter. "Nothing more."

He cocks his head. In disbelief or challenge, I'm not sure.

"If anyone knew I'd gone to Winter Court... If my uncle knew..." I shiver. "None would trust me from then on."

He balances the basket in one hand and signs with the other. "You're the Crown Princess. It'd be educational."

"I sat beside the Oak Throne as my grandfather passed judgement from the age of four until I was sent to St. Clotilde's. I've been educated in the ways of government."

"But what of the ways of politics?" Frustration pinches his face as he signs. "Do you know how to turn an opponent into an ally? Do you know how to push past differences, find the thing you have in common, and develop that into a partnership? Do you know how to compromise? To give up something you want for something you cannot live without?" Frustration shifts to longing, yet I ignore the leap of my heart and match that frustration.

"I know how to listen. To watch. To wait for the attention lapse so I can dart in and snatch what I need." How many times have I done that? "I know *not* to want anything extra, because I cannot *ever* have it."

I cannot ever have *him*.

I must live my life without his wit and sunshine.

My heart twists as if the Fates themselves reach down and grip my chest; as if I'm once again knocked flat on the hard-packed road, meeting Tys' eyes and unable to breathe.

"Could you..." Tys reaches up. His hand brushes my cheek.

I step back, though I want to lean in. Want to smell him, to feel his lips on mine.

"I cannot have both you and Valonia." I swipe at my damp cheek as

I laugh. "A Perdrix and a VandeBrandt, together? It's an impossibility even the Fates can't muster."

"We could try." I love him for the willful hope in his eyes.

"I can't. I'd be a traitor."

He looks down at the ring once more before glaring at me. "Can't? Or won't."

I look away. "I won't."

He turns then and busies himself tying the basket behind the horse's saddle. I peek at his face, at the muscle jumping in his cheek. I wait for his rebuttal. I ache for one more protest, even as I dread it.

When he finishes, though, he turns his back on me, stalking towards the house. I scoop up a pebble and throw it, hitting his shoulder before he reaches the door.

"Mattias VandeBrandt!"

He turns, stone-faced.

I can't profess my love to him. I'm leaving. I'm making the hardest choice of my life. The right choice. For my kingdom. For my people. For my father.

"Will you tell me what's coming for Valonia?"

His hands move back and forth like a battling army. A sign we've rarely used. "War."

Merde. I pull in a shaky breath as my mind leaps forward, trying to find solutions to a problem I don't know the dimensions for. I gesture for Tys to elaborate. He just shrugs.

Taut as a thread, I'm ready to snap. "Anything more specific? A date, a location, anything?"

A pained expression. "I don't even..." He breaks off and signs, "I can't tell you."

"Can't or won't?"

He resumes his stony mask. "Won't." Then he turns on his heel and leaves.

I'M on the road before Terce bells. When I'm outside the city, I release my tears. I sob to the rhythm of the horse's hooves pounding against the road until there's nothing left but emptiness weighing heavy in my chest and a headache.

The gray abbey-clothes, the pigeons, and the ring keep me safe enough from guards and patrols. My stomach clenches each time I show it, sending up plenty of prayers for the Fates' protection. Once I enter Brandt, though, soldiers seem to sprout like mushrooms. It's not just the green and gray Brandt uniform; there's soldiers in uniforms from several countries within the Haps-Burdian empire. Gray and black. Brown and blue. Black and green. Every tiny village has its half dozen, but some have as many as twenty-five men mustering on the packed snow of the village green.

Anxiety turns to dread. Tys didn't lie. The bloody Duke of Brandt is readying for a spring campaign against Valonia.

CHAPTER ELEVEN

WHEN I REACH THE MUSE RIVER, I skulk in the alleyways of Nemeaux until I spot a Mirvray ferryman. Exchanging hand language, he agrees to take me to Isle Dinant after sundown. Darkness falls. We muffle our oars. Tensions are high, he informs me. The Brandt military no longer turns a blind eye to any kind of river crossing.

When Tanja answers her front door, my hands tremble so much I can't get the governor's ring off my finger.

"Melt it into something else," I ask. "Please, I can't..." The words don't survive the storm of emotion that surges over me. "I... I..."

Tanja opens her arms.

I fall into them, releasing a long wail of heartache and fear. It resonates through my chest. She strokes my back. How did I ever feel awkward in her embrace? She lets me cry. When I've soaked her blouse, she escorts me into her workroom, and I collapse onto a stool. She stokes a brazier, listening as I pour out the tangled story of Tys and me, Renata and Sister Treuda, Tys and the Governor, pigeons and a ring, worries about my father, and Tys' final farewell.

When I finish, she slips the ring off my finger. She makes it look easy as she melts it into a golden puddle and pours it into a mold. She settles at her workbench as I continue talking. She takes up a spool of gold wire; she twists, clips, hammers, and solders, as her Otherlight glows brighter and brighter.

When I subside into silence, she looks up from her work and signs, "So, it is an impossible thing? You and Tys?"

I frown. "Yes." *Was she not listening?*

"More impossible than when he was an acrobat?"

"Then I... I didn't feel so..." I press my lips together. "It's different now. His father will be *invading* Valonia. Should I give Brandt what they haven't taken already?"

She puts away her tools and signs. "Understanding the obstacles is wise, but fully examine the possibilities. Bargains. Alliances. While here, Tys showed good character and a strong Gift of magic. He could bring much to a partnership. However, do you wish to yoke yourself to *anyone* yet? Perhaps in a year, or five, or ten, you will be ready. It is not a decision for *this* moment. For now, you must claim your birthright."

She lifts her handiwork, turning it this way and that. What I thought was a torque of bundled gold wire is a slender crown. The golden twists mimic a wreath, diverting this way and that to suggest oak leaves and small acorns. She beckons me forward. When I stand before her, she rests the coronet upon my head and speaks.

"You do not need hearing to lead, but this might be a useful tool since none of those poor Valonians bother with hand language." Her voice is warm. Tender.

My eyes prick with tears. "Like my combs!" After so many months, to hear again...

I throw my arms around her and bury my face against her. "Thank you."

But Tanja's not finished. From a chest in the corner, she pulls out a crimson gown with black and golden embroidery. The trunk is full of the gowns we embroidered last summer.

"You fled Valonia as a scared girl. You shall return as the crown princess. As you grow into that role, these will help others recognize your authority."

I bathe and change into the gown. I settle the coronet once more upon my head. Tanja returns with the recast ring, now shaped like the Mirvraan life-debt ring my grandfather gave me all those months ago. As dawn lightens the sky, she escorts me to a ferry where a horse awaits, my trunk of gowns and basket of pigeons tied up behind. She squeezes my hand and kisses the new ring on my finger.

"Be brave," she signs, then I'm ferried across the river and deposited on Valonian soil.

ANXIOUS TO GET HOME, I urge my mount up the snow-crusted path of the Boispierre Pass. The sharp scent of evergreen pricks my nose, so different from the loamy, muggy scent of the Lowlands. An outsider might feel intimidated, trekking deeper into the rocky pass, yet my shoulders relax as the Valon Mountains enfold me in their rocky embrace.

An arrow sprouts, thrumming in the road. I gasp. My mare sidles.

"State your business," someone shouts from up the twisted road. A scout, perhaps sent ahead from the sentinel tower on the ridge.

"I am Marguerite de Perdrix, returning home after a long absence." I pull my hood back, revealing my face and my new coronet.

The scout steps out of the woods, lowering his nocked arrow. He bows, then guides me to the first sentinel tower, reports in, and escorts me all the way to Chateau Boispierre. I go directly to the council chamber. A dozen noblemen stand around the grand table in the center of the room, a familiar scene. Now, the King's Council encircles my father instead of my grandfather. In the past, I'd skulk in the background, but I slip past wide-shouldered uniforms and stout men in velvet.

"Father."

He looks up from the map-strewn table. "Marguerite?" Surprise is chased by fear. "Why...?" I wish I could whisper my news in his ear, but I wear a coronet, so I lift my chin.

"I've traveled far to bring you news of war."

I tell him of my observations of troops and squadrons, their locations and uniforms. I point across the table of maps and my father adjusts small clay icons onto the correlating marks. When I finish, the men in the council chamber silently assess me. A few shift, as if ready to question my report, but my father strikes first, moving to my side.

"This confirms our spies' reports. Well done." As if he had given me this task.

He kisses my forehead and I wrap my arms tight around him. I am home. He isn't my grandfather, but I can grow to love and trust him. This tenderness, the security he offers, it feels the same. I want to protect that feeling however I can. I send my magic into the thick velvet of his tunic. *Strength. Protection.* He pulls back with a curious look.

"Further conversation must wait until supper, *mignon.*"

I accept the dismissal and leave. I unpack my gowns, reveling in their beauty and the power that shimmers from them, then care for the pigeons. I take them to the pigeon loft, hiding them in plain sight. Cages fill two walls, open nests a third, and a large window without glass takes up much of the fourth. Each occupied cage is labeled with the birds' destination. I transfer the birds to an unused cage and label it Ariegny, after Renata's village.

Another obligation I must take care of. But first things first.

The throne room calls me. It's dark and empty, for everyone's still in the council chamber. I tiptoe to the throne, a remnant of the Valonian Oak, and run my hand along the wood's carved surface. The first time I was allowed to sit with my grandfather as he held court, my bandaged left hand traced the strange whorls and curves. This room became a haven from fear, where my uncle couldn't harm me.

"I'm home," I whisper. The same warmth I felt as a child tickles gently beneath my fingers. Back then, I imagined it was the spirit of the ancient oak speaking to me. It's only the heat from my own fingers, of course, but it brings comfort. The tightness I've kept tucked in my chest for months breaks open like an egg. My sight blurs from tears. "I'm so sorry I couldn't save him. I tried." I kneel beside the throne and press my forehead against the wood. "I tried."

THAT NIGHT, after dinner, my father and I retreat to his study. Surrounded by maps and books, we argue over my uncle's banishment. Roc Ursgueule seemed like an inescapable fortress last autumn and my father refuses to see any weaknesses in his plan now that winter's half over.

"Those unscalable, uncrossable crevasses that have kept us safe from Pranzia's army might be perfectly accessible to a few men," I challenge. "The distance from ravine to fortress is only half a league." He only shrugs and peels an orange. I raise my voice. "What of pigeons?"

"Pigeons?" He finishes and hands half to me. Around the pieces of orange, I repeat each word I overheard between Sister Treuda and the mysterious man. He's unconvinced. "Secret messages have been exchanged across the continent for years. I know Reichard is devious, but this feels too complex, too far-reaching, even for him."

I rise and pound on his desk. "No. It's clear—"

"Stop jumping at shadows, *mignon*. Mundane facts are painful enough without the extra embellishment." He chuckles. "Stars, you never argued so vehemently with your grandfather."

"Grandpère believed me."

He pauses in lifting his last slice of orange to his mouth

"You think I'm silly for racing home at the first sign of trouble," I state.

"I didn't say that."

"You may not believe what I saw or what I heard, but I'm trying to protect you."

"A little girl should not be—"

"I'm not so little. Stop pushing me away."

He sighs and stands, coming around the desk to place his hands on my shoulders. "Pax, *mignon*. I will send men to check on your uncle's confinement." He leans forward to kiss my forehead, but I step away. His hands drop to his sides. "War is at our gates. Let's not start another within our walls."

THE NEXT DAY, before the King's Council convenes, I'm settled beside the window, less than five ells from their strategy table, busily embroidering. I intend to make my father's linen armor even stronger. I smile at each man who enters the room as my needle darts in and out. Lord Cygnetroit greets me kindly and offers to give my regards to his daughter, Isabeau.

My heart squeezes. "Please tell her I've missed her company."

When my father joins us, my smile retreats, but I don't avoid the kiss he drops on my forehead. "Adding military tactics to your curriculum?"

"The abbey didn't think it necessary." I shrug. "So I'm in want of a bit of strategy."

He smiles, as if it's a joke. Perhaps he plays to the councilors' expectations. They're quite silent. I thread more silk through my needle.

Stilted conversation starts. I've never eavesdropped so obviously. My needle work is jagged. My jaw aches. I want to hide or be standing shoulder to shoulder with the council, studying the strategy table. A crown prince wouldn't be bent over embroidery, five ells away. They eventually seem to forget my presence; their talk flows more naturally. My needlework smooths.

When I've emptied all the magic I can into the linen tunic, I pull out the Governor's Broid Cypher syllabary. I stitch what looks like a practice piece young abbey girls make as they learn new techniques. I smother my tickling unease. I'm only informing her of my safe arrival. And asking for any more news regarding my uncle. At mid-day I climb to the pigeon lofts. I roll the cloth tight, but it won't fit into the ankle canister of the Governor's pigeon. I peer closer and discover a paper message already inside. I pull it free, unroll it.

A hundred glances, words we shared, you try to cut asunder.

I fumble with the pigeon. It flutters out of my hands and out the wide window.

Merde. I only have five pigeons now.

More carefully, I examine the remaining birds and find a message in each ankle canister. I rearrange the slips of paper until I decide how it should read.

Rope is but a hundred threads, twisted to a tether.

Strength it has from union, not compelled, but drawn together.

Raveled close, entwined with you, what could have been, I wonder.

A hundred glances, words we shared, you now cut asunder.

I would have bound myself to you, Companion all and ever.

The Gordian knot that defied the blade, your tongue now has severed.

"Damn you, Tys." I'm not sure if it's a poem of his own making or borrowed words from another, but it cuts me to the quick. Doesn't he know what it cost me to leave him? To leave the hope of him behind? How could he? Everything in a future union would be to *his* advantage.

I pull a needle from the cuff of my sleeve. I thread it with truth-telling black thread as well as a strand of crimson that matches Valonia's flag. The color of love, of anger, of passion. I embroider the three letters of his name onto the corner of my message to the Governor. Then I pull out two more needles and thread all three. Black, red, and the pale green of loss. I maneuver them in a tricky bit of needle weaving that results in the raised triangular icon of sacrifice. The Queen's Snare. I want him to know what leaving cost me.

Perhaps then he'll leave me alone, so I can heal.

THE NEXT DAY, it's time to cut away the stitches in my leg. Jacco's bite has healed with no sign of infection, thanks to Renata's handiwork. When my father sends his spies up toward Roc Ursqueule fortress to check on my uncle, I convince him to let me go along; I have a favor to repay.

The spies disguise themselves as servants, traveling with my retinue to the village of Ariegny. I'm not subtle in my teal gown, gold coronet, and a dozen outriders. They leave us before we reach the village. I find Renata's family. I admire her father's carpentry work, and commission a new embroidery stand and a few chairs. Privately, I give them news of Renata and Lilou. They're true mountain folk, hardly showing emotion, except for Renata's mother, who hides her face in her apron. Her strong blue Otherlight wavers as she silently sobs. A son puts his arm around her. He's as red-headed as Renata, as tall as his father, but with the same Otherlight glow as his mother.

He's the kind of boy I should've fallen for. A good Valonian boy from a caring family, who loves the mountains and swears allegiance to the partridge and oak.

I give my farewells and return home with an aching heart.

Four days later, a servant brings a scrap of fabric, delivered by pigeon. I coo over the 'new stitch patterns from the abbey' to allay suspicions. A green silk vine wraps drunkenly around its border. The message reads: *Man disappeared. Source reports Reichard works with others outside Valonia. Discussing construction.*

No answer from Tys.

The Governor's message has too much of nothing. Construction is all my uncle should be doing up at Roc Ursgueule, but the materials should be locally sourced. There's no shortage of Valonian stone.

I stitch another message. *Please elaborate regarding Reichard.*

Days crawl by until a new message arrives. *Whispers of discord in Perdrix family. Possible cooperation of R with a Haps-Burdian hunter.*

I'm more confused. And still no response from Tys. Which I shouldn't even care about.

I set aside my other embroidery and take this scrap to the window of the council chamber. I've become a common enough sight to now be invisible. In the winter sunlight, it's plain there's nothing more to the message except the border, a frame with odd hatches all the way around. I run my fingers over it, puzzling over my uncle's reported actions.

The lowlands are still in the grip of winter. Travel isn't ideal, except over frozen rivers. In the high mountains, it's impossible. Or should be.

Wandering over to the table, I drink in the map, a bird's-eye view. The only way my uncle could communicate outside of Roc Ursgueule is by messenger pigeons. But if he's dealing with dangerous folk outside our borders, he'd need payment. Pigeons can't carry coin. Information, though, secret information, can sometimes be as good as gold.

But would my uncle ever turn traitor? To his family, yes. But to Valonia?

My fingers rub the nubby surface of the border. *Nubby?* I study the embroidery again. It's amateurish, doubling the stitches in places. Unless it's purposeful. I peer closer and pinch my lips against a gasp. I retrieve my scissors and return to the window.

I might ruin what's underneath if I cut the wrong thread. I suck in a breath, place the tiny scissor blade under the top-most thread and snip. Using a needle, I carefully pull the extra thread away. Stitch by stitch. I turn the cloth. Squint. Remove more stitches. There, buried under the extra bulk, is a message.

War comes. Beware St. Ione.

My hands tremble. My scissors drop. The clatter summons startled gazes from the gathered men. Flushing, I apologize for disturbing them, but catch my father's eye. I want to pour out the news that Haps-Burdia will invade on St. Ione's feast day. Within a fortnight.

"*Mignon?*"

That means explaining how I know this. Explaining that I've exchanged private messages with the Governor-General of the Haps-Burdian lowlands. The emperor's own sister. At best, it's a deceptive omission that would damage my father's trust. At worst...

"It's nothing," I say, returning to my seat.

I can't stay silent, though.

That evening, with a prayer in my pounding heart, I visit my father in his study. I bring both scraps of cloth and lay them on his desk.

"What is this?"

I tiptoe carefully through the truth, omitting the identity of the woman who embroidered the messages. "At first, I thought to just learn Broid Cypher, but she had more information. Now, she says Haps-Burdia will attack on St Ione's day."

My father doesn't answer immediately. He studies the embroidery pieces. Turns them over. "This doesn't look good, *mignon*."

"I know..."

"If your uncle thought—" He pinches the bridge of his nose. "Let's be certain he *never* discovers you communicated with anyone beyond the Muse. Too easy to call it treason."

"I thought you'd *want* to know when they'll attack."

"The King's Council knows it'll be soon. It's the wisest time strategically; the ground won't be sodden and the rivers not yet swollen with snow melt." He pulls out a map. "The question is which front will they choose? Wurtz, Kohlne, Brandt, Hlaandrs? I doubt they'll march in through Pranzia; they've had uneasy peace since that betrothal debacle."

"I warned you about the southern ravines."

"Stop crowing. Yes, you did."

On his map, I trace the southern border, stopping at the words *Roc Ursgueule*. "Bridges could be made if desperate enough."

"Your little bird said he was in league with someone outside of

Valonia." He taps the northern border. "Why not the Duke of Brandt or the Governor herself?"

"No, he couldn't."

"It would be bold and devious. Reichard excels at both."

"He hates Brandt too much."

We argue for another hour. My father listens more than talks and doesn't laugh. Finally, he stands and kisses my forehead. "Don't send anymore messages without my approval."

I open my mouth, half-ready to protest. I understand the wisdom of his prohibition, yet there are so many possibilities when a message *could* prove useful.

He cups my cheek. *"Mignon?"*

"I promise."

⁂

THREE DAYS BEFORE ST. Ione's feast day, a soldier bursts into the Council room, breathless.

"Boats... crossing the Muse... Isle Dinant. Counted five large ferries."

My heart clenches. I flee the room even as it fills with questions and commands. I hurry to the courtyard and mount an already saddled horse, then commandeer a spyglass from a junior officer. I feel guilty as I ride out the gates toward the pass, but I don't pause until I reach the first sentinel tower and ask for news.

"Alarm bells ringing on the island. There's smoke."

"Smoke?" I ask.

"Brandt soldiers have torches. They started on the north side of the island, burning what they can to flush 'em out."

I train my borrowed spyglass but am too far away to make out details, except for a few bright blossoms of flame and the rising smoke from the fires.

"I'm going closer, to the lower sentinel tower." I leave before he can protest.

If Tanja or her people need help, Valonia will provide. Part of me wants to wait and organize a better response; more people, food, blankets, boats. Yet aid will be slowed by the parallel preparations for an invasion, for that's what my father and his councilors will see, I'm sure. If I wait for them, it might be hours or even days before help is sent. What might happen in the meantime?

I reach the lower sentinel tower and dismount.

"Can you see what's happening down there?" I shout to the men up in the tower.

"They've fired off catapults, but did little good stopping Brandt," a scout answers. "Some Mirvray men are fighting back. Mostly the soldiers seem to be herding those rats to our side of the island."

I freeze at that word, then my anger propels me up the outer stairs to the lookout.

"Never," I gasp, mustering authority as I stare at the two scouts, "use that word again. They are people, not rats."

They seemed startled by my arrival in their aerie, but nod. The grizzled one clenches his jaw and mutters, "As you say."

I accept their submission, then train my spyglass on the island. Fires burn in several buildings, including the weavers' lodge. All those bolts of magic-infused cloth, up in flame. My hands fist around the glass. I see figures but not faces.

"Your telescope must be better than this?" I say it as a question, but the younger one reacts as if I've given an order, stepping back from the large cylinder mounted on a tripod. I give him my glass in exchange, then stand on my toes to peer through the eyepiece.

Men and women. Children. They race through the streets, down toward the river. My heart squeezes. I try to discern faces. It's difficult. They're moving too fast. Buildings and greenery often block my view. I step away from the telescope and squint at the island. More smoke billows up and out.

The grizzled scout takes my place. I fidget until he steps away again.

The magnified Mirvray gather along the river. They pile into two ferries. The boats look overloaded. One pushes off, then another. Still, people line the bank. The boats will need to deposit the first passengers quickly, then return for those waiting. I know what I must do, what I and my father promised Tanja months ago.

I stand back from the telescope and explain briefly. "We must help them. Offer sanctuary. Help any wounded. I'll take some supplies from your quarters downstairs. Blankets and your extra horse. You" —I point to the younger scout— "ride to the upper sentinel tower and ask for more help."

The older scout steps forward. "Sorry, Your Highness. We can't."

"Because they're rats?"

His mouth tightens at my scorn, but he points toward the island. "*That's* Valonian soil. If Brandt crosses the river and invades, Valonia will retaliate, but rescue a bunch of squatters?" He shakes his head. "Our duty is to watch and report."

"Watch *me* then and report the princess is an arrow's flight from the Brandt army, helping a band of homeless Mirvray."

I race down the stairs. Scouts always have a horse saddled, bridled, and ready to go. I gather an armful of supplies and dump them in the waiting horse's saddle bags. I grab a couple of blankets and strap them on. I mount my horse, leading the scout's horse with its life-saving baggage, and race as fast as I dare down the mountain pass.

When I glance at the river, though, the Mirvray boats aren't coming straight across. They're heading farther downstream. Perhaps there's a better mooring place, but it'll be decidedly more difficult to row back across against the current. It makes no sense.

Finally, I reach the muddy, pebbly bank of the river. The second ferry is just going around the bend of the river, out of my sight. I put the spyglass back to my eye and scan the island shore. There are still a few dozen standing on the dock. Waiting.

Stars! Why don't we keep any boats on this side of the river? What I wouldn't give for one and a strong set of arms to row it. I hate feeling useless. I search along the streets and rooftops of Isle Dinant, hoping for some sort of inspiration. Movement. I shift the spyglass. Focus. Soldiers in green and gray. Just come over the crest. Carrying torches. A gleam of sunlight on metal. A sword held by an officer.

"Tys?" I jerk and lose the image. My horse sidles. I almost drop the lead reins of the sentinels' horse. Can I believe what I saw? Tys— dressed in a dark green uniform, metal breastplate and plumed helmet —running down the street with the soldiers. Yelling.

I shiver. Impossible. Tys would *never* chase Mirvray folk out of their home.

I raise the spyglass. Find him again. Teeth bared. Clearly shouting. Swinging his sword as if he means to kill every Mirvray he meets.

My mount sidesteps, trying to turn back toward the pass. I drop the spyglass. As I regain control, smoke roils up from the island. My chest aches. My lungs can't fill—as if I'm there in the smoke and the chaos, facing Tys. Waiting for his sword to sweep through me.

I shake my head to clear it and peer across the river. A longboat has been procured; it's overloaded, people hanging over the sides as it noses into the icy river. There are still folk left on the bank of the island. I grab a blanket and wave it above my head. The ferryman ignores me, heading downstream instead.

I dismount, tie the horses to a tree branch, and reclaim my spyglass from the riverbank. The lens is cracked, but it still magnifies. I peer across at the small crowd left on the island. Some faces I recognize; Gaspar's sons, a weaver, two children who played with Henk. And in the back, Tanja, her baby in her arms, stands beside Gaspar.

My chest constricts. How close are Tys' soldiers? I search, only catching movements between buildings and under trees. I refocus on Tanja's group, trying to estimate how quickly they'll meet. Tanja's folk all focus upstream, agitated and waving. I pull the spyglass away.

A lithe, small craft races toward the dock. The ferryman's back bends low to get a few more ells from each stroke of the oars. He's nearly there. I put the spyglass back to my eye. Gaspar reaches out and grabs the side of the boat. They don't bother to moor it as folk pile into the boat. Tanja sits; I release my breath.

Brandt soldiers stream down the hillside. So many soldiers. They race toward the dock. *No!*

Gaspar climbs aboard and pushes off.

Tears blur my eyes. I wipe them hastily and bring the glass up again.

Several soldiers reach the dock. They gesticulate, but the river's pushed the boat beyond their reach. A soldier, still carrying a torch, pulls his arm back and throws it.

I drop the spyglass.

The torch arcs across the distance, then falls neatly into the mass of Mirvray packed in the boat.

"No!"

The screams of the Mirvray take several heartbeats to reach me, faint and shrill. Frenzied movement—trying to put out flames. Those boats are sealed with pitch. Highly flammable pitch.

I lift the spyglass again. The crack is wider, the lens out of focus. I toss it away and squint across the water. Gaspar goes over the side, clinging to the gunnels of the boat. The others follow, so quickly the boat rocks dangerously. The flames are visible from here. Nearly everyone's out. The last is Tanja, her baby snugged close in a sling. As I watch, Tanja's foot catches on something. She tumbles over the side and into the ice-cold river. Vanishing beneath the water.

"Tanja!"

Gaspar leaves the side of the boat. Dives.

I run forward until I'm waist deep in the river. It pushes against my legs, pulls my skirts. I can't swim. The water is freezing. I will drown.

But Tanja...

I return to land and wrestle myself atop my horse once more. I race along the bank, but the river runs faster. Gaspar comes up for air a dozen ells downstream. Dives again. Flames dance in the center of the boat.

I search for Gaspar or Tanja. Nothing breaks the surface. *Heaven help them.*

The current sweeps the boat around the bend. I pursue it.

A copse of trees grows all the way down to the water's edge. An old fallen tree is caught up against it, extending branches out into the fast current. I urge my horse deeper into the water.

My mount suddenly plunges neck deep. I'm thrown forward. Nearly tumble off. I clutch at reins, mane, as tree branches claw and the horse scrabbles for footing. Then we're up but going the wrong direction. Back towards the other horse and the pass.

"No!"

The horse won't obey. She's panicking, racing toward safety. I let her run until we reach the wider bank where the other horse is still tethered. She starts to slow, and I regain control.

The heavy hoofbeats do not stop. I look around. Up toward the pass. They arrive before I come to a halt, three bands of thirty-five, thundering down the twisted road like a long red centipede, led by my father. His gleaming breastplate lists askew over his scarlet uniform. I trot forward to meet him.

"Tanja. Her people evacuated the island. One boat is on fire. We *must* help."

"Yes." He scans the river. "I'll send men downstream once the situation is safe. Which it currently isn't. That island is crawling with Brandt soldiers. We're within their arrow range." He gives a few terse orders before his gaze focuses on me. "Go home, Marguerite. Battle is no place—"

The arrows come swift and silent, falling upon us as we stand on the riverbank.

"Shields!" a commander bellows.

Panic skitters through my veins. My father dismounts and pulls me down with him, protecting me with his own body. My coronet topples off and rolls in the dust. Silence fills my ears as surely as if I'd plunged headfirst into water. Horses rear silently. Soldiers mutely topple off their mounts. Quiet chaos ripples through the ranks. The moment the air is clear, my father moves. He snatches the coronet. Presses it onto my head then tugs at his breastplate. Trying to pull it over his head.

"Wear this. Get up the pass, to the safety of the castle." He pulls me toward the only horse not prancing about, the one I'd tethered, still with a blanket strapped behind its saddle.

"Wait." I push the breastplate back over his chest. "Keep that. I'll use the blanket as armor."

"No."

"It will be enough." I pull the blanket free and let my power flow into the woven wool. *Ward. Protect. Shield.* It won't last long without any anchoring stitches, but it will protect me long enough to get to safety. My father looks like he wants to protest, but I push the blanket against his palm. His eyes widen and he nods. He throws me atop the horse and I'm clinging to reins and wool as we gallop up the pass.

Another volley of arrows, but not from across the river. They come from a ridge upstream of where my father and his men have taken shelter. On the Valonian side of the River Muse. No. That can't be. No troop of Brandt soldiers could have come across that wide water without being seen... unless the attack on Isle Dinant was a distraction.

My gut twists into a horrible knot at such a thought. And all that it implies.

A painful thump strikes my shoulder. I turn. An arrow tumbles to the ground. My blanket armor worked! But I must get to real safety and warn others.

I reach the lower sentinel tower and find a troop of soldiers in command. I give my news and they send a horseman off towards the castle.

"Now, get off home with you, Your Highness," the commander tells me.

The grizzled scout shouts down from the top of the tower. "Brandt soldiers advancing up the west ravine. Will be here in a trice."

The commander sees only a girl with a blanket wrapped around her for protection and pulls me from my mount and bundles me into the tower. "Bar the door."

I slam the sturdy oak door, pull the bar into place, and press my forehead against the cold, reinforcing strips of iron. Everything hushes as if I'm not wearing the coronet at all. I pace the floor, begging the Seven Sisters to protect my father, Tanja, her baby, Gaspar, the scouts and soldiers. Asking them for a good explanation for Tys' presence in *that* uniform with *that* expression.

My mind spins the fibers of thought until it becomes one long thread of hope. It's all a ruse. There must be a mistake. Perhaps I imagined it. Tys will contact me soon. He'll explain. We'll laugh over my misunderstanding. I relax against the door, then shake off my stupor and kneel in prayer.

I beg the Fates again on behalf of my father, Tanja, her baby, Gaspar…

Time is long and meaningless. There are no windows; the tower is built for strength and the sentinels always watch from the top. No bells chime away the hours.

Pounding on the door signals the end. Either we won, or we've been defeated.

"Who is it?" I yell.

The muffled voice speaks Langue-Valon. I open the door.

The brass insignia on his red uniform show he's a colonel. Rusty stains and bandages indicate it was a rough battle. His shoulders settle as he looks me over. "Your Highness, thank the Stars you're safe."

"Yes." I look past him and his companions. Bodies stretch inert on the road. Red uniforms and green. "What happened? How did they take us by surprise?"

The colonel's face twists. "It seems they came up the hunters' paths from the river while we were watching the fires on Isle Dinant."

"Does anyone know what happened to the burning boat's survivors?"

"I… I've no news of that, Your Highness, but…"

"You must send men to search downstream." His expression collapses into disapproval. I trail off, my gaze switching to the fallen men and the carrion birds already circling in the sky. Dread shivers through me. "My father, where is he?"

"Your father's safe in Boispierre."

I let out a sigh, but the colonel's chin lifts. His eyes focus over my head. "I regret to inform you, however, that Bishop-Princep Reichard is dead."

"My uncle? In Roc Ursgueule?"

He clears his throat. "Apparently, the Bishop-Princep left Roc Ursgueule, arriving at Boispierre the same time as the news of Brandt's movements. King Julien discovered his brother already wearing his uniform. Reichard convinced him Valonia couldn't lose another king." He clears his throat again. My gut wriggles with dread. "Your uncle led this company, Your Highness, not your father. Your uncle took five arrows as he rallied our men to scour the mountains for the Brandt vermin. He died of blood loss an hour ago. We all thought it was the king. We called truce. Brandt retreated to the river. We're clearing the dead as we speak."

I lean against the door frame, not trusting the stone beneath me. "My father... my uncle."

"They always did look a bit alike," the colonel offers.

I let out a broken sound.

"It was a brave thing, to sacrifice himself for his brother," he continues. "For his king."

I nod as my thoughts whirl. "It's the second time in less than a year the *Mors Regiis* pact has been put to use."

"Yes. A brave thing." His voice cracks.

I should be relieved. A joyful daughter. But would my uncle have shielded me with his own body? Or tried to give up his own armor for me? I'm suspicious.

"Please," I push words through my tight throat, "can you take me to my father?"

※

I DEBATE ALL the way back to Chateau Boispierre what to say to my father. Or uncle.

I can't be sure until I see him, but I suspect my uncle's handiwork.

In the council chamber, he bends over the table of maps, surrounded by councilors and generals. From the back he looks just like he should.

"Father?"

He turns. "Marguerite, *mignon*." His face is my father's. Worried. Relieved. He holds his arms out to me. I fall into his embrace. His clothes smell like him. Cedar and oranges.

Yet, he releases me *without* a kiss on my forehead.

I collect my embroidery from where I left it, wondering how to prove which man stands in this room. I turn and find him watching me.

"The last boatload of Mirvray, they were in peril when they floated out of sight," I say. "We must search for survivors and give assistance to any refugees."

He shakes his head sadly. "*Mignon*, the truce is fragile. I cannot risk sending our men that close to Brandt. Not now. It may be seen as an instigation."

"Then send women. You promised…"

He pats my cheek. "I'm grateful you're safe, *mignon*, but I must discuss military matters without distraction." A dismissal.

I leave, my jaw tight, my hand clenched around my embroidery hoop. My father promised on his life and mine, before the Fates, that he'd aid any Mirvray in need.

This is my *uncle*.

Now I need tangible proof.

CHAPTER TWELVE

Hardanger: embroidery openwork having elaborate symmetrical designs created by blocks of satin stitches within which threads of the fabric are removed

THE CASTLE IS CROWDED WITH UNIFORMED MEN AND worried nobles. The garden is a better place to order my thoughts. When I reach it, however, it's been transformed by orderly rows of bodies. Dozens of soldiers who were alive this morning. They might be sleeping, except they're not. They face the sky, awaiting the Fates' final blessing tonight before they're buried tomorrow.

As I stare, more are brought in. The lower level is filled. The second terrace grows crowded. I edge toward the far gate. I don't want to look at their faces. They're too young—not much older than me—and they're gone—spark and spirit vacated from their flesh. There are older ones too, of course. Men who might be husbands, fathers. I wonder who they left behind. There's so many. One dozen, two dozen. Five dozen. All dead defending the Boispierre Pass.

Then I stop.

A familiar face. One of the men who shadowed my father. His uniform marks him as a member of the King's Guard. But he wouldn't go on sortie with my father, would he? I scan the uniformed corpses. I find three more. I scurry to the gate and out into the courtyard. A temporary hospital has sprung up. The cries of the wounded echo off the battlement walls; the scent of blood and offal is as thick as on hog butchering day.

I hurry to the nearest entrance and flee blindly up the stairs, trying not to retch. I collide with a broad chest. Before I can apologize, I vomit all over the floor. A large handkerchief is pushed into my hands. It glows a subtle blue.

"Mop your face with that, *chérie*."

Through my tears, I recognize the portly frame of Lord Beauchamp. He was a close friend of my grandfather's, and a longtime member of the King's Council.

"I was on my way to the chapel to pay my respects to your uncle," he said. "I would ask you to accompany me, but that seems cruel when you're already in such a state. Let's find Lady Ulrica to tend to you."

"No." I grasp his hand. "I want to see him. I'll go with you."

He looks doubtful.

"Please."

The chapel is guarded by two soldiers. As we approach, one speaks.

"The body hasn't been cleaned or prepared, Your Highness."

"I understand."

The tang of blood fills the small chapel. The body is covered in it, the red of his uniform pale under the wine-red stains on his chest, shoulders and legs.

"Tell me what happened."

A soldier speaks, his voice steady. "He was a brave man. Charged right into the fray, he did. Took one arrow in the shoulder, there. Another in his side. Broke the shafts and kept riding. Farther west, we came upon a mess of Greenies. They were all over us with pikes and knives before we could bugle for help. He took a pike to the leg and one to the other shoulder. Dropped his sword then. Someone pulled him off his horse. I didn't see him again 'til it was all over."

I kneel beside the body, taking his hand in mine. It's cold, but not yet stiff. I place my left hand on the tunic sleeve. There is no magic humming. No Otherlight glinting. No magic in his clothing at all. Could it be my uncle? Hastily, I pull back his sleeve. No, there is my handiwork. My father wears the linen armor I made him. It just wasn't strong enough. I didn't pour enough magic into its threads to withstand the onslaught of pikes and arrows.

I failed.

"Stay here with me. Please—"

I rub my fingers over his cold flesh. Stop. There, at the base of his thumb, is a scar. From when I tried to prove I was strong enough to start sword training. I wasn't yet six years old. I whipped a smallsword through the air, not knowing my father was behind me. I turned. The sword sliced through the meat of his thumb. He bled badly, and I learned an embarrassing number of expletives.

A primal, guttural howl wells up and bursts from me. I can't control it with lips or tongue. I scream. Cry. Beat my fists against the stone bier.

My father.

I've lost him.

He's gone.

He was taken.

…While my uncle deceived everyone into thinking *he* was the dead hero. My uncle, the deceiver. Like Tys deceived me. Tricked me into believing he was something more than my enemy. He played with my heart, convinced me of his caring.

The smothered pain swells, threatening to tear me apart. I won't think about Tys. Not now. This is about my father. And my uncle.

I use Lord Beauchamp's handkerchief thoroughly and lift my head, addressing the soldiers standing nearby. "Where were the King's Guard when the Brandt soldiers attacked?"

The soldiers exchange a glance. "The King's Guard never go to battle, Your Highness. They guard the king in his duties. Here in the castle and traveling about the kingdom."

"Can you explain then" —my damp gaze includes Lord Beauchamp — "why there are at least four men in King's Guard uniform out in the garden with the rest of the battle-dead?"

"There shouldn't be."

"No." I stand and swipe the last of the tears from my cheeks. "Nor should there be a scar across my uncle's thumb." I lift it to show them. "When I'm the one who accidentally gave it to my father eleven years ago."

The chapel is silent.

Lord Beauchamp runs a hand through his gray hair. "These are serious charges."

"They always were the very likeness…" The guard trails off at the lord's stern look.

"Come, Your Highness." He escorts me toward the door. "We shall look into this."

WE FIND the uniformed bodies of the King's Guard where I left them. It's growing dark. Lord Beauchamp directs servants to bring them into the castle. Laid out in the Great Hall under candlelight, they're a grizzly sight. I shadow Lord Beauchamp as he examines them.

"All four throats were cut," I comment. "Not by sword in the heat of battle. Look at the skin at the edges. An assassination, rather than a battle wound."

"*Chérie*," Lord Beauchamp scolds. "Your grandfather allowed you in the throne room while he sat in judgement, but those are not things for young ladies, or princesses for that matter, to know anything about."

"It's unpleasant, but kings must know such things," I say. "Queens as well, for that matter." I'm frightened and thrilled at my own boldness.

Lord Beauchamp only has a moment to consider my argument, for my uncle and the King's Council enter the Great Hall. He pauses at the sight of the corpses.

"Heaven's sake, the valiant dead belong under the Stars, not ogled before supper."

"Why were your King's Guard assassinated?" I ask.

"My Guard is here, as you can see." He indicates the four men standing close to him. No gleam of triumph in his eyes or satisfaction in his voice. He plays his part well.

"Then how did your other men end up dead with the battle-wounded?"

"They must have bravely followed my brother into battle."

"No, because the King's Guard never go to battle. Ask any soldier in the army."

"Today was an exception in many ways, including that the princess was closer to battle than the king. The strain has gotten to you, *mignon*."

"No. King Julien lies dead in the chapel. He has a scar on his left thumb. You are Reichard, the Bishop-Princep."

"*Mignon*," he remonstrates. "Such wild accusations."

"Your Majesty." Lord Beauchamp steps forward. "Let us hear her out. Justice is the meat of the law, as your father always said. If you will observe the wounds here—"

"Enough!" My uncle finally shows anger. "I'll not allow the brave dead to be handled such to prove a whimsical, half-baked idea formed by my daughter's weak brain." He makes a regretful face and turns to his councilors. "Since her grandfather's untimely death, she's been easily upset, insisting he's still alive. She's been sequestered with medically trained nornes since his death. I thought she'd made a full recovery, but it's clear she remains unwell."

I gape at such bold lies. "No, Uncle. You'll not push blame on me. I tell you, he's—"

My uncle makes a brief gesture. Soldiers grasp me.

"What are you doing? Unhand me."

"I'm sorry, *mignon*. You'll stay confined to your chamber until you can control yourself."

The soldiers wrestle me away from the Great Hall.

"No, I am telling the truth. *That* is Reichard."

They pull me up the stairs.

"My father died bravely in battle," I shout down at him. "*You* snuck out of your banishment and took advantage of his death."

One soldier covers my mouth. I twist away, determined to shout one more truth.

"You do not deserve the title of king!"

⁊

I SPEND my first day trying to find a way out. The latch for the doorway to the secret passage has been broken and won't open, no matter how I maneuver hairpins in the mechanism. The doorway to the corridor is barred. The window is four stories above the busy courtyard. I'm imprisoned in my chamber.

Ulrica and her maid bring food; they change out my chamber pot and my laundry. They are accompanied by my uncle's new guards. My first whispered plea to Ulrica, and a guard places a knife against the maid's throat. I don't ask for help again.

No one takes my embroidery things, so I measure my days with the needle. I mourn my father, writing my memories of him in stitches. Composing thread sketches of his face that I never can get quite right. I tear long strips of cloth to use for messages. I waste several, anguishing over Tys leading those soldiers on Isle Dinant. I burn those. I knew Tys was an enemy of Valonia when I ventured out on Yule Night, when I joined him on his tightrope. I let the Fates intoxicate me with his charms, but that's all it was. Starlight and charm.

I switch to stitching facts: my uncle masquerades as king, and I'm imprisoned for telling the truth. All in Broid Cypher, in case the messages are discovered. I wish to the Stars I kept those stupid pigeons in my room. I plot how to get to the loft and tie these to as many birds as possible.

After seven days, Ulrica arrives with servants and a large basin of hot water. "I thought you'd like a bath before you leave your chamber."

"I'm being released?"

"It is Nemeaux Memorial Day. Folk have already started gathering outside the castle."

It is a holiday like no other: one of mourning, for the loss of our land and our neighbors, and also celebration for the birth of their princess. Me. It is a strange, paradoxical day. Food vendors hawk their wares to somber folk wearing black ribbons and armbands. Small posies of early spring flowers are presented to me, and afterward my grandfather always gave a somber speech. Which will now be given by my uncle, I suppose.

It is my seventeenth birthday. There *must* be a way for me to make the truth known today. My spirits lift until a maid reaches to help me undress. I have strips of Broid Cypher hidden in my bodice, Tanja's necklace still around my calf, and Tys' ring I've not yet had the will to remove from my foot. I step back.

"Thank you." I smile. "When I'm finished, perhaps you can advise regarding my hairstyle?" Lady Ulrica lifts her chin, understanding the dismissal, and leaves, maids trailing after. After shutting the door, I lean against it and let out a sigh. Dare I trust Ulrica? No. She's my uncle's partner or his cat's paw. No matter how bad she felt, she never saved my grandfather.

Once clean, I pick out a blush-pink dress from Isle Dinant. Wine-red embroidered flowers and green oak leaves twist around the square neckline and cuffs and blossom along the hemline. Feroulka said it's the perfect dress to impress a boy. *It accentuates your assets while still maintaining your innocence.* I don't care about boys today, but perhaps I can emphasize being old enough to know my mind, and innocent enough to be trusted. The dress fills me with tingles of magic and confidence.

The maids dress my hair under Ulrica's expert guidance. It's so thick, the curls so unruly, I usually keep it in a simple style, but today, they coax it into a loose pile of twisted curls tucked around my coronet. Sophisticated, without being severe. I feel elegant and smile at Ulrica, despite my wariness.

"Thank you."

She smiles in return. "You're now seventeen, yes? No longer a little girl." She's never been demonstrative, but she tenderly squeezes my shoulders. "Felicitations on your birthday."

MY HOPE TO speak out does not go as planned. Instead of going down into the square and mingling with the people while collecting my posies, I'm escorted to the castle walls overlooking the festivities. A different maid stands off to the side, clearly thrilled to be so close to the royal party on such an occasion. Something to tell her future children, I'm sure. She doesn't see the blade held by the guard behind her.

My uncle makes certain I do. "Look pretty. Say nothing."

I do.

The speech is exactly what the people expect. My uncle gives the dreadful recounting of the battle of Nemeaux, as it's written in our history books: the retreat across fields and into the city, running between the streets to the great bridge, my father carrying his limp wife across his saddle and my uncle carrying me in his arms. The Brandt army at their heels. The tide of green uniforms was nearly to the bridge when the two princes set off an explosion of black powder, and the hopes of the greedy empire were denied. At a cost. He reads off a list of the villages and towns that are now governed by the empire and ends with the city of Nemeaux.

"We will never forget our people on the other side of the river. We continue to pray for the day when we will be reunited again as one land. One people. One Valonia!"

All the folk cheer.

"All hail the Fates!" my uncle calls out.

"All hail the Fates!" the people answer.

I'm hustled away before the crowd quiets again. When my guards release me in the Great Hall, they remember their manners. "Wherever you wish to go, Your Highness, we are happy to escort you."

I dare not go directly to the pigeon lofts, so I visit Etoile in the stables. She's healed from our travels last summer and is plump from not being ridden often enough. I visit the gardens next. They're nothing but brown stalks and half-frozen earth. All the bodies from last week's battle are gone. They must be buried by now. I wander through the *orangerie* and pluck a piece of fruit. I peel and eat it, the scent bringing sharp memories of my father. I pick another. My guards become bored. I return inside and climb the east tower stairs.

"The pigeon loft, Your Highness?"

"I just need fresh air. I can't stay in the garden." I give a delicate shiver. "And the *orangerie* is too cloying."

Up in the pigeon loft, the wide stone window ledge is speckled with white droppings. I lean against the upper frame. The courtyard below is an anthill of activity. Beyond the castle walls, the twisting streets are less busy. The movements I do see are quick, careful. I stand there as the sun climbs, ignoring the bitter wind, as I think through chess moves against my uncle. Against the Governor, the Bloody Duke, and possibly Tys.

A guard clears his throat. "If you don't mind, Your Highness, we'll wait on the stairs."

I smile. "Make yourselves comfortable." They descend the stairs, avoiding the wind's teeth. I hurry to the cage I labeled, pull out a pigeon, and carefully tie one of my messages around its leg. I toss it out the window.

Below, my uncle strides purposefully across the courtyard. *Falling Stars.*

I pull out another pigeon. Knot the cloth strip twice.

I launch the bird as my uncle enters the tower four stories below. I grasp a third pigeon. This knot is hasty, but I've time for nothing more before tossing it in the air.

I hear a clatter that might be my uncle coming up the stairs. I secure the cage and return to lean against the window casement again. I watch the birds' flight. A pale, ribbon-like length of cloth flutters in their wake, falling slowly towards the earth.

Merde.

Only two pigeons escaped with my messages.

"Marguerite."

I turn. It's my uncle.

"Only hours out of confinement and you're up to mischief."

I keep my breath even. "Mischief? After a week in one room, I need to fill my lungs with air and my eyes with the beauty of our mountains."

He studies me, then the wicker cages.

"You do not fool me, Marguerite. Confess your true intentions before it is too late."

"You want me to confess? I'll happily tell the world what I'm doing up here as soon as you tell the Valonian people why you wear your brother's crown." I speak loudly.

His eyes narrow. "The guards are on the first floor. They can't hear you." He shakes his head. "You've been trouble since the day you were born. Ill-timed and half-deaf. The Fates must have been toying with me, but no matter. I will ensure their plans are fulfilled."

"*Their* plans?" I ask. "Since when do you speak for the Seven Sisters?"

"I am upholding the destiny they determined for our family seven generations ago." His eyes burn. "My brother became the weak link. Julien let that lying whore entrap him with her magic and wiles. I was the only one to see it. I tried every way possible to warn him, but he wouldn't heed me. I didn't act with enough strength then, but I do so now."

I push past distorted logic to the truth worth shouting. "You admit you're not my father?"

His nose wrinkles. "I'd never dirty myself coupling with such *filth*."

"Don't speak of my mother that way."

"*She* was the reason we lost a third of Valonia seventeen years ago. You both pulled Julien out of orbit. Away from me. Away from his duty to Valonia."

"He handed over command to General Dupuis because his wife was *dying*," I say.

"He didn't know that when he left his post." My uncle bites off each word. "We'd devised a plan. A brilliant strategy to isolate the Red Duke. To cut him off from the rest of his battalion." His hands move as if a map is laid before him, pointing out locations in the air. "We'd informed our generals. After we'd taken position half a league from each other, a messenger came. Told him the baby was coming early. *Not* that his wife was in danger." He paces to the window ledge. "Women give birth every day. Why did he go? Because he was ensorcelled by her magical entanglements."

Anger, simmering all week, bubbles up inside of me. "He *loved* her. She was having his baby. Of course he wanted to—"

His face twists. "Julien had a duty. To his men. To Valonia. To me. He acted like that was nothing but dross when he entrusted the battle plan to Dupuis and left." He thrusts his arm through the wide opening, pointing northward. "He left."

"He sent a messenger," I defend him.

It *was* terrible that my father left his post. Any soldier, any officer, would've been whipped publicly and demoted for doing the same. Yet, he was the crown prince. Leaving for the birth of the royal heir could be easily forgiven. Except everything went wrong.

"We were vulnerable when the Red Duke attacked."

"Vulnerable, Uncle? You had more than a thousand men. You were on home territory."

"We failed because Julien brought the Fates' displeasure down upon us. He embraced magic, even so far as to using it himself."

I blink, certain I've not heard right. "My father used magic? No. He—"

"—hid it well, but there was no doubt at the Nemeaux retreat."

The annual speech tells of soldiers and farmers, women and children, fleeing before the Brandt army, but no one tells the awful details of my birth. My uncle and his men arrived at Nemeaux Manor to find my father holding me in one arm as he knelt beside my mother's bed. She was hemorrhaging. The midwife said Ruxandra shouldn't be moved and my father refused to leave the manor.

My uncle scooped up my mother and carried her to the waiting horses. All the wagons were gone, so he placed her on horseback. She was weak. My father mounted behind her and thrust me into his brother's arms. They raced the horses through the streets of Nemeaux to the great bridge that crossed the Muse River.

"The Nemeaux retreat?" I repeat. "No magic was used then."

"When we crossed the bridge, the Duke's army was already in the city." He shakes his head. "I ordered barricades, but Julien called them back. Told everyone to make for Boispierre. His expression... I knew Ruxandra was gone. He placed her body under a nearby oak, then told me to care for you, like a farewell."

My uncle's eyes glitter with anger. Tears spill onto his cheeks. He doesn't wipe them away, letting the icy wind dry them.

"He climbed down the bank and under the bridge. I handed you off and chased after. There in the shadows, my brother glowed like a witch. It was unnatural. It shouldn't have been possible. I asked what he was doing. He only said to keep the bridge clear. I didn't leave. He pulled off his doublet and shirt, waded out to the nearest support column. He pressed himself against it like a limpet. That rumbling, like an avalanche hurtling down the mountain. I'd never have guessed it was the bridge itself."

I speak slowly. "It was black powder explosives."

"A story I perpetuated. We had some, but not enough to collapse that bridge."

I frown. "My father brought it down? With magic? He was a mage?"

My uncle's face compresses into its familiar lines of disapproval. "I can only guess how he became Gifted. The witchcraft radiated from him—cracks in the masonry from where he touched the support, up through the arch and into the body of the bridge."

"My father broke the Nemeaux bridge with magic." I can barely believe it.

"Not just broke. It crumbled like goat cheese." Awe and distaste mingle on his face.

What kind of power could produce such a feat? He was a mage. With an affinity toward Stonecraft, perhaps? "Magic runs in the Perdrix family," I murmur.

"No." His gaze is unnerving. "The Perdrix line is *void* of magic. There's proof. Up in Roc Ursgueule. We defend the land *against* magic. The taint came from your conniving mother." He steps closer.

I should've retreated from the window earlier, for I've no way to escape now. I back against the low ledge, too aware of the ells of open air between me and the ground below.

"It's already brought ruin upon one generation." He seizes my shoulders. "Perhaps it's contaminated the next?"

He pushes. I grab his doublet with one hand. My curled left fingers claw his face, even as I twist. My shoulder hits the stone post. I pivot, and he swings toward the wide opening.

"No," he bellows, yet it's a whisper.

My crown is gone. The weight of it, missing.

I can't worry about my useless ears as we hang, clutching and pushing at each other, teetering on the edge of the pigeon loft. It's perhaps only a few heartbeats. I can't be sure, for my heart stops beating.

Guards are suddenly there, pulling us back into the tower.

"Thank you," I gasp. "You saved me."

They don't look at me, but at my uncle, who points an accusing finger in my direction, then at the window.

"What? No. My uncle pushed *me*."

He's two moves ahead, wiping his cheek where I raked him with my nails. He shakes his head sadly and taps his skull.

"He's lying," I shout. "He admitted to me just now that he's masquerading as my father."

The soldiers look between us, uncertainty in their expressions.

My uncle slips on his tender, regretful mask. I watch his lips carefully. "Believe I'm her father or uncle" —he shrugs— "...but we must keep her safe." He pulls his cuff from his cheek. The scarlet blood draws the men's gaze. "...Before she harms someone else..."

They turn toward me, and I know I've lost.

CHAPTER THIRTEEN

Crewelwork: decorative embroidery done with crewel or
worsted yarn on cotton or linen, using simple stitches
traditionally worked in floral or pastoral designs

I CATCH THE WORD *TEMPORARY* ON MY UNCLE'S LIPS. My
stomach knots, sensing the lie.

The guards grip my arms tight, hauling me down several sets of
stairs toward the dungeon. I twist and arch against their grip as we
plunge into the gloom reeking of mildew and fear. This is the blacksmith's anvil all over again. But instead of crushing my hand, my
uncle intends to crush my soul.

It was never about being deaf, or left-handed, or even witchcraft.
It's about power, and I stand in the way. I won't wait for the hammer
to fall.

I fight. Struggle. Bite.

A blow. My head rings with pain I can almost hear.

I blink and find myself slumped in a cell surrounded by stone walls
and one ironwork door. The room is lit indirectly from a torch in the
corridor. I pull myself to the door. The cell across from me is empty. I
can only see a short distance down the hallway. The guards are not in
sight, and without my coronet, I can't discern how far away they are.

Despair threatens. I keep it at bay with remembrances of other dark places within the castle. There might be a secret passage nearby. In the gloom, I search for discrepancies in the stonework. It makes no sense to build a secret passage where they'd imprison enemies, yet there are direct passages to the royal bedchambers. I dwell on these possibilities, inflating myself with hope, even as the moist walls and the scent of fetid, rotting things fills me with dread. I fear what I might become down here, so I determinedly focus on escape.

I WILL NEVER ESCAPE.

Perhaps a day has passed since I was locked in my cell; I'm not certain.

I am certain there's no access to a secret passage from my cell. I pressed and dug into the mortar around each stone. No hidden door. I saved a chicken bone from my first meal to shape it into a makeshift lock pick, but the iron mechanism is heavy and more complicated than the locks I've picked before. The chicken bone breaks.

I lean my head against the cold metal bars and pull my arms back into my cell.

Stars above, help me.

The desire, the need to escape beats like a pulse as I squeeze the iron bars, wishing I had the Gift of Forgecraft to manipulate the bars and lock. I retreat to my cot. It's better than the pile of straw in the other cell. I'm grateful. Barely.

Perhaps...

Perhaps I'm too limited in my perspective. I want to leave this cold, damp dungeon *now*. But my uncle hasn't achieved all he has in a few days. Neither has the Governor, nor Tanja. I didn't learn embroidery or Skeincraft immediately. Some things take time.

I breathe deeply and let the air slowly leave my lungs. This is a long game. I need to adjust my expectations and strengthen my patience.

Seaux de merde. I don't want to be patient.

THE DUNGEON COULD DRIVE me mad without needle and thread. I've kept needles in my sleeve cuff since St. Beatricia's. For thread, I unpick a small section of embroidery from my gown. It can't be obvious enough for the guards to notice.

First, I add warming spells to my dress and blanket. I add a sleeping charm to the blanket as well. It'll make it easier to bear the isolation if I'm awake only a few hours of the day. With so much time alone with my thoughts, I'm forced to examine the problem of Tys.

Mattias VandeBrandt.

I go over and over what I saw on the island. I'm *certain* that was Tys leading those Brandt soldiers. Not his father or brother or some other blond Brandt fellow. *Tys* was on the island. He attacked Tanja and her people.

Still, I can't understand why. If he found it impossible to refuse his father's commands, he could've ducked away from the soldiers. Or slipped to the back of the pack, searching for survivors. Put out fires the soldiers had started. Nothing I imagine explains the fierceness I saw through the telescope. The way his lips curled as he yelled.

After sifting through the ashes of excuse, I'm left with only a singular explanation. He's different from what I thought. I was blind to his true character, or he manipulated me into seeing someone he wasn't. Perhaps, once he learned my true identity, he decided to play me for a fool, because I'm the easiest pathway for Brandt to gain what it wants most—all of Valonia and her people.

This thought carves me hollow.

Tears and misery fill me until I drown. Until I cannot stand myself any longer. I double my sleeping spell stitches. Triple them.

My few wakeful moments are haunted by Tys' betrayal. Did he feel no obligation to Tanja or the Mirvray? How could he not warn them? They healed his leg and offered him lengthy hospitality.

I mourn Tanja and her baby, even as I mourn my father and grand-father. Each day is its own special torture, trying to piece my heart back together. It seems impossible.

THEN COMES the day when my uncle visits the dungeon. He studies me with narrowed eyes through the bars of the cell doors. I'm grateful for that barrier, but the guards soon unlock it. He strides in, then stops halfway to my cot.

"What is it?" I ask.

I can't read his lips in the gloom until a guard brings in a torch.

"...Accusations and half-truths... wormed your way... my King's Council."

Those few words spark hope. "What do you mean?"

He stands stiff as a statue. "You planted doubt... Lord Beauchamp... Lord Cyngetroit... the others... no peace... pester me... finding holes."

I have allies. All is not lost. Relief spreads like a tide. I can't stop it from heating my cheeks, lifting the corners of my mouth.

He pounces, gripping my face. My head hits the stone wall of my cell. Stars erupt behind my eyelids. When I can see again, his tight, angry face is inches from mine. He shoves my head against the wall again. His palm presses against my nostrils, blocking my breath. My heart pounds. I claw at his arms, trying to push him away. The fine wool doublet slips under my fingers. Instinct, or inspiration, recalls the itching charm in Renata's blanket. I curl my fingers into his cuffs and shove that same magic into my uncle's doublet.

He leaps back as if burned. I wheeze, pulling in a great lungful of air.

He shouts at the guards. A new one appears in the doorway with a birdcage made of metal. My uncle's pleased expression as he handles it makes my skin prickle.

Past him, the cell door is open.

I jump sideways off the cot, running around him and through the open door. The guards in the corridor face away. I run past them, up the stairs, two at a time. Halfway up, my muscles protest, but desperation pushes me onward. I'm nearly to the top when someone hurtles into me. I tumble in an avalanche of pain and everything turns black.

I WAKE TO A THUMPING HEADACHE.

I'm bound. Sitting on my cot. In my cell.

My uncle faces me with that iron bird cage. He refuses to come close enough for me to touch him. I scared him. Little comfort. I'm more frightened than I've ever been.

It's not a bird cage.

He hands it to a guard who approaches cautiously. He opens it like a sideways oyster.

My gaze darts between the cage and my uncle, who smiles as if we're chatting in the garden. "...Used for troublesome women... keep their tongue... lesson." He bends closer, and my gaze fixes on him as he enunciates the message he wants me to understand.

"The King's Council is for the king to counsel. Not his daughter, nor anyone else."

The guard brings the cage closer. I shake my head, making my head throb worse.

"No. Please don't." The other guard grabs my shoulders to keep me still. The cage fits over my head, a long iron piece jutting into my mouth. A spike protrudes from its bottom side. My tongue convulses against the intrusion. I taste blood. I whimper as the guard snaps the padlock into place at the base of my neck. It lies cold and heavy against my spine.

"Plzzz." My begging is muzzled. My uncle shrugs as if he doesn't understand, and leaves with the guards, slamming the cell door shut behind them.

I give a long, desperate screech, but their shadows retreat. I curse him. Silently and with all the hatred in my body, I curse him to all seven levels of Hell.

A GUARD UNTIES me after the first night so I can feed myself.

The cage remains.

I note the days with tally stitches on my cuff. The weight of the cage hurts my tongue if I tilt my head to embroider, so tallies are the only stitching I do. Most of the time, I hold up the cage, alleviating the weight from my tongue. When I grow tired, it sits on my shoulders. That hurts so badly, I can't do it for very long. Even laying down is painful. The iron protrusion pushes against my teeth and tongue. I taste blood all the time.

The meals of bread, vegetables, and meat become soup. It's the only way to feed me through the cage, but the soup is thin. I suspect my uncle keeps my meals scant on purpose, for soon it grows difficult to use magic. I struggle to hold it in a thread.

I can't escape my hunger or the pain in my mouth. I leach power from Tanja's necklace, my sleep-soaked blanket, and my pink gown. A little to ease my stomach growling, and a little to ease the torment of my tongue. I'll deplete it eventually, but it's the only way I can bear it.

That day arrives.

I try to pull strength from my dress. There's nothing. Panic darts through me. I try the necklace. There's barely any power left. I take the last little bit, like a child licking a bowl, and pray the Heavens will send help.

I DESCEND INTO HELL. I mark each day with a single stitch in my sleeve. I'm not sure it *is* a new day each time I wake, but this helps me feel closer to release. My tongue swells with infection. A nasty taste develops. By the fourth day, when I spit, it's milky with pus. Two days later, my tongue is so swollen, I must breathe through my nose. Pain is constant. I hold the cage high, the bottom against my jaw, to get relief. I stumble to the door. I can't shape words to beg the guards for mercy. I take off Tanja's necklace, wrap it around my fist, and bang the iron bars.

The guards ignore me. Then they shout through the cell door, but I don't quiet. When the next set comes, they thrust their halberds through the bars. One snags the necklace from my fingers. I scramble, reach for it, but they're too swift. They pull Tanja's gold ring off my bony finger before driving me away, halberd blades sharp as razors.

I retreat to my cot, holding up the cage, voicing my pain and hopelessness in long, keening wails. The guards stand at the cell door, yelling words I can't hear, banging against the door themselves. They don't come in. I wonder, distantly, if they're under orders not to enter without my uncle. They gesture violently, threatening to beat me, I assume, but I don't stop. Unconsciousness is better than the torment inside my mouth.

The pain becomes so intense, my mind drifts elsewhere.

When I come to myself, Tanja stands at my cell door. My keening stutters.

I try to speak but scrape my tongue against the spike.

I lift my hands in supplication, begging with insistent wails. She comes to my side, and it's not Tanja, but Lady Ulrica. I squeeze my eyes against the truth for two breaths, continuing my beseeching. As she kneels beside me, whimpers escape from my throat.

A guard brings a lantern. Ulrica examines the torture device, discovering the padlock. She argues with the guards—a waste of time. I tug on her sleeve, pointing to my mouth. I open it so she can see. She steps back, hand covering her mouth and nose.

Lady Ulrica walks around me. She speaks, but I don't understand. She gives a sad smile. A hopeless shrug. She turns away.

No!

I clutch her sleeve. Fingers curled, I pull her closer. I want to speak, but all that escapes is a low, desperate growl. Ulrica's eyes widen. The guards lower their halberds; blades press against my throat. My growl becomes a whine.

I can die, right now, if I make the slightest violent gesture. I've not considered that option before. My pulse quickens. The pain—I long for release. As I decide that death is preferable, Ulrica's pale face and straight nose waver, becoming Tanja's dark eyes and knowing mouth.

She shakes her head. I can't die. Not like this. Not for this.

I came back for Valonia. For my father. For my grandfather.

I straighten my fingers in what is the slowest, most agonizing movement of my life. I remove my hands from her clothing. My eyes fill with tears.

Trembling, I press my palms together. *Please.*

Lady Ulrica touches my shoulders, then lifts the cage to ease the pressure of the spike against my tongue. I blink so I can see her expression. Grim.

She gives orders. The guards hesitate. She snaps. One leaves. Ulrica holds the cage for the entire eternity it takes for him to return. He brings brandy and a much smaller bottle.

More orders. The guards hold the cage. Ulrica tips the smaller bottle, and shakes out two tiny, brown cloves. Double barbs and Otherlight mark them as vigor-cloves. Older men use them when they take a young bride. Soldiers use them during long battles. They have natural efficacy, but when harvested by folk versed in Othercraft, they become worth their weight in gold.

I tilt my head back; she drops them into my mouth. The heat spreads quickly. My eyes water. When I look up, she holds a third, as if debating my need for one more. One guard reaches for it. Ulrica gives a quelling look, returns it to the bottle, corks it, and tucks it into her pocket.

Next is the brandy bottle. She wedges its neck through the cage and presses it against the side of my mouth. I twitch my lips. Cool liquid pours in. For a moment, it soothes. Then my mouth ignites on fire, burning worse than it did before. I choke and spit it out. The guards and Lady Ulrica step back. The cage crashes against my shoulders, the spike stabs my tongue.

I roar with pain and push the cage up off my tongue.

Ulrica waits, the bottle offered. I tilt my head back and accept the fiery liquid, letting it fill my mouth. I resist the urge to spit it out.

I take mouthful after mouthful until numbness sets in. When the brandy dribbles down my lips, Ulrica stops pouring.

WHEN I WAKE, she sits beside me, her huge ring of keys in her lap. They'd once been my grandmother's, but after her death, my grandfather gave them to Ulrica, elevating her to chatelaine of Chateau Boispierre. She has power and authority, no matter her unmarried state.

I turn my head, but pain and Ulrica's hand on my shoulder stop me. Movement shivers through the cage. I brace myself. The padlock jiggles.

I hiss.

The cage shifts. The hinge in front of my nose moves. The bar scrapes against my top teeth, and the spike drags along the length of my tongue. I moan.

Then it's gone. My mouth is empty.

Except for the swollen mass of my tongue.

Eyes watering, I turn to thank Ulrica. She holds two slender pieces of metal. I blink. When I focus again, they're gone. With a whole ring of keys, why would she need lock picks? My vision is blurred. Perhaps I saw one long key. Perhaps.

LADY ULRICA POURS all sorts of medicines down my throat and feeds me thick stews. A part of me worries about where my uncle is and what he will do when he finds out, but I'm grateful for every scrap offered and do nothing to dissuade her generosity. I can't speak yet, so I use hand language to convey a few thoughts to her. *Please. Thank you. Eat. Drink. Hungry. Thirsty.* She's amused as she learns each one.

She lingers sometimes, handing me parchment with stories written about her childhood with my father and uncle. I read them, translating them into hand language.

Once, when the other noble girls made fun of my Luthian accent, I vowed never to speak again. Your hand language would have been useful then. I went nearly two weeks without speaking. Your father played games, trying to coax me to speak. Offering me sweets he stole from the kitchen. He even brought me a puppy from the kennels for my very own. He was kind.

There's nothing else written. I jostle her knee and sign, "What happened?"

"Reichard," she signs. "He kissed me. I was so startled, I spoke."

"And..." I sign.

"When he smirked, I smacked his face." She blushes. "And said words your grandmother never taught me."

I smile over proper Lady Ulrica cursing out my uncle. I wonder, if she and I had been the same age, could we have been friends? And why was she ever attracted to my uncle?

HE RETURNS A FEW DAYS LATER. When my uncle finds me freed from the cage, he shouts at the guards. They're quick to lay blame at Lady Ulrica's feet. She's brought to the dungeon.

Though she seems calm standing there in the corridor, my stomach tangles in knots. As my uncle points at me, she nods, then ticks reasons off on her fingers. His anger simmers. She remains cooperative, stressing the word *daughter* several times, as if reminding him of his own lie. As his anger increases, she becomes more serene. Eventually, he brings the Fates into the argument, pointing to the Heavens.

Her lips form the word *mercy*.

His lips speak the word *mischief*.

Lady Ulrica draws herself up to her considerable height. He pauses then. Studies her. Fear tightens around her eyes. Her lips barely move, in a plea perhaps, or a warning. He steps back and points a long finger at me. I catch the word *treason*.

His next words make her shrink back.

"Reichard, no!"

He's flushed, gesturing for his guards to take her to the far end of the dungeon. The Questioning Room. The men hesitate a moment, then grasp her shoulders.

She struggles, screams at him, but the guards guide her firmly.

My uncle swings his gaze towards me, focusing on the deformed fingers of my left hand. He nods, then follows the guards toward the bowels of the dungeon.

Chapter Fourteen

Madder: *rubia tinctoria* and related plants of the
Rubia family, a viney, low-growing herb, which are a
source of permanent red dyes

I WENT INSIDE THE QUESTIONING ROOM once when I was little, exploring the castle. It looks like a scary underground kitchen. It has two fireplaces, one at each end, for heating water or oil or one of the iron tools that hang from the rafters. One wall is lined with shelves holding pans, basins, and bowls. Another wall has shelves full of knives, hooks, and strange metal implements. The space is filled with three long tables, just the right size for an adult to lie upon. It was dusty and unused when I was a girl, but perhaps it is not so dusty today.

I sit on my cot, imagining what he's doing to Ulrica. I attempt distraction with embroidery, constant prayer on my lips. The back of my neck prickles, as if I sense the screams I cannot hear. I put away my needle and return to the door. I stand there, skeins of fear wrapped around me. Tight. Suffocating. A long time passes. A flicker of torches, then the guards appear with Lady Ulrica. She cradles her left arm with her right. Around her wrist is wrapped a white linen bandage. Where her hand should be, there's nothing.

My heart plummets to my toes.

My uncle emerges behind her, radiating grim satisfaction.

They stop at my door. Is it my turn to lose a hand? I scuttle away.

They only open the door and wait. My uncle stares at Ulrica. She seems numb, unaware of her surroundings. Finally, he speaks, his mouth curling in condescension.

Ulrica seems to wake. The hurt, the betrayal, is on her face, but there's something more, something worse. She shakes her head again and again, then hugs herself with her whole and damaged arms. "I *loved* you, Reichard."

He advances, as if to silence her.

Her face contorts. "I loved you—"

His hand leaps to her cheek. Her head snaps to the side. The guards hold her upright. Ulrica turns a murderous glare on my uncle, then steps into the cell. A muscle jumps in her cheek as she retreats to my cot. I want to take up her verbal sparring with my uncle, but I cannot curse him without sounding like an animal. I know, instinctively, that I must *seem* harmless.

I huddle beside Ulrica.

My uncle stands at my cell door. Studies us. Nods. Then marches away.

I examine Ulrica's linen-wrapped stump. Because of the extra nourishment Ulrica provided the past few days, I have a tiny lump of power resting behind my navel. It's not much, but I spin it long, narrow and healing, twisting it into the thread on my needle. I stitch the length of it through the bandages until they glow a soft blue. Ulrica lifts her head. Her face still radiates anger.

With her remaining fingers, she attempts hand language.

"He'll not live long, I swear by the Stars." She takes a steadying breath, searching for the right signs. "To see him dead, I must live." Her gaze bores into mine. "We'll pretend to be meek. We'll be patient. We'll wait for…"

I know the word she wants by the look in her eyes. I show her the sign.

"...Revenge."

As we sit in the cell together, Ulrica uses a chicken bone to write out her tumultuous feelings in the dirt on the floor, examining how she'd been so blind. She could talk to herself, but she goes to the effort to be sure I understand. As her rage spills over, she kicks at the dirt, stomping upon the floor until all her confessions are obliterated.

I've had shimmering moments when I thought I loved Mattias VandeBrandt. Have I been as stubbornly blind? Did I fall for him because he thumbed his nose at my uncle? Was it after he revealed his father's name that I wanted the challenge of loving my enemy? Or was it simply because he was the first boy to tell me I'm beautiful?

Am I as big a fool as Ulrica?

Three days later, Ulrica is released. For a moment, I believe I'll return to the upper floors of the castle with her, but the guards shut the door in my face. Ulrica gives me a steady look.

"Patience." Her eyes share extra meaning and I nod, but I have thirty-five stitches in my left sleeve. I don't know how to withstand another thirty-five days. Or more. The uncertainty sits upon my chest, suffocating me.

That night, my dreams feel so real.

I'm back in Godesbrouk, sitting across a chessboard from the Governor. We're discussing embroidery. *Check*, I say. My pieces have her king cornered. She lifts an eyebrow, then moves her queen. *Check-mate*, she replies. Then I'm playing chess with my uncle. The pieces are huge. I'm chasing him through the castle and into the courtyard. I'm in the smithy. It's hot. I sign that I don't like it. I want to go. He grabs my hands, tells me to stop speaking with them. The Fates gave me a mouth and I should use it. I wriggle and pull, but he holds me fast.

Tell me with your words and I'll let you go.

I shake my head.

Then I'll do what I must. No princess should behave in such a way. He places my hand on the warm anvil, and the hammer swings downward.

There's no pain in my dream.

Everything shifts, and I'm sitting on my grandfather's lap, my left hand bandaged. It doesn't hurt as it should. My grandfather carefully unwraps the linen. He spreads my fingers wide and moves my joints experimentally.

It's healed. You should try using it.

I protest. It will hurt.

Hurt and healing go hand in hand, mignon. *If you never use it, then your uncle has won.*

※

WHEN I WAKE, his words rattle around in my head. Hungry for his presence, I linger on the dream, even as it crumbles into the corners of my memory. I pick up my needle to put another stitch in my sleeve. I pause. Grit my teeth. Carefully, I grasp the needle with the thumb and finger of my left hand. It feels unnatural.

The first stitch is crooked. I study that single stitch in my right sleeve. I need practice. I tear the wide, bottom-most ruffle from my undershift and practice embroidery with my left hand. It's awkward. The stitches look like a beginner made them. Yet, here in my cell, I can't throw the linen away, or even burn it. I'll embroider the entire strip. Day after day, I make one stitch in my right sleeve, then ply my needle on the practice cloth. I fill it with wildflowers as I imagine Spring creeping her green fingers from Lake Clair up the five valleys. I stitch cows and goats moving to the high pastures. I stitch a lithe, arching tree with little pear blossoms. Its boughs stretch wide and embracing. I add hundreds of heart-shaped leaves, then force myself to unstitch it all. I smooth out the fabric and stitch a different tree. An oak, broad and steady, with a partridge nestled in its branches. This is home. I shouldn't thirst for what I can't have, what was never mine. I'll look within my own borders for love, for hope, for strength. There's a way to stop my uncle, and I'll find it. *Fates, so let it be!*

There are forty-nine stitches in my right sleeve on the day I fill the last corner with left-handed embroidery. I tuck my needle away, stretch my fingers and smile at my work. Despite the dim torchlight, it's clear my skills have increased. The stitches are no longer crooked or awkward. I nod, warmed with pride.

I unpick a new strand of thread from my gown and decide on my next venture. I'll record my uncle's misdeeds; his wrongs against me, my family and Valonia. The underside of my skirts is a wide enough expanse for this long list, and I'll use Broid Cypher, so my uncle can't ever read it. I begin with the edict on witchcraft the summer before.

Twenty-three days later, as my testimony weighs down my skirts, the guards' behavior shifts. They're fidgety. I stay near my door and watch the corridor, so I'm there when new prisoners arrive. They're a subdued bunch. Heads down. Shoulders slumped. Clothes torn, as if from fighting.

They're all children. The youngest is about five. She clings to an older boy who can't be more than eight; the poor fellow's wet himself. A child of about ten sucks her thumb unashamedly. A girl about Renata's age mutters a prayer. A few glow with Otherlight. Golden, blue, green. The blue-haloed one is my age with hair the color of marmalade. Renata's brother.

"Why are these children here?" I ask.

The guards don't look my way, but the prisoners do. Perhaps my words sound strange because of the hole in my tongue. I blush.

Then I shiver. Their left sleeves have been ripped half-off, and each child has a crusted, circular sore on that shoulder. Not sores. They've been branded. Even the little ones.

My uncle once threatened to brand the Forgewitch's children.

"Who did this?" I indicate their shoulders. "Was it my uncle? Did he order these children taken from their families? Branded like cattle? Thrown in prison?"

I can't hear them if they answer, but the horror of what they've done should prick them. All I get is a lazy sneer.

"You'll roast in Hell," I tell them, "for what you've done this day."

One unlocks the ironwork door of the cell across from me and chivvies the children inside. "They're witches." His lips continue moving as he locks them inside. Two of the little ones start crying.

"They are *children*," I shout.

He spits to the side but says no more as they retreat down the corridor to the corner where they play dice or cards. In the cell, most of the children sink against the wall, or curl on the straw. Three grip the door's bars, staring at me. I want to offer hope; they need a spark of fight.

"I am Marguerite de Perdrix." I speak carefully, conscious of how I form my silent, vibrating words. "I've lived in my ancestor's dungeon for one hundred and seven days. My uncle tortured me and cut off the hand of the one person who helped me."

I look into their eyes, willing them to take the strength I'm offering.

"I'm not broken. I'm not dead. I'm still a witch. No one can drive the magic out of me. Its power was woven into me by the Fates above."

I offer a chicken bone so they can write to me on the dirt-crusted floor between our cells. Conversing is time consuming, but we have time. They scratch messages and I whisper back. They each write their names, family names and village or town. Each witnessed his or her mother burn. Some, like Renata's brothers Luc and Georgie, watched fathers beaten for defending their wives and children. I wonder how to tell Renata if ever I see her again.

Others, though, watched fathers do nothing. I know which is worse.

I record their accounts on the underside of my skirts.

I tell them my story: hiding my abilities, living in a castle and two abbeys. I tell them how magic is permitted in St. Beatricia's, unlike St. Clotilde's. I share what I've learned from Tanja, how magic is a gift from the Fates, to bless and benefit, to intercede when the Fates can't immediately do so. I explain how to store power in objects for later use. I describe the difference between witches and mages and how some boys can do magic, too.

Georgie looks at Luc, who shakes his head slightly. Georgie stares at the floor, as if mortified. He's learning how easy it is to endanger another's life.

"I have a... friend who's a Rope-mage," I say, trying to ease the tension. "Very talented." I describe Tys' rope juggling, how knots obey him. I account, in detail, of his performance on Yule Eve. They listen, rapt. As I finish, I find my fingers tracing the knotted twine necklace that reach from Tys' ring on my toe to where it wraps around my ankle. I clear my throat.

"I have an idea..."

I don't dare speak my thoughts aloud. Using the chicken bone, I write out the plan. It depends on a Forgewitch, a Kitchenwitch, and a Skeinwitch. I can tell who they are in the cell across from mine but keep my plan theoretical. I draw maps of the castle, the secret passages, and of Valonia itself. The younger children become excited; the older ones steady them with words and nudges. Finally, Luc, Geneve, and Bernelle exchange glances.

"Need to discuss privately," Geneve writes.

I motion to go ahead and wipe the floor clean of my scribblings.

The guards deliver our next meal before the others share their decision. Yet when the seventeen bowls of thin soup are brought to their cell, fourteen of them drink only half. They line up their half-full bowls in front of Luc, Geneve and Bernelle. With sheepish posture, but determined expressions, the three drink their extra measures.

Bernelle sips the last bowlful as Luc holds out his hand for my needle. I toss it across the corridor.

He mends the other children's shoulder seams. The illusion he stitches into the sleeves is well-done. Each child looks more pink-cheeked and less disheveled, and somehow unremarkable. A useful charm.

Meanwhile, Bernelle fingers the lock.

The next time I look her way, she's ripped the tin buttons off the cuffs of her sleeves. Tin. Of course. I've plenty of buttons I can sacrifice. I remove five pewter buttons from each cuff and toss them to Bernelle. Two others have tin buttons and offer them. She holds the buttons tight between her hands and waits.

As she glows golden, and Luc glows blue, Geneve sits quietly in the corner. As the day plods on, she becomes restless. When Luc stitches up the last sleeve, she gathers the bowls and scrapes the last drops into one. The resulting amount isn't more than a tablespoon, but as Geneve stirs it with her finger, she glows a deep, vibrant green.

"No," I hiss. "You'll need your strength to find and make food once you're in the mountains."

She speaks, and another writes her response. *If Bernelle can't get us out, it won't matter.* Geneve lifts the bowl to the forgewitch's lips and urges her to drink the last mouthful.

When Bernelle finally pulls her hands apart, she has a pliable lump of metal. She kneads it like dough, then forms it into a key-like shape. She tries the lock. She reshapes it.

It turns in the lock.

Jules must've cried out, for Blanche covers his mouth. They slip out the door. Bernelle crosses to my cell, but the key doesn't fit. I catch her hand before she reshapes it.

"Keep your strength for the other two locks."

She insists. I grip her hands. Since the idea formed, I've known I can't go with them. For hours, I've wrestled with this desire to escape with them. It binds me, suffocates me, but I force the words out. "If I go, nothing will keep Reichard from hunting me down. We will *all* die."

They crowd around, touching my hands and cheeks through the bars. Whispering thanks I can't hear. Luc presses the needle back into my hand. He left some of his power stored within.

"Go," I whisper. "The guards can't play dice forever."

They leave.

I cry then, counting out time in prayers for their protection, as I imagine them passing the guard room, the stairs, the door, the secret passage to the bed chamber corridors, my father's old room, the long passage, the hut, the meadow. Wishing, wishing I was with them.

When ten thousand moments pass and they aren't brought back, I retreat to my bed and pretend to sleep, tracing their names with my finger as I beg the Seven Sisters to keep them alive and safe. Luc, Georgie, Anne, Pauline, Oscar, Rose, Susane, Bernelle, Jules, Blanche, Patrice, Claudette, Felicitie, Vincent, Julienne, Pascale and Geneve.

Hours later, when new guards bring food, I feign shock at the empty cell across from mine. I ask what happened to the children. Ask if they've killed them. I beg on their behalf, until my throat hurts, embroidering the illusion that they disappeared without my knowledge.

The next day, my rations are cut.

I TRACE the children's route along my thumb and imagine them crossing into Hlaandrs, receiving help from Sister Famke and the Governor, Renata's joy at being reunited with Luc and Georgie. The ache in my chest is nearly unbearable. It's ridiculous to feel jealousy for something I offered freely.

A week later, a dozen men are brought in. Their clothes are torn and smeared but are obviously smocks and trousers of the mountain folk. The urge to help them, to grasp this new opportunity, burns within me. If we escape together, they'll be faster, stronger. When the hounds chase us, I'll not feel as responsible to linger if one falls behind. It'll be every man for himself.

But none glow with magic. With cut rations, I've no power either. Disappointment howls inside me, tempting me to succumb to despair. I listen to the rational voice that reminds me of Tanja, advising me to find purpose in their presence. I wait until the night shift guards settle, then creep to my cell door.

One prisoner notices, nudging the fellow beside him, who nudges the next and the next. By the time I crouch, the half-dozen men across the corridor stare at me. A few ells down, hands clutch at the bars of the next cell, waiting.

"Tell me your names," I say.

One opens his mouth. Another claps a hand over it.

I wait until they finish arguing. "I cannot hear you, so you must write in the dirt."

The closest one asks, "Why?" followed by dozens of words too fast for me to understand.

I hold up a hand. "I record Reichard de Perdrix's crimes, his predations upon Valonia and her people." It's my new purpose, until the Fates offer an opportunity to escape.

A man with a long black beard moves closer to the door and writes, *We heard rumors King Julien died, not Reichard. Is it true?*

"Yes."

How do you know?

"I saw his corpse. I recognized a telltale scar. It was Julien who died, not Reichard."

That gets them talking. A different man swipes at the dirt and writes a new message. *Have you seen a girl? 15. Name of Bernelle.*

"Bernelle de Ferr?" I ask. "Of Champetroit village?"

"Yes." Hope blooms on his face. *You saw my daughter? You know where she is?*

I'm not sure what to admit. The black-bearded man mutters in his ear; the father's expression falters. Crumples in despair. I can't bear it.

"She escaped," I whisper.

They gather tighter around the bars.

"I can't hear if the guards come. Be my ears, and I will tell you." I release a sigh. "There were seventeen of them." I recite their names. I tell of the buttons, the skeincraft, the escape, but after that I can only guess. Too much depends on the whims of the Fates. "When the war is over, go to St. Beatricia's Abbey in Hlaandrs. They should have record of your daughter."

Hlaandrs? The father writes. *We're at war with Hlaandrs.*

"They're safer in Hlaandrs than in their own village. What does that say about Valonia?"

They mutter over that. Another man pushes to the front, his expression cynical.

Why didn't you escape?

"If Reichard discovered I escaped, he'd have hunted us until we were caught."

Who are you then?

The black-bearded man pushes forward and writes, *Your Highness?* They argue.

Exhausted by the conversation, I stand. "I'm supposedly crazy because I insisted the king was dead. If you believe Reichard wears the crown, then perhaps I'm not insane."

Before I retreat, Black-beard gestures for me to wait. *Why do you need our names?*

"I'm recording my uncle's crimes." I won't say *victims*. "Those he has assaulted, arrested, tortured… or killed." It gives me something to live for. My own revenge.

He nods, and it's permission.

Jean-Paul. My wife used herbs. Made tonics. Delivered babes. Never did no big magic. They called her a witch. Took her. He swipes his face with his sleeve. *Her name was Sofia.*

I repeat back the information as I stitch both their names, then their village. I take my time, knowing there's no hurry. They're husbands of witches. Or fathers. When their womenfolk were taken by the king's guards, they refused to disavow them. They know the executioner's ax awaits. Each man tells me his name and those in his family who were killed, or taken, when accused of witchcraft. It's a long list.

I don't cry.

CHAPTER FIFTEEN

Scrollstitch: a beautiful embroidery stitch which creates a line of knots along the surface of the fabric, producing a graceful, scroll-like effect

OVER THE NEXT WEEKS, MORE MEN COME.

I stitch names.

Each man.

The woman he loved.

Their children taken.

I never cry again.

Not even when the guards take seven at a time and return without them.

THE MARKS of days inch up my sleeves.

Both left and right. Straight stitches. Groups of seven.

The underside of my skirt fills with thread.

Through the thinness of the linen, the knots of names press against my skin.

They haunt my dreams with whispers.

I see them amid the scratches on the floor, telling me of battles between Brandt and Valonian forces. Skirmishes. Raids. So much death. So much blood.

New prisoners bring word of a truce. It must be September, for it's called so both lands can bring in the harvests. There are thirty-five men in the dungeon. The air is thick and rank. The guards will take seven men up the dungeon steps today. Another seven in three days. Next week there'll be another trial. Another burning. More men will be brought. I wonder how folk can gather the harvest, if my uncle squanders men's lives in warfare and witchcraft trials.

MY UNCLE MIGHT'VE THOUGHT the same thing, for those thirty-five men are taken out of the dungeons, but not replaced for a month and a half. I'm alone with hundreds of names stitched into my clothing until the beginning of November. They fill my dreams. I embellish the lists with embroidered illustrations of the mountains, houses with flowers in the windows, oak trees. Anything to make their cloth Elysium more comfortable.

The next handful of men are a thin lot. They give their names. Report all they witnessed. It's the same story. Women are accused. Resistance by family or neighbors results in punishment. Women burn. Men are imprisoned and, everyone assumes, executed privately. Children are branded, then taken away to be "educated."

Stars, they twist my heart!

They share rumors; the truce was called because of increasing desertion by Valonian soldiers. They leave their ranks to check on their families. They escape into Pranzia, or cross into Haps-Burdian lands. It's wrecking army morale. Deserters are now killed without trial.

My jaw aches with anger. My uncle is destroying Valonia, ruining it in every way. Frustration itches at me to find a way out of this dungeon, to be in the council room learning all the news for myself. I long to pit my wits against the Duke of Brandt, using Valonia's natural defenses and the gifts of her people to keep us one step ahead of his army. Some nights I dream I'm there, leading the council. Sometimes Tanja's beside me, sometimes Sister Famke, sometimes my father and grandfather. Each time I wake, I'm startled to find myself in the dungeon. The dreams feel so real. I wonder if they're visions from the Fates.

Yet the dungeon remains too well guarded, the men guarding it too intractable. No tool comes to my hand. If the Fates want me to do anything for Valonia, they're too patient.

THE DUNGEON'S empty again in a week.

Empty, except for me.

I'm alone for the next week and the week after. I should be relieved, but it feels wrong. Like the quiet afternoon build-up of a storm. It's coming, but unseen until midnight when lightning dances in the high peaks, or the next morning, when flash floods ravage the riverbeds.

I can't sit easy, and it's more than the lice.

My uncle is up to something.

For once, embroidery can't soothe me. Since the children's escape, I've had so little nourishment that magic is a faint memory. I recognize the names I've recorded in Broid Cypher as what they truly are. A graveyard. I can't bear to re-read them. My restless fingers instead trace and retrace the knotted necklace that holds Tys' ring. I finally untie it from around my ankle. I fiddle with it, twirl it, twist it around my fingers.

I'm not lonely. Especially not for Tys.

I don't miss him.

Yet no matter how much I play with the ring and its necklace, I can't get past a handful of facts. I saw Tys chasing the Mirvray, snarling, sword in one hand, torch in the other. I sent pigeons to the

Governor a week later, asking for help. Boispierre dungeon is less than two leagues from Nemeaux Manor. I've been trapped here for nearly three hundred days. If Tys, or anyone else, was going to help me escape, they'd have come long ago.

Knot by knot, I unravel the cord necklace until the ring slides into the palm of my hand. I hold it for a few more hours, but it does nothing. Can do nothing. It's a symbol of my foolish, trusting heart. I harden my jaw and throw the ring into the darkest corner of my cell. I turn my back and shred the remaining cord, pulling it apart strand by strand.

CHAPTER SIXTEEN

Indigo: *indigofera*, a pinnate leafed legume, which is a source of dark, violet-blue dye

I PUT THREE MORE TALLY STITCHES IN MY SLEEVE, EACH more difficult than the last. Though I sleep and wake and eat, I don't pick up my needle again.

DAYS PASS. Nothing matters.

CHAPTER SEVENTEEN

Mordant: a substance in dyeing to fix the coloring
matter that combines with the organic dye and forms
an insoluble compound in the fiber

ULRICA STANDS AT MY CELL DOOR WHEN I WAKE. I CLOSE MY
eyes, certain it's a dream. When I open them again, she's beside me, a
cup of water pressed against my lips. I drink. My eyes clear enough to
focus on her moving fingers. She spells something. Slowly.

It makes no sense. I close my eyes.

My shoulder is shaken. I push back. Strike out. More shaking. I
scream. "Leave me be!"

They take my hands. Bind them. *No!* They'll not take my hands!

I open my eyes. Ulrica sits before me, an ugly welt on her cheek.
Her hand grips my wrists tight against her chest. Her mouth moves as
she stares into my eyes. Everything's silent and shadowed. My gaze
slides away. She shakes me.

Listen. Her lips form the word several times. Her fear-tight eyes and
glances toward the two guards flanking her make me nod. She loosens
her grip, moves her hand.

"Eat. Drink. You must."

"Why?" I sign.

"Your uncle. He insists."

I narrow my eyes. "My uncle can't force me."

"I..." She points insistently to herself. "I beg you. Please eat. Please live."

"Why?" I glance at the guards. Wondering why they used to scare me so. Then I remember something from the dusty past. "Will they cut off your other hand?"

Her face tightens. "It's not only for me. There are others you must save."

"Who?" There's no one dear to me that my uncle can kill or maim or threaten.

"Your people." She hunches her shoulders, shielding her signs from the soldiers, as if they know hand language. "Valonia," she spells out. "She needs her queen."

A strange feeling tears at my lungs, at my ribs, like an animal trying to free itself. Perhaps it's regret. Or fear. Or possibly hope.

I command the feeling to stop; it reduces itself to gnawing at my sternum.

"Valonia has a king." I sign without expression.

"Valonia has a rapist." She places the stub of her wrist against my cheek before signing, "Save her."

She holds out a bowl of soup. It's little more than broth. I drink it all.

They leave, and I sit in my cell wondering how much of the truth Ulrica gave me.

※

I EAT every drop of the soup at the next meal. I'm licking the bowl when I notice the guard who delivered it never left. He stands outside the cell door, watching. My cheeks heat with shame, but I continue. I need every morsel.

The next meal, he watches me eat again. I ignore him and lick the bowl clean once more. He leaves, but the next time he passes, he throws a chunk of bread through the bars of my door. It's nearly the size of my fist, but it lands too close to the door. I stay on my cot, wary, waiting for a trick. Finally, temptation wins. I scuttle forward, snatch the bread, and retreat.

The bread still has softness to it. I almost groan with pleasure. I try to make it last, to savor every crumb, but it's gone too soon. Still, as hours wear on, I sense the extra nourishment from the bread. After I devour my next meal, I've enough strength to spend a little on magic.

I close my eyes and spread my fingers across the cloth of my skirt. The remainder of the embroidery I stitched last year is mundane, all its magic sucked away months ago. I turn the hem and feel for the beginning of the Broid Cypher. It's also powerless, but I let a little magic trickle out of my fingertips and onto those threads. I release as much magic as I dare, then wait as it soaks into the threads.

I remember the catapult in the tower on Isle Dinant. How a twitch of a mechanism sent a stone hurtling through the air, its force multiplied by tens. I keep my breath deep and regular. When I sense my little ration of magic has been absorbed, I imagine all my Broid Cypher stitches vanishing from sight. I exhale sharply, as if blowing out a dozen candles.

Hide.

I don't look immediately. I let my fingers wander over the stitches, making sure they're still there, then slowly crack one eye. Before me is a wide expanse of pink silk, seemingly uninterrupted. It worked.

My cheeks spread wide, and it takes a moment to realize I'm smiling.

Whatever my uncle does next, my record of his crimes is safe.

Chapter Eighteen

Blind Stitch Hem: stitches which are visible on one side only

I TALLY DAYS ON MY SLEEVE AGAIN. THE END OF THE YEAR draws near, but I'm not certain of the date. Three more marks, and the guards behave differently as they change shift. Their backs are straighter, their steps more exact.

My throat prickles as if I swallowed nettles.

I unfold myself from the sagging cot. Leaning against the icy stone wall, I stand on wobbling legs. If this is death, I'll face it on my feet.

My cell fills with cold torchlight. Men in red uniforms stand at attention outside my cell. A shadow darkens the center of the corridor. Unhurried. Confident. My uncle steps into view. I shiver, but I don't cower. As a soldier twists the key, I push away from the wall and step forward.

The door swings open.

The soldier strikes his halberd against the floor, announcing the king. I remain still for a heartbeat. Sharp words, swallowed for months, almost slip out. I keep them behind my teeth and bend my knees in a clumsy curtsy. I'll play along until I can see sunlight again.

I wobble. Tip forward.

Guards grab my arms and march me out into the torchlight. I force myself not to squint as my eyes travel up my uncle's burgundy velvet doublet. A chain mail shirt peeks out from underneath, protection he can touch and heft. What havoc I could play if I got my needle into his linen undershirt. Something more than pretend fleabites. A tightening around his chest? The sensation of drowning on dry land? A hundred more miserable ideas flash through my mind. I raise my gaze to his face. His eyes narrow, as if he can hear my thoughts.

"Dearest daughter..." He speaks for the benefit of the others. "It pained me... restrain you... many months. My heart overflows... Fates softened your heart... you've recanted."

I blink. *What does he mean?*

"Brandt... your birth... steal... third of our land... Fates... regain... lost... Seventeen... years we've waited... make amends... tragedy." He speaks of Brandt's invasion, but otherwise...

"I don't understand." The words scrape against my rusty throat.

"You shall marry," he pronounces.

I must have read his lips wrong.

"The Fates decree... marry and raise up sons... glory to Valonia. All hail the Fates."

"All hail the Fates," the soldiers repeat, thumping their forest of halberds.

Marry. My eyes slide shut. I exhale heavily. I will live.

I should smile or burst into tears of relief, but I'm tired. Like a war-weary soldier, these many months I've prepared myself for death.

The Fates granted me a stay of execution, and I'm not quite grateful.

THEY CARRY me up the stairs. I couldn't have climbed them on my own. They dump me on my feet in a utilitarian room. Ulrica follows. She glances over her shoulder meaningfully at the two guards standing inside the doorway. Guarding the exit, not the entrance. And watching.

Signing close to my body, I ask Ulrica why we're in this room. In answer, she tugs at my hair, then shows the dead louse between her fingers. Shame heats my body. She gestures for me to stand on a large canvas sheet spread across the floor. I obey. At each corner, a brazier burns merrily. Ulrica motions for me to undress.

I stiffen. "No."

She speaks to the guards. Their gazes slide away.

Still signing covertly, I touch my dress. "Save this."

She nods. With her one hand, she helps me unfasten all the bindings. Finally, we slip the dirty silk over my head, then my torn linen shift. They reek of sweat and ten months of mildewed despair. Ulrica wads the bundle, tossing it in the corner as if it means nothing.

She speaks to the guards. One leaves. Goose flesh pricks the length of my body as I wait. I purposefully keep my eyes from my wrinkled record. I focus instead on the window, which had been as dark as the stone walls. Now it's lightened to pearl gray.

I glance away briefly when the guard returns with three maids. I kneel at Ulrica's behest. I begin to shiver, but not because of the maids removing the tiny vermin that made their home on my body. Not because I'm naked in midwinter while they rub poppy oil into my skin. Not because of combs tugging against stubborn snarls.

Dawn shows pink through the windows.

The windows are narrow and leaded with little diamond panes, but I watch with firm concentration. Emotion swells within me like Renata's rising bread dough as the sky lightens to peach, then pale yellow. It's not joy I feel. I might never feel joy again. But perhaps it's joy's cousin—twice removed.

Ulrica strokes my long, matted curls. "We must cut it."

I nod impatiently.

There's no mistaking the gold as the sun crests the stone ledge. Its beauty tugs a gasp from my lips. I don't wipe away the tears that fall.

A maid pats my arm, commiserating the loss of my hair. Her back is to the window. How easily she ignores sunlight. Ten months I've gone without even a glimpse.

The maids alternate between soap and saltwater, vinegar and herbs, until Ulrica pronounces me clean. The sun climbs. The maids leave. Ulrica follows, a wad of dirty silk under her useless arm.

I force myself to look away. That bundle, precious as any scroll in the Emperor's library, *must* appear like any other bit of laundry. I feel the guards' eyes upon me. Gooseflesh pricks my naked, hunger-pinched body. I scoot closer to a brazier and angle my back toward the doorway.

I peek over my shoulder. One shifts his halberd to bar Ulrica's way. The other guard, a little slower than his counterpart, moves his halberd to form an X before the door. Ulrica shakes the bundled clothing at them. They don't shift. They won't let her out.

Ulrica plants her feet, draws herself up tall. The second guard lifts his halberd, but the first won't budge. My stomach knots as the second returns his halberd to block the door.

Ulrica points at the door, measuring her stubbornness against theirs.

One guard speaks. Ulrica's chin lifts.

A heartbeat. Two. Ulrica shakes out the once-beautiful pink silk and secures one end of it between her teeth. With her remaining hand, she tears the gown. Neckline to hem, it splinters like rotten cloth.

My uncle. His crimes. My stitches.

She tosses half in the brazier closest to her and sweeps towards another.

"No!" I fling myself at her, trying to wrestle the other half from her hands. I touch it, hold it for a moment. But Ulrica hasn't languished a year in a dungeon; she's stronger. She wrenches it away and easily pushes me to the floor. She flips the rest of the gown into the brazier while I scramble to my feet.

"No, no, no..." I reach for the brazier. The dirty, embroidered silk flares and blackens. Ulrica hauls me back by the shoulders before I touch the flame. I jerk and twist and slip out of her grip.

Dash to the other brazier.

That portion of my dress is already curled and charred.

I sag to the floor. My purpose is consumed. Burnt to an unrecognizable crisp. I bow myself in half and sob. Frustration, exhaustion, and months of despair fully claim me. When my shoulders stop shaking, Ulrica gives one a sympathetic squeeze. "I'm sorry," she signs and looks over her shoulder. "It was forbidden to keep."

"All that work…" I sign. "I'm tired of fighting."

"Revenge," she answers. "You survived. You can win."

I turn away. Revenge is salt with no meat.

She grips my arm until I look up. "Snatch Valonia from him, and spit on his bones."

Snatch Valonia. My embroidered names, the stitched mountains and homes aren't lost. They're here. Outside this castle. *Save Valonia.*

I nod.

Ulrica pulls me upright, onto my knees. My gaze wanders to the smoking brazier. My belly cramps, but I nod once more. I'll not fall victim to my uncle's schemes. I'll defeat him at his own game. Using my magic, I'll topple him, and I'll spit upon his bones.

The maids return, unaware of what's passed. They carry a freshly pressed dress of crimson, blue Otherlight emanating from the black, cream, and teal embroidery. Another of Feroulka's creations that we embroidered together. The maids lace me into its folds, and the magic soaks into my thirsty skin. I'm warmed by the color, its power, its potential. It will hold my back straight as I face my uncle and this mad scheme of his.

Ulrica produces a mirror. The maids use cosmetics to add a healthy tint to my sunken cheeks, for they can't add plumpness. They cluck over my hair as they twist it into short ringlets that graze my ears and neck. Then, Ulrica brings forward something almost as golden and beautiful as the sun—my coronet. She sets it atop my head.

"Where did you find it?" My voice sounds hoarse.

"In the courtyard, beneath the pigeon loft." She hushes my thanks and dismisses the maids. The guards lift their halberds, finally willing to let us leave. Ulrica makes a small adjustment to the coronet and mutters, "Lord Beauchamp called it prime evidence in your favor. When he died, I made certain it didn't... disappear."

⁊

THE GUARDS ESCORT Ulrica and me through corridors decorated with evergreens, the air heavy with the sharp scent of their sap.

"It's Yuletide, then?" I ask.

She nods. "First day."

Memories from last year come unbidden of skating icy canals with Tys. His tightrope performance. Our kiss. I battle those memories with what I saw through the telescope.

I'm better off without him.

We arrive in the throne room as baritone bells chime Terce. My uncle stands before the Oak Throne. I stumble to a stop, then force my feet forward. I keep my face expressionless and swallow words that want to leap from me. His eyes dart towards the coronet, but he only tightens his lips.

He reaches for my hand. I tuck it against my side.

He firmly takes it, leading me to stand beside the throne, almost exactly where I sat when my grandfather reigned. He places my left hand on the back of it, then inspects me, as if I'm a statue he might consider purchasing.

"Decorative, yet supportive." His gaze sharpens on my face. "If you have thoughts of sabotaging my efforts, allow me to dissuade you." He snaps his fingers. A servant steps forward with a large, octagonal, lacquered box, which he opens.

Sitting upon the padded pink silk is the iron cage.

Cramping fear shakes my newly remade determination. My tongue throbs. I tremble, unable to disguise my emotions as he watches. Finally, he snaps his fingers once more. The servant closes the box and retreats.

"Be such a pity to use this again. I hope its presence is enough of a deterrent." He leans forward. "Look pretty. Say nothing."

I tighten my grip on the carved throne. *I will save Valonia. I will spit upon you.*

He sits. "Bring in our guests."

Velvet and fur-clad men file into the room. All are bearded, some handsome, some cragged and gray. Perhaps they're new members of the King's Council, here to witness my nuptials. Lord Beauchamp is gone, as Ulrica told me, and I see that Isabeau's father is also missing. *None* of these men in front of me are familiar.

My uncle relaxes into the throne's embrace. "Honored suitors, I'm pleased you have decided to join my little... tournament."

Suitors, plural? Tournament? *Merde.*

"...I present to you my daughter, Marguerite Julianna Ruxandra de Perdrix, my heir."

Bearded faces turn toward me. My uncle's voice rises and falls, weaving promises of power as eyes skim over my face and hair and body, measuring my worth against their ambition. I want to shrink, but I watch them back, memorizing their faces. If they're in league with my uncle, their names will be stitched alongside his in my next record.

Except I know none of these men. That broken nose, that lazy eye, those drooping jowls aren't familiar. I sat in this throne room; I've lingered behind this castle's tapestries and peepholes for too many years. I know the courtiers that plied my father and grandfather for favors. These lords are not Valonian.

I press my fingers into the divots and curves of the throne, wishing for answers, for the wit to slip from my uncle's snare. And the cunning to trap him in my own.

The wood warms under my fingers.

My uncle sits up a little straighter and stumbles on his words. "... most happy to welcome you, Lord Ostenvoorde." The jowly man.

I sharpen my gaze. Listen to their names. The Count of Waldenfeucht (lazy eye), the Duke of Gelter (bow-legged), the Duke of Schelte (broken nose), the three barons of Hlaandrs (reminiscent of a rooster, a piglet and a mule) and that graybeard, Lord Elchen. My suitors are not Valonian, but noblemen of Haps-Burdia. Sworn enemies.

"... Lord Van Yvren." My uncle addresses the youngest of the pack, a black-bearded giant who must be at least thirty. "Welcome to Chateau Boispierre." He turns to the next suitor, a middle-aged man wearing a white ruff and a heavy gold chain of office, the Lord Chancellor of Aemsterhaven. My uncle acknowledges them as if they're his closest friends and settles back into the throne.

This must be a trick, an elaborate double-cross. Why else seek a union with Haps-Burdia? It's antithetical to every principle he espouses, to bring an enemy into his family. To ally with the empire. To give away Valonia. Unless the war's gone so badly....

Is this the only way to salvage Valonia from the clutches of the Red Duke of Brandt? The only way to gain peace and keep a semblance of pride? My insides twist.

He sits up straight once more. He tosses a quick glance over his shoulder at me, catching my stony expression.

"Look pretty."

I soften my mouth into a curve. I grit my teeth behind my smile and wish *he* could have a week wearing his thrice-cursed iron cage on his head. He shifts, as if my emotions needle him.

My thoughts twist into seething, angry knots. Everything wrong happened because of my uncle's deception and betrayals. I rehearse the list I stitched in my gown. I won't forget those names. I can't forget his crimes. I might be the only one left with a comprehensive knowledge of my uncle's wrongdoings. I'll recreate my record. As soon as possible.

The throne heats under my fingers, as if ready to burst into flames. My uncle perches on its edge.

Movement at the far doors brings him to his feet. His commands tangle as guards from around the room rush to the entrance. The Haps-Burdian noblemen shout, and perhaps fearing betrayal, circle up back-to-back, rapiers drawn. But the red-liveried knot of Valonian guards, pikes pointed inward, nudge forward a trio of men in black caps and surcoats carrying a tree.

The sapling stretches above the men's heads. Ells of scarlet wool, shimmering in pale Otherlight, drape through branches, which are fully leafed as if it's still summer. Our guards step back, revealing the men's black livery, embroidered with the pear tree of Brandt.

Merde!

Brandt servants? Here?

Valonian guards nudge them with halberd-points. The two men carrying the sapling's burlap-wrapped root ball shuffle forward. The third lifts his palms, showing he's unarmed.

"I can't imagine why anyone in House VandeBrandt would think it safe to venture onto Valonian soil." My uncle's voice slinks dangerously. "What errand brings you to your death?"

The unarmed servant produces a scroll, unrolls it and speaks in the distinctive Lowland accent. "Gracious greetings we offer to our esteemed neighbor, the kingdom of Valonia and her magnificent ruler, King Julien. We humbly request to be numbered among those offering suit to thy honored daughter."

Is this on behalf of Mattias or his terrible brother?

"As a token of goodwill, we offer this sapling, a prized Brandt pear tree, in the hopes that it might add to the adornment of thy gardens. In addition, we offer this partridge, one of the many faunae which find refuge in our fields and forests."

I grip the Oak Throne as I peer into the sapling's branches. Indeed, a live partridge roosts there, ribbons binding its feet to the branch. It's a skewed reflection of the sigil embroidered on the flags around the room, and on the red surcoats of my uncle's guards. The golden-brown Valonian oak adorns them all, a partridge nestled in its branches.

The messenger finishes. "Signed, Mattias Eustatius VandeBrandt, Graaf of Nemeaux."

This gift symbolizes more than a traditional marriage alliance. I am the partridge. Mattias VandeBrandt tempts me to leave my home and make a nest with him. A year ago, I might've thrown caution to the winds and flown to his side.

But I witnessed what he did on Isle Dinant. He'll never get Valonia through me.

My uncle drapes an arm around my shoulder. "My daughter attracts a thirteenth suitor?" He adds a convincing chuckle as I clamp my teeth tight. "I'm bound by oath to kill any VandeBrandt who sets foot on my land, but I'm not unreasonable."

The room seems to shift as the Haps-Burdian men lean forward. There are tensions in this room beyond mine, and the appearance of the Brandt representatives seems to make these dozen men *very* nervous.

"I grant his servants free passage. I'll even declare Mattias Vande-Brandt this year's Lord of Misrule *in absentia*." My uncle continues, "For the twelve days when the world is upside down, my enemy's spawn may offer suit for my daughter, but come Twelfth Night, my generosity will have worn thin. The youngling had best not attempt to claim her, for there's nothing in Valonia for a VandeBrandt except death."

In rare agreement with my uncle, I nod.

‡

THAT NIGHT, I ignore my soft, inviting bed. I kneel at my prayer desk, consulting with the Fates as I make plans. I must defeat my uncle. I must do so in a way that keeps others from suffering the blade. And I must make sure that if it results in my own death, there will be a record of Reichard de Perdrix's crimes. I need cloth, needles and thread to recreate my record. It must be on something easily transportable. A clothing item, then. Memories of Mattias Vande-Brandt interrupt my prayers and snag my thoughts. That ridiculous tree with its excess of cloth. And that poor bird. All to thumb his nose at me, or to woo me in the most false and embarrassing method possible. I'm ignoring his overtures.

Yet, I need cloth—and a dozen ells of magic-soaked, scarlet wool lie two stories below.

The secret passages are the best route, but that door is still broken. I'll need to traverse a corridor and the balcony over the Great Hall to get to the nearest working entrance. I throw a cloak over myself and slip out my door. My guard stands near the stairwell. I pray to the Fates to evade his gaze as I round the corner. Behind that balcony's tapestry, a well-hidden door leads to a narrow staircase. Except I'm not ready for the dark, silent space, or how my heart crashes against my ribcage. The damp scent transports me back to my cell. Fear paralyzes me.

I fight to control my breath...

My thoughts...

A hollow thump startles me. Cool air pours into my lungs.

I pull away from the secret passage.

Below, in the Great Hall, at the edges of moonlight slanting through the large window, there's movement. The shadows are thick under the musician's gallery, but someone's there. A foot backs into the light, followed by a swinging arm.

A fight?

A man stumbles into view. He clutches at a table to keep from falling. Three more men emerge. They circle the other one, pinning him against the table. A beating.

"You!" I hiss. "Leave that man alone."

Three look up. Their victim takes advantage of their distraction, swinging and kicking. Two go down, but the third hauls him close and twists his arm behind his back. He squints up into the darkness.

"It's one of those Greenie servants, Lady Ulrica. Accent and everything. Paying him back a bit for the good men we've lost."

I don't correct the mistaken identity. "I sympathize, but hospitality rules extend even to our enemies."

The three exchange mulish glances.

"The king offered twelve days of hospitality. All in this castle must uphold his word."

"Twelve days, no more," one says.

"He was sneaking around," another protests.

My thoughts scamper. What if it Tys had sent him to… No, not possible…

"I'll double the guard. Now, find your beds."

They release the man, giving him an extra shove and lingering just inside the shadows.

I harden my tone. "Must I call the guards to remove you from the castle?" They leave, none willing to risk their wages. "Now you, man of Brandt." I explain where bandages and vinegar are stored. "Clean your wounds, then find your bed."

"A thousand thanks, milady." His voice is gravelly, like an old man's. Difficult to hear at this distance.

"Enjoy Valonia's hospitality. It won't last long."

He hobbles away. I'm left with the dark passageway at my back. Its threat has somehow lessened. Breathing through my mouth, I duck into its narrow confines. I hurry around corners, whispering the names I'll embroider once more.

Once in the laundry, I light a candle and go hunting. I find the scarlet fabric tucked beside a length of gray wool. I'm prepared to cut what I need, but my hand returns to the gray wool. It doesn't glow, but it has something… else. The cloth's dyed with oak galls and iron, but the color came out uneven, mottled with green and black streaks —nearly five ells of it—an expensive mistake. I measure out five ells of the scarlet and take both. I filch two needles and a handful of silk skeins, hardly bothering to discern their color before slipping away with my plunder.

I hurry back to my chamber and lay out my treasures. I slide the wool between my fingers, remembering those decorative stitches Feroulka taught me that kept us from men's notice as we traveled. I recall Sister Famke's embroidered dragon that rippled with Skeincraft. I think of the Governor's necklace that offered anonymity. I remember Tanja catapulting a stone across the island. *More focus. Less effort.*

A cloak. I remove the one I'm wearing and study its construction. A simple garment, really. But I have enough cloth for two cloaks, one of red, and one of gray. Or perhaps a lined cloak. I cut each length into pieces. I hold up one behind my prayer desk. I'll pretend to spend my days embroidering scarlet cloth to decorate my prayer alcove. Innocent enough, but it will become the cloak's scarlet lining, filled with names in Broid Cypher.

Perhaps I'll try that obscuring charm on the cloak itself. The gray wool, dyed the color of twilight shadows, will hide me from unwanted notice, keeping my secrets hidden until I'm ready to reveal them.

ON THE SECOND day of Yuletide, I pick out a blue gown that Feroulka and I embroidered. It's the shade of Lake Clair, full of snow melt. The pale, greenish-blue gives me a sense of clarity, and I can use that. Black and red embroidery line the collar, cuffs and hem.

It glows with power. If there is a voyant in the castle, this gown will draw his notice, sure as rain. However, I've not seen a single voyant since leaving the dungeons, or since I returned to Valonia. Perhaps my uncle keeps them elsewhere so as not to mar his charade as King Julien. Still, I'd rather be caught with this dress than without.

Once the maids leave the breakfast tray, I pull out the gray wool and start my work. I stitch a protective, obscuring pattern in blue using my left hand. As my needle slips in and out, I imagine myself moving through the castle, unseen by others. *Invisible.* Power hums through me like it did in St. Beatricia's. I complete an ell before Terce bells.

Flanked by my guards, I join my uncle and his men in the Great Hall. I sit beside the fire, in case any voyants appear; its light might obscure some of my Otherlight. I fasten an embroidery hoop on the red wool and prepare a length of dark green thread. I embroider boldly before them all. I want no scent of deception.

The entertainment is meager, only a handful of musicians and a single acrobat. The fellow juggles and walks across the balcony balustrade above our heads. I can't help comparing him to Tys and find the fellow wanting. My uncle spends the morning meeting with each suitor. He's only across the room. Each time I look up, his attention rests upon me. Instinct commands me to flee, to hide from my predator, but I will myself to stay, to smile, to stitch.

While I regain my strength, I must find an unexpected path to defeating my uncle. Like the Governor's puzzle box. As the suitors take turns sitting beside me, eager to begin their pursuit, their legs brush up against my skirts. I send out calm, tranquil emotions through the cloth, calling for their trust and their secrets.

It seems not all the men vie for my hand; some come representing sons or younger brothers 'of a marrying age.' They produce tiny portraits of their unattached relatives, extolling virtues as I lay down stitches. Surprisingly, they seem genuine in their efforts to gain my interest. A few are visibly relieved when VanderZee is knocked out of the running after his meeting across the room. Compared to the other suitors' gifts of jewels and fur cloaks, VanderZee's barrels of pickled herring did not please my uncle. It was better than the partridge in a pear tree, but not by much.

The Brandt representative never shows his face.

There is, however, another gift waiting on the table at mid-day. The wicker cage, a foot tall, has two occupants, a pair of gray and buff birds. My uncle reaches the table before me and reads the attached note. He glances between it and me with narrowed eyes.

"Your thirteenth suitor sent another gift." He glances at the note once more. "A pair of turtledoves 'to symbolize love and faithfulness,'" he quotes, and crumples the parchment in his fist. "Love! The war *his father* started was not—" He breaks off, glancing around the room. The Haps-Burdian suitors stand in a half circle around the dais, silently staring at him. Their faces are solemn as granite statues. My uncle composes himself. "The animosity between our countries casts a long shadow. Come, eat. I'll join you shortly."

He stalks from the room.

The suitors converse amongst each other with glances. As the servants bring in meat and pastry, they settle at the table with an air of cordiality. The decorated "throne" for the Lord of Misrule remains empty, with no Brandt servant. I put a few tiny stitches in the tablecloth. Broid Cypher stitches that mean 'princess' with black threads of truth, and purple threads of mistrust that form the word 'king,' and send my power trickling through it.

I study the birds as I eat. If one expects turtledoves, one sees turtledoves. Yet, I've sent too many messages to mistake these as anything but pigeons.

A torn bit of the parchment note dangles from a square knot—the same type of knot Tys once tied around my wrist. *You've not seen the last of me.* The pastry in my mouth turns dry as wool. Pigeons are for messages and can only be sent one way. What message did Tys want from me? I snip a bit of the scarlet cloth under cover of the table and tuck it in my sleeve beside my needle. There's something I've needed to tell Tys for months.

I can't send the birds from the pigeon loft. That would give away the secret. I can't take them to my chamber; it would be misconstrued as embracing the Brandt suitor. Leaving the cage on the table means rejecting it. If a Brandt servant was beaten last night, the whole lot could be horsewhipped by morning.

I must tread the narrow middle. I lift the cage and call a servant to fetch my cloak.

"I'll release these birds."

"Would you like company?" the lazy-eyed lord asks, standing.

"I won't be gone long enough to merit company." I smile sweetly.

I go to the snowy garden, climbing to the highest terrace where I can work in private. My stitches are hasty, but the letters are clear.

Tys. I witnessed your betrayal of the Mirvray.

I tie it to the first pigeon's leg then launch the bird into the sky. There. He'll know he'll find no welcome in Valonia.

I release the other as well, for I've nothing more to tell Mattias VandeBrandt. Ever.

⚜

I STAY in the garden until the bitter wind sends me inside. I find the suitors gathered in the library, away from the musicians and the acrobat. From their silence, I suspect they've been discussing me, or my uncle. I pretend not to notice, greeting each in turn. As my wide skirts brush up against their leggings, I focus on icy Lake Clair. All the mountains' waters, all their secrets, flow downward into her depths. I let my smile echo that tranquility as I settle beside the fire with my embroidery. As shadows lengthen outside the windows, the men relax. Conversation hums; some in Haps-tongue, others in carefully worded Langue-Valon.

Between stitches, I watch lips, catching snatches of honesty. Lord VanderZee and Baron Van Leuden have heavy mustaches curtaining their mouths; I ignore them. Others, thankfully, are better trimmed. The Lord Chancellor of Aemsterhaven, eliminated from the tournament today because my uncle found his conversation "insipid," says he'd hoped to be sent home, but was told to remain for all twelve days. In fact, he'd thought it strange to be summoned to Valonia in the first place and hadn't immediately responded to the invitation.

"And then?" jowly Lord Ostenvoorde prompts.

"I was convinced it would be worth my time."

"I, too, was *convinced*," Lord Ostenvoorde says mournfully.

My neck prickles. The suitors hadn't instigated this visit?

Lord Van Yvren, the broad-shouldered noble, sits down beside me, blocking my view.

I smile around gritted teeth. The man leans closer. My neck prickles for new reasons.

I pin my smile in place as we chat: yes, it *is* cold. The mountains *are* tall. The lake is *very* wide. Yes, I heard the hunting is good this year. All the while, he watches me, like my uncle so often watches me, and my heart throws itself against my ribs as if trying to escape. His gaze finally slides away, but only as far as the embroidery on my lap.

"That's very pretty." Lord Van Yvren traces stitches with his finger, but only those glowing with faint blue Otherlight.

I gasp. *A voyant.* A skilled one. I press a finger to my lips, pretending I pricked myself. I beg an excuse and flee.

My chamber is the closest I have to a sanctuary. I lock myself in and push a chest in front of the door before I bury myself under the bedclothes. There's no reason for my tears. Or for my shaking. Lord Van Yvren's done nothing except sit too close and touch my embroidery.

He's not a voyant. He's not scarred. He doesn't have a long, iron knife. He just has the Sight. Perhaps, Lord Van Yvren won't tell my uncle about my Otherlight. The Lowlanders seem to have some… reserve… regarding the king, despite joining this marriage tournament. Whatever the rules are, they're careful playing it.

I force myself to climb out from under the covers.

I brush my hands over the scarlet wool, soaking up the magic I let fall into its stitches. I pull a little extra strength from the cloth itself, enough to dim its shine. I exchange the scarlet for the gray and stitch more of the obscuring charm along its hem.

When I reach the end, I turn to the gown laid out for tomorrow: the fine, white wool is embellished only with red ribbons and gold embroidery along the hem, cuffs, and neckline. I must keep Lord Van Yvren from seeing my telltale shine, so I thread white silk on my needle and wind the stitches around the gold embroidery using Feroulka's obscuring charms. When my strength fades, I pause to eat the nuts and sweetmeats left by Ulrica. She worries over the plump-ness stolen by my months in prison. I continue working on the dress until the candle's a quarter of what it was. My eyes are gritty, but I pull out the next length of gray wool. Everything stitched on the first piece I duplicate on the second.

This is the way I've chosen to escape my uncle's grasp, with my needle, my magic, and soon, all the truth.

CHAPTER NINETEEN

Quilt: to stitch together two layers of cloth with a
soft interlining, usually in an ornamented pattern, to
prevent the filling from shifting

ON THE THIRD DAY OF YULETIDE, I PULL THE WHITE GOWN
over my head. It's white as the snow that tops the Valon mountains—
pure and untouched, just as I'm not tainted by whatever mischief my
uncle is stirring. Despite the obscuring charms, the gown glows a
steady, pale blue. Fear of Lord Van Yvren and his voyancy makes me
shiver. If my uncle bends him to his will, learns what he sees... *Stars!*
If my uncle brings back *any* of the voyants he's hidden away, I'd be
named a witch. My magic is too clear, too blatant.

My insides twist in debate until I straighten my spine. I am a
witch. I am my mother's daughter. I am my father's heir, and my
uncle's enemy. I'll walk proudly into that room, like the princess I am.

When I reach the main floor, the men are milling around in heavy
cloaks and boots.

Lord Van Yvren bows and greets me first. The rest turn. That
moment stretches like a fine thread of silk that won't break. Every
man stares. Some look calculating, others have mouths agape. So
much for Feroulka's obscuring charm.

My uncle pushes his way through the mass. "We hunt today, *mignon*. Say farewell quickly, for the hounds are pulling at their leads."

I long to join them, to have an excuse to see more of Valonia, to see the reality of my uncle's rule. Yet my record *must* be finished before my desire to mend Valonia sweeps me into a confrontation that might prove deadly. "I'll be waiting for your return this evening."

After each nobleman kisses my hand, they depart. I retreat, my guards in tow, passing Ulrica at the center of a knot of servants in various liveries giving out assignments. I pause and study the group. No black uniforms with a green-leafed pear tree.

I haven't seen *any* Brandt servants since the first day.

I suspect meddling.

When Ulrica acknowledges me, I ask if the foreign servants are all accounted for. She ticks them off on her fingers. Twelve sets.

"And the Brandt servants?"

My question draws silence. They look at one another, expressions varying from puzzlement to wariness. Ulrica shows me the room they were given; no beds were slept in. Finally, a maid speaks up.

"Ask the acrobat, the one with the scar on his face."

"There's more than one acrobat?"

"There were two yesterday morning. The scarred one cornered the Brandt servants then." She describes him. "Dark hair. Burn on his cheek."

I tell the servants to find the man and send him to me in the *orangerie*. I stalk through the corridors. If one of our own broke hospitality bonds, all our safety is in jeopardy.

I settle with my embroidery between the orange trees, sunshine pouring in from the many windows. My guards watch from the doorway. They examine a man dressed in motley, a patchwork tunic of green, black, and red diamonds, then allow him in. He carries a large wicker cage; within, a few bundles of feathers cackle protests. I peer through the bars.

"Chickens," he says. "Just arrived."

He hands me a scroll tied with another square knot. I harden my jaw, crack the seal and skip the opening, flowery compliments. *I give unto you three fine hens as a symbol of the benefits that will come to Valonia from a union with Brandt.*

An old man on Isle Dinant raised this variety with twice as many feathers as normal ones, drooping over beak and feet. He'd gotten his first breeding pair from an obscure valley in Pranzia. I frown. Why would Tys give these? Has he made amends with the Mirvray? Was he allied with Pranzia? Should I watch the Pranzian border? I throw my hands up in frustration. Tys is being obscure, and I'll not gain a headache over it.

I turn my attention to the young man before me. He's tall. His hair is cut unfashionably short and the left side of his face is marred with a shiny scar that wrinkles from his hairline to below his jaw.

"You're an acrobat?"

"As you see, Your Highness."

"The Brandt delegation has disappeared. You were perhaps the last to have a conversation with them. Do you know where they've gone?"

"Departed, Your Highness. Back to Brandt."

"Why is that?"

"Felt it dangerous to stay in Boispierre, Your Highness."

His low voice is distinctively raspy, though his face slips from my memory like a rat into the shadows. All I can sense is the scar and short hair. My core becomes as taut as the silk on my needle; I know this sort of magic.

"Who are you truly?" He's taller than Tys. Wiry, where Tys had more muscle padding his shoulders. And scarred.

"Dare not say, Your Highness."

"You wear some sort of charm to keep your face less memorable."

"Some folk would kill me as soon as look at me, Your Highness." His voice is distinctive. Memorable where his face isn't.

I lower my voice. "You're the Brandt servant from the first night of Yule."

He whispers back, "You're *not* Lady Ulrica."

"As you say. So, you transformed into an acrobat to avoid being pummeled."

"'Twas Master Mattias' idea."

Angry words want to burst from the boil covering my heart. Instead, I manage, "This charm, may I see it?"

He hesitates.

"I've seen his handiwork before. I'm just curious how the charm works."

He pulls it from under his tunic. I stand to get a better view. It's an intricate web of twine looped and knotted in a pattern difficult to imitate. It glows with Tys' white Otherlight and is anchored with five small stones that glow violet, placed around the necklace at critical points of intersection. Impressive work. I still don't like it.

"When will you have contact next with your master?" I study his face for lies.

"Won't," he says. "Receive the gifts he sends and try to give them without being seen."

"I don't want them."

He shrugs. His charm makes it impossible to detect the normal signs of deceit.

"Can you remove the charm?"

"Master Mattias fastened it around my neck. If untied…"

"You'll lose your anonymity."

"Chicken in a den of foxes."

I want to ask him about the chickens. I want to know if Mattias salvaged them from Isle Dinant. A sliver of my heart hopes they were given to him by the Mirvray after he explained how he'd tricked everyone in an elaborate hoax. I shake my head. The servant wouldn't know. Instead, I ask a question he *can* answer.

"What happened to your face?"

His chin goes up. His shoulders straighten. His gaze that was downcast now focuses over my head. "Burned, Your Highness."

It's too personal a question, but I can observe his behavior as he tells uncomfortable truths. "Yes, but how?"

"Was sailing on the *Baalhoek Meid*. Cook's mate checked the level of brandy in the cask. Spark fell in the bung hole. Brandy caught fire inside the cask. Cook and mate raised the alarm, but not before the fire spread to the *buskruitmagazijn*.... er..."

"The gunpowder stores?" I guess.

"*Ja*. Blown into the sky, then fell into the sea. Some of us survived. Held onto salvaged wood. Happened in the shipping lanes, so we were found in a few days. Lucky."

It's a terrible story but told honestly enough. I nod. Approaching the question of Tys, I must tread carefully. As I open my mouth, a maid enters the *orangerie*.

"A visitor for Your Highness."

"For me?" I put away my needlework. The Brandt servant remains standing before me. "You may go, though I do have more questions."

"Yes, Your Highness." He bows and retreats.

I've no time to be curious before the guards allow a dark-haired woman into the *orangerie*. In the winter sunlight, her face is more angular than I remember from when we shared a room in St. Clotilde's.

"Isabeau?" I embrace her. "I didn't know you were coming for Yuletide."

"I was invited." Her smile doesn't quite reach her eyes. "His Majesty himself asked for his daughter's particular friend" —she gestures toward herself— "to keep her company during this festive time of year." She's being careful, deliberate. Why? She meets my gaze. "I need your promise to not speak of... certain things."

"Isabeau..."

"The king dueled my father nine months ago and defeated him."

I'd forgotten that her father was one of the Council members who followed up on my accusations.

Her words are measured. "Dishonored, he left the Council and retreated to our estate. He's tutoring my younger brother to inherit."

"What happened to your older brothers?"

"The war."

"All three of them?"

Her eyes tighten. "Nothing is the same."

I squeeze her hand. She looks away.

"This is the only way to help my family. To regain our honor." I've never heard her voice wobble in all the time I've known her. The past year must have been as terrible for Isabeau as it was for me. I decide to be stoutly cheerful.

"I'm glad my friend came to visit." I pick up my embroidery. We make small talk. She admires the *orangerie* and its contents.

"Except, that one isn't... Is that an apple tree?"

I prick my finger. Pressing it to my mouth, I shake my head. "Brandt pear."

"What in Heaven's name is it doing in your *orangerie*?"

I tell her of the twelve suitors, and the extra one from Brandt.

Her eyebrows rise higher. "Valonia allying with provinces of Haps-Burdia?" She shakes her head. "A partridge in a pear tree? The stars will slide backwards now, I suppose?"

"It was foolhardy," I say, as if I don't care a whit about my thirteenth suitor.

"You're not furious?" Isabeau stares. "If they hear about this in Ligeron, the folk will be up in arms. My brothers fought in that battle. The Duke gave no quarter." She crosses her arms. "Folk are dead-set against Brandt, and Haps-Burdia only slightly less."

I frown. How could my uncle try to pull off this marriage tournament if rancor runs so deep against Haps-Burdia? I pester Isabeau to tell me of the war months. The battles, the losses, the hardships. Her words come slowly at first, each story dyed deep in sorrow.

We held our borders, but the cost was high.

"My father estimates we lost a quarter of our able-bodied men. Fates know how we'll plant and harvest next year." She says nothing about witch trials. I don't mention the dungeon. It's like skating on Lake Clair two weeks before springtime. I can't trust the surface beneath my feet. It's too easy to crack.

Isabeau sits forward. "Remember those puppet shows we'd put on for the girls at St. Clotilde's?" The long winter nights in the dormitory bored Isabeau. She made puppet frames from filched kitchen utensils and wire and convinced me to sew their cloth bodies. "Let's do another. Tomorrow night. For your guests."

I glance up, wary. "You want to entertain the men with stories of maidens and princes?" But really, I have too much to do. Too much to undo.

"Surely you've heard some new ones since leaving St. Clotilde's."

"With only a day to make the puppets?" I have so much more to record.

She tugs away my embroidery. "Plenty of time. Now, what story should we tell?"

The talk of war reminds me of a tale from Isle Dinant. It won't make an audience laugh, but as much as Yuletide is about hope in a new year, it's also about reflecting on hard-earned truths. It might serve other purposes as well. If I told the story, with all attention on me, I could weave powerful Skeincraft in the room.

"What do you think of the puppets being birds?"

"Bird puppets," she says. "We've never tried that before." We work until late afternoon, Isabeau constructing the framework while I sew wings and beaks.

That night, the feast is raucous. The men's spirits are high after a successful hunt. Their spoils roast ostentatiously over the fire, and they boast shamelessly. The rooster-looking baron from Hlaandrs is chaffed, for he only managed to kill a brace of rabbits instead of larger game. He joins VanderZee and the Chamberlain of Aemsterhaven as my uncle's rejects.

I congratulate each man, my hand touching their sleeves as I try to learn their motivations. Nine remaining men compete for my hand, and though some seem desperate for… something… their emotional attachment towards me is shallow. I'll not marry any of them. I'll rescue Valonia and myself before my uncle can perform the ceremony.

Once in my chamber, I pray the Stars will help me do so as I empty my magic into the gray wool stitch by stitch. I pick up the red wool and record more names. My heart beats heavily as I think of all the names I've not learned—the battle-fallen and the wounded. Are these names I should lay at my uncle's feet? Or does the blame for their deaths lie squarely with the Bloody Duke of Brandt?

I don't know. And I should. I'll learn the facts of those battles. I'll find ways for my kingdom to heal.

Once my uncle faces his punishment.

***

ON THE FOURTH day of Yuletide, my uncle takes the other men out to race horses. There's a long stretch of the Pilgrim Road nearby that has so many close-growing trees, the road is almost free of snow. Again, I'm tempted to go. I wilt under such confinement, but I rely upon my Skeincraft. I have nine days. I must finish the cloak, ferret out and foil my uncle's larger purpose, and escape his wrath unscathed.

There's still too much empty cloth around my embroidery hoop. I hurry through my ablutions and don a twilight-blue dress decorated with extra obscuring charms amongst its embroidered stars. Entrenching myself in the *orangerie*, I record two dozen more names before Terce bells. Isabeau finds me as I finish eating an apple. I'm like a fire needing fuel every few hours. She joins me. We share honeyed nuts and a wedge of cheese as we plan the stagecraft for our evening's theatrics.

After lunch, I return to my embroidery while she prepares the stage. Hours later, as the sun retreats behind the mountains, the puppets and stage are ready. A frisson of anticipation ripples through me.

***

"TONIGHT, you'll hear the Tale of the Four Colley Birds." I let my voice become mysterious. "Listen."

We lift our bird puppets on their long metal posts and maneuver the mechanisms to flutter their wings. We swoop the puppets back and forth around the tin trees Isabeau made. I tell of four nestling brothers and how the youngest had an itch for new surroundings. The tale goes from adventure to tragedy. I didn't enjoy the story the first time I heard it, for sadness bleeds through the tale, but after these many months it feels truer than others.

"Only Iancu returned home that day." I wrap up the story. "And he never left the forest again."

The room is silent, heavy with potential.

"Many nights he couldn't sleep." I perch the puppet in a tree, willing the story, my stitches, and my voice to call forth the bravery within each member of the audience. "As he fathered one nestful of chicks, then another, he told the story of his brothers. Each generation learned of Nelu the Explorer, Petru the Protective, and Radu the Valiant. And so, in this way, Iancu gave his brothers a life that stretched beyond their mortality. Eventually, he grew old; his feathers became gray and thin, and one day, he never roused from his nest."

Tears leaking down her face, Isabeau maneuvers the trees to veil the puppet's removal, then pulls them apart. Only the trees are left on stage, as they were at the beginning.

"When his descendants gathered to honor him, they named him Iancu the Enduring. They understood that surviving with the memory of the fallen is as difficult a task as dying bravely. And so, this tale is shared with each generation in the dark forests beyond the seas, and now you've heard it too."

My voice dies away, and the fire at my back scorches in the lingering silence. Finally, the applause begins. There's a few *huzzah*s tossed in. Isabeau's face smooths into a smile. We stand, revealing ourselves to our audience. The firelight reflects on bright faces; tears leave glistening telltale tracks on cheeks before hiding in the men's beards.

"A grand tale," the bow-legged duke declares. "I'd never have thought it of two such young ladies. I'd have expected more... stardust and romance."

We duck our faces in pretend bashfulness.

I say, "It seemed a proper tale for a castle full of men."

"A proper tale, indeed." My uncle comes forward.

My small smile freezes. I force it wider. "You liked it, Father?"

"Of course, *mignon*. Puppeteering must agree with you. You're practically glowing."

I stiffen, but Isabeau saves us with an obvious fanning of her pink cheeks. "It's the roaring fire. Please, Your Majesty, do not point out our unladylike perspiration."

My uncle makes a gallant bow. "I'd never dream to, my dear." He holds her hand a fraction longer than he should, and her eyes widen. My neck prickles.

Before I can puzzle this out, I'm distracted by the count with the lazy eye. He's effusive with his compliments now that he's been eliminated. His horse came in last, three races in a row.

I'm exhausted by all the magic I've used, but I focus on exuding the aura of a hero. I must have these men on my side before my uncle's plans come to fruition. His gaze travels between me and Isabeau. I remind myself that he can't see magic and that, according to castle gossip, all his voyants are at Roc Ursgueule.

"Clever puppets," he comments. "You girls didn't make them yourselves, did you?"

I grasp Isabeau's hand, quickly constructing a falsehood. "We bought them years ago, from a wandering minstrel in Tillroux. We added a few embellishments to distinguish one from another." I gesture toward the stage, but the puppets aren't where we left them.

"Isabeau, did you...?"

She frowns. "No. I left them there. Perhaps a servant put them away."

My embroidery bag's gone, too. Panic rises, howling like a winter storm. I only allow a mask of fretful worry. My uncle's gaze follows mine. I pray his gift of voyance is truly gone. After questioning the servants, searching as well as possible without seeming frenzied, and chatting with each of the men, Isabeau, I, and our ever-present guards leave.

"A *fine* performance," she whispers when we're in the hallway. "Bravo, Marguerite."

I let my mask slip so she can see my true anxiety. "If you took my bag, Isabeau, please give it back."

She blinks. "I thought you whisked it under your skirts when I wasn't looking."

"No." Misery drenches the word.

She squeezes my arm. "I'm certain you'll get your hands on more embroidery supplies."

We separate to go to our chambers. I pause. I ache to share my secrets. Is there some way to stretch these hours of collaboration into real trust? We were roommates for years. Surely, there must be some clever, coded phrase that could tell her the truth without the guards understanding. Yet, I find no words. I've carried my burden of silence so long, it seems impossible to trust her, or perhaps anyone. I force my feet to march all the way to my chamber.

I hold myself together until I leave my red-uniformed shadows in the corridor. I close my chamber door and slide to the floor. The tears come hot and burning, but I press my hands hard against my mouth to muffle the sound. When the storm subsides, I remove my hands and bury my face in my skirt.

There is a cool shift in the air. My head jerks up. I blink away the obscuring tears. A man stands on the far side of my chamber, between the window and my bed.

I stand abruptly, half my skirts still under my feet. Brought up short, I stumble. The man rushes forward. I fend him off with one hand and grab the doorframe with the other.

"Stay back."

He pauses. Candlelight reflects off his scarred cheek. The acrobatic sailor.

"Why are you in my chamber?"

He retreats to the bed and pulls my embroidery bag out of hiding. His lips move as he holds it out to me. I straighten my coronet and press it tighter against my skull.

"... Didn't think you'd want them examined," he says. "Glowing brighter than an autumn sunrise you were. Puppets, too. If anyone with the Gift saw them..."

The thousand angry words avalanching toward my tongue catch in my throat. I untangle myself from my skirts and wipe the tears from my cheeks.

"Thank you." I take the bag from his outstretched hand, tucking its reassuring weight against my chest. "Why?"

"You were given a VandeBrandt ring." He bows. "My duty is to protect and assist you."

"Your duty from Mattias VandeBrandt?" His name hisses through my teeth. The man flinches, but I barrel on. "I'll take no more of his aid."

"Why? You've no friends here who'll put you before themselves."

"I have friends–"

"Lady Isabeau doesn't count. She's conferring with your uncle as we speak." It's a slap of surprise. "As for Lady Ulrica," he continues, "she doesn't lift a finger to help, despite her recent estrangement from the king." He knows more than I'd expect a landed seaman to learn in a foreign castle. He's a spy or something equally dangerous.

"You called the king 'your uncle,' just now."

His lips tighten, but he doesn't explain himself as he stands at the foot of my bed. How did he gain entrance? Door, window, the broken secret door? I study him, but other than his scar, his features slip away into unremarkable blandness. The knotted charm. I can't discern the full truth from his expression, but I have another way.

I march to my bed and pull the gray wool, dyed in oak galls, from under the mattress. I thrust it at the VandeBrandt servant. He takes one end as I hold the other.

"You've heard the official story?"

His fingers tighten around the cloth. "The princess was distressed after the death of her uncle. So distressed, she claimed it was her father who died and that her uncle usurped the throne." He moistens his lips. "Heard she was taken to an isolated castle, perhaps Roc Ursgueule, to be cared for by medically trained nornes." No flicker of deception.

"Your master heard this?"

He nods.

"Then why, in all the seven levels of Hell, did Mattias leave me to languish?"

His throat bobs. "Couldn't at first. He was… detained."

"Detained?"

"Forcibly."

"By whom?"

"His half-brother."

"Why?"

"If you knew Willem…" His voice wobbles and goes high as he says the name. Honest fear. It settles my tumultuous thoughts.

"What happened?"

"Willem told the duke his younger son was consorting… er… behaving treasonously with the princess."

Heat floods my neck. The kiss during last year's Yuletide? Hardly consorting *or* treasonous. And how did Willem know of it?

"The duke thought the relationship to Brandt's advantage. Wanted to use it. It didn't sit well with my master. He spoke his mind. The duke grew angry, sent him to the invasion's front line, to the raid on Isle Dinant. 'Prove yourself a VandeBrandt, or don't come back,' he said."

"Stars." The wool in my hand turns clammy. "That's why Tys turned on his friends."

"No, Your Highness." He shakes his head. "The duke placed him with Willem's soldiers. To watch him and report back. Master Mattias told them he knew curses in Mirvray-tongue. Taught them a few. They were doubtful, but they landed on the island shouting *'Fugi!'* and

'Pericol vine!' Folk fled before them, so the soldiers believed Mattias VandeBrandt obeyed his father's orders."

"That means *run*." I swallow. "That danger is coming." The pieces stitch together. "He was warning them. Telling them to flee."

"Yes." I catch a smile as he ducks his head. The warm glow filling my chest falters.

"How do you know this?"

"Told me, three days later, when he was stuffed in the hold of the *Baalhoek Meid*. Hour before she sailed out of Aemsterhaven harbor."

"What?"

"Willem didn't like his brother's success. Told you, Your Highness. Forcibly detained."

I fit this new story into the space I carved for the story I thought I knew. My head jerks up. "The fire in the brandy cask. Tys... did he survive?"

"He lives, Your Highness." He seems ready to say more but pinches his lips together instead. The unspoken *however* hovers in the air.

"What is it?"

"Injured."

I suck in a breath. "How badly?"

"Bad enough. Couldn't come to your rescue, 'til now."

A dozen thoughts wrestle for precedence, but the most unexpected escapes my mouth. "*This* is a rescue?"

The servant's posture straightens, then sags. "Happenings in Valonia have been well-cloaked. Plans were made for a... different situation. Tried a rescue last month. It... failed."

I want details, but I don't. I want to rage against the unfairness of what I endured. Tell of the horror and abuse I suffered. I swallow that down. "I've made plans for myself." It's an exaggeration, but my pride won't allow me to admit I'm floundering through this as best I can.

He doesn't respond. He just stands there, waiting like a good servant. Yet I sense he's waiting for something else. Perhaps it's the way he stands, for his expression's still concealed. Perhaps the oak-infused cloth nudges me with truth, for it's as if the sun rose and I can finally see the land spread before me.

The world might see an acrobat, a servant, a sailor. They'd see a scar, a charm-obscured face, and the deferential air, but I see the man behind the mask.

"Tys!"

"*Kleintje.*" His head comes up, his shoulders relax. "I'm so sorry."

"You're taller."

"Still had more growing to do. Even on ship's rations."

"Why is your voice so different?"

"Smoke and seawater."

My grip around my anger slips, but I tighten it. He stood by while someone sent a fiery arrow into Tanja's boat. He could have stopped... Or maybe helped... I wrestle my desire for justice, for mercy, and the burning question: How much truth can I truly detect? The charm keeps his expression from me. His raspy voice obscures the inflections I knew.

Only his scar proves he was in an explosion. I move slowly, my hand outstretched. He stands like a soldier as my fingers trace the wide, pink scar. The skin is smooth and hairless, with a rippled texture. I lift my other hand to his uninjured side. His cheekbone and jaw curve under my fingers in familiar ways. The muscle jumps in his jaw, the way it does when he pretends to be brave.

The ice around my heart melts and I push away the hurt I've nurtured for months. Stepping closer, I press my cheek against his chest. His arms envelop me.

"I missed you," I whisper. His embrace tightens. I look up, and his eyes stare into mine.

"Stars, *kleintje.* Can't have any idea how I wanted to be here. Wanted to sprout wings, to fly to your side." His face is still... indistinct. I can't read his expression. Even with the charm, the scar's unmistakable.

"Does it hurt?"

"Sensitive to heat and I want no more Valonians pummeling my face…" He trails off as I stand on tiptoe, pressing a kiss against his damaged cheek.

"We've both been ill-handled." I tell him of the cage around my head and the spike. I shudder at the memory but extend my tongue to show him the resulting concavity.

Tys sucks in a breath. "Marguerite."

"It doesn't hurt now, but some foods aren't as flavorful as before." I try to speak lightly, but my voice wobbles. His fingers knead my shoulder. I close my eyes and let his touch soothe my taut muscles. I lean my forehead against his motley tunic. The massage migrates up the back of my neck, then to the sensitive hollow behind my ear and jaw.

"Mmm."

His fingers caress my jaw and tip it upwards. His lips brush mine, then press against them. Blood rushes through my veins with the power of a waterfall. My fingers spread across the warmth of his chest, then curl into his tunic, pulling him closer. Our lips carry on a dialogue of longing and loss, sweetness and sorrow, in a language only we two could understand.

As our kiss lengthens and deepens, moisture slips down my cheek. I pull back. The tears aren't mine. Tys' cheeks gleam in the candlelight. I murmur his name, smoothing them dry, then press a lingering kiss against his lips. His arms wrap around my shoulders and snug me close.

"I was willing to trade my soul for a chance to see you, to be sure you were safe." His lips brush my left ear. "Powerless, I was, out on that ocean. A thousand times I praised the Fates for that stray spark that fell into the brandy, and again for the schooner which found us. Fretted every hour these past ten months, trying to get back to you."

"So you recently returned, then?"

"No." He falls silent. I pull back to see his expression. It does me no good.

"Can you take off that charm? I hate not seeing your face."

"Infinity chain. Only way is to cut it. Can't do that until this caper is finished."

"Caper?"

He unwraps his arms from around me and we sit on my bed. "Spent nearly three months on the Iferian coast, healing" —he points to his face— "and waiting for a homeward-bound ship." Tys notices where we're sitting and jumps to his feet. He starts pacing, stops, then leans against the bedpost. "First two wouldn't take me. I was in no shape to work. Finally convinced a captain to take me on, but I had no say at which harbor we docked, what cargo was taken on, and what new destination the captain chose. I was at the mercy of the Fates. Finally arrived in Aemsterhaven two months ago. Didn't try to find my father or brother. Went straight to the Governor to learn how the war went, and if she had news of you."

He rubs the back of his neck. "Since the treaty was made, more news trickled in. Last she heard was that Princess Marguerite had become... *ill* and taken to Roc Ursgueule to heal. I went there, *kleintje*."

His throat bobs.

"Castle's been rebuilt, but something's wrong there." His fingers pull a bit of cordage from somewhere and he ties anxious knots as he speaks. "Searched for you everywhere, but no women there. Only dozens of voyants and workmen. Went into the valleys and the villages. Discovered Rotten Reichard's plague of witch trials. Burnings. Coerced confessions. Children taken from their families. Tracked every thread, hoping it led to you. And that necklace I gave you with the ring?"

Wary, I nod.

"Whole time, I felt like you still had it. Still wore it. It was thin, like a rope worn down to a single strand holding the weight of that hope. Then, it was gone." He covers his face.

Guilt floods me. "Tys, I—I gave up. I thought I knew what I'd seen. And you didn't come."

"I know, but Stars! Returning to Nemeaux empty-handed—" He

drops his hands. "Then I recognized a few lords lingering in our taverns. Heard rumors they'd be crossing the Muse, by invitation of King Julien. There were whispers of a nuptial alliance."

Tys kneels at my feet, gathering my hands in his.

"It was the first time I smiled in months." He places my hand against his scar. "Hurt like the shifting of Hell's foundations, but I didn't care. Knew you must be alive." He kisses my palm, then the other. "Nearly lost hope."

"What did you do?"

"Grabbed my nearest comrades, crossed the border, infiltrated Boispierre, and got caught before we found you." His face is impossible to read, but his shoulders are stiff, knuckles white. "People died, *kleintje*." His voice rasps. "It was my fault. Stefan and Gina—"

"Stefan, Gaspar's son?" Heat and cold rush through me. "You've seen the Mirvray? How do they fare? Did... did Tanja and her baby survive?"

Tys nods. "By the Fates' good grace and Gaspar's skills."

I release a huge breath.

Tys lifts a strand of twine from beneath his collar and reveals a silver ring of tiny cartwheels like the one I received from my grandfather. The token of a debt-gift. My last shreds of doubt flutter away. "Gaspar nearly killed himself trying to bring the baby back from death. Still, Tanja's become a shadow of her former self. Trauma stole her Gift."

My belly falls to my toes. I didn't know that was possible. "Forever?"

"For now, at least." He tells how they settled in a forest in Haps-Burdia. "Been rough, but the Governor and I provided necessities. Winter supplies."

Supplies are good, but they lost their home. When I finish with my uncle, I'll invite them back. I'll protect them the same as any Valonian, for they're my people, too. Silence settles between Tys and me. He leans against one of the tall bedposts, playing with the life-debt ring.

"Reichard's wily." He tucks it under his tunic collar again. "I couldn't bear the weight of more lives, so I'm coming at this sideways with the suitor business. Driving Rotten Reichard mad with what he can't see and can't catch. Nipping at his heels. Like that damn dog, Jacco."

"Jacco." I laugh, and give the old back-handed blessing, "Stars, keep his life interesting."

"Oh, they did. He's at Chateau Nemeaux. Henk discovered the rascal at the Governor's manor and was determined to love the dog to flinders. Jacco put up a fight, but the lad won him over. The devil dog still hates everyone else, but..." His lopsided smile fades as he stares at me. "Come home with me, *kleintje*. Tonight."

"I can't. Valonia..."

"You're a pawn in your uncle's game. Get to safety first. Then we can save your land. Enough people have died."

"Stefan. Gina." I'll add them to the list of my uncle's victims.

"Thought you might try to escape these past few days."

I bristle. "I was as weak as a newborn. Guards watch my every move."

"What about that first night? You stopped those fellows from thrashing me thoroughly. Why not leave then...?"

My expression stops his words. "Mattias VandeBrandt, if I hadn't just forgiven you, I'd bloody your nose." I let out a heavy breath. "Where am I to go? Nowhere in Valonia is safe, with voyants out there hunting. I can't cross into Brandt or Hlaandrs because we're at war."

"There's a treaty."

"A fragile treaty. And something's afoot with the suitors."

"Why not go south to Pranzia?" It isn't a challenge, but I stand.

"And how would I get there? Fly like a bird across the southern ravines? Travel round through Hlaandrs for dozens of leagues?"

Tys holds his hands in a surrendering motion. "So fierce, *kleintje*."

But my anger flares, in part because I've already come up short seeking ways out from under my uncle's thumb. I don't know how to fight him from leagues away. I have no allies. The King's Council is disbanded. Valonian witches are dead or in hiding. Folk are too scared or desperate to rise up. At least not without a bold move by me first. And that move, whatever it might be, will most likely result in my death. Honestly, I'm scrambling. What I have accomplished with the suitors is merely sweet-talking and political wooing. Not enough to make a difference. My uncle has a hold on them I haven't discovered yet. Do I have a plan?

No.

I sigh and cross my arms around myself. Tys reaches out, strokes my shoulder.

"Let me collect a few things. I'll be back before the next bell chime. You'll be ready?"

I hold my breath, feeling like a failure, feeling the weight of the Fates' notice. Then I nod and lace my fingers with his. We walk towards the door, but he stops halfway across the floor and jerks a thumb toward the window.

"Came that way."

Laughter burbles out of me. "Of course you did."

He pulls me tight against him. Kisses me. Tells me of his love with every move of his lips. I melt against him as I answer with my affection. When he steps away, I want to pull him back. Instead, I brace myself against the bedpost where he stood moments before and watch him lower himself out my window with a rope he mysteriously produces.

CHAPTER TWENTY

Chainstitch: ornamental hand stitching in which each
stitch forms a loop through the forward end of the
next

I HAVE LITTLE TO GATHER. SOON, I'M SITTING ON MY BED, eating nuts, replenishing my energy and feeling stupid. I should have just left with him out the window, but that felt too much like giving up. Sitting here with my embroidery, the remains of my haphazard plan that relies almost entirely on Skeincraft and my wits, I realize what a fool I've been.

Naïve. Overconfident.

Why *didn't* I just run? Am I so used to being afraid and complacent that I couldn't work up the courage to leave? Yes, I've had two guards following my every movement when I'm out of my chamber, but why didn't I try to put a sleeping charm on their uniforms? Or the itching charm?

And now, I'm just leaving, without trying to help Isabeau escape?

That feels cowardly.

I stand. I must at least warn Isabeau, even if she won't leave with us. I wrap my regular cloak around me and ease my chamber door open. One of my guards is leaning against the far wall, his head sunk against his chest. Sleeping. The other is gone.

I move as silently as possible through the corridor. Up the half staircase. I scratch at her door. No answer. I try tapping. Nothing. I try opening it, but it's locked.

Nothing to do but return to my chamber.

I'm nearly there when my uncle emerges from the shadows. On either side of him stand two white-uniformed voyants, returned from Roc Ursgueule or wherever they've been. I freeze right where I stand, like a rabbit caught in the open by a predator.

"Marguerite, *mignon*, you're up early. Or late."

"I heard something in the corridor. I... I..." My words dry up as both voyants step closer, hands on their sheathed long knives. My skin prickles, as if sensing them reading the shine of my Otherlight. Each nods to my uncle.

I can't spin a tale to escape this.

"A nightmare, I'd wager." My uncle pulls me into his arms, as my father used to. Lavender and incense surround me. I gag. Struggle. He releases me but keeps his fingers tight around my arm. "Come to my chambers. Perhaps some tea to calm your nerves?"

Panic pounds through every vein. "No, thank you."

"I insist." Though his smile is warm, his grip is unrelenting, pulling me into his chamber, the room where my grandfather once slept. Where he died.

"No, I'll just go to sleep. I'm tired." I use Feroulka's tricks to break free, but the voyants block the doorway.

There's still two ways out of the room. I flee towards the tapestry. Ten ells. Five. Two.

I yank back the tapestry—

They tackle me against the wall. Everything goes white. Then black. Then... skewed, like a badly stitched tapestry where the figures' proportions are all wrong. Silently, they pull me to my feet. Sit me down. I struggle as they tie my arms and legs, binding me to the chair.

I'm bound. The world is silent... I know what comes next.

"No, no, no. Not the cage. Please, no, not the cage."

A slap stings my face. My breath leaves me.

Pressure on my skull, and sound returns. The cage? No…

"Sure you want to do that, sire?" a voyant says. "Lots of magic in that crown thing."

"She stopped screaming, didn't she? Now listen…" My uncle steps into view and sits facing me. "We will discuss this calmly, like two adults."

I tremble.

"I'm glad the cage was so effective, but we're beyond that now. You, *mignon*, seem to be… a witch." His eyes narrow, as if trying to see my Otherlight glow. "Perhaps you were one all along." He glances toward my left hand. "You've been embroidering with your left hand since I released you from the dungeon."

Merde!

"We can't have you passing on that curse to future heirs of Valonia, now can we?" I don't like his smile. "Not to worry. A few adjustments to my plans and all will be just as it should. Don't tell your suitors, though. Our little secret, yes?"

"I won't keep any more of your secrets, Uncle," I grind out.

"I think you will, *mignon*."

"That cage cannot silence me." I hope those words are true.

"A cage may not, but perhaps a castle."

What?

"Roc Ursgueule has always dampened magic, but with the help of my voyants, I've made the entire structure a void of magic. No charm is effective, and no magic can be done. You shall go there tomorrow. On Twelfth Night, you'll be wed. And you will remain in residence until it is time for your demise." He speaks so calmly.

"You cannot possibly…" I shake my head.

"You should be thanking me, *mignon*. It's far more comfortable than the dungeon."

"No. I will not go. I'll not marry any of these men you've duped into joining you. I'll tell them the truth. They'll know you for who you are. For what you are."

"There's always the iron cage."

I can't let that threat silence me. "I'll always speak truth. For myself and for Valonia."

"Valonia isn't yours."

"It is my home. It's in my blood."

"Valonia will never be yours. You will *never* rule!" He leans over me, menacing. He's taut with anger. "You are a witch!"

His spittle sprinkles my face. I can't wipe it away.

"I never thought you should rule. Female *and* deaf. You couldn't talk properly. You were always moving your hands, the left one in particular. Why should the Fates let such a creature be born into our royal line? A deaf girl can't rule. How can she learn the principles of government? How can she guide her people if she can't even hear them? You were broken, cursed since the day you were born. Then I realized why the Fates hadn't let you die in your cradle. You're a challenge. A symbol of how the Perdrix family had gone wrong. If I could right those wrongs, prove myself worthy, the Fates would remove all my obstacles." He leans closer. "Now, when I can finally put you to some practical use, I find you truly *are* a witch, not just the daughter of one." He flicks his fingernail against the crown. "... And consorting with other witches?"

He grasps my left hand. Bends my fingers back. I hold my breath. I won't cry out.

Bends them further. Pain—I can't escape; knots bind my wrists to the chair.

A whimper escapes my lips. He smiles.

No.

I pitch forward, taking the chair with me, and ram him aside. With my legs trussed to chair legs, I hobble toward the barred door. The ropes loosen with each step. Impossible!

My desperation, or my Gift? Perhaps rope's not so different from thread, as Tys said so many months ago.

Six steps. Seven.

A shove and a yank. I fall, wrestling rope and furniture.

Crawling.

My uncle's boot is the last thing I see before everything fades into blackness.

WAKING IS PAINFUL. My eyelids are weighted with stone, but my uncle's voice pounds between my ears.

"... found my daughter stretched out in the corridor... huge knot on her head."

He seems outraged. Distantly, I wonder why.

Other voices join my uncle's. Men's voices. Soft, muddy accents.

"Attacked her, didn't they?" he interrupts. "Leaving her... sending a message."

Pieces of memories float through my mind like jumbled bits of thread. I heave my eyelids open and stare up at the ceiling of the Great Hall. I'm on a pallet or a stretcher.

"All are accounted for, except the Brandt servants. They vanished after they did the deed." My uncle's accusation agitates the men around him. He continues bellowing about the audacity of Brandt's suit, treachery, the need for medical care, when a sharp, unfamiliar sound interrupts him. Everyone rushes to the far side of the room. Twinkling starlight covers the floor, where a stone the size of a man's head rolls to a stop. A rope is tied around it like a tail. It was thrown or catapulted through the great window, shattering it. My uncle crosses the broken glass. He cuts the rope. The stone splits open.

He bends, pulling a folded bit of parchment from it. The other men move forward. My uncle extracts a ring from its folds. His face darkens with anger as he reads. He crumples it in his fist before anyone else has a chance to read it.

"Death to Brandt!"

He stalks to the fireplace and throws the ring and message atop the

Yule log. He stares down at the flames as the parchment flares, burns and crumbles. When it's reduced to ash, he faces us. The suitors stand as if awaiting a whipping. He addresses them first.

"If you want to side with Brandt, you are free to leave. At noon, I ride with my daughter to the fortress of Roc Ursgueule. There, we'll be safe from Brandt spies, and she'll receive the healing she needs. Come with us if you wish."

He turns on his heel and leaves.

No threats. No haranguing. Simply an invitation.

Reichard de Perdrix is skilled in manipulation.

※

I HAVE no opportunity to turn the tables or to escape.

Isabeau gives me a posset. She spoons it into me as I whisper my uncle's plans. She assures me we'll escape my uncle as soon as my headache eases. The tonic is hot and well-spiced. Perhaps that covers the flavor of whatever drug my dear friend uses to augment it.

※

I WAKE IN THE SLEDGE. The creak and jangle of dismounting men surrounds me. Still immobile, I'm well-covered with furs. Other furs beside me are still warm, as if someone just left. I crane my neck, but whatever reason we've stopped is blocked by tall men and their horses.

I look to the mountains to determine our location. We're in a high valley, far from Boispierre. Hammertoe Peak is over my left shoulder. Roc Ursgueule's up ahead, golden in the late afternoon sunshine. We're in the center valley, heading south towards the fortress, but too far away to make it before midwinter sundown.

Isabeau returns to the sledge. She frowns when she sees I am awake.

"My headache's gone," I tell her. "But somehow I doubt you'll help me escape."

She flushes. "We're almost to the hunting lodge. The king says we'll overnight there. Perhaps if you—"

"I've no use of my limbs. How can I escape?"

"The effects were unknown to me," she says as the driver urges the horses forward. We pass a pool of water that should be frozen, but several swans swim away from red-liveried servants trying to net them.

"Is that why we stopped?" I ask.

"More gifts from Brandt." She nods. "A wagon blocked the road at the entrance to the valley with six geese nestled into its straw. Then these swans. Both came with notes. The king let no one else read them." A sidelong glance and a whisper. "He's furious."

She wants sympathy, but I've none to spare. "That's why I wanted to escape, but you and your quest to regain your family's honor made that impossible."

"You knew this was going to happen?" she asks. "You *are* in league with Brandt?"

"Of course I'm not in league with Brandt. I know my uncle."

She pinches her lips together and says nothing. We approach a village, the first I've seen since my release from the dungeon. I can turn my head now, but no matter where I look, there are no people. They must've heard our approach, but no faces peek behind windows or doors. The only signs that folk live here are fresh, snowy footprints and smoke drifting from the chimneys.

"They used to come out and greet us." I speak mostly to myself, but Isabeau answers.

"It's been a long, terrible year."

"Yes, it has."

When we leave the village behind, she asks, "Where've you been, Marguerite?"

Feeling creeps into my fingers and toes. I must piece this together just right. What do I tell her? The truth? She's in my uncle's pocket. What would she believe? "Boispierre dungeon."

"For a year and a half?"

"No. Since a week after the battle of Boispierre, when my uncle had my father killed and took his place as king."

She's silent.

"I guess you believe the news that I've been insane this past year?"

"N-no."

I wait for her explanation. Wait for the burning prickles in my legs to reach my toes. I'll not stay in my uncle's power for long.

My uncle materializes beside our sledge.

"Isabeau, *chérie.*" He smiles as his stallion keeps pace with us. "Don't let my daughter tire herself in these high altitudes. Another posset, I think, shall keep her in good health."

"No," I growl.

But Isabeau doesn't focus on me. Her wide eyes look past me to my uncle. Frightened. Caught. Perhaps screwing up her courage. But I can't wait.

I stand on numb feet and clutch the side of the sledge as I swing my legs toward the opening farthest from my uncle, the side Isabeau half-blocks. Her arms stretch out. Snatch me from the open air that promises freedom. Wrestles me back into my place.

"Traitor," I spit as she pours the syrup down my throat.

※

THE NEXT MORNING, vague memories of the royal hunting lodge are overlaid with the sweetness of Isabeau's medicine and the bitter aftertaste of her betrayal. My uncle carries me to the sledge himself. I want to scream, to escape his touch, but am caged within my own unresponsive body.

Damn Isabeau!

As she sits beside me, tucking the furs securely, I only manage the smallest movements. Flared nostrils and narrowed eyes. She catches my expression, flushes, and looks away. Good. She *should* feel uncomfortable.

My thoughts move back and forth, a shuttle weaving cloth infinitesimally longer with each pass. I'm sure Tys will attempt a rescue. However, judging by the livestock he's littering along the path, any rescue will be unconventional. I've only a few more leagues before I'm trapped for good. I dare not wait on him.

The mounted men, my uncle, suitors, guards and servants, flank us in front and behind, guiding their horses through the snow. Isabeau's the only person within reach. I must either convince her to help me or warn her of what it means to be my enemy. Under the furs covering our laps, I twitch my fingers. My hand shifts. Twitch. Shift. Twitch. My hand reaches the edge of my thigh and slips off.

Onto the upholstered cushion of the sledge.

My fingertips press against the cloth. I close my eyes and exhale. I breathe in again. Slowly. Savoring the crisp taste of snow, pine sap, horse sweat, nervous men. I let those scents, those emotions, twist together like wool fibers tightening into thread. Let the tension hold it together, but I need more. I send my Skeincraft senses through the upholstered cloth to other cloth pressed against it. Clothing that holds a secret tight.

Secrets? Yes. Power. Dampened. Hidden.

The tang of steel. Isabeau's charms, masking her Gift.

I twitch a thread here. Another there. Isabeau shifts her weight. She probably feels something, but I keep my face expressionless, my eyes closed. Another tug with my Skeincraft, and the needle charms slip from her dress. Isabeau jerks. I must act before she does.

I inhale, guiding the power residing in her clothing, ready to shine and tattle, through weave and weft of threads to my palm pressed against the upholstery.

Leave her... Come to me... I'll set you free... Let you...

A hand grips my shoulder, breaking my concentration. I open my eyes. Isabeau, pale and trembling, murmurs something. Speaks more forcefully but is still silent. My coronet was never placed on my head this morning. I stare at her lips.

"Stop. Now."

I harden my jaw and look away. I'll take no more magic from her, but I'll let her wonder what I'll try next.

The siphoned power aches against my skin, ready to be used. That's good, because Roc Ursgueule looms closer. My efforts took longer than expected. I must act now, for in half a league the road will make the final climb. The snow fields up there are steep; the danger of an avalanche is quite real. What a pity if my uncle were to be swept away.

As for me... The last of the tree line grows conveniently close to the road. Tys managed several escapades through branches...

I have no rope.

I have threads in my gown. Still, I'll need a good breeze and the most luck the Fates could ever grant a person. I lift my thoughts to the Heavens, to the Sisters, sleeping during the sun's reign. Remind them of the tiny spiders that send silk on the breeze to catch on branches and make them airborne. It should be impossible, but with all the magic swimming through my veins, I feel capable of anything.

Isabeau grabs my chin and forces me to look at her. That's foolish. Arrogant. Rude.

I narrow my eyes and send the fleabite charm through the threads of the upholstery to her clothing. She jerks. Pulls away.

"Don't. Touch. Me." My tongue is heavy with the drug, but Isabeau understands.

Her lips form, *I'm sorry.* She keeps talking. I stare at her face, but magic floats through my thoughts, unraveling threads. The length of a finger, a hand, a cubit, an ell. They trail from my neckline, sleeves, and shoulders, floating behind me like an invisible train. The speed of the sledge lifts the weightless threads upwards. *Yes, up. More.* That low-hanging branch the riders swerve to avoid will be perfect. I just need a distraction...

The sledge slows. *Stars, no!*

The driver urges the horses to the far side of the road. *No, no, no...*

No! The road curves around a shoulder of rock and disappears into... a tunnel? Stonework forms a massive arch. I shiver as my magic retreats from the trailing, enchanted threads. They're of no use now.

Merde.

The lead horsemen ride into the tunnel side-by-side without ducking. Did my uncle build this last year? An egress from Roc Ursgueule, usable even in mid-winter? Was this how he escaped to switch places with my father? *Seaux de merde.*

My fingers fist. Too little, too late.

The sledge slips into the shadows of the tunnel. Torches light the road every ten ells, but the silent darkness is too much, cousin to my months in the dungeon.

No end visible. A whimper crawls out of my throat.

Isabeau's hand takes mine. I don't want her touch, but I need that hope.

The air grows heavy. Difficult to breathe. I squeeze Isabeau's fingers. She squeezes back. My breath grows more constricted, as if the tunnel is collapsing onto my chest, though the passing torches indicate we still move forward.

I gasp like a landed fish. My unoccupied hand twists my gown; perhaps all my excess magic can loosen this tightness. Yet, as I focus on stretching fibers and thread, an ache spreads throughout my body, as if *I'm* being stretched.

I lift my hands. The ache subsides. I still struggle for breath, but it's not gotten worse. I take a handful of cloth once more. Nothing. I inhale and again focus on stretching. The dull, aching pain returns.

Merde. This was what my uncle meant.

I hold enough magic to free myself but can't use it without pain. I'm caged as sure as if he locked me up. *Damn him!*

The end of the tunnel lightens to twilight and then to gray. I extract my hand from Isabeau's. We emerge into the dazzling snowfield surrounding the fortress of Roc Ursgueule. Breathing is still difficult, but I settle my face into an impassive mask.

Isabeau's not looking at me though; she stares at my uncle. He's already dismounted and is in conference with the majordomo. His expression is livid as he bites off words.

"…Eight head of cattle cannot just disappear."

The majordomo looks miserable, pointing south across the snow-field. "…Ravines…"

My uncle's not appeased. "…Tumble into the ravines… middle of the night? …Secure?"

The majordomo slowly holds up a piece of parchment. My uncle's face turns an astonishing shade of puce as he snatches it, reads it, then storms into the fortress. My rush of glee at his anger is quickly smothered by annoyance with Tys. Why spend efforts on such matters when there's more urgent demands? *My rescue*, for instance.

Isabeau steps out of the sledge, but though my hands and lips can move, I'm still immobile. Two voyants step forward, ready to lift me, but Lord Van Yvren arrives at my side and scoops me up. I'm not sure which is worse until the nobleman slips a bit of parchment into my hand. His expression doesn't change as he carries me up the stairs and deposits me in a tower room. He bows briefly and leaves.

When I'm alone, I pull the parchment into view, unfolding it one-handed. "We regret stepping foot in Valonia. If I can be of assistance, I am your servant."

I crumple the note in my fist. My world is upside down. Magic feels impossible. Friends are enemies. Enemies are allies. Rescuers are absent. I turn my face into my pillow and cry.

⁂

I WAKE to late afternoon sunshine streaming through the narrow windows. I wiggle my fingers and toes. I grin. I can move! The suffo-cating tightness remains, but I'm able to stand and tiptoe across the room. I try the door. Locked. Possibly with a guard on the other side. I check the windows, which are old arrow loops, impossible to squeeze through. They only reveal views of snow-covered rocks and gray sky.

The cold drives me back to the bed. The pillow feels odd. Adjusting it, I find it not full of feathers, but folded wool—bumpy with excess thread. I laugh and pull free familiar lengths of embroidered gray and scarlet wool. Tucked inside is my hoop, needle, scissors, my skeins of thread... and a note.

We leave in two days. –T

I scowl at the note, then press it close to my face, as if I can inhale his essence from the paper and ink. I'll begin with the gray wool. With dozens of men crawling around the castle, I must remain inconspicuous. Invisible. But the first stitch drives pain through my skin, as if I pierced myself with the needle. Right above my heart. I take a steadying breath and shepherd my thoughts as Tanja taught me. More focus, less effort. I've enough magic to spare. Surely, I can...

The bite of the next stitch makes me gasp.

No. I knot the stitch and fold up the gray wool.

Instead, I'll finish recording the names on the scarlet. I'm certain that whatever Tys or I do will go sideways. There is too much chance that I will be killed with my uncle's secrets still tucked within my memory. Broid Cypher uses no magic. I thread my needle again, searching for where I left off. The cloth is uncooperative, the thread easily tangled, but nothing hurts as I slide my needle in and out.

The orange sunlight turns crimson. I move the braziers closer to my bed. The sunset fades to shadows. Still, no one sends for me. No one comes. I keep the haunting, silent darkness at bay with the bright braziers and the names of the dead.

I HAVE no way to mark the time. If there are bells in the fortress, I can't hear them. Throughout the night I stitch the names of Valonia's fallen and wronged. The weight of the Stars presses upon me; just when I think I've exhausted the list, more names whisper through my memory. I add Stefan and Gina's names and feel the pierce of guilt.

Finally, finally, there are no more names. I sit on my bed, needle poised in a sort of stupor, reading all I've recorded.

It's done.

There are more, of course. Others I've never heard of. I'll seek them out in every valley of our kingdom when I leave here. But these are all I know.

The windows are still dark. Perhaps because of the late hour or the trance-like state I've worked in for hours, I pick up the gray wool and thread my needle. Fear sits just under my breastbone. The magic is here too, just under my skin. Pricking the wool, I feel a corresponding prick within. I cry out, then bite down on it. The magic seeps out of me a drop at a time. It's awful and a relief, like the easing of a blister, as the power soaks into the cloth, stitch by stitch.

I select colors at random from my limited selection of skeins. Yet a picture forms under my needle. I peer at the cloth curiously as I work. Yes, the Valon mountains do have that shape and hue. The gray-green pines do clad their slopes just that way. That warmer shade of green hints at spring meadows, where cattle and goats feast. As my needle darts, the pain becomes less a pricking and a more generalized hurt. But I don't stop.

Eventually my arm slows.

The stitches become excruciating. I must be deliberate with where I place each one.

I'm tiring. I've used all my reserves. My fingers ache. My shoulders hurt. My stomach growls. My breath wheezes as if I've climbed a dozen flights of stairs. I have no reserves of magical strength left. I pause long enough to rub my eyes, and find the braziers burned down to ashes, pallid sunlight shining through the arrow slit windows.

Time to turn these cloth panels into a cloak.

The simple stitches do not demand any Skeincraft. I'm not trying to give the cloak extra strength, durability or other qualities. Still, my magical efforts of the night, or just exhaustion, make it difficult to sew a straight seam. I only finish an ell before I fold it and tuck it under my head. Stars know, I can do nothing more.

I wake to vibrations and mid-day sun reflecting off snow.

The door flies open. The chaos and colors of a market fair burst into the room with a horde of Mirvray girls dressed in their best and brightest clothing. They're about my age, ranging from a pale, freckled blonde to a dark-skinned beauty with braids swinging behind her. My mouth falls open. From their midst, Feroulka emerges.

She winks over her shoulder at the guards who peek around the doorframe, her hands moving as she speaks. "… and shut the door so she can dress without you all gawping at her."

The door closes. Feroulka makes a commanding motion. Half the girls linger there, chatting and giggling. They're a curtain of sound, hiding Feroulka's mischief from the guards.

"Are we leaving now?" I ask.

"Not yet," she signs.

I gesture at her companions. "What are you doing, then?"

She grins. "We're the distraction, before the sleight of hand." I frown, and she continues. "A castle full of men, stuck here for months on end. They're hungry for entertainment."

"What *sort* of entertainment?"

"Get your mind out of the pig muck." She smacks my arm. "Dancing and pretty acrobatics. Enough to keep the menfolk blind to other happenings around them. Including this."

She brings a packet from under her skirts—a loaf of oatbread. I tear off a chunk and stuff it in my mouth, signing my thanks.

"A few other things." One by one, the others approach, laying small bundles on my bed. Apples. Nuts. Braided bread. Cheese. Hard-boiled eggs. "Fuel, to keep up your strength. This castle…" She shivers. "Tys told me it suffocates magic, but I didn't understand."

"Tys? You've seen him?"

She nods, tucking food under my pillow. She finds the embroidery, grins, and places the items under the puddling folds of the bed curtains instead. "Eat it all by tonight."

I'm not sure I can.

Feroulka pulls me out of bed. "Come, we've only a few hours to sow more discord and distraction. When we leave, it'll be in opposite directions."

I dress in a gown of vermillion, edged with warm brown, black, and ashy white embroidery. It reminds me of glowing coals buried deep in a brazier. I smile grimly. The truth burning deep within me won't die.

"Where's Tys?"

"Here but caring for other business." She produces my coronet from a fold of her skirt and places it upon my head.

"My coronet! Wait, what other business?"

"You know how many voyants your uncle has crawling around this place? To keep the magic flowing backward in this cursed castle? More than *two dozen*. The charm to impede their Gift can't be forced upon them; it must be offered and accepted."

"There's a charm to—"

"The point is, Tys can only lose so much coin in card games before he falls under suspicion. That's the reason *we're* here."

"Because they'll willingly take money from a pretty girl?"

"Men will take anything from a pretty girl." She twists her wrist and a silk kerchief appears in her palm.

"I saw you pull it from your sleeve."

"In Valonia," a girl with straight black hair speaks up, "none want to be mistaken for a real magic-wielder."

I understand. "What must I do?"

"If we miss any voyant, you must give them a charm." She holds out a few coins and a pair of ladies' gloves. When I reach to take them, Feroulka jerks them back. "You want to lose your ability to sense magic? Remember. Accepting the charms rouses their power."

"Then how...?"

"These coins were given to me by a soldier last month." Feroulka loses her jovial mask. "To pay for... something... I didn't want to give him." She drops the coins in a glove and tucks the gloves under my belt. "The gloves... don't ask."

I shudder. "Feroulka. I'm so sorry—" I search for comforting words but have none.

"Be sure every man that is, or could be, a voyant has a charm." With that, she sails out of the room, the other eight girls sweeping me along in her wake.

CHAPTER TWENTY-ONE

Slipstitch: used to sew a seam from the outside of a
garment or item in which the seam is almost invisible

THE BUNDLE AT MY WAIST IS DIFFICULT TO IGNORE, BUT I
focus on the changes made to Roc Ursgueule since I visited years ago.
The fortress is smaller than Boispierre, and its layout simpler—thick
walls and narrow windows built around a central, circular Great Hall.
When I enter the Hall, though, I gasp. When I visited last, the single-
story walls were open to the sky. Now it has two more stories. Its new
design imitates a classical cathedral; instead of a pitched roof, it has a
domed ceiling with a glass window over the oculus.

Yet it's not a cathedral. It's a rotunda, encircling the original Oak
Throne, still rooted in the center of the room. It's the stump of the
Valonian Oak my ancestor felled two centuries ago, hewn into a
massive chair. With no carved adornments, it looks like the stump it
is. The roots splay out from its base, across the floor tiles, and thrust
into the soil beneath the castle.

As we parade in, my uncle calls from the balcony above. "So, this is
the entertainment the Graaf of Nemeaux sends as a gift?" The suitors
join him at the railing, a circle of men looking down upon us. He

frowns at the guards who finally catch up to us. "Mirvray trollops, dressed better than they deserve. Is this the low regard with which he esteems my daughter?"

Feroulka, if seething, doesn't show it. Instead, she and the others bow deeply. "We seek no quarrel with you, mighty king. We only beg your patience while we perform, and shelter until the sun rises on the morrow."

"You'll not tell me how you arrived?"

The doorways on either side fill with guards and voyants.

"We're obliged to remain silent on this, Your Majesty. However" — Feroulka's mouth quirks— "if you're willing to offer us hospitality for a second night, our previous obligation will be satisfied. We'll happily tell you all you wish to know."

My uncle's eyes narrow. The undercurrent of temptation she offers this hall full of men is obvious. "Do not besmirch this noble gathering with your pandering. You may dance, but that is the limit of my toleration."

"As you command, Your Majesty."

She makes a gesture, and the others fan out around the Hall. A tall Mirvraan woman stomps her foot. The sound rings out across the room. The other girls echo the stomp. She begins a syncopated rhythm that seems simple, but quickly grows complicated. The others offer counterpoint. They move in a circle dance, seen often enough in village squares. Yet their extra flair is something never seen in the villages.

The men at the doorways move into the Hall. The suitors migrate down the wide curved staircase to get a better view. Feroulka and the other women smile up at them winningly. My uncle scowls with suspicion, but the suitors react with interest. Only Lord Van Yvren seems unaffected. His face is pinched; perhaps he's also affected by the void of magic. The voyants, however, don't seem to be bothered.

The rhythm changes. Castanets appear. The dancers twirl, weaving around the pillars that hold up the circular balcony. As they kick and curl around each other, more men migrate to the Hall. They press in behind the guards and voyants.

The nine dancing women mingle with the men. Smiling, brushing up against them. The blonde urges Lord Van Yvren to join them. He affixes a smile, but his steps are heavy. Once all the suitors circle the Oak Throne, the rhythm slows.

The dancers form a circle right up against the throne. The women appear to swim in a circle around the throne as they produce blue and green scarves from their sleeves. The water illusion is complete as the silk floats slowly through the air, blossoms, and floats again. I glimpse no Otherlight. The dancers create the illusions with *legerdemain* alone. Impressive.

Even more impressive is the way the scarves disappear. First one, then five, then all. I catch a few of the suitors' movements, as they tuck the scarves in sleeves or pockets. Lord Van Yvren doesn't accept one. He'll need a gift from me. No sooner does the scarf dance end than the Mirvray produce ribbons. They swirl through the air as the women break ranks and dance throughout the room. The ribbons are distributed among the voyants this time. Two voyants don't take one.

The women continue dancing, slow and fast, until time seems to have no meaning. Eventually, though, they finish, curtsying to thunderous applause and appreciative shouts. When they curtsy to me, I give a nod. Then they're gone, led away by Roc Ursgueule's majordomo.

I position myself near the two voyants without keepsakes and tap them on their shoulders. "Did one of you drop these?" I hold the coins out on my palm.

"I did," they both answer.

"Oh." I pretend to be flummoxed, then offer half to each. "There."

They eye one another but don't argue as they snatch up the money.

I draw near Lord Van Yvren and bump into him, pretending to stumble. "How clumsy of me, I apologize." He catches my elbow then spots the glove I 'dropped.' He retrieves it. When it's offered, I give a bashful smile. "Please, keep it."

Then I turn and make my way to the opposite side of the Hall. As I pass the Oak Throne, however, I trip for real. Reaching out to steady my fall, my palms slap against the wood. At that moment, the scene around me disappears. I see a tall man with an ax striking the Oak Throne when it was a huge tree, filling the Hall. Lifeless bodies lay strewn around its roots. My stomach heaves. One at a time, crowned men pass into my vision. Each sits upon an oak throne. Four have colored auras of Otherlight around them. Gold, green, purple, silver. The next one doesn't. Neither does the next, my grandfather.

The vision shifts, and I'm a child sitting beside the oak throne in Boispierre; my chubby fingers trace the carvings in the wood. My grandfather speaks. *Always live so you can sit comfortably upon the throne. It never pays to do otherwise.*

Then, my uncle sits upon the throne, expression cold. *I don't care how many,* he says, *I want them dead. The Fates cannot bless us until all witch-craft is removed from Valonia.* As he relaxes against the throne, he sits forward again, his face startled. Pained.

Then I'm back in Roc Ursgueule, in the middle of the Great Hall. My knees ache, and my palms are scraped. Guards assist me to my feet. I've heard of magic-wielders having visions, but never expected to have one myself in the middle of Roc Usgueule surrounded by my uncle's men. I barely recover my balance before my uncle bears down on me.

"Poor *mignon!* You mustn't be fully recovered. Come, return to your chambers so you can rest." His words are honey, but his shuttered, angry expression bodes ill.

I don't protest. My mind hums from the strange vision.

When I'm snugly locked into my chamber with a newly stoked brazier, I fill my belly with Feroulka's food and ponder what I saw. I'm still puzzling over it as I spread my items on the coverlet and start constructing my new cloak in earnest. I work steadily, tucking, basting, then sewing it all together. My fingers ache, but I keep going until I place the last knot, letting out a weary laugh. It's finished.

The sun's slipping low on the horizon as I whirl the cloak around my shoulders. Red wool whispers names against my skin, while gray wool shields me from bitter cold and, hopefully, others' gazes. I wish for a mirror, but the closest thing is the glass in the old arrow loops. They offer only a narrow glimpse of my reflection.

Unfortunately, there's no distortion or disappearance of my form.

Merde.

Seaux de Merde.

I heave out a long, weary sigh. I untie the clasps at the front and drag it from my shoulders. I touch the embroidery. It's fine work. I used all the skills I learned from Tanja, Feroulka, Sister Famke, and the Governor. But it's not enough. I'm not enough.

I crumple onto the bed, letting this new misery wash over me. I eat a few nuts. Then an apple. Then cheese with a chunk of bread. The food pushes back my hunger.

My resolution creeps back.

I'm not weak.

It doesn't matter what my uncle says.

Mirvraan. Deaf. Female. Witch. Why do those qualities make me unsuitable?

I want the best for my country. I'm ready to care for the wounds he inflicted upon our people. I'm deaf, but I know things he doesn't want told. I know who he truly is and what he's done. And with this power, this magic he says is antithetical to faith, I can tell the world.

First, though, I must escape.

Tys and Feroulka have their plans, but I'll give invisibility one more try. I pull out a fat skein of blue that seems to fade into the wool. I thread my needle, set my embroidery hoop, and begin. The pain's worse than I remember. I don't stop.

I embroider the obscuring motif, only pausing to nibble more food. I persist as my skin prickles, my joints protest, and my head pounds. Tears fall, for myself and for those who've been hurt, taken. The gray wool absorbs each drop.

I must've fallen asleep, for I open my eyes to pain and a new day.

I make one last knot, clip the final thread, and survey the mottled blue-gray cloth. There's no Otherlight glow. I sigh. It may never be a cloak of invisibility, but it holds the truth on its underside. I must be satisfied with that.

I pull the last gown from the bottom of my trunk. It's dark as pine forests, lined with warm fur at the neck and embroidered with black, red, and gold. It's nowhere near the bright hue of Brandt green, but still dangerous. But if I escape my uncle today, while holding hands with Tys VandeBrandt, this is the dress to wear. I place my coronet on my head, tuck my needle in my cuff, and fasten the cloak around my waist under the skirts, ready for whenever I need it.

WHEN I JOIN the morning meal, everyone seems short-tempered. The other two barons from Hlaandrs, jowly Lord Ostenvoorde, and bowlegged Lord Gelter have been eliminated in the past few days. Only four men remain eligible for my hand, but that's not the reason for the tension. Something's shifted. The suitors have an aura of resentment.

I find an empty seat beside Lord Van Yvren. He has no plate before him, but holds his head, massaging his temples. He barely peeks at me between his fingers, then stands clumsily and sketches a bow.

"My apologies, Your Highness. I'm not currently fit company."

"You seem ill. Would you prefer to rest in your chamber?"

"Unfortunately, that would bring worse consequences."

I can almost taste the truth lying in wait under his words. "How so?"

"Your father forbids it. I cannot jeopardize—" He breaks off.

"Jeopardize what?"

He lifts his head to meet my gaze. His complexion is gray, his pupils shrunken. "Don't you know what price we pay to court, Your Highness?" His mouth twists bitterly. "Don't you know we each have something held over our heads?"

I dare not drop my façade. Still, I need Lord Van Yvren to keep speaking. I pretend to busy myself cutting the meat on my plate while whispering, "I was kept in Boispierre dungeon for nearly a year because I spoke the truth that everyone was blind to."

He sucks in a breath. "The rumor is true."

"If the rumor states I was imprisoned by my uncle, then yes, it is."

A servant approaches with a pitcher. I accept a glass, then turn more obviously toward Lord Van Yvren. "Drink, sir. I'm sure it can only help your headache."

He accepts, brings it to his lips, then asks, "Why did you choose to speak now?"

I gesture at the domed ceiling as if extolling its beauty. "I won't die of suffocation—real or otherwise."

"What if your resistance" —he also gestures toward the oculus— "places someone dear to you in danger?"

"It already has." *Tanja. The Mirvraans. My father. Grandfather. Isabeau. My people.*

His self-control snags, tears. "Your father, or whatever he is," he growls, "took my son. He's not yet five years old. I cannot see him unless I fully cooperate in this... venture."

Questions form on my tongue, then melt at the sight of my uncle.

"Something troubling you, *mignon*?"

"Yes." I scramble for an innocent answer. "Poor Lord Van Yvren has struggled under the burden of a headache for nearly two days, and he's been offered no herbal tonic. I'm aghast at our poor hospitality."

My uncle gives an order to a nearby servant, then maneuvers his chair between Lord Van Yvren and me. "I hope no one's brought contagion from the Lowlands. Thank the Fates no children are here. They're so fragile." Newly aware, I hear the threat. He turns and pats my cheek. "Go show Isabeau your new dress, *mignon*." It's a dismissal.

Isabeau stands on the balcony, observing the company below. I greet each suitor on my way, prolonging the moment before confrontation. All her humming purposefulness seems to have seeped out of her. She won't meet my eyes.

"Isabeau..."

"Look happy," she commands, and fixes a false smile upon her face. "He watches. Right now, I'm telling you that after your own wedding, I shall have one, too." She grips my hands, foretelling terrible news. "I've been betrothed to King Julien of Valonia. I shall be the next queen and… your new step-mother."

Merde. I just stare until she throws her arms around me. Is this her way of making peace?

"Act pleased, excited."

"Your family's honor depends upon it, I know."

She pulls back, giggling shrilly, before hissing, "My family's *lives* depend upon it. The king noticed Cyngetroit lands had fewer witch burnings than other holdings. He'll station a troop of voyants in my home if…" She shakes her head. "I shall not watch my mother and sister burn."

Seaux de merde. I can't forgive her treachery, but…

"That means that whoever marries you won't ever become king of Valonia." Isabeau's voice is heavy through her smile. "The king shall announce our engagement *after* your wedding when Lord Whomever is truly stuck being your husband."

Not for long, if my uncle successfully manages my death. "I'm not sure now how many *want* to make an alliance. They're all being coerced to go behind the Empire's back."

"How do you know?"

I'm not sure Isabeau won't tattle to her new fiancé. "One suitor's been forced to pay court; a family member held against his will. I suspect the others are also under duress. If the treaty's already on shaky ground, the emperor would be apoplectic to know twelve provincial lords had come here."

"He'll find out soon enough." Isabeau's hands fist. "Within a week all will be signed and sealed, wedded and bedded." I would be married to the Duke of Schelte with the broken nose, Baron Van Leuden and his overgrown mustache, gray-bearded Elchin, or unhappy Van Yvren.

"The Fates made us to be more than this," I mutter.

Isabeau looks towards my uncle. "Then the Fates should have made certain *that* twin died."

I nod, but I can't fully trust her.

Below, a servant makes an announcement. It's impossible to understand in the noise.

Isabeau sees my puzzled look. "The latest gift from Mattias Vande-Brandt. Come!" She pulls me to the stairway, and we descend halfway. "He's graduated from fowl to cattle to dancing girls. What else is up his sleeve?"

Tys' note *had* said we'd leave today.

Men march into the room. Nearly a dozen Mirvray. They're well-bundled against the cold but even so, they hold themselves in a way that betrays strength and confidence. Like the dancers, their band is a mix of ethnicities, and each is handsome. From their midst steps Tys. He no longer wears the charm that obscured his face. Every detail is clear, but I doubt the Lowland nobles will recognize Mattias Vande-Brandt. His hair's still dyed dark and cut short, but it's his scar that draws one's gaze. Pink, wrinkled skin spreads across his left cheek from jaw to temple. His ear curls a little askew. I wince in sympathy. Yet the way the other men surround him makes it clear he's not a person to be pitied, but to be honored.

Emotion clogs my throat. I want to wave, to catch his eye. I want to shout, *This is the man I've chosen. This is my Tys.*

I stay silent though, waiting for the lump to melt, pride shining in my eyes.

My uncle stands, imitating respect while establishing his superiority. "So, what has the Brandt whelp sent today? A troupe of actors? A band of wrestlers? This can't be all that remains of the Brandt army, is it?"

The Valonian guards and servants give him the laughter he wants, but the Lowland nobles and the Mirvray men remain straight-faced.

Tys offers a bow not nearly as low as etiquette demands. "Mattias VandeBrandt, Graaf of Nemeaux, sends us to share our talents of mid-air acrobatics."

The room shifts with interest, but my uncle remains stony-faced.

Tys continues. "You played host to our sisters yesterday, yes?"

He waves up at the balcony, where the dancers lean against the balustrade. They wave back. As his gaze slides past me, he winks. My breath stops, my heart gallops, and I make certain not a single muscle in my face twitches.

My uncle is speaking. "... *mid-air* acrobatics? Have you wings hidden under your coats?"

"We'll use ropes," Tys answers. Memories from last year flood my mind.

"Isn't that cheating?" my uncle taunts.

Tys takes two steps forward and focuses on the Lowland nobles sitting around the tables. "No one cheats unless they have to."

Stars! He's poking the hornets' nest.

"But I don't have to," he continues. "None will be disappointed in our performance. I promise." That must be a cue, for the men step away from each other and each toss a coil of rope up to the balcony. The dancers catch them. Tys makes another, deeper bow. "With your permission, of course."

My uncle may not like it, but surely he can read the anticipation of the room. He makes a careless gesture. "Go ahead. We'll watch you break your necks as we feast."

Everyone, from the scullions to the majordomo, crowds into the room to watch. The dancers and acrobats string the ropes across the great circular space, until they crisscross overhead like a spider's web.

A movement at floor level distracts me; a guard, dusted with snow, whispers to my uncle. He nods and follows the man out. My guards have grown lax and are ogling the dancers. I slip through the throng until I enter the empty corridor. They must be outside. I hurriedly pull my new cloak from under the skirts of my gown and fasten it around my shoulders, gray side out. It'll give me warmth and, if not invisibility, less notice than the green gown.

I follow the corridor to the outer door. No guards in sight. I peer outside. The world is white; snow swirls through the air. A knot of men in red and brown guard uniforms mill by the gatehouse. I creep outside, near enough to see what they're doing. Who they're watching.

My uncle stands a stone's throw from the gate, arguing with a man dressed in leather hunting gear and a waist-length cloak of loden-green. The man's face is hidden by the deep cowl of his cloak's hood. Just when my uncle looks ready to hit him, the fellow indicates his satchel; the tension subsides. He claps my uncle on the shoulder and turns toward the fortress.

I hurry back inside, kick the snow off my shoes, then scurry up the narrow staircase and wait in the shadows. My uncle and his guest enter. The man removes his cloak and shakes the snow from it. I bite my lip to keep from gasping. Even from this angle, crouched halfway up the stairs, the visitor looks too much like Tys. He's older by a half-dozen years. His cheeks are angular, his hair a reddish-blond and not as curly. Still, the similarities are uncanny. This must be Tys' brother, Willem.

Willem swings the cloak over his shoulders once more and continues their conversation. "Convince... heel-draggers... Don't worry... my little brother stirred up trouble?"

"Mischief only," my uncle says irritably. "I might've thought you guided his hand, except he was too brash... a flair for pageantry... didn't seem your style."

"I'm hip-deep in Valonia, masquerading... Pageantry must run in the family."

My uncle studies him. "Incognito charms won't work in this fortress. Keep that hood up. Come... signatures, the sooner... can move ahead."

Willem pulls his hood over his head again and follows my uncle toward the Hall. I race up the staircase and go the back way to the rotunda balcony. I slide behind a pillar as the Mirvraan performers descend from their perches on the ropes and file down the grand stair-case. When they're out of sight, I move to the balustrade. Peering through its gaps, I witness my uncle chivvying the Mirvray as well as servants and guards out the lower doors. The only folk left are my uncle, Willem, and the Lowland nobles.

My uncle takes a large scroll from a table. Together, he and Willem unroll it until they stand a few of paces from each other.

"Here is a map of what we can become..." His voice fades as he turns away, pointing to the other side of the vellum, then becomes audible again. "Each man keeps... enough land and men to stand up to the Emperor. No need... trodden under his boot."

"You've never been included in the empire." The bow-legged lord stands. "How is it you think we're oppressed? We have voice in our own councils."

"Led by a woman," my uncle scoffs.

"Led by the emperor's sister, who's strong but fair."

"Are you infants, unable to leave your mother's kitchen?... Take back what's yours?"

Gray bearded Lord Elchen doesn't seem impressed. He barks out arguments. My uncle meets them with audacity, the scope of his scheming both surprising and impressive. The nobles tell him how wealthy and comfortable they are. He offers visions of riches to be had by exploring further. He reminds them of gold, ivory and silver found by previous seafarers.

Van Yvren states Valonia is landlocked. "Perhaps you have a covetous eye?"

My uncle bats away his arguments with logic and temptation. Still, the nobles won't risk the displeasure of the empire. They seem wary of the Duke of Brandt.

The Lord Chancellor takes a swipe. "Can you imagine how the Red Duke could retaliate? He knows our strengths and weaknesses intimately. He's been in our homes, entertained in our castles, traveled our roads and harbors with his army. He'd rout us before the end of spring."

The others agree fervently. Fear of the Red Duke seems to be the core of their resistance. My uncle answers their concerns as Willem says nothing. I trust nothing about his presence here.

"Did you not notice the Duke's son in the running, just as you are?"

Lord Elchen cackles. "Blood runs hot when land and a pretty wife are there for the taking. Yet the boy's not here, nor has his father sent word."

The others back his argument. My uncle raises his voice to counter, but the noblemen speak over him. Their words tangle in my ears until Willem lets his side of the map snap back into my uncle's hands and steps forward. With his hood up, he presents a mysterious figure. The men fall silent.

"Perhaps I'll remind you why you should ally yourselves with the King of Valonia." His Lowland accent is clear, even to me. The men exchange surprised glances as my uncle scrambles to retake control.

"May I introduce the Huntsman, or as you might say, *de Jager*."

The noblemen are alert, like deer who've sensed danger, and only wait to see which direction it comes from.

My uncle continues, half-apologetic. "*He* has possession of your... valuables."

The men leap to their feet, demands and questions snarling around each other.

My uncle holds up a hand for quiet as Willem pulls a folded paper from his satchel. "Lord Chancellor of Aemsterhaven."

The man snatches it eagerly.

"The Duke of Schelt."

He takes his packet with shaking hands.

Willem distributes one to each man. Their masks drop as they pour over the letters. Each includes a lock of hair, a bit of ribbon, or other ephemera that must have personal meaning. My uncle watches their expressions as if studying castle defenses for weakness.

Finally, he claps his hands. "We've delayed long enough. Winter Court is next week, and this declaration of intent" —he holds up another vellum, not nearly so large— "must be given to the Governor, so she may acquiesce before spring when the Red Duke returns with his army. Come, who shall be first?"

CHAPTER TWENTY-TWO

Whipstitch: stitches passing over an edge, in joining,
finishing, or gathering

LORD VAN YVREN STANDS. "THIS IS EXTORTION."

"Extortion implies theft," my uncle says. "I've taken nothing. Only offered opportunity."

"Coercion, then."

"I've threatened nothing. I sent an invitation... *You* arrived at my doorstep. I simply offer another invitation. I'll never force you to accept it." Yet two dozen guards form a half circle around the balcony rim, crossbows aimed at the Lowland nobles' backs.

"That was the ransom though, when you took my son." Van Yvren steps around the table and approaches the two men. He's nearly a head taller than both and well-built. "I was told if I want my son returned without hurt or harm, then I must come for the full twelve days of Yule. I'm fulfilling that."

"I am grateful for your presence... However, my friend" —my uncle points to Willem— "feels strongly that secession from the empire will greatly benefit all your provinces... He created this opportunity... agreement... mutually beneficial."

"You speak out of both sides of your mouth." The jowly one was quiet up until now. "I want truth."

"Truth." My uncle tosses the vellum on the table and crosses to the Oak Throne. He reaches out but doesn't quite touch it. "Seven generations ago, my ancestor wrested Valonia from an incompetent fool who trusted magic and an impregnable fortress... My family increased our borders wider yet..." He paces around the throne, mute, until he faces me again. "For a hundred years we were mighty, until the Haps-Burdian empire encroached... bit by bit."

"You want your own empire?" Van Yvren guesses. "We'll trade one emperor for another."

"No. I won't scramble for land that isn't mine." My uncle's voice rises. "I seek comrades to stand with me against the voracious appetite of Haps-Burdia. It's consuming the whole of our continent. Am I the only one with vision? With foresight? The only one who doesn't wish to dance like a puppet on a string?" He places a hand against his heart. "I love my kingdom. Valonia is beautiful, from her mountains to her lakes to her peaceful valleys...Valonia is my home. It's where I am rooted and from which I gain my strength. I'll do all within my power to defend her and preserve her from danger. Everything I do is because of my love of Valonia."

His face radiates with passion. His words ring true. They echo the feelings of my heart. My throat tightens. I love Valonia, too. I'm willing to do what's necessary to protect and defend her. But not this. Not any of this.

To be so cruel and claim innocence, to stand beside his sworn enemy, calling him friend, when I was willing to sacrifice the person I loved for...

Tys. I must warn him. Willem will recognize him, even with the scar.

Perhaps if we reveal Willem is the Huntsman, that will knock the wind from his sail. No one will trust Reichard or Willem, Brandt or Valonia. They won't sign that agreement. They won't secede, or declare war, or whatever that vellum says comes with signing it.

Now. I'll do it now.

I don't move.

There are two dozen crossbows on the other side of the balcony, and my uncle below.

I swallow against my panic, against the push to act. I breathe as deeply as possible. I'm not responsible for Van Yvren or the others. I'm responsible for Valonia. And I can do more for her and her neighbors if I walk out of this fortress.

Except dozens of guards watch the gates and the walls.

The men argue. Enticement. Refusal. Coercion. Frustration. Convincing. Resentment. By the time the bell rings for Vespers, all the men sign with various levels of mistrust. My uncle opens the Hall's doors wide, demanding a feast to best all the other nights.

I REFASTEN my cloak under my skirts and search for the Mirvray, but they've gone to ground. I return to the Great Hall and walk around the rotunda balcony, worrying over Tys and Willem meeting at the worst possible moment, and scrutinize the newest revelation.

How in the name of Heaven had my uncle met Willem Vande-Brandt, and not murdered him before they cooked up this scheme to destabilize the western quarter of the Haps-Burdian empire? If successful, does my uncle plan to take back Valonia's other lands from Brandt? Certainly, he must, despite his friendly appearance.

I stop pacing. Perhaps Willem has similar plans to claim Valonia for himself. How would his plans move forward with Tys wooing me on his own? If the king's discovered to be false, or is killed, then I'll take my rightful place as queen.

I can remain unmarried and perhaps hold the political reigns, but if I do marry... My cheeks heat, and I begin pacing again. *If* I marry Tys, then aren't I giving Valonia to Brandt one way or another? Tys' father will be pleased, but what about Willem? Will he try to wrest Valonia from me, from Tys and I both? Would he resort to murder? If Tys and I have a child, they will have claim in both lands. If orphaned, that child would inherit Valonia, and be just behind Willem for the duchy of Brandt. It'd be logical if Willem became regent for his niece or nephew.

I hit the stone balustrade with my palm. Valonia won't hang in the balance, now or later. Not because of me.

The Mirvray burst into the Great Hall with exultant shouts. Feroulka sees me, waves, and the entire herd races up the stairway to join me. The women embrace me, offering messages in hand language.

"No matter how good they look, don't eat the poppyseed cakes."

"Be ready to fly."

"After the lullaby."

"Don't even taste the poppyseed cakes."

I hold up a hand and sign, "Are they poisoned?"

"No." Feroulka's fingers fly. "Drugged. One of Gaspar's concoctions, but it won't work until their skin touches the fake snow."

"Snow?"

"It will go everywhere. So…"

"Don't eat the poppyseed cakes," I finish.

"But don't be obvious about it either."

"I can be discreet."

Just then, she shifts, and Tys is in my line of sight as he jogs up the stairs. His close-fitting clothing is well-suited for acrobatics. I wonder if he'll repeat any of his performance from last year, or if this will be something new.

Feroulka pinches my arm and signs, "Discreet about some things. Obvious about others."

I stick out my tongue and move toward Tys.

She grips my sleeve. "Anyone with eyeballs can see the sparks between you two. Don't speak now."

"But his brother is here," I sign.

"Willem? How?"

The noblemen return to the Hall. A lengthy conversation is impossible.

"He's known as the Huntsman. Green cape. Hood up to disguise himself."

She nods and is off, darting into the lower ropes of the cobweb before I can say more. I descend the stairs as she flirts with the first fellow she meets up there. Leaning forward, her signs are barely visible. She laughs, shimmies away along the ratline and returns to the balcony on the far side. Her little escapade draws notice from the men, but nothing more than amused chuckles.

My uncle and Willem join us, and the atmosphere grows uneasy. Willem keeps his face hidden within his cowl and sits at the table's end where no light illuminates his features. The rest of us make small talk as we nibble appetizers and turn our faces upwards.

The Mirvraan entertainment hasn't started in earnest yet. The men roost in various spots among the intersecting ropes overhead. Two juggle apples lazily, occasionally tossing them back and forth. The women sit on the balustrade around the balcony, swinging their legs and attracting gazes from nobles, guards and servants.

The feast truly begins with the presentation of a boar's head, followed by platters of beef, swan, goose, chicken, and small fowl I suspect are pigeon. Last of all comes a platter of roasted pheasant. It's placed before my uncle and he stands to make the first ceremonial cut of meat.

"This particular partridge won't be flying off to any pear trees, here or elsewhere." He smiles with satisfaction as he employs the carving knife and places the white meat on a plate. "Give that to my daughter. She is the one we honor this Yuletide season."

I stare at the plate put before me. Not pheasant. Partridge.

"Go ahead. Eat."

I cut a small piece and put it in my mouth. I chew. It's prepared like *coq au vin*, but I nearly choke. The partridge is *protected* in Valonia. It's the only fowl banned from hunting. It's on our flag. It was killed and roasted and is now in my mouth. I swallow and feel like a traitor.

"Delicious, eh?" He turns to the others. "Who else wants a taste?" He distributes it among the men. Willem especially seems to relish it.

The other meats are carved and served. Delicacies circulate around the table. I take a wide sampling but pretend not to notice the poppy-seed cakes. I've lost my appetite, but I eat heartily. We'll leave Roc Ursgueule tonight, perhaps traveling on foot. I need my strength.

When the Mirvray begin their acrobatics, my shoulders ease. I sit back in my chair, tilt my head, and try to forget about the meal. The men are talented. They leap and tumble across the space, catching themselves at the last possible, exhilarating moment.

Tys takes his place on the ropes. Worried frustration retreats to the far part of my mind.

He doesn't do anything extravagantly different than the other men. Yet his confidence is palpable as he hurtles himself from a column to a rope, to another rope, to another column. Such strength and with seemingly very little effort. It stirs my blood. All the feelings from that Yuletide night a year ago flood through me. I yearn to be up there with him.

The girls, who've been dancing barefoot along the narrow beam of the balustrade, clinking their castanets and twitching their skirts, all hush. Feroulka and another girl, standing on opposite sides of the rotunda balcony, toss slender lengths of fabric out over our heads. One's bright red silk, the other black, a tribute to the Valonian flag. They leap from the balcony, swinging out over our heads, holding nothing but the fabric. They twist in their cloth swings, arms and legs free, looking for all the world like soaring birds. We all gasp and applaud. Then the other girls run out onto the network of ropes. They each meet a partner and begin dancing, if it can be called that. They twist and tumble, holding each other in tight embraces.

Stars, how I want to hold Tys like that, to press against him and not care who watches.

I squint into the cobweb of ropes and count couples. Nine men and women. Tys is nowhere to be seen. No. There he is, near the oculus, on the highest rope of all. He walks alone, holding a long pole weighted with burlap sacks at either end. Against the glare of the candles, white powder drifts downward from the sacks, like flour mist in a mill.

The fake snow.

It's nearly reached the table. The noblemen notice. Some laugh. Then the 'snow' dusts the food and drink and the murmurs grow suspicious. Lord Van Yvren puts a small amount on his finger and delicately tastes it.

"It's sweet." He turns a skeptical gaze upward and calls. "What is this?"

The answer drifts down with more powder. "Mixture of fine-ground flour and sugar. Safe as honey."

Some accept this answer, licking fingers, while others, like my uncle and Willem, blow the dust off their food before eating more. Yet the powder coats everything. I eat and drink, giving confidence to a few suspicious ones to carry on with their own repast.

The Mirvray continue their mid-air antics.

Dessert is brought in, a huge confection of sweetmeats stacked precariously and lit on fire by the majordomo. It's impressive, but the applause is languid. The nobles are relaxed, almost drowsy. Even my uncle appears serene. The time is approaching. I adopt a tranquil expression as I eat my dessert.

The Mirvray women begin a sweet song of love and loss, enhancing the placid mood. The men slow their acrobatics. One song bleeds into the other, and soon the men are slowly swinging on long swaths of cloth as the women descend the stairs, singing a lullaby-like tune. They spread across the floor, twirling leisurely. Feroulka gives me a significant look, incorporating hand language into her dance movements.

"Join us. Up the stairs. Then put on your cloak."

I ease from the table. I join them, mimicking their rhythmic steps. I pass through their ranks to the base of the stairs. We dance up the steps as the girls sing a haunting song of farewell.

When I reach the balcony, I retreat into the shadows. I'm loosening the ties of the cloak around my waist when Isabeau slips out of a nearby chamber.

"Marguerite? What are you doing?"

Panic washes over me. Then I frown. That room's not hers.

"Where've *you* been? Why weren't you at the feast?"

"I was detained." Puffy eyes and trembling mouth tell another tale.

"Isabeau, what happened?"

She pinches her lips in a determined line.

Feroulka motions for me to come. I give a single hand sign. *Wait.*

Isabeau straightens her shoulders. "I've poisoned your father," she mouths. "Or uncle. Whoever he is."

"What?"

"I'll not let him continue to threaten me. I'm finished." She drags me farther from the balcony edge. "I thought I could be his wife. His queen." She swallows. Her eyes are frightened, but her chin is set. "I cannot."

I couldn't trust her before, but… perhaps… "We're escaping. Now. Come with us."

"No." Isabeau steps back. "I must be sure he drinks the wine I left in our… his room."

She says nothing else, but I think I understand. Sympathy wars with calculated planning.

"We've just drugged everyone down there," I tell her. "They'll sleep soon. I doubt my uncle will trust any cup prepared by another after this. He might force *you* to drink it."

Isabeau doesn't seem to hear me. Feroulka signs for me to hurry.

"You'll be safe." I pull on Isabeau's hand, but she jerks away.

"My family won't." Her expression is fierce. "They'll pay the price. I'll see this through."

"If you kill him, you'll lose your magic."

"Magic's done me little good these past eighteen years."

Feroulka draws me away. "She said no. Each must make her own choice."

I look back to Isabeau, but she's already crossing to the stairs.

"Come. Save yourself." Feroulka places the cloak around my shoulders, covering my coronet with the hood. "Save Tys. The besotted fool won't leave unless you're beside him."

She pushes me toward the lowest tightrope. The distant floor is too far away, and the rope is only the width of my biggest toe.

"I can't do this."

"Yes, you can." Tys walks toward me on the rope and holds out his hands. "I'm beside you. Look at me. Nothing else matters right now."

I swallow my fear and lock my gaze with his. I step off the balustrade and onto the tightrope. It's easy to feel through the thin soles of my slippers, but it seems insubstantial. "How can you trust something so thin?"

His grin peeks out, sending my blood skipping. "You trust thread. Even thinner."

I place one foot before another. I'd longed to be up here with him, to feel the exhilaration of flight. Wanted to defy all the elements beside him. Now, I'm full of doubt and fear, knowing my uncle and an unforgiving granite floor await eight ells below.

"You're thinking of all the things that could go wrong." Tys' eyes twinkle. "Let's think of all the things that could go right." He boosts me to a higher rope, and a Mirvray pulls me to my feet. He has a loop of cloth fashioned into a swing, ready for me.

"Think of this as an adventure," Tys says.

"Without blood or danger?" I ask.

"Without blood, anyway." He grabs the swing and leans in close. "A little danger adds to the feeling of adventure, doesn't it?"

My breath catches at his smile. I nod. And lift my lips against his. *Stars!* There's nothing in the world like a kiss from Tys VandeBrandt. My Tys. After a moment, he breaks away.

"Time to fly." He nods to someone and pushes us out into the middle of nothingness. The two of us swing out and upwards.

"How are we...?" My gaze follows the rope to which our swing is attached, to the pulley system affixed just below the oculus. Two fellows hold the other end of the rope, sinking past us towards the floor as we soar upward.

"Pulleys. Ropes. Counterbalance." Tys shrugs. "Basics of sailing life put to good use."

"Impressive." My throat tightens. We're fast approaching the oculus. "Now what?"

"We escape, like rabbits from the fox's den."

We slow. Tys grasps a ledge, pulling himself up. I rise higher. The knot between the rope and the cloth sticks in the opening of the pulley. The swing stops. I carefully step onto the ledge beside Tys, not looking down. I focus on the glass just over our heads. It's thick and framed in brass fittings with a wide hinge on one side the length of Tys' forearm. He raps on the glass and it swings upwards. The Mirvray on the other side offers his hand as Tys boosts me up.

I crawl out onto the top of the fortress. The cold is stunning, as is the view. The full moon soars high, illuminating the wide snow field around us, as well as the broad shoulders and summits of the surrounding mountains. *Stars above!* I've missed my mountains all these months. Nothing compares with their strength and immensity. It dwarfs me and fills me with power all at once. Tys pulls himself out and busies himself on the other side of the oculus.

"*Kleintje…*"

"I'm trying to remember my land."

"It's beautiful."

"And dangerous, but it's *home*."

"We'll return."

I want to believe that. "How do we get down?"

"Over here." I scramble to the other side of the oculus. A cable-thick rope is tied to the brass fittings. It shines with Tys' tell-tale white glow. He produces a device that looks like the pulley we just used, but with handles. "This fits over the rope and you hold here, or you can sit upon it. You'll slide down this rope to the far end. Then we'll cross the ravines and be safe enough in Pranzia."

I nod and follow his directions, getting situated. Other Mirvray emerge from the oculus. They each produce their own sliding devices. Two go ahead of me. I launch off the edge of the great dome of Roc Ursgueule fortress and into the icy darkness of the Valon Mountains.

CHAPTER TWENTY-THREE

Fugitive: dyed colors that are prone to fading when
exposed to sunlight or washing

I'VE NEVER FELT COLD LIKE THIS BEFORE, NOT EVEN IN THE
dungeon of Boispierre. This whipping wind drives all heat from me. It
numbs and invigorates simultaneously. The bulky fortress vanishes
behind me. Fields of moon-kissed snow flee past. I soar onward,
finally plunging between trees into the forest. The darkness feels absolute for a breath or two, then, as my momentum slackens, a clearing
opens before me. I'm still traveling as fast as a trotting horse when the
rope curves upward and slows enough for a Mirvray to leap up and
grab my foot. He brings me to a stop, and I disembark by falling into a
mound of powdery snow.

He pulls me away from the rope as it trembles and hisses. I wait by
the tree line and wrap my cloak around me. Tys flies into the clearing,
his teeth white and shining. He sets foot on the hillside and releases
an exultant laugh as he detaches his device.

When he turns, his posture changes, tenses. "Where's Marguerite?
Did she fall off?"

The fellow who assisted me looks up. "She's here. She's fine." He turns in my direction, then pauses. "Was there a moment ago." The moonlight must be tricking his eyes.

I open my cloak enough to wave my hand. "I'm right here." Tys and the other man draw closer. I pull the hood down, and they both let out a deep breath.

"Now that's some magic, *kleintje*." Tys seems impressed.

"Completely invisible," murmurs the other fellow.

It works! I harnessed invisibility with Skeincraft.

"Yet I saw her soaring toward me on the cable."

"My cloak was blown backward then," I offer. "And it didn't seem to work within Roc Ursgueule. That place…" I shake my head. "I can finally breathe free again." The weighted, suffocating feeling is gone.

Other Mirvray arrive, dropping into the drifted snow.

"Here, we've got heavy cloaks and boots for everyone." Tys gestures for all to gather at the base of a large pine where branches have kept the ground relatively bare. We huddle there, layering on thick woolens and stamping into sturdy boots. I place my cloak over my new layers, but don't put the hood up—that seems to fully acti-vate the magic. Tys goes to the far side of the clearing, ready to untie the cable when the last man arrives. The Mirvray chuckle over how soundly the noblemen were sleeping. Then everyone's head turns.

"What?" I ask.

No one answers. They all run to the cable, peering back towards Roc Ursgueule.

"What is it?" I ask.

Feroulka answers. "The Huntsman."

I have more questions, but the others dash away. Tys stands alone by the cable anchor, doing some sort of magic. A Mirvray sails into view, shouting.

A flare of white Otherlight from Tys' hands. The cable sags, then snaps like a drover's whip. I duck. The cable sweeps through the air, fleeing the clearing. The Mirvraan fellow rolls on the ground, then he's on his feet, racing toward us. Tys snatches my hand, grabs the sack of clothes, and runs. When the fellow catches up, Tys tosses the sack to him.

"Karel, what happened?"

"The Huntsman." The man pants out his story. I only catch bits. "That cloak protected... powder... Georg and I... out the window... then he's climbing the rope like the devil himself... Tried shutting the window... too fast."

Tys shakes his head. "Willem always was quick on the ratlines."

"He took Georg's coaster... shoved him off the roof... close behind me."

"I hope Willem broke his neck," Tys says.

We race towards safety, through the moonlit woods, following the trail left by the Mirvray who went before us. I feel blind, not fully knowing the plan, but for the moment I don't care. I'm with Tys. We escaped my uncle's grasp. We have truth that could ruin him. Soon, we'll set things right for Valonia.

We run until we reach a wide snowfield intermittent with large black rocks. I know, even by moonlight, what we're approaching. The Ravines are massive cracks nearly a furlong deep. The old tales say that when invaders tried to attack this border, centuries ago, the guardians of the mountains shook the earth, dividing the land. It frightened the invaders, and the fissure kept them from returning. It's forty miles long and never less than ten ells across, so any land with an eye on Valonia must find alternative ways to attempt invasion.

"How did you find a way across the ravines?" I gasp as we finally slow our pace.

"Ropes."

Of course. "How much farther?"

"We're close."

Karel stumbles to a halt. "Do you hear that?"

We stop. Tys cocks his head. "No. Can't be." He meets my gaze. "Hounds."

"How can they be on our trail so quickly?" Karel asks.

"Willem must have woken my uncle before he went out the oculus," I say.

Tys looks skyward. "May the Fates torment my half-brother for a *very* long time."

We continue running. Karel gives Tys a worried look. "They'll find the bridges."

"Only the footbridge."

"*Dumbkopf.* If they don't find us, they'll search in earnest… They'll find them before the Governor's in position."

Did I hear wrong? "What's he talking about?" I pant.

"I made three bridges. The Governor has gone through Pranzia with her own forces—"

"What?" *Haps-Burdian troops here?* "You're working with the Governor?"

"When I failed at Boispierre, and learned King Julien was inviting our nobles, I sent to her for help. She knew nothing of it. Her spies had failed her, but she offered to help me. She made an agreement with Pranzia to come through Valonia's back gate, so to speak."

"I can't believe—"

"Was only if we couldn't manage to free you before Twelfth Night. She'll cross the bridges then. Help Van Yvren and the others to stand up to Rotten Reichard or—"

"Or what?" I ask.

"Or else take them into custody and off your hands."

I stop. "I trusted the Governor. I trusted you…" Tys returns to my side. Karel keeps running. I focus on the boy I've trusted with my life, with the truth, with my country. "You invited her to come into my lands? You made a bridge for her? For her army?"

"She's helping."

"Perhaps," I say. "Perhaps not." His eyes dart toward the baying I can't hear. "Tys, you must destroy those bridges."

"What about when the Governor arrives?"

"If she must parley with the men in Roc Ursgueule, rebuild that footbridge you mentioned." I grab his cloak and pull his face close to mine. "But no imperial soldiers."

"As you say." He nods somberly and presses his cold lips to mine. "To bind my word."

I frown. "I hope you didn't seal your promise with the Governor with a kiss, too."

"No." He laughs, then turns serious again. I hear the hounds this time, too. "We must run longer then." We clasp hands once more and follow the tracks of Karel and the other Mirvray.

We reach the footbridge. It's little more than three ropes strung across the ravine. One's a sturdy cable to walk on, the other two are only as thick as a man's finger. They're placed at waist height as a railing of sorts. Only a brave person would trust themselves to this.

"How do we take it apart?"

"I must unbind the knots." His fingers work fast, glowing with his Otherlight. The hounds are gaining, like the nightmare of our first adventure.

"Let me help you." I stand behind him, wrapping my arms around his chest. I press my hands into the folds of his thick woolen jacket. I close my eyes and let the power that fills me flow into the wool threads.

Tys gasps. "I didn't know you could do that."

"Keep working," I mutter into his jacket. His muscles flex and move under the wool. I enjoy it too much and my flow of magic quickens. "Tys?"

"Finished."

I look up in time to see the last rope slip around the trunk of the tree and into the dark chasm. I suck in a shuddering breath. Whatever I just felt holding him, there are no words for it. I silently hold his hand as we run along the edge of the ravine.

Our pace slows now that we're breaking trail. After a while, I ask how far we have to go.

"Still a ways. Had to be sure the Ursgueule guards won't stumble upon it."

"I wish we had a horse."

"Fates, so do I."

Snow seeps into my boots, numbing my toes. The wind digs its claws into the gaps of my clothing and scrapes my fingers until they ache. I pull the hood across my nose and mouth, so breathing won't hurt so much.

"This was a stupid choice," I say. "We should've gone across the first bridge, undone it, then moved on to the other two."

He nods in agreement. We keep going. No other choice now. The hounds have our scent and we'll not be safe until we cross the ravine. My teeth are chattering when Tys points.

"There."

The hounds seem to be right behind us. Tys hears hoofbeats. We hurry to the large boulders that anchor the bridge. This one is wider, with wooden planks. Three men, shoulder-to-shoulder, could cross at once. We scurry out upon it, our hands tightly clasped. The bridge sways with our movement. I yelp and reach for the rope railing. Tys' hand tightens, even as he glows brighter with Otherlight. The bridge steadies as we continue onward.

A shout from the Valonian side. The air hums. An arrow lodges in the wooden plank just in front of my feet. I stop.

"Lucky shot." Tys pulls me forward. "Even with the moonlight, they're shooting blind."

"Tys," I hiss, "you glow like a lighthouse. Any voyant with good aim can hit you."

"We gave charms to every voyant in Roc Ursgueule, and a few besides."

"What about Willem?"

Tys nearly stumbles.

"Is he a voyant?"

No answer. He only pulls me quickly along the bridge planks. Until he twists. Cries out.

"Tys!"

An arrow shaft protrudes from his back. *Fates and all the stars above!*

"Tys!" I pull him to his feet. "We're almost there." I ignore the location of the arrow. Pretend his mouth isn't opening and shutting like a landed fish. I pull him forward. We just need a good healer, like Gaspar. Then Tys will be fine.

"Get on the far side," Tys signs. "Use your cloak. They won't see you."

"I won't abandon you."

"I'll cut the ropes from here."

"You'll fall."

"The ropes will save me."

"Mattias VandeBrandt," I hiss. "I'll not lose you again."

A shadow of his rakish grin peeks out. "You won't." He presses a kiss to my palm. "Go."

I do.

I go.

I leave him.

I stand on the Pranzian side of the ravine, wrapped in my cloak, watching him glow brighter. I squint against the Otherlight. *Please*, I pray, *keep him safe—*

He sags against the bridge. His Otherlight falters. Another arrow?

"Tys."

"Stay there," he signs.

The hounds arrive, but they won't venture onto the bridge. The men, though, have no qualms. They march out to the middle, where Tys lies. Where the bridge is weakened. I hold my breath, waiting for the bridge to break, for the ropes to save Tys while the others fall.

It doesn't happen.

The men haul Tys into their arms and off the bridge... to the Valonian side.

Merde.

CHAPTER TWENTY-FOUR

Stumpwork: a style of embroidery in which the
stitched figures are raised from the surface of the
work to form a three-dimensional effect

I WANT TO CRY. I WANT TO CURSE AND STAMP MY FEET. I DO neither.

I take one step forward and then another. Imagining I'm light as silk thread, I walk across the bridge. I walk past the guards who now stand sentry at the ravine's edge.

The hounds scent me, though. They turn as I approach.

My heart hammers. Nothing's woven into my cloak to mask my odor.

I pause, breathing as gently as a butterfly on a milkweed pod. Tys is on the other side of the pack of dogs. I wait. Watch. Willem's there, his hood thrown back, bow in hand. My uncle sits unsteadily on his mount, arguing and looking down his nose at him. Servants toss Tys over a horse's saddle like a corpse.

Seven Sisters, I shout my thoughts to the glittering Heavens. *If you only answer one prayer of mine, please let him live.*

The houndmaster moves his rowdy charges farther from the ravine. Upwind. I take the opportunity to approach the three men who interest me most. As I pass the hound pack, I gather my cloak about me, hoping to do the same with my scent. I think of snow and its crisp, odorless quality, let that sense fill me as I walk carefully past.

One long arrow protrudes from Tys' back. Another protrudes from his leg, just above the back of his knee. His hose is dark and damp with blood. Several drops stain the snow around the horse's hooves. Tys groans. He's alive. Tears freeze on my cheeks as I examine his wounds, wishing I had the gift of healing.

I poured all my Gift and skill into this cloak of invisibility and it can save only one.

It feels so useless.

Willem and my uncle stop arguing and start barking orders. Without second thoughts, I hoist myself up onto Tys' horse. I make sure my cloak covers all of me from feet to forehead.

Tys detects my presence. "*Kleintje?*"

"Shhh."

The men start riding, and our mount follows, pulled along by a lead rope. If I can just twitch it out of that soldier's hand… I lean over Tys' body, but I'm still the small girl I've always been. My arm is too short. Tys reaches out, gasps. Tries again.

"Don't," I whisper.

I direct the horse with my knees, nudging it around the outside of the group. I dig my heels into its flank, pulling the bridle sideways. We break away. I urge the horse forward, clinging to Tys with one hand and keeping my cloak tight around me with the other. We don't make it far before a guard catches up, snags the bridle with his long arms, and leads our mount from the mouth of the dark woods back to the party heading toward the fortress.

Stars, can I have one *night of good fortune?*

I could leap from the horse's back, but I can't take Tys with me. He can't walk, and I can't carry him. Landing wrong, the arrow might be pushed further in, puncturing his lung, if it's not already. I can save myself or I can doom myself to whatever the Fates have in store for him.

I've already chosen—since the moment I walked off that bridge. I stay with Tys.

I sense when we enter to the domain of Roc Ursgueule; the suffocating weight returns. My invisibility cloak might keep me from being noticed, but not from sight. Our horse is the last in the party. I wait until we slow, passing under the gatehouse. I squeeze Tys' hand as I slip off the horse's back and into the shadows. I watch. Wait. My uncle leans against his horse, still unsteady from the drugged cakes and powdered sugar, giving commands. He gestures at Tys, then at the tower where I slept.

Willem negates that order. "His magic is with ropes and cords... vanishing into thin air. Don't put him in the tower." My uncle clearly doesn't like to be corrected, but Willem continues, pointing to the ground. "...You have a dungeon? My brother's afraid of dark, enclosed spaces."

"Afraid? But will he escape?"

Willem smacks Tys' head as he walks past the horse. "He's used witchcraft to escape towers, traps, even ships in the middle of the ocean. Yet, whenever I've put him underground, there he stays."

My uncle studies his partner with an odd look. "You regularly imprison your brother?"

"*Half*-brother." Willem steps closer. "He's a witch. Don't you regularly burn those?"

They bicker until Willem grabs Tys' hair, lifting his head to face my uncle, and speaks directly. "Send for a healer. I want Mattje incapacitated, not dead."

My uncle stares him down, then nods. Men remove Tys from the horse and haul him by his arms and legs down the stairs that lead to the dungeon. My heart shrivels at the thought of Tys finding himself there, but I turn away and go to the kitchens. I loiter in the corner until I spy the items I need. Food, of course, but also herbs for healing. Again, I wish for more knowledge and skill. I wait until all the kitchen workers are busy with their tasks, then glide behind and between them, gathering the items I need. I'm almost finished when a tall cook takes a step backward.

"My apologies," he sputters as he turns. His hazel eyes look down into mine. The man seems familiar, but I can't place him. I nod and say naught. I walk out of the kitchen, taking nothing more than what I already have in the sack beneath my cloak.

I tremble, as if I can feel the Fates fully turn their attention on me.

I walk out into the courtyard and look up. The Pleiades constellation gleams directly overhead. I want to shout at them, to shrink from their notice, and to plead for their help. I tremble. I face another dungeon—the gullet of the beast that has already gnawed my bones. I stare into the Heavens as grooms and houndsmen pass around me, as the fear swirls. Yet the light of the Stars strikes an answering spark within me.

I am here because of the Gifts you endowed upon me. I am here because of the love I have for my grandfather, my father, my friends, my land, and for Tys. This is who I am. I know the trueness of that love and that it demands action. I will do whatever is necessary to be a blessing to them and to bring goodness into the world through my Gifts. I cast off my fear. Let me be a Light shining in the darkness.

I walk forward across the courtyard. The men don't seem to see me, but they part nonetheless. I pass the sentries and descend the stairwell into the dungeon. Memory of starlight holds me steady against the darkness. The door is new, a replacement for the one destroyed two centuries ago. No lock. Only a large plank placed in metal fittings bars the door.

I remove it. Set it aside. Enter.

It doesn't smell like a prison, perhaps because it hasn't been used in so long. There are no cells or ironwork bars separating one part from another. The dungeon is cavern-like, with only enormous footings supporting the castle above interrupting the open space. Tys sprawls beside the moss-covered one in the center. In a few places, the stone's tumbled away, and dirt spills in.

I take the only torch and go to his side. He lies on his stomach.

Someone's tended his wounds. The arrows have been removed, and blood-soaked bandages wrap around his back and leg. I'm no healer, but I know a man can die from blood loss.

"Tys."

A low moan only, yet his breathing seems normal. Perhaps the arrow did less damage than I thought. I brace the torch against the footings, then pour strong cider down Tys' throat. Retrieving a needle from my sleeve cuff, I pass it through the torch flame before threading it. I ready the sack's contents within easy reach. Take a deep breath.

"This will hurt."

I peel away the bandages and his shirt. Blood leaks from his wound. I press the hem of my cloak against it. The bleeding finally slows enough that I can stitch it shut. Taking a bundle of leaves from my stash, I press them against the wound. He needs a new bandage. I pull at my skirt but pause. I need more than ordinary cloth.

I need cloth heavy with magic.

I untie my cloak, holding it as I war with myself. Then, with the kitchen knife, I cut the seams binding gray and scarlet wool together. Loss envelopes me. I still have my record. I'm only sacrificing the invisibility portion. Perhaps the blood stains will wash out. I can restitch it...

"But there'll never be another Tys Owlymirror, greatest acrobat south of the North Sea," I mutter as I cut the seam down the middle of the gray wool.

I bind one long piece around his chest and fasten it tight. I blink away tears and focus on his leg. The arrow sliced an important bit of muscle. He'll need crutches before it heals. I mop the blood, stitch it up, then wrap it. I finger both bandages, letting my thoughts spin healing into the fibers, until I grow drowsy and can't resist collapsing beside Tys.

My hand curls around his chest and rests on the bandage.

I WAKE TO A CARESS. Fingers slide down my cheek and cup my chin. I open my eyes. Tys smiles down into my face.

"Brave *kleintje*."

He brushes a tendril of root away from my hair and kisses my nose. I tilt my face upward for a real kiss. He obliges me. Thoroughly. I sigh.

"Now, how to leave this hell-hole?" His expression is taut, but he's not petrified.

"I have no more invisibility cloak."

"Noticed that." He plants a soft kiss on my swollen lips. "Thank you."

I collect my thoughts from where they scattered. "I left the door unbarred."

"Thought you'd been tossed in here with me."

"I snuck in."

He lets out a shaky breath. "When we've escaped, I might call you a froth-headed, foolish girl. Don't believe me. Braver than the stars, you are." Another thorough kiss warms me to my toes as I help him to his feet. He grimaces.

"Fates, that hurts!" Still, he hobbles beside me.

When we reach the door, he leans against the wall, his face pale and sweaty. I pull the door handle. It moves, but only the width of my smallest finger. Tys chews his lip. I suggest banging on the door until the sentries come to check. Tys shakes his head.

"The torch is almost burnt down," I say. "We'll ask them for more light."

"Wicked Willem will take the torch all the sooner."

I rub my temples, calling myself seven kinds of fool.

Tys straightens. "Get the gray hood of your cloak."

I do, also bringing the sack and torch.

"Thread and rope are our *modus operandi*. Try to use them somehow to shift the bar."

We slip cloth and twine under the door. The distance is too far; the gap between the door and its frame too narrow. We empty the sack, searching for any useful items. A deep vibration rattles the ground under our feet. The stone walls ripple. I wrap my arms around Tys as the entire dungeon shakes, trembles, then stills. The air dims, tasting of soil and dust.

I've heard of earthquakes but never experienced one before.

Tys tries the door. It doesn't budge. He raises his fist and pounds on it. "Hey! Hey there, sentries!" He turns to me, his eyes wide and dilated. "When Willem opens the door, hide behind those far footings. No matter *what* happens, don't come out. When his fun is finished, Willem will leave. That's how his games always work. We'll crawl out."

He's bridling his panic, but it'll break loose soon, trampling his dignity.

"I won't let him hurt you any further." I keep my voice calm.

"Marguerite. Willem's capable of… no idea… He…"

"Breathe," I remind him. "Right now, he has other plans. Other victims. The family members of those twelve men up there. You're not his focus." I tell him of the ransoms that drove the Lowlander nobles to accept my uncle's invitation. His breathing slows. He limps from the door, back to the center of the dungeon.

"That's good for them. They won't face immediate charges of treason from the Governor if she crosses my bridge. Rotten Reichard and Wicked Willem are to blame. She'll punish them."

I avoid the roots that now protrude from more cracks in the footings. "She has no authority over my uncle. What can she do?"

"He's an ordained Bishop-Princep. She'll hand him over to the Seer of Stars."

"The Seer is hundreds of leagues away." I brush away a hairy root dangling before my face, following Tys as he hobbles around the dungeon, talking of transportation of my uncle or the Seer. We circle back toward the door. Tys tries it again. It doesn't move. He lets out a long, juddering breath.

My gaze is on the central footing, else I'd have missed it. Three of the newly exposed roots flutter, as if Tys' breath traveled all the way across the dungeon to blow against them. The back of my neck prickles.

"Tys?" I put a hand on his arm before he returns to the center of the dungeon. He gives me a questioning look. I point to the roots. "Watch those." I blow a puff of air, as if trying to enliven a shovel full of coals.

The roots shiver, then uncurl their tips toward us, as if reaching, seeking.

"What in all the levels of–"

"It's the Valonian Oak," I breathe.

"I thought that was a throne."

"It is. Seven thrones. Before that, it was a tree. It grew in the middle of Roc Ursgueule before one of my ancestors hewed it down and made the other six thrones. When I've touched its wood, I've felt magic… seen things."

Tys shifts to look at me. "By all the suckled Sisters–"

I smack his arm. "Stop swearing."

"You never said *anything* about–"

"You're in the presence of something powerful."

He studies the roots again. They wave now, beckoning. I take a step forward. Tys grabs my arm. "You think it's safe?"

"My grandfather said it pricks those who rule with a black heart. It's impossible to lie in its presence, and my uncle sits uncomfortably upon it."

Tys doesn't argue further, but slips his hand into mine. Together, we slowly approach the waving roots. All the hairs on my arms stand tall. I'm in the presence of something older and more powerful than I can explain.

"*Kleintje.*" Tys tightens his grip. His face is taut. His arm and bandaged leg half-lift toward the tree roots. "Your embroidery. My knots." His cord bracelets gather tight against the bones of his wrist, ready to slip off as soon as he relaxes his hand. "It's hungry for magic."

I won't fear it.

"Think it caused the earthquake?" he asks.

"Tys. I'm trying to be brave, and you're not helping."

"Let's not sacrifice anything we don't need to. Especially you. I can't sacrifice you."

"I must communicate with it, Tys. Just… don't let go."

He twines his fingers through mine and nods.

I step forward and stretch out my left hand. The roots wrap like tendrils around my fingers. Up my arm. One snakes around my waist and brings me closer to the central footing.

"Stars above!" Tys tightens his grip and steps closer. "Marguerite—"

His voice fades. My mind fills with images. A vision. *Colors, textures. Embroidery. A tapestry. I'm inside a tapestry world. I see tangles and knots, the beauty and harmony of the stitches. I see everything. The history of my land. The land that's been for eons before anyone ever called it Valonia. I witness folk who lived in harmony with the stars and the seasons and the magic rich within this fold of the mountains. Sometimes the magic was abused by prideful women and selfish men. I watch people cycle through these ebbs and flows. The tapestry wrinkles, folds, and I stand in the branches of a tree overlooking a village square. I witness five women herded to the center. They glow brightly with Otherlight colors. Their trial is brief, their death longer and more ghastly. Their children stand beneath my branches, watching with crumpled faces. Their husbands are pressed against my trunk, held back with pikes.*

The horror of the scene opens all my scabbed-over wounds.

"Noooooo. No. No. No," I sob. *My agony pours out like late-winter sap. I'm a powerless witness.* "What do I do? How do I fix this? How do I heal?"

My roots are tainted with the blood of those men, the tears of those children, the ashes of those women. They call for justice.

The wind murmurs through my leaves, telling of a girl. A girl of the blood that did this sin. Yet she did not sin against me. She knows the names of these women, these children, these men. She uses her Star-endowed Gift to stitch their names upon her garments. She says their names. She remembers their stories. She knows their pain. She suffered under the same persecutor. She seeks justice.

Where is that girl? Can she be found? Has she been found? Am I her?

The fingers of the roots question my skin, tangle in my hair, rummage in the folds of my clothing, trying to find the truth.

"I am she." A whisper, but the tree hears me. It trembles the roots of the mountain we stand upon. "The names are here. I embroidered them into my cloak."

I turn my attention from the tree to Tys. He anchors me to this place with his grasp. I open my eyes. There he is, the face I love. His eyes are wide, staring at me.

"Tys?"

Half a dozen roots explore his skin, but he doesn't seem to notice. "You're so... bright."

My mind is still caught in the vision. "We must help Valonia remember."

"Remember what?"

"The terrible things that we've done."

"What'd we do?"

"Not you and me, the Valonian people. We let someone frighten us into allowing our mothers to be murdered. We let fear tear our families and our villages apart. Our country is in tatters. We must mend it."

He opens his mouth to protest, to state he isn't Valonian.

"We must mend *our* country," I say.

His face softens. "How?"

"My cloak. I stitched the names of my uncle's victims into it. We must tell those names to the tree." It sounds ridiculous, but Tys nods.

I unravel the remaining cloth of the hood while he knots those strands of oak-dyed wool to the exposed tree roots and each other. This is the foundation. I whisper all the things I love about Valonia. The waterfalls and wildflowers, the crisp snow and gorgeous sunsets, the tall trees and the smell of a brewing storm. When it resembles a monstrous cobweb, we switch roles. Tys deconstructs the cloth, telling me how Valonia looks to a stranger, learning to love her, while I weave the strands until it becomes a strange, primeval cloth.

We start reading the names from my cloak. Tys catches on to Broid

Cypher quickly, so he reads them while I stitch their initials into the rooty weave. I tell what I know of each person's imprisonment or punishment, while he picks colored threads from his bandages for me to use.

"Should never have happened," he says after each one.

Each time, I respond, "Never in Valonia. Never in any land."

Tys says the wind whistles through cracks in the foundation. He says it sounds like the piping of a funeral dirge. As we work, the oppressive constriction that's been present since our arrival eases, and the keening wind grows loud enough I can hear its mournful accompaniment. We work on, until Tys reads the last name.

I stare at the strange tapestry we made.

"We done now?" Tys asks.

I prod at my inner feelings that have led us this far. "Not… yet."

"What do you need?" Tys kneels beside me, his eyelids at half-mast. Exhaustion pulls at me, too, yet I'm not finished.

"Just hold me."

Tys kneels behind me, wrapping his arms around my waist, resting his head against my shoulder. I taste his magic as it flows through the weave of my clothing and into my skin. The scent of salt and free wind, the sweet taste of pears and the laughter of pine trees twist together. Hope and longing pumps through my veins, diluting my grief, his magic mixing with mine. I clutch roots and threads. Pale blue Otherlight slips from my fingertips into the cloth, creating something new. Unmaking something else.

We stay there until our legs grow numb. I give our handiwork a little pat, and we stretch out on my red cloak to sleep.

I WAKE to the glare of sunlight.

I blink and sit up. "Tys—the dungeon—there's a way out!" I stare at our surroundings and pat the hand that snugs my waist close to his. "Tys, you must see this."

We're cradled in a web of roots, cloth and thread seven times as large as anything we did yesterday. Long tendrils of roots wrap around Tys' thigh and chest, and the remains of the invisibility cloak bandages are nowhere to be seen. Other roots tangle into a pillow-like form under his scarred cheek and tangle in his hair, which lost the dark dye and seems to have grown an inch overnight. I'm certain the roots are benevolent; still, it's startling. And Tys doesn't wake.

I retrieve my coronet, then reach out toward the largest mass and stroke it. The roots tangle around my fingers lightly, the way two deaf-blind nornes at St. Beatricia's signed into each other's hands.

"We must leave," I sign to the tree. It should seem strange, yet it feels perfectly natural. The memory of yesterday's vision is clear and fresh. I know the tree has thoughts. It has power. It can communicate when it wishes. "Thank you for letting us make restitution on behalf of my... family."

The roots undulate in a way that could be a nod or a shrug or perhaps just a wakening jostle for Tys. He stirs. Stretches. Squints into the glory of the sunlight. "Escape's possible?"

"I suspect help from the Valonian Oak." My words feel different. My tongue. The damage in my mouth from my uncle's cage is... healed.

Tys eases himself to his feet. The roots relinquish him, like a mother releasing her baby taking his first steps. He rolls his shoulders, bends his knees, testing his strength.

"My wounds!" He studies the Oak's roots, then bows. "Thousand thanks." He turns a wondrous smile at me, then touches his cheek. "It doesn't hurt when I smile." The scar looks the same. His fingers explore as far as his ear. It still curls forward, shrunken.

"Perhaps, if I'd let you sleep longer," I say, "the Oak could have repaired it further."

"Don't apologize." He gives me a brief kiss, then turns to the mass of roots and thread. He bows again, more deeply. "It's more than I deserve."

"A thousand thanks." I give the roots a fond tug as they curl around my left hand. I flex those fingers, deformed since I was four years old, and laugh. It still looks wrong, unlike my whole right hand, but the pain and stiffness I've grown used to is practically gone. I give my own heartfelt curtsy. The roots undulate as they did before and then retreat into the massive column of the footings, thread, and all.

I stand, breathless. In awe.

The Oak left something behind, though, at the base of the column. Half hidden in shadow is a wreath of roots surrounding a squat, round box. We peer at the items, then Tys laughs and snatches up the wreath.

"It's rope." He pulls one end free. "A rope of tree roots."

The box is burled oak, mottled with irregular swirls of gold, brown and black. I open it and gasp. A fat skein of black wool thread curls against the gray felted lining. Tucked into the lining are three needles of different lengths, each made of slender, golden wood. I touch one, and a shiver of magic runs through my body.

"Thank you," I whisper. "A thousand, thousand thanks."

I shake out my scarlet cloak and fasten it around my neck, then join Tys at the opening. It's just wide enough for a person. On the other side, we discover why the Oak gave Tys a rope. The mountainside that once surrounded this side of Roc Ursgueule has fallen away. Half a furlong of empty air hangs between us and the rubble below. Above, little is visible past the curve of the fortress walls.

Tys considers the stone wall and the rope in his hands, then nods. He steps back and twirls the end. He gives the rope all his thought. Even in the morning sunlight, Otherlight sparks through him. The rope soars until the end tangles around a jutted stone. I tuck my box of needles into my cloak's hood. Tys wraps his rope around me, then around himself, snugging us close and tight. His breath warms my cheek as he smiles.

"Marguerite de Perdrix, you're a bewitching girl. Never do I want to part from you." The humor in his expression melts into an honesty that's achingly vulnerable. "Say we can be together for always?"

"Until the stars fall from the sky and the last tree withers."

And with that, Tys grins in the cocky, brilliant way that first caught my eye in Tillroux square. "Then come fly with me."

We kick off the wall and make our way up and around the stone fortress of Roc Ursgueule with nothing but a root rope, each other, and magic.

CHAPTER TWENTY-FIVE

Whitework: monochromatic embroidery in which
white thread is used on white cloth; the texture of the
stitches as well as moving aside or removing base
threads create the pattern

WE ARRIVE AT THE TOP OF THE FORTRESS WALL TO FIND NO guards within a stone's throw. Everyone in Valonian livery is clustered on the far side of Roc Ursgueule, pikes and trebuchets ready. Tys stows his rope and we hurry forward. As we run, thunder rumbles, though the sky is clear. Tys grabs my hand.

"Drums." He points south, towards the ravines.

"The Governor?"

Tys' mouth is a grim line. "The bridges were never unfastened."

When we reach the tower, joining the west and south walls, I feel the vibrations of the drums as well. We peer over the parapet. The snowfields beyond are filled with an army. They don't wear Brandt green and black, but the gold and chestnut of the Haps-Burdian Empire. The drums reach a crescendo, then stop. The sudden stillness seems too quiet. A horse and rider emerge from their ranks.

"They convinced her horse to cross that bridge?" Tys signs.

I squint. Yes, a woman sits upon it. She's impressive, wrapped in her deep golden cloak that drapes over the horse's flanks. Three soldiers come forward, carrying the white parley flag. They march to the gate of Roc Ursgueule as the Governor looks on.

"We should do something," I sign. Tys shakes his head.

"Hear her terms. Know what she offers—and threatens—before we act."

The white flag stops within arrow range. The central soldier produces a brass speaking trumpet and lists the demands of the Haps-Burdian Empire. Tys interprets for me. First is the release of 'all people subject to Imperial laws.'

"The suitors," I sign.

"And their servants."

The demands continue. "To recompense the insult of holding fealty-sworn men against their will, you shall give the city of Ligeron and its environs to the Emperor of Haps-Burdia."

Heated discussion erupts on the adjacent wall. The men shift, and there's my uncle and Willem, side by side. Tys' brother once again wears his hood up to disguise himself.

Tys continues interpreting the Governor's demands. "If these are not met before the sun's zenith on this day, it's understood the Kingdom of Valonia purposefully offers insult and discourtesy to its neighbor. If the ruler of Valonia doubts the retribution given to those who offend the House of Haps-Burdia, we respectfully remind him of the current state of Cromacia, Temegovia, the lands of the Dauphin of Savonie..." Tys struggles signing all the lands and abbreviates it. "... and so forth. Do not test our Imperial will, or your country will suffer."

My uncle's not pleased, but not intimidated either. He calls down to the courtyard. Servants scurry. He and Willem confer. Someone brings a speaking trumpet. Another brings a tight roll of vellum.

"We offer our compliments to Her Excellency for her unparalleled but unnecessary military action." Tys interprets my uncle's words. "The men she refers to have broken fealty with the Emperor of their own accord. They dine in comfort at my table. They sleep in soft beds and have been offered the finest entertainment. Her Excellency must be misinformed."

His flowery words soon lose their substance. Tys signs polite words but shows mocking expressions, giving the message a double entendre.

"That's what he's saying?" I ask. "How he's saying it?" Tys nods and continues.

"There is danger in my mountains and ravines that you've not planned for. All you can bring across those fragile bridges are men and a few horses. Cannon, siege-engine, trebuchet... all are too heavy for ropes and sticks. So, this" —Reichard gestures to the ranks of gold-uniformed men— "must be all you have. No more than four hundred men who've been up all night crossing into my kingdom. They're exhausted, freezing, unused to the brutality of my mountains.

"It doesn't matter if you outnumber us two-to-one or ten-to-one. This fortress has stood for six hundred years and will stand for another six hundred. Nothing you can tote across those bridges can damage it. Feel free to pitch your tents and freeze. You'll have an unpleasant siege."

He lowers the speaking horn and Tys lowers his hands until the Haps-Burdian messenger speaks. "Is that your complete answer?"

"You want more?" My uncle snatches up the speaking horn again and shouts down to the Governor. "How dare you, a woman, the *sister* of the emperor, try to threaten me? Don't you know your place? Your brother should have married you off again when your first husband was fool enough to get himself killed. Perhaps no one wanted you." Tys struggles to keep up with the rapid speech. The insults descend into vulgarity. Tys' face flames as he repeats threats centering around the Governor's womanhood and all the ways a man could hurt or defile her.

I motion for Tys to stop. I stare at my uncle. His face contorts as he shouts through the speaking trumpet. It's as if all the anger he's hidden beneath his fine manners finally bursts from him like pus from a boil. I close my eyes. Tys' arm wraps around my shoulder.

A moment later, he pulls back. I open my eyes to find Tys interpreting once more.

"Perhaps you need a little help remembering your place." My uncle snatches the vellum from a servant and an arrow from a nearby archer. He wraps the declaration around the arrow shaft. "Tie it," he commands, giving it back to the archer. "Shoot. Don't kill anyone. Yet."

The arrow arches over the walls and plants itself in the snow at the soldiers' feet.

My uncle makes one more vile suggestion as to how soldiers should treat a female commander. "If none of you are man enough, then start with that," my uncle shouts one last time into the speaking horn, then turns away, giving orders. "Post archers along the wall. Keep the pikemen in reserve. Make sure the Lowlanders are secured."

"And what of my brother?" Willem asks. My uncle shrugs.

"If we can't get in, he can't get out. Let him stew a little longer."

Willem nods, as if this is the natural answer to such a problem. Tys turns away, his jaw set. I touch his arm.

"We must get Van Yvren and the rest out of here."

He nods. "And that declaration. Once the Governor has both, she can destroy them."

"When she hears their story, do you think she'll retreat?" *Stars, let it be so.*

"Possible. But with such insults, she might try settling the score with Reichard."

"She *must* leave Valonia. I recognize an invasion, even if my uncle doesn't."

Men in Valonian red scurry throughout the courtyard. We need to blend in. I find a smelly, discarded uniform in the corner of the armory for Tys.

"Do you think I look enough like Isabeau?" I turn. Tys' mouth is in a funny shape. "What?"

"You…" Laughter escapes. "Don't look like Isabeau."

I make a face and pull my hood over my hair. "My hair is shorter and curlier."

"She's a lot *taller* than you are."

"I'm a girl." I huff. "They're running about trying not to die. It's enough for now."

We cross the courtyard to the circular keep but find no Lowlanders.

"Second floor?" Tys suggests.

"The tower rooms," I counter. He nods.

Two sentries stand guard outside the first door. Tys whips his rope toward them. It cracks once, twice, and both men drop their halberds with a yelp. I scoop up the weapons and hold them threateningly as Tys secures the men. When I reach to unbolt the door, he grabs my arm.

"Want a boot knife in your throat? Best to warn them first."

Tys knocks, speaks in Haps-tongue, then opens the door. The men swarm out, their boot knives ready. The corridor fills with whispered plans, illustrated with hand language, as we come to a consensus. Van Yvren and the broken-nosed fellow put the tunics of the trussed-up sentries over their own clothes. They take the halberds and with Tys as the third guard, they herd the men out of the keep and across the courtyard.

Meanwhile, I dash to the laundry. It's empty, save for a tall servant in the back. I don't make eye contact or say anything as I gather a huge stack of bedsheets and leave.

I reach the armory as the others march up the tower stairs. A pair of soldiers pass, giving me an odd look. I lift my stack of sheets, shielding my face, and scurry up the stairs. Tys is at the tower window. He's fastened his rope. Van Yvren is the first out. Tys takes the top sheet from my pile and tosses it out the window.

Old Lord Elchen pushes himself to the front of the line. "I'm not as slow as you think, and I'll not die on Valonian soil." Then he's out. Tys tosses a sheet after him. The nobles slip out the window, one after the other, without any more comment. Van Yvren and Elchen cover themselves with the sheets and crawl through in the snow. They aren't stupid enough to make for the front lines of the Haps-Burdian army but go towards the tree line at an oblique angle. When all the Lowlanders are out the window, I have three sheets left. For Tys, me and one extra.

"Should I find Isabeau?"

"No." Tys' answer is terse. "She had a chance last night."

"But..."

"Your uncle's not dead, so perhaps he killed her. Perhaps she dumped the wine and is still his pet. If needs must, she'll find her own way out."

It tastes wrong, though his logic is sound. I toss the sheets to the ground and take hold of the rope. I shimmy as far as I dare, then drop to the snow and snatch up a sheet. I spread it over my shoulders, covering my red cloak, and crawl through the drifts, following the tracks of the others. I let power flow into the cloth; let the familiar desire for invisibility soak into the fibers.

I crawl onward. The winter sunshine warms my back, but not my extremities. Toes turn icy. Fingers grow numb. I keep crawling. The tree line is two furlongs from the fortress. I'm almost half that distance. I can keep this up. One hand in front of another.

A shout echoes across the snow. I look back.

Tys signs, "Lowlanders discovered missing."

I look past him to Roc Ursgueule. Perhaps the crawling bedsheets across the snow finally caught someone's eye. Men line the fortress wall. Bows lift. Arrows nock. I scurry forward. I look back again. The snow behind us bristles with two dozen arrows. One lands two feet from Tys' sheet-covered form. We're still within range.

"Hurry!" I stand. We wrap the sheets close around us as we race for the trees. Some camouflage is better than nothing. The other men stand. Scramble. Run.

Another flight of arrows hums through the air. Thud where I'd been a few heartbeats ago.

My legs pump. Tys beside me. Grasps my hand. We run.

A third flight of arrows. They land only a few feet beyond the second group of arrows.

I slow. Press my hand against the stitch in my side. "We're... out of range."

Tys tightens his grip. "Won't feel safe...'til we're in those trees."

I jog to a stop. "No. We won't be safe then. Not until they" —I point back to the fortress— "are gone. Locked up or dead."

"*Kleintje*, whatever you're thinking—"

"I refuse to live like that. To be afraid of him." I leave the trail made by the Lowlanders and head toward the distant mass of dark-gold uniforms. I drop the sheet and pull my cloak from my shoulders. I wave it overhead, once, twice. I'm a smear of scarlet against the white snow.

"Marguerite..." Tys hisses.

"I'm walking parallel to the fortress walls. They can't reach me with arrows." The field stretches before me like an expanse of white cloth, my path as clear as if embroidered upon it. The Queen's Snare requires three needles. Me, my uncle, and... would the Governor engage?

Tys catches up. "They have trebuchet and ballista."

"Which is useless against such a small target."

"Not too small for Reichard." Tys looks toward the wall. My uncle and Willem are easy to pick out. "He'll come for you himself if he has to."

"That's what I'm hoping." The drifts are knee deep. Easy enough to stumble with skirts wrapped around one's ankles, like a partridge trying to lure an enemy far from her nest by feigning injury. "Have they left the wall yet?" I ask, picking myself up again.

"Reichard has."

"We'll need to run, but not yet. Is your rope ready?"

"Yes. Archers have shifted on the wall. They're covering the gate."

"Good. When he comes out, we must run fifty ells farther south and then due east toward the Governor."

"He'll come with other men," Tys warns.

"Take care of their horses with that rope of yours."

"You've a high opinion of what I can do with this rope."

"That I do." I give him a cheeky grin. "Are you ready for an adventure?"

"Plenty of danger and the possibility of blood?"

"Is there any other kind?"

Tys tenderly chucks me under the chin. "Only with you beside me."

Then the gates of Roc Ursgueule open.

I LIFT MY SKIRTS HIGH, and we run. Snow sprays up around us as we plow southward toward the distant ravine. I count our steps, trying not to let the distant hoofbeats throw off my measurement.

"Now!" I huff. "Turn left."

As we turn toward the Governor's army, I'm pleased to see her galloping towards us. The Haps-Burdian banner streams out behind her; soldiers follow. The war drums beat once more. I match my steps to their tattoo. I must keep this pace until my uncle catches us.

I glance towards the fortress. My uncle gains ground, but he must swing westward along our flank to keep out of range of the Haps-Burdian archers. That gives us the time we need. Once he realizes how far he's come, it'll be too late. He has two swordsmen and two archers galloping on either side of him.

"Take down the archers first," I tell Tys. "Break their bows if possible—"

"My father's the Red Duke." He taps his forehead. "Strategy, I understand." He twirls his rope, waiting until they draw near. "Bows drawn," he warns. "Released."

I dart off course, then correct after the arrows land harmlessly. I glance over my shoulder. The air vibrates as Tys' rope picks up speed, then flies from his hand. The loop falls around one's shoulders. A jerk, and it pulls the man from his saddle, careening into the other archer. That one drops his bow, reaches for the saddle horn to steady himself, but topples as well.

I keep running. The archers can be dangerous, but a horseman with a sword is deadly, and three are bearing down on me. The hum of the rope. The change in a horse's gait as it slows without its rider. Still, I run, my lungs aching.

I draw closer to the Governor and her men. Not close enough.

Another hum of rope. The rider dodges it.

The rope whirls once again. Tys can't miss this time. My legs burn, threatening to tumble me into the snow.

"Marguerite!" My uncle's roar is a whisper in my ears, carrying a frustration that scares me as much as it gives me satisfaction.

Tys unseats the second swordsman. I glance back to gauge my uncle's distance one last time, matching it with the one set of hoof-beats vibrating through the snow behind me.

I look ahead. Focus on the oncoming Haps-Burdian soldiers. Watch their reactions. Flickers of hesitation, opening mouths that will warn too late.

I fall face first into the snow as my uncle's mount gallops past.

I look up in time to see Tys' rope sail overhead, wrap around my uncle's body and jerk him from horseback to snowdrift in a heartbeat.

"Beautiful." I pick myself up and settle my coronet back on my head. I glance back at Tys. "Remind me to kiss you when we're finished here."

Tys hauls on his rope, dragging my uncle through the snow like a fighting trout. "Let's get this finished, then."

"Keep the rope tight." I thread one of my new needles with black thread. My uncle spits out a mouthful of snow and shouts profanities as Tys forces him to his knees. I stand behind and whip my needle through the cloth of his sleeves, binding him with my own magic.

"The Valonian Oak guards this land and her people." I speak quietly. No need to shout over him. My words spark the magic of the Oak. "None can stand before the Oak Throne and speak lies. Those who have an unrepentant heart will find sitting on the throne... unpalatable."

He still blusters, but the needle and thread hum in my hands.

"You may cloak your heart, but your deeds are known."

He quiets.

"All will soon know of the women you burned, the men you killed, the children you snatched from their families. They will know how you tried to bleed Valonia of her magic. And how you failed."

The cords on his neck stand out. The thread connecting the two of us thrums.

"All will know how Reichard of Perdrix tried to supersede the Fates. How he poisoned his father, plotted the death of his brother, and seized the throne under a false name."

"And he maliciously crushed the hand of his niece," Tys adds as he stands beside me.

"Yes," I agree, as I finish stitching my uncle's cuffs to the back of his doublet. "But he did not succeed in what he attempted." I knot my thread and pull my needle free.

I step around to face my uncle. I've never faced him on his knees. For once I'm taller. The balance of power is in my favor. The temptation to strike, to hurt him, is strong. I breathe in the cold mountain air and harden myself against it. My uncle gasps, laboring under the strain of truth the Oak is already inflicting upon him. Truth is my justice.

"I am a Skein-mage, Uncle. Your cruelty did not stop the flow of magic in my blood."

"From your... damned... mother." It's an effort for him to speak.

"From the Rjasthani line, yes, but also from the Perdrix family." As I hold the Valonian Oak's gifts, I know the truth. "My father was Star-endowed as well. A mage, who could see *and* do magic. The voyant gift you once had pales in comparison."

"No!" His face purples. "That is not why she rejected me."

I frown. "Who?"

He struggles as if against some other power, some truth he doesn't want to accept.

"Ruxandra. I told her... Julien is weak. I'm the one... she should..." He coughs. "She laughed. Said she wanted... brother with power." He struggles in the sewn-up doublet. "I took that power. I seized it. The throne is mine." He snarls up at the sky. "You hear me, Ruxandra? I have more power!"

His anger is almost tangible. I retreat from his writhing form. From this entire generation of pain. Tys' arm comes around my shoulder. I lean into his comfort.

"What should we do with him?" he asks. "Kill him? Imprison him, torture him?"

For months, I dreamed about killing him. Fantasized about revenge. My uncle seems to be experiencing his own private torture, but is it enough? Should I kill him? Trussed up like a roasted goose? Gaspar said magic abandons killers. Since my experience with the Oak, the hunger for my uncle's blood is diminished. Justice, though, is still needed.

Reichard de Perdrix must pay for the lives he ruined.

The Governor approaches, slowing her mount, and applauds. "Marguerite de Perdrix, you are a wonder. That's the largest Queen's Snare ever, I'd wager."

I give a brief curtsey. "I've had skilled tutors."

"Now, what of your captive? Is he father or uncle?"

"Your Excellency, may I introduce Reichard de Perdrix, my uncle. I claim he's guilty of two counts of regicide, one count of patricide, fratricide through a third party, impersonation of a sitting monarch, over one hundred counts of murder by means of burning." I pause to catch my breath. Tys jerks his head towards the woods where the Lowland noblemen escaped. "Twelve counts of accomplice to kidnapping, and twelve counts of coercion to commit treason."

"Serious charges." The Governor is stone-faced. "How do you answer for these crimes?"

His face is twisted, and when he speaks, it's as if his words are pulled reluctantly past his teeth. "Yes. I did all that, but it was for Va... lo... ni..." He grits his teeth and goes silent.

The Governor frowns. "I would also add slanderous defamation of an Imperial representative. Unfortunately, I've no authority over the king of Valonia."

"False king," I correct.

"Acting king, even if under false pretenses. However, I *can* escort the Bishop-Princep to the Seer of the Stars. The Holy Seer has absolute authority over all who've sworn themselves to the Fate's church. He can mete out punishment for the Bishop-Princep."

Tys turns. The Governor looks up. I follow their glances toward the snow field we just ran across. One of the fallen archers, a tall, thin man, limps toward us.

"No." His protest is high and thin. "You must kill him, to have our revenge."

He shakes his fist at me, except he has no fist. His arm ends at his wrist.

"Ulrica?"

"Reichard filled my ears with flattery. He took me to his bed, then never got around to marrying me. I was chatelaine, never queen. He took everything I offered, and only ever gave me false promises in return. False promises and a sharp sword."

She's nearly upon us. Her eyes are wild. Her hair is short as a man's and I realize I bumped into her in the kitchen yesterday and in the laundry today.

"Ulrica, you're not yourself."

"No, this is myself." She stalks closer. "You understand, Your Excellency, don't you?" She draws near the Governor and her men, voice pleading, yet unrepentant. "How a man can change you—how his love and his life can turn your soft woman's heart to stone?"

Ulrica moves quick as a snake, snagging a halberd from the Governor's guard. She pivots, swinging it in a wide arc that barely pauses when it passes through the bone and sinew of Reichard de Perdrix's neck.

His head tumbles to the snow and rolls briefly. His body remains upright for another heartbeat and then slowly falls like an axed tree.

CHAPTER TWENTY-SIX

Braid Stitch: individual stitches made continuously so
it looks like a braid; though decorative and often used
to fill other embroidery work, it's often used to make
a clear border

EVERYONE STARES. ULRICA THROWS DOWN THE HALBERD
and pelts toward the woods.

"Permission to apprehend, Your Excellency?" the guard who lost
his weapon asks.

The Governor watches Ulrica flee, as if considering the question. I
glance between the two women, then at Tys. He shrugs. When Ulrica's
fifty ells away, the Governor nods. "Permission granted."

Half a dozen men chase after Ulrica, their pace noticeably slow.
The Governor motions for several others to take my uncle's body
away. I avert my gaze from the blood-stained snow.

"An ugly way to end one's life." The Governor motions for us to
follow her back towards the Haps-Burdian line. "Though his life was
spent doing terribly ugly things." She sighs. "It wraps things up
neatly."

"Not everything, Your Excellency," Tys speaks up. "My brother,
Willem, is still in the fortress. He was Reichard's co-conspirator. They
coerced Van Yvren and the others to come."

"He took Van Yvren's son. Each has a family member held captive for ransom," I say.

The Governor stops her horse. Another half-dozen men step forward. "Find Willem VandeBrandt and bring him to me, no matter the cost. Take as many men as you need."

Her men run much more quickly toward Roc Ursgueule.

The Governor, Tys and I follow. Tys peppers the Governor with questions about the rope bridges he constructed and how many companies crossed over. She gives a wry moue.

"We moved three-hundred fifty men over last night, before the earthquakes started. The closest bridge broke apart then. We lost seven men. The rest clung to the remains and climbed to either side. My commanders were wary of using the last bridge. Only two more bands of infantry crossed before the quakes started again."

Fewer than I feared, yet her forces still outnumber the men in the fortress.

"Is the last bridge still standing?" Tys asks.

"No. It was torn apart during the last big quake, just as the sun rose."

"Reichard knew you're cut off," he says. "Perhaps that's why he was so... defiant."

I glance at the Governor. She doesn't show anger. Instead, she stares steadily at me. "I believe we heard a rare disclosure of his true feelings regarding women in general."

I nod.

She halts her mount. Tys and I stop walking. We're fifty ells from the gatehouse.

"I hope you can still bear to trust me when the Haps-Burdian flag flies over Valonia."

Tys reacts first. "What? Taking Valonia? After everything—you can't."

My protest dies, for I see the truth. She's on Valonian soil with an army, albeit a small one, at her back. "Were you grooming me all this time?" I ask. "To become your puppet queen?"

Her expression flickers with regret. "No, Marguerite de Perdrix. When I met you, I saw a curious, clever girl. A girl with spark. I couldn't bear to see that snuffed out."

Tys marches toward her. He might've been intimidating if the Governor wasn't on horseback. "We trusted you."

"And I regret turning that trust upon you like a knife," she says.

I continue walking toward Roc Ursgueule. I can't let her see the betrayal I feel. A dozen options flood my mind. I desperately try to discern the wisest move. My eyes lift to the fortress walls. Though the Governor's small band of soldiers gained entry, I have Valonian archers ready on that wall. The Governor wears no armor, and she's within range.

I stop and spread my arms. My scarlet cloak spreads around me like a peacock's tail, demanding attention. "Listen, you men of Valonia. The king is dead. Killed by a Valonian for crimes against his own people and consorting with enemies."

I point to the army behind me. "The Governor of the Haps-Burdian Lowlands offers us leadership at this vulnerable time. All we must do is submit to the emperor."

More men gather along the wall, listening.

"I, Marguerite Julianna Ruxandra de Perdrix et Rajasthani, offer another choice. Let me claim my blood right." I trace my lineage as they do at the coronation ceremonies. "Barthelemy Cheyne was the first in the Perdrix line, followed by his son, Aloys, who was followed by his son, Leocadie, who was followed by his nephew, Juibert, who was followed by his son, Bernaud, who was followed by his son, Gauthier, who was followed by his eldest son, Julien, who is now followed by his daughter, Marguerite."

The embroidered names vibrate. My cloak flutters and flares, urging me to declare my full identity.

"I stand here, shining with Otherlight, proof to every voyant within those walls that I am a witch. I do not hide what I am. That power was passed down through my father and his ancestors before him." I should be trembling, but my voice resonates through my chest, heavy with authority. "You may doubt what a witch can do for our land, but I love Valonia. I admire her strength and want to protect her vulnerabilities."

I gesture behind me, to the sea of gold uniforms spread across the snowfield.

"The Governor's army stands upon our threshold. I offer safe return of the Haps-Burdian people, but no more. I say, ready your arms. Be sure she takes nothing more than offered."

A heartbeat later, each man has his bow drawn or halberd raised.

"The king is dead," Tys bellows. "Long live the queen!"

"Long live the queen!" The men's response is quiet in my ears, but it warms me.

I march toward the gatehouse. "Send the Lowlanders out without violence." I must ensure no Valonian takes the opportunity to start trouble with fist or blade. I turn to face the Governor. "Respectfully, I must insist our hospitality is at an end."

She answers cordially. I hear some of her words, but Tys' signs make sure I understand more. "I'm afraid, Your Majesty, that I must trespass upon your hospitality a little longer, for the way we came is no longer accessible. Perhaps we'll return home by way of Boispierre castle. I've always wanted to see it in person."

That smells like invasion, or at least an occupying party. I glance at Tys. He stands alone, halfway between me and the Governor. I want him beside me. Want it as much as breath. Yet only he can get my enemy back across the ravine, and it's an opportunity to retreat gracefully, honor intact, if he so chooses.

"I will send my chief engineer to provide the temporary reconstruction of those bridges."

Tys holds my gaze. Telling me something with his eyes. I know what I want that look to mean, but I dare not hope. Then he nods and turns. He gives a courtly bow, indicating for her to return from whence she came.

The Governor holds her ground.

Stars! Is it to be a battle of wills, then?

The silence is broken by the vibrations of hoofbeats. The Lowlander servants exit Roc Ursgueule, leading their masters' horses. They're laden with hurriedly packed saddlebags, one trailing a velvet sleeve and a pair of blue hose. Each bows to me as they pass. The Haps-Burdian soldiers sent to find them bring up the rear. When they pass, the Governor nods.

"I see you have me in check, Your Majesty, but not checkmate. Not yet. My brother has longed for Valonia for too many years. It is the plum just out of reach. Look to your defenses. Strengthen your stratagems. I look forward to matching wits with you again."

"Understood."

Finally, she turns her horse and retreats with her men across the snow. Tys VandeBrandt keeps pace beside her.

Exhausted, toes numb, and barely keeping my emotions from bursting my rib cage, I march alone into the fortress of Roc Ursgueule. The majordomo awaits me; the staff line up behind him. He gives a low bow, but before he can speak, I address the issue that itched since the Lowland servants filed out the gates.

"Where is Willem VandeBrandt?"

"Who?"

"The Huntsman. *De Jager.*"

He pales. "Your Majesty, we searched the fortress thoroughly before the Lowlanders departed. Every person in Roc Ursgueule is here in the courtyard or on the walls."

"You searched *every* room?"

"Yes, Your Majesty. Except for the dungeon. It seems to be sealed shut."

"Quite." I survey the score of men around me. "What of Isabeau de Cyngetroit?"

"She wasn't located during the search either, Your Majesty."

My emotions congeal into a tight ball in my gut. I order one more search. I ask that someone make a coffin for the late king's body. I instruct a small party to search for Georg's body outside the walls. "Take the body to where the engineer is reconstructing the rope bridge. He'll know how to return him to his family."

The rest of the morning, I discuss the logistics of keeping a garrison at Roc Ursgueule, as well as tracking Willem and Isabeau. I shiver at the chance that they travel together.

Finally, I dismiss the men.

They follow my word as if it's law. I'm out of the shadows. I now have the power my grandfather and father held. The power my uncle stole. I wrested it from him.

I won.

I wander, unchallenged, through the fortress and arrive at the Great Hall.

"Fates bless us…"

The tables and chairs are knocked over, perhaps from the earthquakes last night. However, my gaze centers on the Oak Throne. It looks less like a throne today. It's quite obviously the stump of an ancient tree. It curves to form a seat as if it grew that way. Springing up from the back of the seat is a new shoot, waving as if a breeze rustles its two leaves.

I release a long breath as I approach it. As I run my fingers along the rough, bark-covered arm of the throne, warmth seeps into my fingers. Warmth I long for. I sit on the edge of the throne and pull off my wet shoes and stockings. I spread out my sodden skirt hem and tuck my bare feet under me as I curl up on the throne. It isn't nearly as uncomfortable as I thought it would be.

I lean back into the embrace of the throne and brush the new leaves with my fingertip. "There's a heavy task ahead of us."

Movement at the door diverts my gaze. He signs, "Need a shoulder to share the burden?"

"Tys!" Warm shivers flood through me. "You came back."

"Always." He strides across the room, reaches for me and swings me about under the shining light of the oculus. He bends his head close to mine. "Always and always."

I laugh then, dizzy from spinning and from the emotions that blossom within me. He sets me on my feet. I lace my fingers through his golden curls. His face drops temptingly near. I breathe in his scent, but don't kiss him. Not yet.

"The politics are a tangle," I say. "I don't know how I can hold on to you without losing Valonia. Or the other way around."

His eyes never waver from my gaze.

"You're clever with tangled threads. You'll unravel it."

There's no reason not to kiss him. Our lips meet, cautious at first, reminding each other of all we gained in the past day.

"I love you," I whisper against his lips. Tys leans back just enough to look at me. I smile. "From the moment you threw that cabbage at my uncle."

He tosses his head back. "Ha! I've loved you, *mijn kleintje*, since I saw you, glowing blue as any saints' candle."

I shove his shoulder. "You can't. Not from the moment you saw me."

He catches my hand. "Can't? Perhaps when I first touched your hand." He traces a map across it. My pulse jitters. He grazes my thumb and fingertips where the callouses are firm. Then he drops a kiss onto my palm. And another. His lips travel to my wrist. My pulse gallops.

He pauses, a slow, roguish grin spreading across his face. "Hmmm?"

I twist my wrist to hold his face between my hands. "Perhaps." I rise on my tiptoes and press my lips firmly against his. He responds with a slow, enticing movement that draws me even closer. When I have a chance to breathe, he caresses my cheek.

"Marguerite de Perdrix, deliverer of Valonia."

"Tys VandeBrandt, builder of bridges," I whisper.

"The one who thwarts empires."

"The one who defies armies." I smile.

"The one who holds my heart."

And for that, I give him another kiss.

THE END

ACKNOWLEDGEMENTS

In 2020, when so many hopes and plans were shattered, I held this story in my hands and wondered if it was time to tuck it away in a drawer. Over five years, I had written, revised, edited, replotted, revised, queried multiple times, revised, and resubmitted. It didn't fit neatly into a single category. It was both too much and not enough. I took comfort in newer writing projects, but then decided to enter one more Twitter pitch contest. I am eternally grateful to Sword & Silk Books for taking a chance on Marguerite, Tys, and the world of Valonia!

Many, many thanks go to MB Dalto and Laynie Bynum, my publishing fairy godmothers! In addition, so many wonderful people at Sword & Silk helped me along the way: Nicole Bea, who helps pluck manuscripts from the slush pile; Kristin, our social media maven; Jennia, who made editing such a fun experience and whose honest fangirling reminded me why I poured so much love into this book. Celin Chen created the most GORGEOUS book cover I could have dreamed of, sharing a bit of magical Skeincraft with anyone who looks at this cover. Also, Starla Rajavuori and Shania Turner, who are important members of the team. I also have the best pub-siblings through Sword & Silk: Justine Manzano, Haleigh Wenger, Alys Murray, Amanda Pavlov, Ann Miller, Lillah Lawson, and Lauri Sellers.

Before Sword and Silk was a twinkle in my eye, I had fabulous friends who supported me: Emily Willson (my first beta-reader), Tanja Groll, Demere Knecht, and so many other ladies from Virginia, who were my cheerleaders when I first started writing "some stories" in 2009.

A significant turning point was joining SCBWI in 2012, and I will always be grateful to the Goddard family for paying for my first year's membership. I gained many friends and learned good, practical writing skills. I am particularly grateful for my critique groups, including Darcy Pattison, Carla McClafferty, Ramona Wood, Monica Clark-Robinson, Elle Evans, Melissa Clark Bacon, Emily Roberson, Heather Steadham, Annmarie Worthington, and Marc Gray. I have learned so much through your feedback and friendship.

Monica Clark-Robinson and Heather Steadham, no acknowledgements could be complete without homage to your kindness and snark, your editing skills and enthusiasm, the joy of writing retreats and writing conference quests. Long live the Three Witches.

My family is the center of my life. My mother is a retired children's librarian; books and stories surrounded us as I grew up. Mom, your continued confidence in my abilities sometimes baffled me, but your encouragement is truly the bedrock of my life. You always believed I could achieve anything. I am forever grateful for your love. My sister, Elizabeth, was my competitor when it came to reading. You always zipped through Nancy Drews faster than me and you still read more than I do every year, but it's great to have a lifelong friend who's always up for a bookchat. Arick, thanks for your continued cheerleading! Andrew, Wesley, and Alex, thanks for all your love and support, even if this book makes no sense to you whatsoever.

I'm grateful for my sons, Peter, John, Philip, Joseph, and Daniel. You have cheered me on, even when kinda oblivious to what I'm actually doing. You've been chill with hot dog dinners and have great tolerance levels for untidiness because of my writing habit. May that be a benefit to you in the future.

And for my husband, Mark, who's been the most patient of all. Who is great at kissing wrists and is wonderfully distracting even when I have just one more thing to jot down. We are the opposite of Marguerite and Tys. I am the sunshine chaos to your vigilant, loner cinnamon roll. I'm so glad you swept me off my feet that first week we met. Life has been an adventure, but it's so much better with you at my side.

ABOUT THE AUTHOR

Amelia Loken writes Young Adult Fantasy and Contemporary fiction, exploring the courage of women who forge bridges from the shards of old obstacles. Professionally, she's worked in the Deaf community as an ASL/English interpreter and currently in the field of assistive technology. Not only has she studied sign language, but also swordplay, embroidery, theology, disability rights, and the history of pirates; bits of this flotsam turn up in her manuscripts without invitation. She's a member of SCBWI and a superb critique group. Much of her life was spent moving from one town to another, but today she lives in Arkansas on the edge of a wood with her husband, five sons, and no other animals.

COMING SOON
FROM SWORD AND SILK

Coming June 2022

Beneath the Starlit Sea

By: Nicole Bea

Coming August 2022

A Heartbeat Away From You

By: Ann M. Miller

Coming October 2022

Poison Forest

By: Lauri Starling

A Special Thank You to Our Kickstarter Backers

Alexa James, Mary Beth Case, Jasmine, Morgan, Elayorna, Brynn, Lane R, Rhiannon Raphael, Sara Collins, Tabitha Clancy, Erica L Frank, Jen Schultz, Tao Neuendorffer, Kyle "kaz409" Kelly, Patrick Lofgren, Rebecca Fischer, Bridh Blanchard, William Spreadbury, Wm Chamberlainq, Adam Bertocci, Susan Hamm, Paula Rosenberg, Morgan Rider, Elizabeth Sargent, Greg Jayson, Jamie Kramer, Karen Gemin, Jonathan Rice, Bonnie Lechner, Katherine Pocock, Mary Anne Hinkle, Marlena Frank, Melissa Goldman, Stacy Psaros, Meghan Sommers, Marisa Greenfield, Anne-Sophie Sicotte, S. L. Puma, Jenn Thresher, Caley, Jim Cox, Kris McCormick, Jamie Provencher, Melody Hall, Ara James, Leigh W. Stuart, Sarah Lampkin, Stuart Chaplin, Amanda Le, Rae Alley, Arec Rain, Megan Van Dyke, Hannah Clement, Kathleen MacKinnon, Paul Senatillaka, Christine Kayser, Jennifer Crymes, Christa McDonald, Debra Goelz, Amber Hodges, Thuy M Nguyen, Jess Scott, Ella Burt, Sarah Ziemer, Mel Young, and Claire Jenkins.

CPSIA information can be obtained
at www.ICGtesting.com
Printed in the USA
LVHW031740140322
713412LV00005B/212